Dear QPB Member,

I am thrilled *The Barbarians Are Coming* is a selection of QPB. Back in the days when I was on the outside looking in, this was the sort of thing that seemed to happen only to other authors, the super lucky ones, those who by virtue of reputation, merit, or blood ties to a book club's editorial board caught all the breaks.

Soon after the publication of *Barbarians* my wife and I were walking in San Francisco's Chinatown when she asked if my father had ever been there. Her question literally stopped me in my tracks. Not knowing the details of my father's life that I wasn't on hand to witness was nothing new. My father has always been a blur. He died when I was a freshman in college, nearly two decades ago. At that time I had neither the inclination nor the wherewithal to ask about his life in China or the U.S. (not that he would've told me anything of consequence). When he was alive he was the apotheosis of the strong, silent type. You didn't crowd the guy with questions, especially not personal ones. Once for an eighth grade social studies assignment I tried to interview him on his immigration experience. "Who wants to know?" he snapped, and that was the end of that. In fact he didn't play with or talk to us (except for the occasional "when I was a boy in China . . ." variety of word snapshots meant to instruct or admonish). He was not a pal. He wasn't going to chat about his day at the dinner table. This was his privilege in the family hierarchy: As the father he was under no obligation to talk to us, and I accepted this without question.

From the outset one of the main motivations for writing *Barbarians* was a desire to explore this gap in my knowledge. In particular I was intrigued by the ten-year span that he spent alone in this country before my mother's arrival in the early 1950s. There is virtually no record of that time, except for a few photographs and discharge papers from the U.S. Army. When I asked my mother what he did during those years, she responded, "He worked!" Which was, perhaps, the same brusque answer he had given her. I wanted to fill in the hole in his narrative, if not factually, then at least emotionally.

Barbarians is a coming-of-age novel, even though its protagonist Sterling is twenty-six years old, not the usual angst-ridden teenager. Here, Sterling grows into his role as son to his father, Genius, and later into his role as father to his own sons. Sterling and Genius have a lot more going on than what I had with my father. Genius occupies a much bigger place of Sterling's consciousness. Even if he regards him as a thorn. Throughout the novel they miss many chances to connect, make their peace, because of their stubbornness or respective blindness to one another. But at least they had those moments. This is the beauty of fiction. Giving your characters what you never had, which then comes around and is a vicarious gift to yourself.

Sincerely,

David Wong Louie
Venice, California

Also by David Wong Louie

Pangs of Love

David Wong LOUIE

A MARIAN WOOD Book

published by

G. P. PUTNAM'S SONS
a member of Penguin Putnam Inc. | *New York*

The BARBARIANS
Are Coming | *A Novel*

This is a work of fiction. Names, characters, places, and incidents either are the product of the author's imagination or are used fictitiously, and any resemblance to actual persons, living or dead, business establishments, events, or locales is entirely coincidental.

A Marian Wood Book
Published by G. P. Putnam's Sons
Publishers Since 1838
a member of
Penguin Putnam Inc.
375 Hudson Street
New York, NY 10014

Portions of this book have appeared, in somewhat different form, in *Los Angeles Times Magazine.*

Grateful acknowledgment is made to Marilyn Chin for permission to quote from "The Barbarians Are Coming," from *The Phoenix Gone, the Terrace Empty* (Minneapolis: Milkweed Editions, 1994).

Library of Congress Cataloging-in-Publication Data

Louie, David Wong, date.
    The barbarians are coming / David Wong Louie.
    p.   cm.
"A Marian Wood book."
ISBN 0-399-14603-2
1. Chinese-Americans. Fiction.   I. Title.
PS3562.O818 B37   2000   99-36902 CIP
813'.54—dc21

Printed in the United States of America

10   9   8   7   6   5   4   3   2

This book is printed on acid-free paper. ∞

BOOK DESIGN AND ORNAMENT BY
JUDITH STAGNITTO ABBATE

In memory of my mother

The barbarians are coming:

If you call me a horse, I must be a horse.
If you call me a bison, I am equally guilty.

MARILYN CHIN, "THE BARBARIANS ARE COMING"

Part One

Tell me what you eat: I will tell you what you are.

— Jean-Anthelme Brillat-Savarin

Chapter 1

FEAST OR FAMINE. My plate is suddenly full. One day my Bliss is in Iowa, studying dentistry, gazing at the gums and decay of hog farmers and their kin. She claims she can eyeball a patient's teeth and see through to what's rotten. And now she's coming home for a quick visit, a thousand miles, without even the excuse of a national holiday or school calendar break. "Don't you have teeth to clean?" I asked hopefully when she called with the news. At my insistence we use long-distance sparingly, only when something truly important comes up. Since I'm still up in the air about our future as a couple, why throw away good money until I'm sure about what I'm doing: it's the difference between carnations for her birthday and a cashmere sweater. I have us writing postcards back and forth. Short and sweet, public enough so things can never get too involved or serious. A picture's worth a thousand words.

Here's the rest of the picture: I am twenty-six years old, and was recently anointed the new resident chef at the Richfield Ladies' Club in Richfield, Connecticut. I make lunch and tea, and in the evenings I'm on my own. A few weeks back, an old classmate at the CIA (that's the Culinary Institute of America), Jim King, now pastry chef for one of the Kennedy widows, and *hating* it, told an acquaintance of his who had just started her course work at the Yale Graduate School of Design to call me if she ever wanted a great home-cooked meal. Her name is Lisa Lee, and as she put it when she phoned and invited herself to dinner, "Sterling Lung, King says you're fabulous. He said I'd like you even if you couldn't cook." I was flattered, of course, but as soon as we hung up, I felt crowded by her presumptions, as I do whenever some know-it-all enters my kitchen and counsels me on ways to improve whatever I have on the stove: more salt, more pepper, or once even more *cardamom*.

To my credit, I did try to discourage her with the warning that New Haven is clear across the state, a solid two-and-a-half-hour drive away. "How can that be?" she said. "We're in the same area code." I couldn't imagine what Jim King might have told her; Lisa Lee was undaunted. "I'm sure you'll make the drive worthwhile."

In bed that night I puzzled over the phone call. Why had Lisa Lee been put up to this? I tried to contact Jim King, but was unsuccessful; the alumni office at the CIA wouldn't divulge his exact whereabouts, a condition of his employment. I mulled over the facts, scarce as they were. Finally I decided: Jim King must have a stake in this, he must be in pursuit of this Lisa Lee and is simply using me as bait. My role is that of a culinary Cupid. Fair enough. One day I'll call in the favor, have King set me up with a Kennedy.

I was so pleased with my revelation that I bounced out of bed and wrote to Bliss. On the back of a John and Yoko postcard (it's their wedding day), I should've known better, but I spilled the beans. I put it all down, except the bit about King and the debt he'll repay with a Kennedy.

I'm innocent; totally up-front, right? But honesty isn't enough for Bliss. She'll never admit it, but some corn-yellow tooth is going to go unpulled because she's jealous, in love, and coming east to protect what she believes is hers.

So it goes, the laden table, the overflowing cup.

I'm TALKING TO FUCHS, the butcher I buy from. "How about a nice capon?" Fuchs says. He has muttonchop sideburns and a nose with hairs like alfalfa sprouts. I grimace; with his talk of capons, Fuchs suddenly assumes a sinister, perverted cast.

I've never cooked capon before. Serving castrated rooster isn't my bag. All I want is a four-, four-and-a-half-pounder, a biggish bird so Lisa Lee won't think I'm going cheap on her.

Fuchs tears off a square of orange butcher paper, which he lays on the scale, then plops the bird on top. "Fresh," he says. "Be my guest, take a whiff. Fuchs won't steer you wrong. Pound for pound, you can't buy better than this."

Cool refrigerated air rises off the dank yellow skin. "I'm surprised at you, Fuchs. I would think you'd be more sympathetic to his plight," I say, fingering the ex-rooster.

"Why? Because I'm a member of the tribe? Because I was circumcised?"

"No. Because you have one to circumcise." I poke the bird. "Us guys have got to stick together, Fuchs. Think about it: *Snip!* And as if that's not bad enough, they throw him back in with the others to plump, big and fat, and he struts around like cocks do, big man in barnyard, only the hens are snickering behind his back. Think how he must've felt."

"Sterling, what gives? Since when did you become psychologist to the poultry world?" He wraps the capon, ties the bundle with brown twine. "Hey, speaking of snip, how about what's-her-name, the one they let play against the ladies at the U.S. Open last year. Whatever happened to her—or should I say 'him'?" Renee Richards, tennis pro, who in a recent former life was Richard Raskind, medical doctor. I remember the first time I saw her in the newspaper, she was in her tennis whites, in one of those ridiculously skimpy skirts female players wear in order to show off their panties. I was immediately drawn to her looks, found her rather sexy even, that is, until I read the accompanying article detailing her surgical transformation. "Can't tell a she from a he?" I scolded myself. "What kind of man are you?"

A woman enters the store. A young housewife dressed in an outfit; her shoes, belt, and lipstick match. Fuchs snaps back to his business mode: "So how many of these capons would you like, sir? I guarantee you, the ladies at the club will adore this flesh."

The new customer is browsing the beef-pork-lamb end of the refrigerated case. I look at her, then at Fuchs, who rolls his eyes and whispers, "That one was never a *doctor*."

I nod; he's got that right! "That's it for today," I say.

"Hey, these birds are meaty," Fuchs says, "but just one won't feed that crowd at the club."

"It's not for the ladies." I laugh nervously. "I have this art student from Yale, a total stranger, coming for dinner. A friend of a friend, that sort of thing."

"Why so glum? Yale, you say. At least she's smart."

"How do you know she's a she?"

"Because a guy gets hamburger. She," he indicates the housewife, with a tip of his head, "gets the bird."

"You're right, she's a she. Lisa Lee."

"Chinese too, Sterling! Better than good."

I stare at Fuchs as though he were a freak, natural or manmade, himself a capon.

"Why're you looking at me like Madame Chiang Kai-shek just burst from my forehead?"

I shake the shock from my eyes. "I never imagined she might be Chinese."

"Madame Chiang?"

"No, Lisa Lee."

The other customer sets her purse on top of the meat case.

To her Fuchs says, "I'm almost through here, miss." To me he says, "Lee's a Chinese name. Am I right?"

"Sure, but I've been thinking Robert E. Lee. Vivien Leigh. Sara Lee."

"And don't forget Richard Day-*lee* and F. *Lee* Bay-*lee*."

"Be serious."

"And there's that jujitsu guy—Bruce Lee." Fuchs scratches his bald spot. "Geez, when you think of it, hardly anyone's Chinese."

I hand over some money. Fuchs offers to charge the purchase to the Ladies' Club account.

"Personal use."

"Boy, you Chinese are honest," Fuchs says. "Well, I wish I was in your shoes, having a blind date like that." He winks, and at that moment, as half his face collapses, I see him as a man from an earlier time in human history, someone who could effortlessly tilt back the chin of a lamb and slash its throat.

Leaving the store, I hear Fuchs say to his customer, "So, I see you like looking at meat—"

I WALK to the Ladies' Club with the capon bundle under my arm. I know Fuchs must be right. Hanging around death as he does all day, he sees things. Lisa Lee *is* Chinese, which explains why Jim King has put her up to our meeting; he thinks we'll make a cute couple together, a pair of matching bookends.

I try to imagine Lisa Lee and immediately conjure up my sisters. I see them, one after the other, their faces like post office mug shots, and under their chins, instead of a serial number, is a plaque that reads "Lisa Lee." I know it's wrongheaded, even a bit spooky, and entirely indicative of bad wiring inside me, but in my heart every Chinese woman registers as an aunt, my mother, my sisters, or the Hong Kong girl whose picture my mother keeps taped to the kitchen mirror. They hold no romantic interest for me.

I pass Kim the greengrocer. People in town think he is Chinese. I backtrack, enter the store. Lisa Lee: bean sprouts, snow peas. I rarely do business with Kim, who charges four times wholesale and won't cut me a break, ripping me off, his Asian brother, along with everyone else. Six bucks a pound for snow peas! Kim's making a mint and getting fat, even his wire-rims look fat. And he speaks only enough English to kiss up to the housewives with his "America is good place," "You look nice," "Cheap, cheap" stuff. With me, he doesn't bother—what is another Oriental going to get him?

I pay, and feel pickpocketed. My own money, and what's it going to get me? "Not so cheap," I say to Kim, with a smile, angling for a discount. But he just eyes me, a stray that's wandered in off the street.

"You not have to buy," he says, and shrugs.

Normally I have no use for bean sprouts and snow peas, even at half the price. They are not part of who I am as a chef. But just as tennis requires a can of balls, a milkshake a drinking straw, a dinner guest named Lisa Lee requires the appropriate vegetable matter. "Blind date," I say, holding my purchases up by my ear. I can see from Kim's blank expression that he has failed to grasp my meaning: he can't see that my hands are tied, that I must go against the grain, that under routine circumstances I wouldn't tolerate this economic exploitation.

Kim says, "America is land of plenty. Why you want a blind girl for?"

WHEN I GET HOME—that is, the small apartment that comes with the job, four hundred square feet, the top floor of the carriage house in the rear of the Ladies' Club property—I find a postcard from Bliss in the mail. A giant ear of corn that takes up the entire length of a flatbed truck. She alternates between sending the mutant-corn postcard and sending the one of the colossal hog with antelope horns. She writes: "A guy comes in complaining about a toothache but he doesn't know which tooth aches. The X rays don't know any better, and neither do my professors. But then I had a hunch, this feeling; I borrowed a light and checked his eyes and his ears. And *bingo!* There was a moth in there *and* a foot of yarn! When it was all over, Moth Ears asked me out for a beer. He said, 'Are you spoken for?' I had never heard it put that way. Sterling, have you spoken for me? I love you. See you Friday, the 16th."

I check the calendar. Today is Friday, the fifteenth. Is she coming today, or tomorrow, the sixteenth? Friday, as she says, or Saturday? Something's wrong. As much as I hate having to do so, I have to phone her, paying premium daytime rates, no less. When she doesn't answer, I'm relieved, spared the toll charges—though I know that's an inappropriate response. She's probably already in the air. I need to straighten the matter out. I try Lisa Lee's number; she isn't at home either. Perhaps both are speeding, in opposite directions—Lisa Lee from the east, Bliss from the west—to the same trembling destination.

I RINSE THE BIRD, salt its body cavity, and curse Fuchs. Before Fuchs, Lisa Lee was just a hungry student coming for a home-cooked meal; a stranger shows up uninvited at your door, you feed him. Or her. There's a right and a wrong, and I was prepared to do the right thing. In the end even Bliss wouldn't have objected to that. But talking to Fuchs has put me in a fix. Now my innocent little dinner, my mission of mercy, has transformed into a date. With a Chinese girl, of all things!

Bliss and I had been seeing each other on a regular basis for only a few months when she asked me to move with her to Iowa and set up house. I told her no, I had my job with the ladies. She then offered to defer the start of her second year of dental school and stay with me. Fearing the escalation in the level of our commitment to each other such a sacrifice would signify, I had to tell her no again. I was flattered, but was even more bewildered by her eagerness to alter her plans. In my eyes we were, at best, a fringe couple. Yes, we were going out. Sleeping together. I was happy to have her in my life. I was new in town, knocking myself out trying to impress my employers, and if I'd been living close to friends, in familiar surroundings, I might not have indulged the relationship as I did. We were pals, we hung out, we ate lots of food, we drank good wine, we had sex occasionally. But moving in together, in the Midwest? Was she kidding? That was far beyond where I was. The trouble then, as now, was that I never meant for things to get too serious. At the risk of sounding like a junior high schooler: I liked her but I didn't love her.

I towel off the capon, massage mustard onto its skin. It feels no different from any of the hundreds of chickens I've cooked, but I can't get used to touching this thing. Bliss would have no qualms; after all, she wants to drill teeth for a living. Nothing seems to bother her. When she wedged her way into my life, arriving unannounced like an angel with a pot of soup, I was sick, a vibrating mass of germs, but she laid on her hands and helped me undress and made my bed and massaged my back and sat nearby, singing French folk songs and Joni Mitchell. I couldn't sleep because of the singing but was too polite, indeed, too beholden, indeed, too afraid to ask her to cut short her concert—that was what it was, for she seemed to pause between songs for imaginary applause. The moment came when I dislodged my arm, which was pillowing my head, and swung it down to my hip, cutting wide arcs that I hoped would alert her to the fact I was still awake and miserable, bored, and ready for surrender.

On one of these sweeps she grabbed my hand—later she would argue I had offered it to her—and when my arm pendulumed up toward my head, she leapt out of her chair like a fish from the sea. Without the slightest break in her song she was lured into my bed—so goes her version of how we ended up making love that first time. As we lay naked between the sheets, chills from the fever stiffening my body, she held me to her enormous heat and asked if she might come again, another day, with more soup, and unsteadily, I said, "Yes."

I admit I was the one who had made first contact. Soon after I arrived in Richfield, I saw her name in our college alumni magazine and called her. We had been marginal friends at Swarthmore, both art history majors, but she was a couple of classes ahead of me, and we traveled in different social circles (her group was acid and orgies; mine was wine and one-night stands). After running hard with the "in crowd" her first four semesters, she turned serious as a junior, finding peace in the study of Gothic cathedrals. At the art history majors' costume party during her Senior Week, we spoke for the first time. She went as Notre Dame, a dishwasher box, with splendidly painted details of the original and posterboard flying buttresses hanging off at her sides like spider legs; her face was that of a gargoyle. Guys joked about coming to worship, going on a pilgrimage. I went as Warhol's Brillo box. Our costumes were huge hits but left us on the sidelines, victims of our own genius—what a drag trying to boogie with your body in a cardboard box.

When I tracked her down at her parents' place in New Canaan, she was completely surprised. We met for lunch on one of my first off-days from the Ladies' Club. She was no longer the hippie she'd been in school. While her long, frizzy brown hair was still her most distinguishing attribute, in the four years since I had last seen her she had lost the roundness in her face and had traded in her T-shirts and Indian print skirts for tailored clothing. Between graduation and dental school, she had worked for her father, who owned and managed properties and acquired things. Even though she slept under his roof and received a salary from him, she seemed to harbor boundless hostility toward her father. In her lingo, he was "capitalist pig scum," who apparently felt morally justified in his own brand of bigotry because his parents were Holocaust survivors. After the initial weekend lunches at local restaurants, I invited her to my apartment for dinner. Then came the day she showed up at my door with the soup.

I rub the mustard onto the capon's skin, with its largish pores and nipple-like bumps; the mustard's whole seeds, tiny orbs rolling between my palm and the lubricated skin, produce a highly erotic sensation.

The telephone rings and I jump, embarrassed by the pleasure I'm taking. My mind leaps from the capon to Lisa Lee. She must be calling to cancel our date; perhaps she has a project due and can't come to dinner.

But the instant I lift the receiver I realize I don't want to hear that message at all.

"I'm here! I'm here, I'm here, I'm here!"

It's Bliss. Originally, she explains, she planned to fly in tomorrow, but a classmate, Ray, has a wedding to attend in Greenwich, and she caught a ride, saving money, his drive-buddy. At this moment they are outside Syracuse, still hours shy of Connecticut.

"I'm skipping my parents," she says. She sounds all juiced up, still speedy from the road. "It's a hit-and-run visit. I'm not even stopping in, they'll want to feed me, take me shopping, you know, monopolize my time. I'm going to stay with you."

Love is a lot like cooking. When either is successful, there's a delicate chemistry in operation, a fine balance between the constituent parts. If you have the perfect recipe for vichyssoise, you don't monkey with it. We've had a workable arrangement. The U.S. Postal Service has kept us connected; we have a standing agreement to take holidays together. That's plenty. Why spoil a good thing?

"We're going to stop by Randazzo's," Bliss says. "Come join us. I'm letting Ray buy me drinks." She informs me that Ray is a third-year dental student; he has been "a good help" to her, and twice has taken her hunting for ring-necked pheasant in the harvested cornfields.

"I'm stuck here," I tell her. "I'm experimenting with a new recipe." Which is the truth.

"Always other women," she says.

I hear the sarcasm in her voice, understand she means the club ladies I have to feed, but suspect she also means Lisa Lee. For a moment I consider putting an end to the intrigue, inviting her and that guy Ray to join us for dinner. A foursome around the table. Me and Bliss. Ray and Lisa Lee. At the mere thought of such a pairing I experience a biting pang of jealousy.

"Silvy, what's the matter?" she says, into the silent line. "It's me, Bliss. Are you upset with me? Come on, tell me. Do you feel threatened by Ray?"

I keep seeing the four of us around the table; Ray, some generic Midwesterner in a hunting cap and ammo vest, and Lisa Lee, who at that moment I imagine as my sister Lucy.

"It's true we spent the night together in the car. But he's just a friend."

I stay silent.

"I'm sorry. Nothing happened. Don't be that way. You know me. I'm already spoken for."

After we hang up I try to reach Lisa Lee again. No answer, of course, she's also on her way. But I don't panic. Bliss has hundreds of miles to go, a couple of hours' drinking at Randazzo's. If I'm really lucky she'll catch dinner there.

S HE FILLS THE DOORWAY, her head and its swirl of dark hair eclipse the early-evening sun. Her face is in shadow. She stabs jugs of wine into the room: "I got Inglenook red and white," she says. "I didn't know how you swing, so I blanketed the field."

I backpedal from the door, and as soon as I vacate a space, Lisa Lee fills it.

She is six feet tall. My first thought is, Where is Lisa Lee, the Chinese Lisa Lee that Fuchs had promised, where is she in this high-rise protoplasm? Still, I can't help noticing her beauty, the cool sort, good American bones and narrow green eyes. I've seen her before, especially the gangliness, the I-beam angularity in her cheeks, through her shoulders.

Then it hits me, like the icicle that fell six stories and opened my head when I was a boy: She can pass for Renee Richards's double.

"Are you all right?" she asks. "Didn't King tell you?"

Tell me what, that she, Lisa Lee, was once a he?

"It's okay. You can stare," she says. "I'm used to it, people are always gawking at my size."

SHE EATS AND DRINKS lustily; she has so much space to fill. I think of horses I've seen, their magnificent dimensions, the monumental daily task of keeping their bodies stoked. For all the energy and attention she gives to her food, she maintains a nonstop conversation, remarkable for its seamless splice of words, breaths, bites, and swallows. "What do you call these?" she says, helping herself to the snow peas.

"Snow peas."

"No," she says. "I mean in Chinese."

I ask about her studies. I don't comprehend much of her response. It's all very abstract, highly theoretical. But in the end she confesses that what she's truly into is interior design. Every designer with a name in Milan and New York, she begins, is a man. She says this has to change. Women are cooped up in their homes all day, surrounded by things designed by men. "Knives and forks," she says, "is macho eating. Stab and cut, out on the hunt." She critiques my flatware, my stemware, my dishes. It's junk, cheap stuff, but she's a grad student and finds things to say, just as Bliss is awed by exotic gum diseases.

She loads up on capon. I've barely touched any of the bird, too much excitement, and I'm still too squeamish. Call it cross-species male solidarity. But I love watching someone enjoy my cooking, especially a woman, one who eats (there's no other way of putting it) like a man, with pig-at-the-trough mindlessness, so different from Bliss, with her on-again, off-again diets, her sensitivity to ingredients, her likes and dislikes, allergies, calorie counts, moral guidelines.

Lisa Lee takes on a leg, itself almost a pound of flesh. As she sinks her teeth into the perfectly browned skin, my mind explodes with the inevitable question: Why Bliss? How can she say she loves me if she doesn't love all of me, including my food? What am I but a cook? You love me, love what I cook! How should I regard a so-called lover who would extract essential ingredients from my dishes, capers, for instance, her fingers pinching the offending orbs like fleas off a dog, then flicking them onto the table, as if she had seen *Warning: Radioactive Materials* printed on each itty-bitty bud. I imagine Bliss encountering the roasted capon, which to a normal diner like Lisa Lee is just a plump bird. But Bliss has an uncanny knack for putting two and two together, even when there isn't a two and two to put together. "What are you trying to do to me?" she would say, her suspicions touching me like the worst accusation, and I would hang my head in shame, accepting responsibility for the rooster's sad fate, feeling the tug of its peppercorn-sized testicles that guilt has strung around my neck. Souvenirs of war. *Men!* Disgusted with me and the bird, she would go on diets: For days, no meat. For weeks, no sex.

Lisa Lee relinquishes her knife and fork. "That was so good! You're everything King said you'd be." She smiles, greasy lips, a fleck of capon skin on her chin like a beauty mark. Her satisfied look pleases me to no end. I start to clear the table. The jug of white she brought is gone. Amazing we choked down so much cheap wine. "If you're a man," she says, "you'll uncap the other bottle." In the kitchen I set down the dishes, and as I open the red, the telephone rings.

"We're on Eighty-four, near Poughkeepsie," Bliss reports. They're at a rest area, making use of the facilities. "I'm going to skip the drinks with Ray. I've already worried you enough about him. I'm so, so sorry."

I watch as Lisa Lee stacks the dirty dishes. What remarkable size! An infinite capacity to consume and thereby to love. Her mastications were gestures of love. She catches me staring, holds a finger perpendicular to her lips, admonishing herself to keep quiet. She seems to know who it is I'm talking to, seems familiar and comfortable with situations of this sort. She steps free of her noisy shoes, and as I watch her move toward me, I wish I could just as easily step from my entanglement with Bliss. Pluck her from my life as cold-bloodedly as she would a bay leaf from a stew I've made, a tooth from someone's head.

"Don't change your plans because of me," I say. "You like Randazzo's. Have some drinks. I'll see you afterwards. I'm not going anywhere."

Lisa Lee takes the opened jug of red from my hands, fishes a glass from the sink, pours, and drinks. I watch her swallow, the little hitch in her throat; if only the hitch were the clasp of a zipper that ran down to her navel, which unzipped revealed Lisa Lee's Chinese self. I want this to happen for Bliss's sake: should she arrive while Lisa Lee is still here, I could simply pass her off as my cousin. Bliss would love her.

I check my watch. With or without drinks they can't possibly get here before I've served coffee and dessert and sent Lisa Lee on her way.

I get off the phone with Bliss. We leave things hanging. I'll take care of business on my end; I can't worry about what I can't control.

"Where does this go?" Lisa Lee holds the platter containing the remains of the capon.

"Let me take that. I'll pack you some leftovers to take home."

"What kind of man are you?" she says, welding hands to hips. "You're going to make me drive all that way, in my condition?"

Do I have a choice? True, the picture of her backing down the driveway is frightening enough, forget the two and a half hours on the interstate. The decent thing to do would be to tuck her safely into my bed for the night. But Bliss stands in the way of such a right and moral act. What Lisa Lee needs is sleep, to pass the hours of her overindulgence out of harm's way. A night's undisturbed digestion, then, upon waking, to eat and love again. Bliss will deny her her well-deserved rest. So much more the pity, sleep the simple thing it is. It's a staggering thought, yet I know that before the night is through I will do Bliss's bidding. She will insist that Lisa Lee must go. And should Lisa Lee, heaven forbid, doze while she's behind the wheel and jump the center divider, a grand jury surely will charge Bliss, not me. Still, what comfort is that?

I BREW A POT of coffee. From the living room Lisa Lee calls, "What kind of wine smells like that?"

Minutes later I carry in a tray with coffee and a rich chocolate torte. She is seated on the pea-green couch. My rickshaw driver lamp gives her skin a yellowish hue. Her eyes narrow in concentration, as she fastidiously rolls a joint.

"What are you doing?"

First her expression is, Don't mess with me; then she says, "You're not chicken, are you? A girl only lives once." She slips the joint into her smiling mouth and slowly reams it through her lips.

We drink the coffee, we eat the chocolate torte. Afterward she seems more together, the alchemy of bread dough in a 375-degree oven. Now I can send her home—Bliss can send her home—with regrets but diminished fear for her safety.

Then she lights up.

The marijuana will counteract the effects of the caffeine in the coffee and the chocolate. When I run this past her she says, "Maybe pot stimulates me. You don't know my body."

But I do know. Her body, her outsized frame, its long rib cage that imprisons the real Lisa Lee, my counterfeit cousin inside her. There's the reason for her vast appetite; she must eat for two, and like her master, the one trapped inside also loves my food, also loves all of me.

She offers me a hit. I scissor the joint, just to get it away from her. She watches me, with a smile that she knows my secrets. "I like your hands," she coos in a hushed tone. "I like what they do to ordinary things. What a miracle that chicken was."

Should I tell her the truth? Straighten her out as to which fowl is which? She doesn't need my help, her powers of perception are unparalleled; after all, she saw the "miracle" in the dish, and the transformation of the capon into something delicious, respectable, beautiful is nothing short of miraculous.

Chicken! I'm the chicken around here. Too chicken to insist that Lisa Lee stay; too chicken to tell Bliss not to come, tell her she's not "spoken for." I'm brave only with my parents; I stared down their anger when (at their nosy insistence) I confessed I was dating someone (Bliss), and they acted hurt and surprised she wasn't Chinese, even though none of my previous girlfriends was of the Asian persuasion either. *What do these girls see in you? You're so stupid, you think they think you're pretty, don't you?* I defended myself with a raging silence. But what *do* they see? I'm a decent enough guy, but there are plenty of decent guys; I'm competent in bed, but competence is rampant. The standard is Robert Redford, and on more than one occasion I've stood before the bathroom mirror with a picture of the actor held up to my face and gauged the extent of my deficiencies. What Bliss sees in me, I can't answer. The mechanics of her fierce affection is a mystery. And it's this mystery that freezes me, makes love cruel. In all my relationships love has felt like charity, needed and hungrily received; I am Pip from *Great Expectations,* fat on another's generosity but crippled by the uncertainty over what motivates my benefactor's heart. With Lisa Lee at least I know she loves my food.

The telephone rings again. Lisa Lee smirks, arches her eyebrows. "Popular guy, aren't you?" she says. "You don't have to answer, you know."

A temptation, a perfect opportunity to bump Bliss from the picture. But I don't have the nerve.

Bliss is at Randazzo's, ahead of schedule. They're going to have drinks and a bite to eat. For a split second I take offense, am actually jealous: eating at a spaghetti joint, when she knows I'm concocting something new and fabulous in my kitchen. I'm shocked by the speed with which they've made Connecticut, but grateful for the regained hours her dining out provides. "That's fine. I'll be here, waiting for you," I say. For reasons unknown, I add, "But tell me, what made you change your mind? You said you were coming here directly."

She says, "At first I thought I had upset you because I was traveling in close quarters with a man. But then I realized I can't upset you. You don't care what I do. So it must be that you'd rather I hadn't come. I'll just go to my parents' house."

"That's silly. It's just that my hands are full." Then I say, "You're spending an awful lot of time with that Ray." And why shouldn't I say this? It costs me nothing, and it's what she wants to hear.

There's a prolonged silence on the other end, after which, with the usual cheerful lilt back in her voice, Bliss says, "You really mean that?"

AFTER I HANG UP I stay in the kitchen and pack a doggie bag for Lisa Lee. Fuchs was right about the capon's size. A lot of meat. Big. And there's never been a blinder date. Wait till I tell him. I can hear him now: "Okay, so she's not Chinese, you can't have everything. Already you got smart. Now you say she's beautiful *and* handsome too! And big! You can't buy any better—"

When I return to the living room she's no longer there. At first I'm relieved, one problem solved. But immediately I realize her absence depresses me.

I find her in my bed, apparently asleep, her jeans on, her blouse off. The top sheet slashes diagonally across her, toga style, leaving her shoulder exposed. When I check, she's taking sleep's slow, steady breaths. "Hey, hey," I say, tapping her on the shoulder.

She opens and closes her eyes. "Mmmmm . . ." she says, but there is no telling why. Asleep again, she shifts her position and does something with her hands, and the sheet flies off, magically, and she's naked for the briefest instant, and I'm not sure if it's happened by accident or design. The fleeting sight of her long, lanky torso burns into my memory, her breasts as tidy as teacups upended on a clear pine board.

I sit on the edge of the mattress. "Lisa," I say softly, "wake up." Lisa Lee yawns, rolls onto her side, curls her body around my spine. It must be the surprise of our bodies touching and the thoroughness of the contact that make me feel enveloped by her. I lean into the heat of her skin, as plants turn toward light, palm her shoulder, and shake her. But my heart isn't behind the business of rousing her, it's something I do, a phantom order I have no choice but to obey. How does this look to someone outside, peeking in through the window? You see a woman in bed—asleep or resting—at peace with her choices in life, safe and secure, and a man on the edge of the mattress, which, to judge from his posture, must seem like the very edge of the world to him; he is alone on the brink, though the woman is there; and you see how worries have fused his vertebrae into a single length of bone, how rest won't come easily to this man, who wants to leap but can't.

Lisa Lee stretches, tightening her muscles, pushing roughly away from me. At once I miss her ardently, it is out of all proportion, but true.

Then it comes to me in a rush. And I feel tricked and double-crossed when I realize that the person I'm missing most right now is Bliss. I miss how she tells me what to think, what to do. Once, back in the early days, when she ate and loved unquestioningly, I prepared a simple dinner, from recipes I can't even recall, and at its conclusion she exclaimed, "That meal is beyond seduction. That, darling, was a proposal of marriage." Weeks later she started dropping hints about living together, about one day marrying, and when I grew exasperated with such talk, she fired back that I, with that meal, had planted the idea of marriage in her head.

I want Bliss to come to my rescue, as she did with soup in the beginning, my personal Red Cross. No one chooses the Red Cross, but when disaster strikes, the Red Cross is there.

Lisa Lee sweetly, softly belches. Her loving appetite! I study the fleck of roasted skin still on her chin, the dark brown of a nipple. I remember some graffiti in the men's room at cooking school:

There once was a girl named Red,
Whose passions were stirred when fed.
A little French wining,
Fine Epicurean dining,
And soon you'll be eating in bed.

But Lisa Lee is not like that girl Red. Lisa Lee isn't about love or pleasure. What's made her so right, all night, is the fact she isn't Bliss.

It's time to act. Time to put my life in order.

I swing my legs onto the bed and slowly slide down next to her. She drapes a heavy arm across my waist and breathes metabolized smoke and wine against my face. When she shifts her weight, her knee scrapes the top of my knee, her pelvis bumps my thigh. She's making all the moves. My record with Bliss is still clean, my hands as good as tied to my sides. But why hold back? Bliss isn't the Red Cross, her soul isn't dressed in nurse's whites. Her habitual kindness, like American foreign aid, comes with strings attached. Around the room I see her touches: the curtains she sewed; the plants she bought and reminds me to water; the Matisse goldfish poster that she framed; the bookcase she knocked together, painted black, and stocked with thin volumes of poetry. This is nothing but interior design. This night's struggle is about *my* interior design, how *I* am configured inside, how *I* want the four chambers of *my* heart arranged, *my* likes and loves, *my* duty and desire, not how she wants those parts to be.

If I accept Lisa Lee's sleepy advances, I can do so with the knowledge that no one is better equipped than Bliss to weather the pain of this bum's indiscretion. She has the recipe for the healing soup, and strong hands to catch herself when she falls. And a heart that all along has loved for two.

Lisa Lee pulls me closer, grinds her nose into my neck, rubs her zipper against my hip, and I sense that it is time. But when I turn to kiss her, her body suddenly goes limp, rubbery-limbed, her joints in aspic, and she softly, undeniably, snores.

I SLIP out of bed. In the kitchen I stand staring at the night's ruins, the capon carcass, the dishes. Lisa Lee's scent lifts from my clothing. That's all I'm doing—standing and staring—my mind blank. Then I realize it isn't quite just standing and staring, I'm actually waiting. For the Red Cross, for 911, for sympathetic Band-Aid-hearted Bliss to tell me what to do with the person in my bed, before she arrives and discovers her herself.

I RUN A BATH. Hide the evidence. Get rid of Lisa Lee's scent, her vague perfume. I can accomplish that much myself.

I look in on Lisa Lee. I call her. She doesn't stir. I shut the bedroom door. Let her sleep. Sleep will protect her.

I undress and climb into the bath. The water is hot, my skin reddens, darkening the way paper stains with oil. I am poached. In a soup. As a boy I cultivated a reputation for my tolerance of discomforts. On car trips I would stand so others could sit; I would eat slightly moldy fruit; I would wait for hours while my parents shopped in Chinatown, would wear my sisters' hand-me-downs and endure scalding bath water, and never complain. It was a boy's notion of heroic duty then, it's a grasp at self-styled absolution now.

Slowly I recline, until I have submerged my shoulders. Soon I pop my legs out—it's too hot—and prop my heels on the edge of the tub, steam swirling off my skin, and I imagine it isn't just steam but some essence of myself that I'm better left without, lifting. Bliss likes my legs, and she has told me so, and with their hair weighted down by water, they are more apparent, better defined. Once she said that I had the body of a Renaissance Christ, his lean, tight torso, evident ribs, and well-muscled legs that reflected a society on the go, exploring seas and deserts, in a time enamored with substantiality, a heavenly earth; it's a Christ fed on game, jungle fowl from new worlds, spiced meats, sesame seeds, saffron, silk, and gold. "There's more there than meets the eye," she said. The muscularity of the Christs in the oils of the Florentine Leonardo and the Venetian Titian and their disciples isn't just an expression of piety, it's also a reflection of their patrons' good fortunes. These paintings achieve paradoxical feats of illusion—substance and spirit; they want you to see what is there, and believe it, and what is not there, and believe it.

When Bliss and I first got together, she told me she could read a person's life simply by looking in his mouth. I loved this idea, my imagination locked on palmists and the articulate lines in hands, or psychics who can predict a life by the shape of a skull. "Tell me about myself," I said. "At one time," she said, "you brushed with a hard toothbrush. The size of your cavities suggests you've had good dental care." And so on. But not a word about my luck, about my destiny, about whether I'm a trustworthy or a dangerous man, about what will happen next.

I close my eyes and sink deeper into the water.

Someone knocks at the apartment door. I sit up, splash water on my face, then lean back, and wait.

The door opens and closes. I could have set the deadbolt, but thought better of doing so. That would not be playing fair.

It's a long time before she comes to the bathroom, and by then, as is her wont, and now her burden, she must've put two and two together: Lisa Lee's car in the drive, the wineglasses, the empty bottle, the dishes, the bird's naked bones. Lisa Lee, of course, in my bed. She has to have figured things out by the time she opens the bathroom door and steps inside, preceded by a rush of the outer room's cooler air.

She stands just this side of the doorway, her brown hair swept high on her head, wearing a long white skirt, a white tank top, a man's unbuttoned workshirt. And a light lipstick because she knows my weakness for girlie things. Now her sane medium build and middling good looks are breathtaking. She hides from me her clenched, polished teeth. *Who is that monster in my bed? You prefer that Amazon to me? How dare you? Get your ass out of that tub and rid our home of that bitch!*

But she says none of these things.

She says, "I don't see why it is that you don't love me," and steps forward, deeper into the bathroom, crossing the small distance between door and tub in four steps, instead of the usual two. With those extra steps she gives me a chance to formulate a response, one that will save the moment, dispute her statement, wash away her hurt. Say, *What do you mean not love you, of course I do, I do, I do.* Or say, *Someone in our bed? Your eyes are playing tricks on you.* Or say, *What did you expect? I am what*

I am, a twenty-six-year-old man who naturally dreads the C word, commit-ment, *as others do* cancer.

But I do the worst thing, though I won't know it for years. I close my eyes and allow her to approach.

I feel her steps, feel her kneel by the tub. I smell her citrusy perfume, a fresh, recent application, barely diluted by her own sweat and oils, the fragrance borne by the vapor rising from the bath. She scoops water with her hand hooked like a flamingo's beak, and she might have shared the wildly strange coloring of that fabulous bird just then, so incomprehensible is she. "This is the last," she says. "It's done. There's nothing in me that forgives you." When she brings the water up to my head I cower, as if what rains down were sharp pieces of glass. The water trickles through her fingers and falls on my hair and into my eyes.

She washes my back, shampoos my hair. I lift my head, defying the force of her hands, and look at her amazed through the bubbles. She is two people: she's biting her bottom lip, trembling, though fighting back tears, but on top her big brown eyes have shrunken to tiny pellets of anger and hate. She pushes my head forward, chin to chest, and digging her fingers once again into my soapy hair works such a thick lather that when she massages my scalp it feels as if the top of my head were falling off. As if she has hold of my mind, pulling me this way, then that.

She says, "If I had my pliers here, you know what I'd do? I'd yank every tooth from her fucking head." Strangely enough, her voice is stripped of hurt or passion.

And that is what breaks my heart: I am her earthquake, her hurri-cane, her personal flood. Doesn't she see that? I want to save her. I should know the way, simply follow her example. Tell her to stay angry, let it grow and abscess, until her only alternative is to yank me from her life.

But the moment passes when she starts rinsing my hair, both hands scooping water.

She helps me from the bath. My legs are wobbly, and I have to touch her here and there for support. Everywhere I touch her blue workshirt I leave a dark handprint that spreads.

She grabs a large purple towel. She holds it open, stretched wide between her hands, and after the slightest hesitation I go to her, let her wrap the towel over my head, across my shoulders, let her pull my body against hers. "It's over," she says, working the towel roughly, "it's like you're dead now." I am dazed, spinning wildly inside, losing myself in this dark, sheltering place, under the wing of some strange bird.

Chapter 2

OVER LISA LEE'S slumbering body, Bliss and I slugged it out. We didn't say all that much. The key words: "Love." "Commitment." "Backstabber." "Scumbag." "Her." That was the big one. Every grimace, every squint-eyed look, every "Why?" or "capon" seemed to be followed with a finger-stabbing at prostrate Lisa Lee. Basically, Bliss accused me of not loving her, a charge to which, in the heat of the moment, I fired back denial upon denial. Finally, as if to prove my point, I went to wake Lisa Lee, hustle her out of bed, remove from our lives the presumptive source of our discord. But Bliss wouldn't let me ease the pressure: "Have you no shame?" she said. "After what you've done to her, Jesus, at least let her sleep it off." Okay, fine. Bliss the caregiver wanted her to stay and sleep. But what about the rest of us? I hinted she take my car and go to her parents' place. "You know that was never in my plans," she said. Then she told me she expected me to leave.

"Are you crazy? I live here."

"I just drove all the way from Iowa to see you."

"Whose fault is that?"

"God, I hate myself!" She bit her lower lip. "I came all that way, for this. I'm such an idiot!"

"Hey, come on—"

"But I'm not such an idiot that I'd want to spend another perverted second under the same roof with the two of you."

I EXILE MYSELF to the main house of the Richfield Ladies' Club. I suppose I could sleep in my car, feed the mosquitoes, or shell out for a motel room, but I can't resist the pull of the house. Should a member catch me in here or even hear of my after-hours trespass, my ass will land hard on the street. That's the way it is, the club rules. No matter how much the ladies love me, they won't forgive the trespass.

Except for the chandelier in the foyer and the ambient light it throws, it's dark inside. I use the key to the service entrance, as I do most days. This is no break-in. I have a legitimate claim on the place.

I creep up the staircase. The second floor is new territory for me. Club rules: The staff stays on the bottom level. I try the doors off the long hallway. Most are locked.

I find the master bedroom: vast, frilly, pastel wallpaper, bay windows, canopy bed. On a hulking dresser there's a collection of small crystal bottles, a silver brush-and-comb set, a cloudy drinking glass, and a Chinese silk-covered jewelry box; on the nightstand, a porcelain lamp, hand-painted, a pink-cheeked teen pushing a young woman on a swing. The air is charged with the scent of permanence: mothballs, soap, lace, and upholstered furniture.

For a long time now I've wanted to do this. When I drove up for my job interview and first laid eyes on the big white house, with its dark green shutters, vast lawn, ancient oaks and elms, bounded by imposing stone and wrought-iron fences, I felt I had arrived. After spending the majority of my years growing up in the back of a Chinese laundry, I was on the verge of ascending to a new station in life, home in this stately patrician edifice, planting my feet firmly in the American bedrock. To think my parents would've had things turn out differently.

I remember the day I broke the news to Genius and Zsa Zsa (their American names) that I was planning to attend cooking school. They had aspired to a career in medicine for me, their one and only son. I dutifully took the med boards, applied to schools, even went for a few interviews. But I wanted to cook; I don't know where the idea came from, but it had burned in me since I was a kid, a desire borne in my blood. I was already halfway through my first semester at the CIA when I went home to confess that I wasn't, as they had thought, in medical school. I appeared in my chef's whites, a double-breasted jacket, twin rows of buttons to the neck, an erect Maoist collar, and checkered slacks. They were so proud, seeing what they wanted to see. Genius pumped my hand, as Zsa Zsa watched and applauded us. She was doubly proud: of the uniform, of the blooming affection between her men. "That's the way," Genius said, meaning that I had finally done right by him. "Who'd believe you'd grow up to be a *dock-ee-da*," my mother said, clucking her tongue. I realized then that they, as usual, didn't get it. I excused myself and went out to my car for more obvious props: apron, side towel, and brand-new set of chef's knives. Seeing these, Zsa Zsa sucked air through her teeth, then clucked her tongue again. She thought I was planning to be a surgeon. She pinched the side towel and said, "After he cuts he uses this to wipe his hands." But the standard-issue chef's toque fooled no one. "You a cook?" My parents stared, as if I were a stranger. "Who'd eat your cooking?" Who'd let me, I wanted to say, make an incision in his body? In their eyes I was a scoundrel, a dumb-as-dirt ingrate. This was the reward for their sacrifice, leaving home for America, for lean lives among the barbarians, so I might enjoy penicillin and daily beef and be spared Mao and dreary collectivism, shared destiny, rationed rice, the communal butt-rag at the outhouse door. To make peace, I offered to cook them a meal, show

off what I had already learned. Feeding people is as honorable as healing people. But Genius said he had been fed enough bitterness by me
and my sisters, and he would not eat any more. He said, "I'll never have
appetite for your cooking."

But the ladies do!

I had never prayed before I first laid eyes on the house, never dared
imagine a good life for myself within such walls. Yet I lowered my head
against the steering wheel and pleaded with an anonymous deity, for
my very survival. I got the job, not the house. While I never seriously
considered turning the offer down, I was devastated by the news my
residence would be the carriage house apartment. For weeks I pouted,
banging around the squat square space like a pinball. But eventually I
accepted it as a passable second-best. After all, we shared the same
grounds, the same pipes, the same electrical lines. Still, I was frustrated
that I couldn't live in the big house. So much space going to waste while
I was cramped in my tiny apartment in back. After the ladies had gone
for the day, when I was tired and lonely, I saw things for what they were.
I occupied the servant's quarters. And I was undeniably the servant. In
that way Genius and Zsa Zsa were right: I hadn't come very far at all. I
was doing no better than they were, living in the back of the place where
I worked.

I LIE DOWN on the master bed with the anticipation that accompanies
the uncorking of a Château Latour '61. Expectations of a transformative experience.

As soon as my butt grazes the hand-sewn quilt, a bolt of disappointment sizzles up my spine. The mattress is vinegar. I sink into
its frailty, and its springs drill me back. Shouldn't I have gotten more
in the way of luxury and comfort? Look at where I am—this brass
bed, the grand old house. Who was the last person to sleep here?
Washington?

I take my slacks off, try to get some rest. I'm surprised at how undrunk I feel: blame the bath and the sobering blast of Bliss. I wish the house would spin madly, rise to the stratosphere, and plop me down in Kansas, far from the events of this evening; I wish I'd just pass out. I close my eyes but they open right up again. On the inside of each lid are Lisa Lee and Bliss. When I shut my Bliss eye in order to focus on Lisa Lee, Bliss has usurped her place. When I reverse the process, Bliss is there again. The only time I'm able to see Lisa Lee is with Bliss riding chaperone underneath the other filmy flap.

The longer sleep eludes me, the more uncomfortable I feel in this room. The linens are brittle and musty, the pillows flattened by the accumulated weight of scalp oil, hair spray, and cold cream. No matter how I position my head I catch whiffs of the salts distilled from decades of ladies' perspiration.

My breaths are shallow and rare; the air is thick and ponderous, as foreign as the atmosphere that surrounds another planet. I am an extraterrestrial on Mars, my helmet off, exposed and vulnerable to contagion in the environment. I fear this air will burst my lungs, as I do the incensed air in a cathedral or the cologne in a Protestant church. Suddenly it comes to me, and I drop back down to earth: I am to blame for my discomforts within these walls, evidence of deficiencies in my upbringing. There's nothing wrong with the mattress, this is what a good Puritan mattress should be: austere, temperate, dispassionate, the springs administering purposeful pricks to the sleeper's soul.

I jump out of bed and switch on the lamp (the bedroom faces the rear of the house, so there shouldn't be any problem from the street). I walk across the room to the two paintings hanging side by side on the wall opposite the bed. Portraits of someone's stern ancestors—any one of the club ladies might claim them: a woman in a white lace headpiece, a man in a somber, dense black hat. They stare me down from their oval gold-leaf frames, unhappy with my presence. If they knew what had transpired under their noses tonight, they would bang their heads against their severe pews. I replay my dinner with Lisa Lee, her enthusiasm for my food; I replay Bliss's arrival. In the hierarchy of nightmares,

I wonder, which is worse for her, finding Lisa Lee in my bed or being locked out of my apartment knowing I'm hiding inside?

Then I come to the most disturbing thought of all, one that's only danced at the edges of my consciousness until now: What's happening back in the apartment?

I go to the window. Across the vast lawn, the carriage house windows burn in the night, stingy yellow rectangles, the dull glow of forty-watt bulbs. Lisa Lee's car is in the gravel drive. I am afraid of what Bliss might do to her. Has already done. What a matchup! Lisa Lee has the height and reach advantage, while Bliss is bigger-boned, possessed of a lower center of gravity—she won't go down easily. The winner? I'm surprised that I have no rooting interest, even though logic screams for Lisa Lee to knock Bliss out.

But why worry about Bliss and Lisa Lee? I have this big white house to myself, with its strangeness, the unfamiliar sounds, the ancestors' bed, the musty smells. All day long I'm in this house of women, with their talk of sweets and diets, gynecological procedures and dinner parties, cosmetics and brassieres (to wear or not to wear?); my ears and eyes and nose are so full of them I can almost taste them. In this house of women, with its spacious rooms, carpeted floors, polished banisters, brass fixtures, I am the engine that makes things go. I have no reason to doubt this. They have to eat, and that's why they come daily. And praise my cooking, squeeze my arm, caress my hair, pat my cheeks, pinch my rump. I *have* arrived; I *do* belong here. I *have* come so far! Abe Lincoln had his log cabin, I had my unsanded plywood box of a partitioned room in the back of my parents' laundry.

I throw myself onto the bed. Like a pig rooting for truffles, I sniff the linens for a club lady's scent. Libby Drake, perhaps. Club president, my boss, early fifties, two grown kids, and the body of a college freshman. She's not there.

Nonetheless, I feel myself harden, my prick hooking on a spring, and I begin moving my hips, back and forth, slowly. I think of Libby Drake's rich bosom, Sally Hayes's pouty lips, Millicent Boggs's long calves, Dottie Cone's painted toenails; then I summon up every one of my parents' customers I had a crush on, women who lived in houses as nice as this, who spent their days making their faces and bodies beautiful for men.

I slide off the bed, onto the Oriental rug, seeking friction commensurate with my hardness and longing. My hand is too soft and familiar for this strange urgency. I fuck the rug some more, then the brass bedpost, the armoire, the back of the overstuffed chair; eventually I fuck the entire bedroom. Still unsatisfied, I fuck the runner in the dark hallway, the moldings, the telephone and its stand just outside the bathroom. I fuck the banister, the stairs, the dining room table, where the ladies are most intimately acquainted with me. I leave droplets of myself everywhere, the sticky residue of my love—they won't even know how we've communed, each time they turn a knob, pull up a chair, raise a fork to lips. I fuck the front door like crazy, then the shabby mat at the threshold. When they enter the house their well-heeled feet must cross this very spot. I roll onto my hip, yank the elastic band down, setting myself free, and let loose instantly, long body-shaking shots that seem to originate in my brain.

Someone knocks at the door. I stop breathing. The universe boils down to the sound of knuckles striking wood, my heart leaping against my chest. The police? Libby Drake? I'm on the floor, my sperm all over the threshold, the end of my career at the Ladies' Club, my life in this house just a vibrating oak door away. Bliss was right when she said I'm dead. I'm dead.

The knocks, to my relief, stop. I pull my briefs back into place, roll to my knees, and crawl across the floor. I take the stairs quickly, hands shielding my privates from phantom eyes.

Back in the master bedroom I force my legs into the slacks, zip, and tuck. Outside, someone is calling my name. One of the ladies? My blood's popping so loud in my ears I can't tell which member it is. Not that it matters.

I hear the click of a switch. A thin bar of light shines brightly between the door and the floor. I crouch behind the bed, and listen to whoever it is work her way down the hall, turning every knob in sight. I wait for my executioner. Inevitably she'll find me.

The door flies open.

"Sterling," she says, "why'd you leave me?"

Lisa Lee! And looking no worse for wear. Her shiny pink-gold blouse where it should be, buttoned and tucked.

"How did you get in here?"

"The back door's open. You know, if you don't want company you should try a lock. Ever hear of that?"

Silhouetted as she is by the light in the hallway Lisa Lee's beauty is lost. Her features are muted, her cheekbones cast bands of shadow across her eyes.

"Well, let me tell you, I was *seriously* out! And once she woke me up there was no turning back. That Bliss can really talk."

"What happened? What did she do to you?"

"Let me put it this way: I was dreaming someone's hand was in my mouth, nothing sinister, but nothing too nice. Like going to the dentist. And when I opened my eyes she's sitting on the bed looking straight down at me, talking away."

I glance out at the carriage house. I can see Bliss's outline in the window. Is she staring at the main house? Just then I realize passersby can see the hall light from the street. "We shouldn't be in here together," I say, stepping quickly past Lisa Lee, then switching off the light. "The ladies will fillet me if they ever find out."

"Why're you so scared? The ladies! They're just rich people. And let me tell you, they need you more than you need them."

"I don't think you know what you're talking about. Who's to say someone hasn't already called the police? I mean, how'd you know I was in here?"

"How do I say this? According to Bliss you're too cheap to go to a motel, so she said check your car and the big house."

"Bliss put you up to this."

"Not really. Actually, she had nothing to do with this. I wanted to thank you for dinner and the unforgettable evening. I have to go home."

"Can you drive?"

"Oh, yeah. I just passed out, is all. Sometimes I just need to be unconscious for a while."

We go downstairs. I lead her through the kitchen, and outside the back door she again thanks me for dinner. She might've kissed me good night. Instead she extends her arm and pumps my hand, in an energetic, mannish way. "You don't have to worry about Bliss," she says.

"I wasn't worried." Truth is, I have been meaning to ask her for a report on Bliss, an assessment of what I'll be up against in the morning.

"Good. I thought I should let you know she's coming with me."

My silence begs for an immediate and elaborate elucidation.

"I'm not sure she knows where she wants to go. She said she might have me drop her off at her parents' house, or she might stay with a guy named Ray, or come all the way to New Haven with me."

"You're kidding."

"Nope," she says. "And I'll tell you something else I'm not kidding about."

That Lisa Lee loves me? She can't wait to see me again?

"But it's a secret. It's a huge secret."

"You can trust me," I say. "Who am I going to tell?"

"What about Bliss?"

Of course! Lisa Lee confesses her love and I'm going to turn around and blab to Bliss. "I won't tell Bliss," I say. "I promise."

"You better. It's her secret." In the yellow bug light Lisa Lee's eyes flutter on her face: she is trying to pry under my skin, sizing me up for the revelations to come.

"*Her* secret. What does that mean?"

"Look, I shouldn't have even started. And I shouldn't keep Bliss waiting any longer. Just tell me you swear to keep her secret a secret."

"I swear."

"Double swear."

"Come on, Lisa. Don't be an infant."

"Double swear."

"I double swear. I triple swear."

"Good."

"Well?"

"You're going to be a father."

Chapter 3

FROM A SMALL HORIZONTAL WINDOW, like an eye slit on the face of the house, I watch the first guests arrive. It is rare to see the ladies after hours, but tonight, the tenth of October, 1978, they are coming, twenty strong, some with their spouses, in spiffy evening attire and long, expensive cars.

It's a big shindig for Libby Drake's husband. He's contemplating a run for the state legislature, and tonight's what Libby Drake calls an "exploratory fund-raiser" for a possible campaign.

I'm standing in the kitchen, my hands blindly working down the row of tomatoes I have set along the cutting board like a string of beauty contestants. I feel not only for firmness but also for elasticity of the flesh; a ripe tomato gives under pressure, then springs to shape again.

I welcome the extra work. Honestly, I wish I had a meal or party or snack to prepare every hour of every day. Work is all that's left that's sane. Since Lisa Lee dropped that bomb on me, I've distracted myself, comforted myself by planning and replanning menus for tonight's function, shopping for the ingredients, and best of all, cooking.

I love the view from this window. A good thing, since I'm here a lot, at the counter, slicing, dicing, chopping. Such an impressive expanse of lawn! A gardener and his son (why isn't he in school?) come once a week to keep it manicured. The gardener is a small Puerto Rican man who wears a straw hat, with a bandanna around his neck, and I like to watch him work. At times, from my position inside the house, I feel as if he were my gardener, working under my orders, keeping each of my blades of grass trimmed to the same height. Except for some giant rosebushes, a birdbath, a decorative Greek column, and a three-foot-high knock-off of Michelangelo's David, the lawn is empty. What a luxury unused land is, a dose of green serenity, instant peace of mind, whenever I squint out the little window as I work. Once, after I first got my driver's license, I took Zsa Zsa for a ride through the narrow, maple-lined streets of split-level houses, fresh paint, and two-car garages where many of my schoolmates and her customers lived. In front of one house she had me stop, and she exited the car and inspected the shiny-leafed bushes and shrubs, clipped at crisp right angles, stately as the Parthenon. I honked and waved her back in. "Why plant so many plants you can't eat?" she said in Chinese. "These people are stupid." She slid her hand under my nose, offering for my inspection dark, odorless leaves she had plucked. "If it were left up to you," I said, sweeping the leaves off her palm and out my window, "those nice garages would be stables, the lawns vegetable gardens." How stupid she was, ignorant of the look of success, of civilization at its height.

Libby Drake, as lustrous as a polished apple, her skin and soul wound as tight as Maureen Dean's, slips past the dark green hedges that rise like a great wall at the rear of the garden. She is accompanied by her husband. Could he be the Drake of Drake's cakes fame? Mr. and Mrs. Ring Ding? Until recently I never realized that some brand names, Kellogg, Heinz, Hertz, for example, are actual surnames later lent to cornflakes, ketchup, rental cars. Such monumental acts of ownership were all but inconceivable to me. Imagine controlling the world's supply of Devil Dogs! Seeing Drake has a strange effect on me. Except for the gardener—he doesn't really count—Drake is the first man I've seen at the club. I've given little thought to this moment, but now that he's here, I feel the sanctity of our home (mine and the ladies') has been violated, a trespasser is on the grounds, an invader in our midst.

The Drakes slowly make their way along the slabs of slate that serve as a path from gravel parking lot to house. As she points, her husband surveys the property. The ancient trees that border it are radiant; the bright fall leaves form a magnificent bracelet of red, yellow, and gold around the land. Drake's black shoes look oiled and hold the day's last sun. The lawn glistens around the couple, each blade of grass, wet from the late-afternoon watering, is studded with diamonds, and my heart fills with gratitude for this woman, who, by hiring me, has made me part of all I behold. Halfway along the path the Drakes stop, and Libby Drake points in my direction. She's probably saying, "That's our brilliant chef, Sterling Lung. He keeps us all, oh, so satisfied!" Her legs gleam in the sun, as my hand alights on the one I'm after, and I lift the tomato, which yields to me its loving weight, its thin-skinned plumpness that molds to the curve of my hand. It is the perfect thing to squeeze.

MORE GUESTS CONVERGE on the club, arriving in their Simonized steel tons, two hundred horses under the hood, commanded by manicured hands, designer-framed eyes, and thin-soled Italian shoes.

In the reception room Fuchs is serving cocktails and hors d'oeuvres. I conscripted him at the last minute; when he came by to deliver the bundle of foie gras for my pâté, I realized I wouldn't survive the evening without some help.

Six swans are lined up on the copper countertop, which shimmers like a toxic stream. I apply the finishing touch on a seventh, pinching the aluminum foil between my thumb, fore-, and middle fingers to form its beak. Inside each swan is a roll of tender Dover sole, stuffed with julienned scallions, sliced mushrooms, diced tomatoes, and minced fresh herbs. I want to do something special for the Drakes, especially Libby Drake, but the swans are a drag to assemble, so labor intensive, costly in time and energy, and worse, she didn't even want the *cygnes* to begin with. "Something Chinese would be nice," she said. "You promised when I hired you that you would cook Chinese someday." Of course I had lied—I would've promised her Chairman Mao's head on a platter, just to land the job. What was I going to say, I am a French chef, my culinary pedigree extends back to the great chefs of Europe, I am the hautest of haute cuisines?

Libby Drake enters the kitchen, a drink with a cherry in her hand. Her hair is combed impeccably across her scalp, slick and gleaming, anchored in back in a massive braid that resembles a lobster tail. She informs me that four more diners are expected. "That won't be a problem," she says. It is, of course, but what am I going to do? She leans against the edge of the stainless-steel sink, a posture of familiarity and friendship. She briefly describes the extra guests, suggests ways of stretching the food, sips on her drink, and comments on the "fabulous swans," the hors d'oeuvres, the peculiar waiter. She is more fumes, perfume and alcohol, than she is flesh and blood. "I feel so small tonight, with men in my club," she says. I abruptly stop work on the swan-in-progress: Aren't I a man? She goes up on a single high-heeled foot, then flips loose the other shoe, which hits the tile floor with such a clatter that I have to stop and take notice, as she massages her toes through the black nylon. "This is my club, right?" she says. "So why do I feel insignificant here?" I know she's not expecting a response, I know it's not my place to answer, but I'm also keenly aware of what she means, because that's how Drake has made me feel ever since he set foot on my property. How does he do that, Drake who might be known worldwide as the man behind a dopey corporate logo: a cartoonish duck wearing a chef's toque.

"Sterling, please." She points with her chin at the runaway pump on the floor.

Is she kidding? What am I, her personal valet?

But it comes naturally, though it rubs me the wrong way. Before I know what's hit me, I drop the swan I'm shaping, dry my hands on the side towel, and kneel to pick up the sleek black shoe, its metallic gold insole grinning at me. I hold the shoe out for her; it is feather light, and when she slips her foot in I feel the heat of her body fill the thin leather and radiate through my palms, up my arms, and into my every part. I'm left momentarily breathless by the sudden weight in my hands. "Thank you," she says, and as I stand *she* loses her balance (a legitimate slip?) and reaches out to me for support. She touches my shoulder, then caresses my ponytail, her fingers running through my hair like a litter of nesting mice. Thank goodness I haven't jumped, embarrassing her. My hair is fine, and as strong as fishing line. Its length has been a longtime source of shame for my parents, especially Genius, who has no problem calling me his fourth daughter, making no allowances for style or prevailing tastes. Bliss is just the opposite; she has said she will terminate our relationship if ever I cut my hair. She likes to roll off the elastic band that holds the ponytail in place and fan my hair across my back and give that black fall a hundred strokes with a pig-bristle brush. She says this is the way Chinese men have traditionally worn their hair, and she likes this quality she sees in me, how I, according to her, honor my forebears, where I come from. My forebears? Think Beatles, Jerry Garcia. The first club lady to touch my hair was Millie Boggs, who joked that my ponytail would make "a delicious whip," as she gave it a playful tug. From time to time a club lady will sneak up and pet me. Some are more welcome than others—I can't stand Sharon Fox, who grabs hold and says, "Giddyup!" Libby Drake is a regular, but her style is high on subterfuge, witness that questionable slip, that relies on my duplicity: neither party can acknowledge what's happening.

Fuchs enters the kitchen noisily and slaps his empty tray onto the counter, sending metal skidding on metal. "Fill 'er up," he says. "They love you out there." Libby Drake abruptly untangles her fingers from my hair, a ring catching a strand. I salivate at the crisp pain. As she rights herself she says, in the stern voice she uses to assert her authority, and now to maintain appearances, "Oh, I almost forgot. Keep an eye on the cars." She peers out the slit window, as if to demonstrate what she wants me to do. "There's been a rash of break-ins in the area."

She rushes past Fuchs and rejoins the party.

"Boss lady?" Fuchs asks, once she's out of earshot. "If you have to have a skirt telling you what to do, she's not too shabby."

"She's great. She's like a friend."

"I see that. She lets you cook *and* guard the cars."

THE OVEN BURSTS with the sweet, briny fragrances of mussels and clams in herb butter; shrimps and bacon; mushrooms stuffed with crab and morels. I quickly try to teach Fuchs the French name for each dish, but it's futile—he butchers the pronunciation.

I push the kitchen's swinging door open for Fuchs. He says, "It's like the *Mayflower* out there." For the first time I see all my guests together. Dark suits and dresses, white shirts and collars.

"They look like the Pilgrims."

"No kidding," Fuchs says. "They *are* the Pilgrims." He launches himself into the crowd, armed with trays of my goodies.

I crack open the door to watch my guests enjoy my food. Fuchs stabs the trays in people's faces, and in a voice out of register with the others says, "I wouldn't know, my people don't eat shellfish." It's strange seeing the ladies all done up. They've undergone an amazing metamorphosis. By day they're pink, yellow, and peach, like those marshmallow chicks that come out at Eastertime. Tonight they look so erotic, with their skyscraper coifs, bare shoulders (sunburnt and freckled), and spiky shoes. What clothes can do! Slap a camouflage jacket and combat boots on Patty Hearst, accessorize with beret and submachine gun: Tanya! I'm reminded of my own prodigious transformation from son of immigrants to denizen of Plymouth Rock. Look at the ladies, each claiming me as her own: each is anchored to a square foot of reception room floor, canapé pinched between fingers; the ladies swivel at the waist, arch their backs, gesticulate with arms and hands—stiff, like hieroglyphic figures set in motion. What they're doing is marking off turf, staking primal territorial claims. Here the territory is the master of the mini-toast smeared with Brie or anchovy paste, the goose-liver pâté, the smoked-salmon terrine; here the contest is over proprietary interest—ten hostesses presiding over the same fabulous dinner party, ten Virgin Mothers and one baby Jesus. Me!

My eyes flit to the men. I struggle to get a fix on them. I feel like a boy again, trying to take my father in, his great intimidating size, overlaid with the constant accusation, as if it was my name, "You're useless, you're useless," which sprang from his smoky lips or seethed off his back, his face stained with regret. From an early age I wondered how to love him if my eyes couldn't hold him. My eyes can't hold these men, because they wear suits that fit; because their cars guzzle gas and they don't care; because their women paint their nails, sign my paycheck, pet my hair; because their shirts (I can tell by their drape) are synthetic, the wash-'n'-wear fabric that's killing the Chinese hand-laundry business, and bringing my father to his starch-stiff knees.

WHILE MY GUESTS are finishing their dinners, Fuchs, rumpled as lettuce left outside the crisper, takes his leave. His duties done, he delivers his parting shot: "Sterling, this gig of yours in this house—you have my condolences."

"It's usually not as crazy as this." I hate having to defend the ladies to him. My head is in the oven, checking on dessert. "The ladies aren't so bad," I'm saying, as I lift from the oven my gorgeous tarte Tatin, your basic no-frills confection, flour, butter, sugar, apples. But Fuchs is gone already. He didn't even let me thank him. He couldn't wait to get out of here.

I TAKE A BITE of fish in the calm and listen to the drift of voices, the sounds of contentment around my table. Fuchs reported that the women loved the swans. But do they know that a young man's gift of a wild swan to his beloved is an invitation to carnal love?

I have ten minutes before the dessert cools properly. I go outside, into the damp evening air, and walk across the lawn to look for sprigs of wild mint. A garnish of the green serrated leaves will set off the gold curves of the caramelized apples beautifully. The wild mint borders the tall hedges marking the property line farthest from the main house, near the carriage house and the driveway, where the guests' cars are parked.

Halfway up the slate path I come upon the David, illuminated eerily by a torchlight spiked in the ground. I stop and stare. Every day when I walk from the carriage house to the kitchen my eyes automatically fall on the statue, and I scrutinize his every inch. Measure myself against him. But if he is the ideal of masculine beauty, where does that leave me? And this guy is just three feet tall. The ladies love him. I have seen them extend their hands as they pass, and casually fondle his curly plaster hair.

ON HANDS AND KNEES I hunt for the wild mint. It is dark but the moon is full, and the fragrance of mint should be tickling the cool air.

I don't smell the mint. The gardener must've weeded or sprayed. I give up the search, and climb the stairs to my apartment to use the bathroom. I check my mailbox—there's a postcard from Bliss. Our first communication since the Lisa Lee night. Without flipping the card I know it's from Bliss—it's a picture of a sow suckling a row of piglets. The legend reads: "Pigging Out in Iowa!" Her handwriting in Bic blue ink is rigidly neat and sane as ever: "It's true, I'm pregnant with your baby. I came east with the news, *but* you were too busy for me. You know the story. I know Lisa spilled the beans. So where the FUCK have you been? (Oops, didn't mean to curse!) Don't you think it's time we talked? Call me collect if you have to. Iowa's hot and muggy and we're waiting for you with open arms."

I look out the window at the great lawn, the spotlighted statue, the house, my guests within, who have given me, as Genius would say, "big face" tonight, coming in their fancy cars and finest clothes (and I have returned the favor tenfold, having lovingly touched every morsel they've ingested, molecules of mine borne on each bite: I am bonded to their insides). And Bliss would have me uproot myself, live in exile from this place, the ladies, my good works here? I feel sick to my stomach. The postcard trembles in my hand. I stare at the pigs, the mother pig's unnervingly pink underside. I keep hoping it's a false alarm. How can she be pregnant? We haven't been together in a couple of months, and when we were together we didn't have sex that often, and when we did it wasn't what anyone would call passionate. Besides, she's an enthusiastic proponent of birth control, famous for doubling up on occasion, mixing in a rubber with her diaphragm, a spermicide with the Pill. Say I have supercharged, high-octane sperm that can burst through all those barriers, does that automatically qualify me as a father? All I have is Genius for a role model. Over the years I've learned his ubiquitous scowl, the leaden disapprobation. I'd hate shooting a child of mine that glare, breaking the baby's back. But maybe it's not too late. Bliss is a smart, liberated woman. She's spoken passionately about overpopulation, man's environmental ruination of the planet. I can trust her to hold true to her political convictions and do the right thing. Get the situation fixed. She has to come to her senses, sooner or later.

I glance out the window at the house again. It tugs at me, like the moon at the tides. Dessert! What a terrible chef I am, leaving my guests unattended for so long. As I leave the apartment and hurry down the stairs, my eyes catch on the streetlights glowing on the dark waxed body of the Drakes' Lincoln Continental. Without hesitation I go to the car and run my finger along its sleek electroplated paint. When I try the driver-side handle the door opens with a stately sucking sound. I slide in behind the wheel. The interior is redolent with cigarettes, perfume, leather, sweat. Drake and I must share the same seam size: the pedals, to my surprise and delight, are perfectly set. We have more in common: Drake has eaten my food; I have eaten Drake's cakes (if he is, indeed, that Drake). In flagrant violation of the pact I made with Bliss to quit smoking (because our professional lives are tied to mouths—I pleasure them, she fixes them), I filch a cigarette from the pack of Benson & Hedges, "a silly millimeter longer," and light up. I'm puffing like crazy, I feel as if I'm driving away from troubles, leaving Bliss behind. She can't touch me. I'm not wronging her: this is Drake's cigarette, and this is Drake's car, and the passenger seat is still warm with Drake's wife. Oh, the privilege of being an American, cars and quick escapes! Until I was fourteen or fifteen my family never owned a car. That fact was consistent with the profile of Chineseness that was forming in my young brain: We don't own cars, we don't live in houses, we don't eat anything but rice. Each one a racial trait. Now I'm right there with Drake.

When I open the door a crack to let the cloud of smoke out, I hear Libby Drake calling my name. I stumble from the car, and slash through the hedges. She is standing on the slate path, next to the statue. One hand planted on hip, a cigarette burning in the other, she looks angry, her body as stiff as the David's. Right then I know I can't face her without an alibi. I retrace my steps to the hedges, and strip a branch clean of its waxy leaves. Who'll notice the difference? For most people mint is toothpaste or chewing gum. I go to Libby Drake, my hand extended, offering her my harvest. I tell her the leaves are a decorative strain of mint, not high on taste or smell, but a nice visual garnish. She looks down her nose at my palm. "I don't know what you're doing out here," she says. "Why are you so determined to make me look bad in front of my husband? Don't tell me you didn't realize these are important people." In the moonlight her hair shines like the back of a Japanese beetle. She brings the cigarette shakily to her lips, then pauses as if trying to align the filter with her mouth. She's been drinking. I can smell white wine in her sweat. She puffs, and as she furiously exhales she stumbles slightly, her heels sinking into the lawn. I reach for her, but she catches herself against the statue. "Are you okay?" I ask, after weighing the pros and cons of calling attention to her tipsiness. "No, I'm not okay. I asked you to serve Chinese food, but you didn't, did you? Have you any idea of the humiliation I endured when Mr. Drake contradicted my claim that the swans are a Chinese dish?"

"You said that?"

"I promised my guests Chinese food, from our very own Chinese chef. And I was justified in doing so. We had talked, Sterling. I told you my conception of the menu." She absently caresses the David, her fingers tickling its curls like a message in Braille.

"But you liked the swans."

"Sterling, that's not the point. And to make matters worse, you disappear, along with that strange waiter you hired. Is he out here with you? I trust there's nothing irregular going on between the two of you. Seriously, Sterling, do you expect *me* to clear the table?"

Her harsh tone pushes the house away from me. I envy the statue her drunken, loving touch; I envy the man I so recently was, loved within the house's walls.

D URING MY LAST WEEK of classes at the CIA—a mere six months ago—my professor took me into his confidence: "When in doubt, Sterling," he said, "just flambé."

To make amends for upsetting Libby Drake, and to climb back into her good graces, I douse the tarte Tatin with Grand Marnier and cognac. I dim the lights in the dining room, ignite one of the cakes, then exit the kitchen, a crown of blue flames in my hands. Oohs and ahhs. Which is the least I can expect. The ladies lean forward in their seats, tightening thighs, flattening feet to the floor to grab a better view. I see it in their faces: I'm their personal lama strolling in their midst, gold robes and etherized grin, god light blazing in my palms. Awe is balanced with delight, in their eyes. This love of small fire—birthday candles, dinner candles, memorial flames—a throwback to primitive times. The ladies and their men fall silent, supplicants awaiting the diviner's word, a nation's destiny burnt into an oracle bone. The durability of a goat shoulder blade reveals who is fertile, who will bear a son. Around the table my guests applaud, as the blue flame fades. Once again, love is in the air.

AFTER DESSERT THEY MOVE into the reception room and look at slides of the Drakes' recent fact-finding trip to China. From the kitchen I see rosy-cheeked babies, toothless octogenarians, bicyclists, guys in Mao jackets, women in Mao jackets, Mao himself, soldiers in streets, swans on a lake, the ubiquitous Great Wall, tombs, rice paddies, birds in bamboo cages, oxen, billboards—the usual suspects I've seen hundreds of times on TV since Nixon visited China six very long years ago.

I'm making the rounds, offering refills on coffee when the slide show ends and the lights come back on.

"Everyone," Libby Drake says, grabbing me by the wrist, tweaking my bones too tightly. "This is Sterling, our very own Chinese chef." She is beaming, flush from her trip to China, as well as from the wine racing through her system. I can read her perfectly: Not only are the slides and the memories they hold hers, so are the people and objects in those pictures. And here I am, as if I'd just stepped off the screen, proof of her assertion.

"That was a fine meal," Drake says, prompting all eyes to alight on my skin, his mere utterance breathing life into my being. "I never would have suspected the hand of a Chinese person in any of those dishes."

"Sterling, tell Mr. Drake about the swans," Libby Drake says.

Tell what? My face is burning: *visage chinois flambé.* Everyone's waiting for me to speak.

"You just told me that the swans is a Chinese dish, didn't you?"

The authority in her voice! Right or wrong, it doesn't matter, have your say and say it with authority. All the ladies are supremely endowed with this skill, an American trait.

I try to do my best imitation of the ladies, and feel for the authority in my throat. "It's as Chinese," I say, "as I am." Flames flare under my collar.

"Ni shuo zhongguo hua ma?" Is Drake making fun of me, talking ching-chong talk? I can't believe he's doing this in front of everyone.

He does it again. "He doesn't speak Chinese," Drake says. "Where are you from?"

"Oh. New York," I answer, hoping people will hear New York City, meaning Manhattan, preferably the Upper West Side, much more glamorous than "Long-guy-lun" and its dull cookie-cutter towns.

"No, where are you *from*?"

Drake's perplexed look unnerves me. I can't risk disappointing him. So finally I confess. "Long Island," I say, taking care to articulate each word clearly.

He shakes his head. "Where. Are. You. From?"

"Lynbrook?"

Sally Hayes says, "He must mean Brooklyn."

"They do that," Kathy Lloyd says. "Flip words around. Kim at the fruit stand does the same charming thing."

Slowing his speech down even further to aid my comprehension, Drake says, "Where are your parents originally from?"

"Canton?"

"You mean Can*ton*," Drake says. "We were there. Have you been back?"

"Back? I was born here." I'm about to give a brief account of my family history, but I quit before I start. And here, in this reception room in Connecticut, I have my first inkling of Zsa Zsa's ordeal on Ellis Island, her entry barred, more than thirty years ago. After three long months in a detention cell, all the waiting and interrogations, she took one look at the dirty streets of lower Manhattan, thought America was nothing but filth and insult, and begged to go home.

"THE CHINESE HAVE a special fondness for Richard Nixon—" Drake is saying as I return from the kitchen with a fresh pot of coffee and an empty tray to bus the dirty china. He has assumed the air of a foreign-affairs expert. He has everybody's attention, and is loving it. His legs are crossed, inches of plaster-pale calf flesh exposed, his nylon socks as sheer as women's hosiery. I am embarrassed for him. "But here, we consider Nixon a criminal."

"No one under this roof does."

Someone praises Ford's pardon. Millie Boggs declares her preference for Betty over Pat. Then Drake says, "Nixon is nothing less than a modern-day Marco Polo. Nixon, one can argue, discovered China."

"Opened her up to the world."

"Brought an outlaw state into the fold."

"They're still communists, but we can like them now."

"The masses I can handle, but not Mao."

"The leader of the free world comes calling, and he doesn't have the decency to put on a suit and tie."

"Mao owes Nixon big-time. Nixon made him a player."

"Ping-Pong diplomacy."

"Nixon just about invented the damn game."

"Everyone was playing Ping-Pong. Someone made a fortune."

"We bought a table."

"Who didn't? Mine still takes up half the den."

"Those Chinese people are such good Ping-Pongers. On *Wide World of Sports* they always kick our butts."

"That must've been what they meant by Ping-Pong diplomacy: we let them win."

I've seen the same matches on TV, and I have to admit I get a charge seeing those wiry Chinese guys knocking the shit out of the Americans.

"It's suited for the whole race of them. Those petite paddles and little balls are perfect for their little hands."

"I agree. It's all in the genes. They're small people, with delicate bones and skinny muscles. That makes them quicker, more agile. They flit around the Ping-Pong table like a bunch of birds. And that's the name of the game. Ping-Pong doesn't require strength."

"I was about to say, I'd like to see one of your Ping-Pongers go up against a Nolan Ryan fastball."

"The physiological differences," Drake breaks in, "are the product of Darwinian adaptations. You see, Chinese culture doesn't value the individual. That's why you always hear them talking about 'the people' or 'the masses.' You saw the slides, you saw how crowded it is over there. They put three or four of their men on a job that one average American can do by himself. For this reason the Chinese have no evolutionary imperative to develop bigger, stronger bodies."

Cindy Nelson says, "But what about our Sterling? I wouldn't call *him* a shrimp."

Things have been going so well. I'm doing my job, minding my own business, making like a part of the decor, blending with the Oriental rug, the velvet couch. But hearing my name boom across the room, I feel I've been found out, a flashlight beam hitting me square in the eyes.

"He's more than average for a Chinese," Drake says, with an assessing eye. "How tall are you, son?"

"Wait!" his wife jumps in. "Don't answer. Let us guess."

"What fun, we'll have a contest!"

"We need a prize."

"That's brilliant!"

"What about Sterling?"

I'm on my way to the kitchen with a tray of dirty cups and dishes. They're crazy, drunk and crazy. I pretend I haven't heard a thing, and hope their contest fades away.

"That's brilliant. Winner gets Sterling—a gourmet meal prepared in your home!"

"What a lot of fun! The winner gets Sterling."

KATHY LLOYD is the last to leave. She's a small woman, about the size of Zsa Zsa in her cork-soled shoes. Her husband has gone home in his own car; she stays to iron out the details. She won me.

We walk together across the lawn, she to her car, me to my apartment. As we approach the David she says, "The Roman god of love. Isn't he beautiful?"

"He doesn't do a thing for me."

"I should hope not," she says. "He's not supposed to." We stop at the statue, and she points out the David's perfection, its claim on the hearts of women, naming the various highly articulated muscle groups, pectorals, deltoids, biceps, abdominals, quadriceps. She doesn't stop there. His buttocks she calls his "buns," his penis is his "cock," which she speculates would be "hung like a goddamn horse" if the manufacturer had made the statue "the size of a real man."

Then she directs my gaze to the statue's hand dangling by his thigh, close to his plumbing. The hand is huge, out of proportion to the rest of his body. She extends her hand—she wants mine planted on hers. "You have beautiful hands," she says, "and that's not just me talking. We all think so. But *I* discovered them first.

"When you come to cook for us," she says, "Mr. Lloyd might not be there. I trust that will be all right with you." She squeezes my hand.

I pull free and continue walking toward the carriage house. I know what's coming: She's going to tell me that theirs is an open marriage, that she's some kind of swinger. "What're you going to make for us?" she says from behind. "I'll eat anything."

When we reach her car, a Buick Riviera, I open the door and she gets in. "Sterling, come closer, I'm not going to bite," she says. Her legs, lit by the amber door lamp, flow from the car.

"I want you to know that I held a positive view of your people long before Nixon ever dreamed of China. I never thought you were as bad as the Russians." In the meager light I can see she wears too much makeup, and the makeup can't hide age or the alcohol she's imbibed this night. I picture her lying in her bed, puffing up on what she reads in *Cosmopolitan*: "Sex, the New Fountain of Youth!" "The Allure of the Experienced Woman!"

But I think of Bliss, and here's my contribution: "Sex Ages You, Takes Something Away Every Time."

LATER THAT NIGHT, I'm lying in bed, trying to figure out how best to stay clear of Kathy Lloyd in the days ahead, when I hear voices outside, kids laughing. Drunk or stoned. I go to the window. Two long-haired guys are carrying the statue of David, one holding the head, the other the base, and a girl with a Marcia Brady look is skipping along, their accomplice. Am I dreaming? The moon shines off the plaster man, and he glows like a giant tube of light. They're coming toward the carriage house, in my direction; they don't see me; they're stealing the David!

I turn on a lamp, open the door, step onto the landing. In the night's stillness, when the boards creak under my weight, they are screaming. The young thieves look up at me and drop the statue, then run back across the lawn, stumbling and falling, laughing and cursing. Leaving beauty behind.

I run downstairs. In the moonlight, against the dark grass, the David a giant bone, the fibula of a prehistoric animal unearthed in a desert, once a primordial sea. I stand the statue up. I hoist it onto my shoulders, Atlas bearing the world. I step toward its usual spot on the lawn, then reverse myself, as if a magnetic force is pulling me back to my apartment. Suddenly I feel all-powerful and break into a gallop, the David almost weightless. We fly up the stairs.

I set the statue on the floor of my bedroom. Now I've got what the ladies want. I clear a space in my closet and put him in there with my other junk. Once he's out of sight, an inexplicable satisfaction settles into my body, a sensation like the glow of twenty-five-year-old Armagnac radiating from my belly, and I feel that the energy driving the world emanates from me.

SOME NIGHTS, in the crease of time before mosquitoes bite, long after the ladies have scratched good-bye kisses alongside one another's cheeks, I venture to the lawn and slide into the slot where several rosebushes converge, not far from where the David once stood. Here the air is thick, cathedral-like, what blood is to water.

The red-black blooms, each the size of a calf heart, cooling after a long day's sun, release their perfume, and closing my eyes I caress handfuls of fallen petals and hold the softness to my nose and inhale deeply. I might think of Libby Drake at these times, or of the customer of my parents' who had starred in an Ivory soap commercial. I'm driven by the same impulse that compelled me to bury my face in piles of strangers' dirty sheets, taking in their layered smell—cologne, deodorant, soap—to a bitter finish, the hint of feminine sweat.

But tonight the roses' musk leads me to Bliss. Should I go visit her in Iowa? Even if I can get the time off—I don't think the ladies will let me out of their sight—what will that prove? I wouldn't mind seeing her, but in the way we used to see each other here. Things between us made a kind of sense back then. We ate and drank and went to movies; once in a while we had sex. We had our own lives. We were a good match—each helping the other tread water, until the right thing came along. Now that has all changed. Me, a husband, a father? I'm still a baby myself!

I can't stand this: Why can't I just be a chef?

This morning when Libby Drake questioned me about the missing statue, I lied. All day long I've thought about the David's hands. They are huge, especially the one that rests on his thigh. That hand is monstrous. Ideal beauty, my ass! They are that way for a reason. Michelangelo isn't selling beauty, but deeds. Like the slaying of Goliath. The David is a monument to work, what's accomplished with one's hands. That's all I want people to consider when they see Sterling Lung: what I do with my hands.

Chapter 4

S HE's COMING. From halfway around the world, and for what? I'm not marrying her, I don't want anything to do with her. My mother is chief architect of the scheme—a picture-bride, a gift to her son, parental obligation done.

She's Genius's girl, because it's all on him; my mother's the brains, but he's the hands and legs of the operation. How can I not blame my father for this ridiculous situation? At this moment he's making his reckless way to the International Arrivals Building at JFK. Why has Genius, of all people, let himself be drawn into the madness? On this side of the globe, he alone had the power to prevent her from boarding the U.S.-bound flight. Zsa Zsa can hatch any plot that duty requires, but without her husband's assistance there's no chance of its success. It's Genius who goes to the bank and withdraws the funds for her ticket; on official papers he is her sponsor, the person who signs the dotted lines, licks the stamps, and swears oaths on her behalf.

At this late stage he can still save the day. He might come to his

senses or lose his will and turn the car around. My best and most real-
istic hope is that Genius, the world's premier bad driver, will have an
average day behind the wheel. Cruising Sunrise Highway at a steady
thirty-five-mile-an-hour clip, he'll piss off other drivers with his skit-
tishness, caution, arbitrary braking. He'll run at least one red light, and
come within inches of his mortality. I should know how awful a driver
he is, I taught him myself. The dubious consequence of flip-flopping
the natural order of things: a son should never try to teach his father
anything. Zsa Zsa was opposed to his learning. Why bother so late in
life? This was about a decade ago, '67, '68? And Genius, then in his
mid-fifties, was freshly discharged from the hospital after surgeons
removed a cancerous kidney—an operation that's left him in my mind
forever lopsided, the lone surviving urine-sodden kidney jerking its
connective tubing low like an overripe pear its limb. The man loses a
vital organ and, naturally, he wants to learn to drive a car. In Genius's
universe there's a perverse logic in the substitution of an internal com-
bustion engine for a kidney, which squeezes piss from the blood: Both
make you go.

I'm rooting Genius is true to form, produces just enough havoc on
the roads to delay his arrival at the airport, and causes my picture-bride
to think no one's coming for her and go away.

I CHECK MY WRISTWATCH. She's scheduled to land in a sweep of the
second hand.

What's funny is, I was scheduled to go to Iowa this week. I'm not
sure what my intentions were, and that's probably why, in the end, Bliss
told me not to bother coming at all. In my strongest moments I imagined myself telling her, I'm sorry, I'm not ready, I've made a mess of
both our lives and don't want to make the mess any worse. Other times
I thought I'd just show up and see how I felt when I saw her again, let
her cue me.

I'm in the kitchen now, my haven from the noise in my life—the threat of a picture-bride; Bliss's blooming belly. I'm deboning the five pounds of chicken breasts that have sprouted like mold in the refrigerator overnight. I have no memory of buying them or seeing before this morning the football-sized bundle, but then, I've been so frazzled recently, I forget and neglect and overlook easily and often. At the CIA I was taught how to anticipate appetites, foresee every contingency that might arise at the table. I learned to calculate a meal to its number of portions, each portion down to the ounce, the olive, the lettuce leaf, in order to minimize waste, to never buy more or less than I would need. But since Bliss's porcine postcard and Libby Drake's wavering love, and with my picture-bride's imminent arrival, I've been listless, not my usual cooking self. Should I expect anything less?

I rinse the chicken under cold water, washing off as much of the sour odor as I can. Who knows how long the meat has been fermenting in the refrigerator? The mere fact I haven't already tossed it in the trash is further evidence of my decline. After all, this is a house of plenty, in the land of plenty, America the beautiful, and its fruity plains, amber waves of grain, chicken in every pot, popcorn-peanuts-and-Cracker Jack. Let the slightly spoiled go to the dogs.

More so than a husband, that's what my picture-bride is after. That's what they're all after, coming over here. Taxiing on the runway, heart in her throat, scared to death of the customs officials and the fake uncle who await her arrival, she hasn't traveled these many miles for love. No one comes so far for the love of a cook; no, she is here for the bounty, for the privilege of throwing away what the starving world would kill for. She has come to be American, to lust after wealth without the slightest bit of shame.

HER NAME IS YUK, which rhymes with *cook,* and which according to Zsa Zsa means "jade." Yip Yuk Hing. And as far as I'm concerned, Genius can keep her as his own virgin bride. For years I've known her simply as "the pretty girl." I first spotted her in a photograph my aunt had sent from Hong Kong, nine females grouped around a banquet table, turquoise- and tangerine-colored dresses, hair piled like torpedoes on their heads, Yip Yuk Hing in the foreground, the largest of the figures, casting a sneaky, flirty sidelong glance at the camera, possessed of more good looks and self-confidence than a fourteen-year-old could possibly know what to do with. Zsa Zsa had taped the photograph to the corner of the kitchen mirror, a place that was a favorite hangout of mine during my high school years. My mistake was asking after the girl, hinting at the tiniest bit of interest. Yip Yuk Hing is the daughter of one of Zsa Zsa's "sisters" back in China. She seems to call every woman she knew a "sister," as if they all came from Toisan, shared the same bed, suckled at the same breasts. While I knew this was just her way of talking (or my own failure to translate her Chinese accurately), I tricked myself into believing that Yip Yuk Hing's mother and mine were indeed sisters, a fact that would render her my first cousin and therefore a genetically dubious mate. So when Zsa Zsa teased about one day introducing me to the pretty girl, I teased back: "Why not? I'm all for it." It was, I thought, low-risk posturing; she was only fourteen, and we were cousins. On my behalf Zsa Zsa sent birthday cards and Christmas presents to Yip Yuk Hing. I humored Zsa Zsa's every proposal: going together to Hong Kong, inviting Yip Yuk Hing to visit, taking her hand in marriage. She would casually float these propositions my way, and I would greet each with a "Sure, sure, sure. Whatever you want."

WHEN I WAS a freshman in college I brought a friend home for a night. He asked about the girl in the photograph, and I, unable to resist the urge, told him that she was my picture-bride, who would come join me, by earlier arrangement, after her eighteenth birthday. The story of my "typically Chinese" engagement was quickly circulated among my friends, and embraced as part of my biography: Sterling has three sisters, he was raised in the back of a laundry, and he's going to marry a girl he's seen only in a photograph. To them, it was all of a piece. No one questioned me—those Chinese people did such things. Put cats in chow mein, piss in the wonton soup. A few months later the Yip Yuk Hing rumor even ended my relationship with Rachel Berg. "How could you?" she said when she heard the story.

"How could I what?"

"You're a bigamist." She started to cry. "I was warned about you."

"Warned about what?"

"Concubines. Asian Studies 101. First wife, second wife, third wife. Your history is full of it. I won't be a part of some harem."

When I opened my arms to her, she said, "Oh, no you don't! This is the United States of America. You get only one. Either she goes or I go."

Obviously I could've easily resolved this predicament with a recitation of the truth. But when some fool wants to believe the earth is flat, you let her fall off the edge every time.

Looking back, now that Yip Yuk Hing's actually coming, I realize I should've just told Zsa Zsa straight out I wasn't interested. But I say "Sure, sure." to a lot of things. Go to medical school! Sure, sure. Get rid of that demon girlfriend! Sure, sure. She knew the drill, and my father knew the drill. So when I said, "Hey, sure, bring her on. You'll have Chinese grandchildren before you know it," I honestly had no reason to suspect Zsa Zsa and Genius would take what I had to say seriously, especially when I had never been less serious.

About the time Bliss was feeding me chicken soup, I received a letter from Yip Yuk Hing, an aerogram from Hong Kong addressed to me, mailed to my parents' place. Before then I used to secretly envy their far-flung correspondence, the nifty featherweight packets, powder blue as if they'd been die-cut from sky; I loved the border of red and navy parallelograms, the stamps with pictures of British royalty. Once Zsa Zsa pressed the letter in my hand I immediately felt the heft of its permanent blue-black ink. Yip Yuk Hing's words, etched into the paper, were like iron shavings scratching my palm. Holding the letter took my breath away. She was so close. No longer just the denizen of the square of photographic paper taped to the mirror. She was a real person, with hopes and desires, a will to reckon with. Zsa Zsa opened the letter and read it out loud. Her voice weighed on me, a thick steel ring hanging from my nose, and every word of Chinese I comprehended was a stern tug on that ring. I was sickened by my mother's gleeful tone, the oppressive strains of a conspiracy that was finally out in the open. I snatched the letter from her hands. "Where's my name?" I asked. Who put those thoughts inside that Hong Kong girl's head? "How do I know this is written to me?" Zsa Zsa pointed at the salutation and said, "Here. She calls you 'sir'." And with this she started to laugh at the silliness of anyone paying such deference to her son.

WHAT KILLS ME IS, they kept her imminent arrival a secret until the very last minute. They waited until they knew she was safely buckled into her seat, with an airsickness bag probably fluffed open in her hands, and then dropped the news on my head. *Oh, by the way, we hope you're not too busy, your bride will be arriving in a few hours.* There's nothing surprising in their act. They've always treated me as they would an infant, as if their will is my will. I might be closing in on my twenty-seventh birthday, but see, they still think they can drop any old kid they want into my playpen with me. With the importation of a picture-bride they've perfected their denial I might have a life of my own. That's why Genius won't eat my cooking; why he always snipes at the way I dress and wear my hair; why he acts as if every girlfriend I've had were a ghost, a figment of my imagination. And speaking of girlfriends, maybe I should drop a bomb on their heads, tell Genius and Zsa Zsa that a grandchild of theirs is already baking in someone's womb. Then what becomes of Yip Yuk Hing? Do they ship her back to Hong Kong, or pretend their grandchild doesn't exist? Who's to say what their response will be? Their most predictable trait is their immigrant oddness, the square-peg-in-a-round-hole quality of their life in America, of their fit in my life. I wouldn't be surprised if in their infinite weirdness they accept the Bliss baby and designate Yip Yuk Hing its Chinese mother, whose influence will purify its tainted bloodline.

As recently as last night I told Zsa Zsa long-distance that I'm not interested in marrying anyone at the present time, particularly not an import. Nowadays, I said, nobody marries someone he doesn't know or love. "I did!" she said. (Zsa Zsa's word for "love" is the same as the one she uses for "hug," so whenever she asked for a hug, in the past, it sounded like "Give me some lovin'.") When I tried to articulate to her my desire to marry a woman I loved, with the caveat *if* I should marry at all, I realized I had never conversed so abstractly with either of my parents. My spoken Chinese is weak. Zsa Zsa talks at me and my sisters only in Chinese; we in turn understand much more than we can speak, and answer her mostly in a tossed salad of bad English and ruptured Chinese. I studied Chinese for seven semesters in college, earning straight A-minuses, costarring in a Chinese-language theatrical production (I played the patriarch whose wayward son goes to the United States and marries an American girl, forsaking his first, Chinese wife at home), and later was an extra in a professional Peking opera. But all that study is wasted on my parents, because their dialect (Toisanese) and the one I learned (Mandarin) are as different as Spanish and French. Still, while I was talking to Zsa Zsa about love I decided to go one hundred percent Chinese: I had to short-circuit her plan, a poor barefooted girl who had done no one any harm was on the verge of having chaos and irreparable damage inflicted upon her innocent life; and in order to do that I wanted to reach Zsa Zsa on her own terms. I thought I had said, in my best Chinese, "If I marry, I want to marry someone I love." She started to laugh, so I knew I must've screwed something up. Even over the phone line I could see her sly-eyed saying, "Of course, of course, every marriage has to have that, no matter what the woman wants."

My mother thought I was talking about sex. My mother with sex on her brain. Remarkable she knew about sex at all. She and Genius seem so sexless I wouldn't be surprised to learn that my sisters and I were selected from a catalogue. Suddenly I had a new mother, one whose arms and legs must've held my father in unimaginable ways; this new mother said, "After you and Yuk are married, go easy on her. There's no hurry, you have a whole lifetime for that." Once my shock wore off I told her, as forcefully as I could in slow baby English, not to monkey around with other people's lives. I refused to share the blame for Yip Yuk Hing's impending unhappiness.

It was as if she didn't hear me: "Should your bride wear the traditional Chinese red gown," she asked, "or do you prefer the American-style white wedding dress?"

"How can you think of such things?" I said, disgusted.

"How can you not?" she answered.

I took a deep breath and delivered what I hoped was the knockout punch: "I'm not going to marry her."

How should I interpret the long silence that followed—bewilderment or indignation? But that was typical of my experience of my parents; I'm never sure which of my words hit their mark and which flew miles wide.

Finally she spoke out. "Bastard," she said. "If you don't want her, I'll keep her for myself."

I CAN'T GET OVER Genius. His capitulation to Zsa Zsa's scheme is all the more stunning because he was once in the very shoes he's squeezing me into. Over the years I've heard Genius enough—yelling at Zsa Zsa, chatting with his friends—to have pieced together his story.

A week before his ship left China, my father took a wife. Marriage was a precondition to his departure, his parents stipulated, and he was glad to comply with their wish as long as it guaranteed a swift, uncomplicated exit. He was twenty-six at the time, my age. His mother arranged everything, hiring a marriage broker, a parched reed with alarmingly red lips, whose motives in the affair seemed to extend beyond the financial. She found him a suitable match, whose one apparent flaw was that she was slightly older than other possible village brides. Everyone agreed she was a beauty, with fair skin, shiny hair, a mare's hips for frequent and easy births, a bearer of sons. An astrologer assured Genius's mother that theirs was a fortuitous union, bliss in the wedding bed, children on demand. To him, age and looks did not matter; his concern was to satisfy his obligations, then off to America, a land of machines not animals. Especially automobiles. Though his impending wedding was nothing more than a means to a long-coveted end, my father couldn't resist the chance, arranged by the marriage broker, to appraise his future wife anonymously at the market.

She was standing, as promised, next to the fishmonger's stall, wearing an embroidered white blouse, unaware which of the men looking her way was her future husband. Her arms were lean but muscular, her hair thick, eyes clear. Incredulous over his good fortune, he wondered what was wrong with her. She must have had a defect that he couldn't see, stone ears, a silent tongue, her womanhood a seamless scar which nothing entered, from which nothing left. He had heard men talk of such things. Or had another already marked her with his claim? Or was she every bit the perfection he saw, her flaw coming, then, from without—a philanderer, an opium addict, or a murderer in the family?

Yet did any of this matter? His duty was to provide his parents with a daughter-in-law to serve them. To that end he had every intention of acting responsibly—checking that her gums were pink, feet broad and sturdy, anus free of worms. He would feel terrible if he burdened them with a problem. For good measure he would give her a big belly before he departed. The stars were pleased, the astrologer said, how could his parents not be?

The wedding ceremony was endless. On the long voyage he would fondly remember the wedding costumes, the banquet, the heads tipping back wine, the music, her electrocuted hair.

Beyond reproach half a world away, his photograph hanging prominently on the wall of his parents' home, he gradually metamorphosed into paper—letters and money orders. His absence transformed into monthly celebrations, a little burst of prosperity in an envelope marked "U.S.A." He had seen the excitement in other families in the village; he could never forget the gray-hair whose bony hand had pinched his arm, pulled him aside to show the letter she had received that day. "Do you know what this means?" she had asked, digging her nail into the paper, under the word "$." Of course, he couldn't read the foreign word, but from the lift of her bosom, the snap in her voice, he reasoned that it must have been her son's good name. Now it was his turn to pay his debts, send pieces of his body back, on the installment plan—here, this is for my eyes; this is for my lungs; this is for my hair. Buy his freedom from the past. And no one would have reason to complain, especially if the baby arrived with a cashew between its legs. An ocean away, a world apart, they were husband and wife under the same vast sky. After his escape he would not forget how public that debt was. And shipboard, below deck and seasick, he heard the lapping waves: *Do honor Do honor Do honor.*

He did. But still his wife wrote letters full of bitterness. When was he sending for her? "Why did you have to marry me, only to leave me this way?" she once asked, like a landowner, that is, like someone who had the right.

GENIUS DELIVERS Yip Yuk Hing safely home from the airport.

Two weeks pass.

I have yet to see my picture-bride. I have been summoned to the laundry but have refused to go. "She's yours," I said on the phone to Genius, resorting to rudeness, a favorite stratagem.

In the short time Yip Yuk Hing has been in the country, she has established herself in my sisters' room. The arrangement smells of incest. Zsa Zsa has no plans for Yuk other than an absolute breakdown in my resistance and our subsequent marriage.

Zsa Zsa calls often, on the verge of tears: If only you saw in person what a pretty and clever girl she is.

FINALLY I AGREE to come home for a visit, making no promises. I might stay for dinner, I might stay a minute. I might just peek at her through the window and go. Before hanging up, an emboldened Zsa Zsa says, "Don't forget to bring her something."

"Like what?"

"Don't be such a dead boy. If it was one of your stinky American girlfriends you'd know what to give her."

The date is set and I'm miserable. I'm feeling so sorry for myself that my mind can't stay off Bliss. Suddenly she's starting to look really good to me. Okay, I don't imagine her with a big belly. I won't allow my mind to wander there. But she looms in my thoughts, like a secret I'm dying to tell someone. At least we have some things in common: an alma mater, American TV, and the English language. In anticipation of meeting Yip Yuk Hing I've been discombobulated at work. For two days running I serve finger sandwiches for lunch. On the third the ladies complain. I worry I have lost my will to cook. At the same time my own diet takes a nosedive. I have abandoned the major food groups for a steady intake of flour and sugar, plenty of Drake's cakes and Hostess Twinkies; my inner tubing—the cute pink intestines and the grim deep-purple bowels—swells with the accumulated dough.

TOMORROW'S MY DAY OFF. The biggest day in Yip Yuk Hing's young life. After I serve the ladies lunch, I'll walk into town and shop Richfield's modest business district for a trinket. I'm heartsick for her: there are hundreds, probably thousands, of Chinese mothers in America, Cuba, Canada, Malaysia, Brazil who could've set her up with an eager (desperate), appreciative (dutiful) son, but she has the lame luck to hook up with Zsa Zsa and Genius and their disobedient, defiant, pigheaded son.

What would Jade want? False promises suckered her into this long, fruitless journey that will end only with her return to where she came from. I am partially to blame for this tragedy, and here is my chance for easy contrition, buy forgiveness with something nice. (But not too nice: she might get the wrong idea.) I step in and out of stores. When Genius used to drag me on errands, everywhere we went the shelves were full of merchandise I coveted, things foreign to the world that my parents, especially he, had made for us: barbecue tongs, wallpaper, curtain rods, pet food, frozen fish sticks, motor oil, garden hoses, flower seeds, deodorant. Symbols of the good life.

I'm standing in front of the hardware store window, contemplating possible gift ideas on display. My favorites are the four-slice toaster, three-speed mixer, electric can opener, and curling iron for Farrah Fawcett–style locks. I try to imagine these appliances through the Chinese girl's eyes. Despite her polished, urbane appearance in the banquet photo, I cling to the notion of Yip Yuk Hing as one of those Chinese I've seen countless times on educational TV—the good, pure, poor child of nature from the countryside, a down-to-earth, salt-of-the-earth princess among the commune set, free of materialistic cravings, Oriental spirit daughter of Max Yasgur, farmer father of the Woodstock Nation. She's bamboo baskets not Wedgwood, cotton shoes not Gucci, tea not Pepsi, boiled water not Perrier; her long black hair is sun-dried in the rice paddies, not blow-dried by General Electric. What would she do with any of these small appliances? She's not a consumer, just as I'm not a socialist. I shift my weight, trying to decide what to do, and I notice my reflection in the shop window. I imagine myself as my father, fresh off the boat, coming face to face for the first time with such an array of American beauties. What a cultural mismatch that must've been. Then I swap places with him: I'm in China, and the natives turn up their noses at my vichyssoise, in favor of a forest-floor stew of medicinal herbs. All my learning and skill wasted. And I pity myself for the difficulty of my new life, in a new land.

Soon enough, I shake free of these thoughts; I was coming dangerously close to finding sympathy with my father, especially his early days in this country, with no money, no degrees, no relations, no language other than what he came over with. I've never considered Genius as young, in possession of a future, a man my age with hopes and desires, ambitions and expectations for this life. As far as I'm concerned, he arrived on the planet a fully formed old man, a head of gray hair, the missing kidney, and the scowl he always wears for me. He's just a parent, and it's unnatural for a child to conceive of a parent in any other way. I can't. I won't. Were it in me to do so, then I'd have to understand that scowl permanently stamped on his face.

A few doors down, at a place called Wig Palace, a shopgirl is rearranging heads in the display window. She has an orange mouth and hair to match. Lucille Ball brightness and an Ann-Margret cut. I can't tell if she's in a wig or not. In a lime-green jumpsuit and red leather shoes she towers above me on the sidewalk. She's switching the hairstyles on the dummy heads, when she notices me and smiles and offers me the blond wig she has in her hands. I shake my head, wave my hands. I'm flustered: Is she suggesting I buy the wig and wear it myself? She turns and goes back to her work. I am walking away when I hear tapping on the glass. The shopgirl motions for me to enter.

The telephone's ringing inside the store. She wags her finger, I'll go get that, I'll be right back. The shelves are lined with heads under wigs cut in the same long, wavy style, in every normal hair color. The faces are identical, with the same high cheekbones, small noses, and big eyes that add up to the same blunt, generic prettiness. Who's buying so many wigs? Where are the bald women? Or are they women going incognito? Women having affairs, hiding from their husbands. Or sick with cancer. In junior high, the girls were into falls, hair extensions: one day they'd show up with their regular hair, the next day it would be long. I felt betrayed by the constant shifting of the visual landscape, and envious of their freedom to become something they were not. I have an idea: Put Yip Yuk Hing under a *Charlie's Angels*–style wig, a big blond thing like Farrah's hair; how much more bearable her American days will be.

"You have great hair," the shopgirl says, coming from behind me. "I know a broker who'll pay lots for hair as thick and straight as yours."

I reach around and finger my ponytail. "Really?"

She closes in. Her manner is that of professional detachment as she aggressively assesses my hair, sensitive to qualities lost on a layman. Her touch reminds me of the barbers of my youth, except her fingertips are painted orange. What she is is a trafficker in body parts. A black-market commerce in human kidneys and lungs and eyes. Contraband. Drugs. Tropical birds and alligator meat. The Chinese are famous in the underground trade: deer antlers, bear claws, tiger testicles.

"I bet it grows back fast. You've got a renewable resource on your head."

"How much?"

"Hundreds," she says. "Maybe more."

"I can't believe it. Who wants to look like this?"

"Well, it's not like you'll be riding on somebody's scalp. Your hair's only the raw material. The manufacturer washes, dyes, cuts, and styles it."

"But it's still my hair on some stranger's head."

"This is hair we're talking about, honey. Strands of dead protein." She twirls my ponytail around her finger. "You've got a cash crop sprouting from your skull."

I STOP BY FUCHS'S on my way home. "*Oy vey,* Sterling!" he says. "What happened to you?"

I bend to locate my reflection in the butcher's scale, and run my hands through my fresh-cropped hair. I look like a young Mao, when his hair was thick and had yet to recede, or like Genius, as I've seen him in pictures taken soon after his arrival in the United States, his hair ink-black, blunt-cut, Brylcreemed back. "I got a haircut, that's all."

Fuchs's eyes narrow as he clamps his gaze on me. "You say it like it's nothing. But if you ask me, Sterling, and I know you're not asking, that hair was to you what those teeth are to Jimmy Carter, what those bosoms are to Raquel Welch."

I reach and feel the rough edge where each individual shaft met its brutal end. I already miss my ponytail, its reassuring weight like an anchor. At least I'll get my parents off my back. Genius hated my long hair, saw it as a shameful billboard that advertised his failure as a father; Zsa Zsa tolerated it, but was always nagging me to have it cut. The ladies at the club loved it, and Bliss said she'd kill me if I ever lopped it off. I tell Fuchs the whole story: The search for a gift for Yip Yuk Hing ("Wait a minute, that's not the Yale student"), the Wig Palace adventure, the cash offer, the Indian guy in the apartment above the store who did the deed ("I'm sorry that you are not satisfied, sir. I never claimed to be a barber"). I lean forward and stare at the prodigious hairs growing from the butcher's nostrils: "You know, you can stand a little trim yourself, Fuchs."

"Don't get personal here."

"Sorry. I'm not myself. All these changes."

"Get a grip, Sterling. It grows back. And you're three hundred smackeroonies for the better. If someone offered me that kind of money, I'd cut my hair too, no problem. But"—he paused a moment—"it's weird, when you think of it, selling off parts of your body like that."

"Who are you to talk? What the hell do you call all this?" I sweep my arms over the refrigerated meat cases.

"I told you once already, don't get personal. Where would these animals be without me? Who'd raise them if it wasn't for me selling them?"

"Oh, I see, you're a humanitarian now."

A customer enters. Fuchs greets her and offers his assistance. It takes a couple of glances before I recognize her, the club's newest member, Barbara Cohen, whose presence there is politically motivated, Drake's play for the Jewish vote, minuscule as it is in these parts. A "trailblazer," that's how Libby Drake officially introduced her to the other ladies, the first club member "of the Hebrew faith." I immediately thought she seemed out of place there. It isn't just the physical difference—she is Fuchs in drag, with heavy eyebrows and stiff wavy hair like a bell-shaped helmet—but a feeling she throws off because she's the only one of her kind there (an olive tree in a grove of maples).

"Mrs. Cohen? I'm Sterling, the chef at the club."

She looks blankly at me, a trace of alarm around her eyes. "I thought it was you. You've cut your hair."

I nod.

"You look . . . better, I guess." Then she scoots closer to me. "Can I ask you something?" She digs a finger into the bend of my elbow. "How do you stand it there? Those women talk without moving their lips. They're so strange."

I feel my brow twist into rigatoni. "What do you mean?"

"I have to tell you?" She shakes her head, but her hair stays in place. "If you can't see for yourself, you better quit before you turn into one of them," she says, then bursts out laughing.

Once she leaves I ask Fuchs, "What's her problem?"

He shrugs. "Who's to say? I can't imagine why she doesn't like her club mates."

I slap my hand on top of the refrigerated case. "Cut the sarcasm, Fuchs. I need your help." I remind him of the bind I'm in, Yip Yuk Hing, the all-purpose gift I need to find that will say to her simultaneously, "Welcome!" and "I'm sorry!" and "Good-bye!"

"This is big, Fuchs. She's come all this way to marry me. You understand? Think of how humiliated she'll feel when she goes back to Hong Kong."

"Don't send her back. It's as simple as that."

"Fuchs, she's Chinese. What am I going to do with a Chinese girl? I'm not attracted to Chinese women. It would be like my mother making me horny. Wouldn't that worry you?"

"Sterling, wake up, she's not your mother."

"I know, I know that. You don't understand. It's not like I've got anything against Chinese women. I'm not saying I *refuse* to find Chinese girls sexy, I'm just born this way. It's in my genes."

"My condolences go out to you and yours."

"And I could easily ruin her life. I can't speak Chinese, she can't speak English, I won't be happy, then she won't be happy, and I won't even know how unhappy she is, because she won't be able to tell me."

Fuchs removes his white cap and brushes his hand over his bald spot. "Boy, you really got it going. I should take up cooking and buy some of your hair from that wig joint and slap it on my head. See if my luck changes."

"What about my luck?"

"I should start charging. You get money for your hair, I should get money for my advice." He puts his elbow on the meat case and drops his cheek in his hand. "From where I'm standing, friend, you seem to be doing everything right. You got luck like the rest of us got facial hair."

"Fuchs," I say, leaning against the meat case, my arms folded on the stainless-steel top. I lay my head heavily on my hands. "My friend, you don't know the half of it." It is then I tell him about Bliss.

"So you see, I have a choice: I can be the good son or the good father."

Another customer enters. "I'll be with you in a moment, madam. Excuse us, please." With his finger Fuchs motions for me to walk around the refrigerated case and join him in the rear of the store. He leads me into the meat locker. It's unbelievably cold, but Fuchs is unfazed. As we stand between two sides of beef hanging from ceiling hooks, he says, "Sterling, I cut meat for a living. I don't know from nothing. Female business is over my head. I can tell you which of my ladies is going to buy tenderloin and which chuck. But I can't say why your girl the dentist makes friends with the lady Goliath from Yale that she finds naked in your bed. Is that what they call love? I don't know too many girls to do that. It sounds to me like she wants you too badly. And that's not good. About the one you got coming from halfway around the world, a total stranger, who you say wants to marry you too, all I've got to say is I've got exactly zero offers on the table. Why're you asking me for advice? If you haven't noticed lately, I'm no Burt Reynolds."

My eyes jump from Fuchs to the carcasses surrounding us. One day not long ago, these steer were hanging out in some pasture, ogling the best-looking cows. "In a not too distant future," I say, "I'm going to be like one of these guys."

"Steak?"

"No, dead. And when that happens I want people to say nice things about me. He was a nice person, a great chef. There's a right thing here I'm supposed to do. I feel like I'm on the verge of screwing up something big that's going to stay with me a long, long time, like the odor of old fried fish. I'll be in my grave, and people will remember me for it, coupled for eternity, like Nixon and Watergate: Sterling Lung, bad son, shithead father."

"Look at the bright side: You'll be dead." Fuchs says this, then disappears, leaving me freezing in the meat locker. He returns with a three-foot-long salami. "Take this," he says. "It's kosher. The best of the best. Dry as Jerusalem."

"What am I supposed to do with it?"

"You need Fuchs to tell you what to do with that salami in your hands, you're in trouble." He steps to the door and stands in front as if blocking my escape. "I want you to give it to her. Sterling, this Chinese girl, you don't have to send her back. We're business associates and we're social associates. Do me a favor. Give her that salami for me. Tell her it's from your good friend Fuchs, tell her he's a wonderful guy. Tell her there's plenty more where that came from. And that there's good money in meat." He winks. "This way everybody's luck changes for the better."

I POUND ON THE DOOR at the rear of my parents' store, and it thunders back: it's an implausibly thick hollow-core metal door, designed to stop bullets, repel flames, shield against radiation. What's so damn precious inside?

I can't just go in, because after I ignored Genius's millionth request that I come claim my bride, he demanded that I mail him my key for Yip Yuk Hing to use. I did so obediently, glad to pay what seemed a cheap price to end the fiasco. But he hasn't given up. According to him, she lives here, I don't. And there's no reason for both of us to carry keys—when we visit in the future, we'll come as a couple.

Genius's Fury isn't in its usual parking space. He and Zsa Zsa never go out during the week. I push up the collar of my jean jacket and circle to the front of the laundry. In the dusk their absence seems even spookier. The sight of idle pressing machines and unmanned ironing boards startles me. With a coin I rap against the plate-glass window, making a sharp, skull-cleaving noise. I hurry to the back door again. I start to worry. Usually the laundry's open for business a twelve-hour day, eight to eight. Between closing and midnight they're often still working. It's only six-thirty. The store should be open, and they in back eating dinner.

The parking lot is empty except for the baker's black Buick. All night his ovens turn out breads, rolls, and cakes, heavy on the vegetable shortening. The air reeks of a mingling of his crude high-profit-margin baking and his dumpsterful of rancid milk and fermented dough.

Standing there I remember the afternoon when I left to start my job at the Ladies' Club. I had just taken a load of my belongings from the laundry to my frog-shaped Valiant, and when I went for more boxes someone had already locked the door.

"Open up!"

"Is that you?" Genius said. "Back so soon?"

"How can I be back when I haven't gone?"

"What are you so mad about? You went outside. When you're outside I don't hear you, I don't see you. You could've died, and I wouldn't even know it. So I locked up."

To register my exasperation with my father's line of reasoning, I slapped the side of my head, the blow landing with such force that my eye flattened against its socket. I hoped that by doing this I might chip away at his intractable dignity, make him feel the sting of his hands that couldn't wait to lock me out. Be rid of me. How does it go on TV? Donna Reed sweeps down the stairs, answers the phone, distributes those neatly packed lunches, and dishes out her unrivaled kisses to her darlings as they leave the house: Here is nutrition; here is red, heart-shaped love; come back for more. And when they do, they find the door unlocked, and Donna aproned, combed, perfumed, breath minty fresh, at the threshold to greet them.

I'M NAPPING in the Valiant, when Genius's Fury pulls up and wakes me. A rear window rolls down. She is framed as in a picture. I rub my sleep-crudded eyes. In the illumination of the parking lot light, Yip Yuk Hing waves. A speedy up-and-down motion like Granny's during the end credits of *The Beverly Hillbillies*.

"Where have you been?" I demand as they unfold from the car. "Isn't it still business hours? Don't you have work to do?"

Zsa Zsa counteracts my irritability with a cloying cheerfulness. "We ate dinner at a restaurant. Very good, very enjoyable."

"Beef restaurant," says Yuk, in an English that surprises me. Confident, only mildly accented. "My favorite. Sizzy-la is name of establishment. Really good food."

I try not to look at her. I'm afraid to. But her beauty has already sunk in deep, a thorn embedded in tissue no tweezer can reach. Hearing her speak, my old ears seem useless; looking at her, my old eyes obsolete. She is taller than Zsa Zsa, slightly shorter than Genius. Her eyes are dark and wildly lucid; they shimmer with intelligence, a light inside that caresses everything they behold. She's wearing blue jeans and a white peasant blouse, gathered slightly just above the bosom, then tenting down to her waist. I recognize it as one of my sisters' shirts. It's obvious from the cotton's flirty lift that she wears it more smartly, amply, ably than any of my skinny sisters ever did.

A beaming Genius, his face flushed the pink of medium-rare, says, "Yuk knows how to eat. We go to restaurants all the time now. *Very enjoyable.*" This is my father's idea of an introduction: Chef Son, meet our future daughter-in-law, your future wife, Propitious Palate. A match blessed by the kitchen god. I can't recall seeing Genius happier or chattier. His bantering is a strange comfort at this awkward moment, one in which, as a matter of pride, I must try to appear indifferent to Yuk. He diverts my gaze from where it keeps wanting to stray: to Yuk, to her eyes, which size me up with darting glances, to her lustrous hair falling loose over her shoulders. I am full of feeling for her, but I'm not sure what, exactly, it is: envy (the way she gets on with my parents), pity (the fact she is stuck with them), or love (she's anything but the barefoot girl with the oily scalp and barbarian tongue who loomed in my imagination).

"Your parents work extremely a lot," Yuk says. "Too many hour, not enough pays. I promote Western ethics: Take it easy. Each week we close laundry early and dine at restaurant."

"Yuk is very good influence. Modern girl," Genius says.

"*We* told you to take it easy," I say, defensively. My sisters and I meant it too; we saw how hard they worked. "But you never listened to us."

"Big difference," Genius adds, switching to English. "You say take it easy because you want to take it easy yourself. You just lazy a kit."

I notice Genius is wearing his suit. He puts it on only for special occasions, weddings, banquets, funerals, and allegedly the day I was born. It's the lone suit he owns, a decades-old double-breasted number straight off the set of *The Untouchables,* with lapels as wide as shark fins and raspberry pinstripes on dark gray wool. In the photos I've seen of his early American days, he's posing: Panama hat, cigarette, leather shoes, the suit, and a mischievous light in his eyes. That was the man he sealed in envelopes and sent across the sea to Zsa Zsa. And for a long time now I have known the suit one day will be mine by default, my sisters posing no competition. It is my inheritance, and that is fine, just as long as it doesn't come with the man inside.

Genius flips through the wad of keys in his hand. The suit makes him look taller, more substantial, even though he bought it a size or so too big, expecting in America he would grow into the broad shoulders and loose waist, the long sleeves and inseam. Watching him unlock the door, I have to remind myself that the surgeons cut out one of his kidneys, not a piece of his brain. He seems more lopsided than ever: off-balance, not all there. How else to explain why he has it in for me? In a family full of females, I should have been his natural ally. And yet the older he gets, the more lopsided he seems.

As soon as I enter the store I head straight for the refrigerators. It is my habit, how it is to be home. One refrigerator, then the next, opening the doors and looking, but knowing there's nothing in there that I'd want to eat. Zsa Zsa runs water for tea, and as she tells me things she has already told me over the phone—how she never would have discovered Texas toast had it not been for Yuk; how everyone who has met Yuk adores Yuk; how they are lucky to have her; and how lucky I am. I take refuge in the machines, absorbed by their contents, and move busily back and forth between these obese twins, set side by side, one motor whirring on, then the other's. On a good day, if I'm lucky, I might find a bottle of Coke stuffed among paper bags of oranges, greens, and roots; bundles of medicinal herbs, twigs, bark, berries, and what look like worms bound with pink cellophane ribbon; see-through boxes of black mushrooms and funky salted fish; cloudy plastic wrappers of duck sausage and waxy pork bellies; takeout cartons with scraps of roast pig, roast liver, roast ribs; jars of oysters, shrimp, wood ears, lily buds; and dishes and bowls, of metal and porcelain, stacked one on top of the other, teeming with leftovers that have been reheated and re-served so many times not a trace of nutrients or flavor lingers in their pale cells. It's barefoot food, eat-with-sticks food. Under harvest moons, rinse off the maggots, slice, and steam. It is squatting-in-still-water food. Pole-across-your-shoulders, hooves-in-the-house food.

It was among the embarrassments of my youth. Thanks to my oldest sister, Lucy, the family flirted occasionally with real food. What real people ate. With forks and knives, your own plate, your own portions, no more dipping into the communal soup bowl. Food from boxes and cans. The best were Swanson TV dinners. Meatloaf, Salisbury steak. I was convinced Salisbury steak was served in the White House every night. Meat in one compartment, vegetable medley in another, apple crisp next door. What a concept! Everything had its own house or its own room. How real people lived. By the time I was nine I had cooked my first meal: roast beef, Green Giant canned corn, Betty Crocker instant mashed potatoes, Pillsbury Poppin' Fresh rolls. Call it the march of generations.

We weren't a family of big eaters. Lily and Patty pecked. Lucy consistently left half her rice. My parents and I were the family jaws, though since his operation my father slacked off from his usual two-bowl pace. Consider this, then: As the household is now constituted, there is a three-to-two diner-to-refrigerator ratio.

I HELPED my father bring home the second refrigerator. It was probably the last time I tried to make a connection with him.

Chinese New Year's Eve, about ten years ago. I returned from school to find my sisters already pressed into service of the New Year, scrubbing and dusting and vacuuming every inch of the store for that clean start, just as we would, for the same reason, wash our feet and hair later that night. In the kitchen my mother was frying the New Year's fish, a porgy for the ancestors, while my father sat like an ancestor himself, stolid, in a nimbus of smoke, his hand serving his Lucky Strike up to his lips, the cigarette like a thick stick of incense, the action a prayer to his own spirit.

"Where have you been?" he asked, pouring hot water into a bowl of broken saltines and Borden condensed milk. I was the only one of his children he made this for; I was the only one who was willing to eat it. He had been waiting for my return, and now motioned for me to eat the warm, sweet concoction.

When I finished, we went out to the backyard, the parking lot, and Pop (that's how I thought of him back then) handed me the keys to the family car. Pop did not drive, and I had only a learner's permit. I turned the ignition, and the engine churned, started, stalled. Ma stuck her head out the metal door, the expression on her face a hybrid of hurt and confusion, and before she could utter a word, the engine coughed, engaging, and I gave her the gas, and she roared at Ma, and Pop yanked down the bill of his orange hunting cap and tapped the gearshift, signaling me to hit the road.

I was a good driver even without a license. I liked the idea that Pop and I might get into trouble together. Bad boys. I didn't see how I could lose: "He made me do it, Officer," I would say, my finger like a gun at the earflap of Pop's cap. And now I got to drive without the encumbrance of a nervous driver's ed teacher or bossy sister. For the briefest instant I wondered why my father hadn't enlisted one of my road-legal sisters instead of waiting for me to come home from school. But hadn't Pop always waited for me? Waited for a son as his wife delivered girl after girl after girl; waited for the son to mature into a second pair of hands to help him with his chores; waited for him to turn into a set of wheels. I knew that was all there was to it. I knew I wasn't singled out as someone special, someone necessary.

I played with the radio dial and was pleased, impressed even, by how adept I was at the maneuver. I switched on the heater, the blower on high, then low, and tried the wipers and upped the volume on the radio. When somebody honked, I honked back, long blasts, as if to say, "You're welcome. I like the way you drive too!" After the rush of that first honk, I clutched the steering wheel at ten o'clock and two o'clock and braced for my father's fierce bark or flying hand or both. But there was no reprimand, no thwack to the back of my head. For a split second I felt cheated. When I finally glanced over at Pop, he was sitting on the edge of the vinyl seat, gripping the dash with both hands, his body so rigid one high-pitched screech and he'd shatter like glass. It was then I realized that in the car the rules that governed our life together had changed. Our common ground had shifted, a tremor strong enough to make you stop and reevaluate your days. As illegal as I was in the car, it looked far worse for my father. Whatever advantage he might have claimed by virtue of his age, he had forfeited it when he slid in next to me and ordered me to go.

Then he told me to stop. We were in the middle of a tree-lined street of brick houses and, up ahead at the intersection, businesses, including a laundry run by a family friend. I eased off the brake, letting the car roll. It only stood to reason that "stop" meant at the corner. "Stop," Pop repeated. "We've arrived."

"What do you mean? Arrived where?"

Pop looked over his shoulder, out the rear window, and I put the car in reverse, driving to meet my father's gaze. "We've arrived," Pop said again excitedly, once, twice. He bounded from the car, circled past the front end, crossed the street. I had never seen him so frisky. Then I saw why: There on the curb was a discarded refrigerator, and Pop was grabbing the handle, as if shaking hands.

The outside air was colder than a refrigerator could ever be. "How do you like it?" my father asked.

I had never thought of a refrigerator as something you liked. It was just there, the way your arms or your teeth were. I shrugged.

"I won it," he said, his breath making steam. "It's all mine."

I wasn't sure, but I thought I heard bragging in Pop's voice. And why shouldn't he brag, I reasoned, a refrigerator is—if nothing else—impressive for its size. This one was an old Frigidaire with rounded corners like a bar of soap, and a dent where its heart would be if this were the body of a man. But I quickly recognized that this particular refrigerator was no prize from *Let's Make a Deal*. What had he won but hundreds of pounds of garbage, a scrap-metal dealer's dream?

Pop removed a homemade dolly from the trunk of the car. Double-thick plywood and black supermarket-cart wheels. Then a length of coarse rope. "Two are always better than one," Pop said. "Has to be that way, except in the case of children." He was pleased with himself, making a joke at others' expense, like the cigar-smoking comedians on *Ed Sullivan*. He said, in English, "I have two kit, I feed two mouth. I have four kit, I feed four mouth. I have two refrigerator, we have more food to eat. Hey, *goong hee faht toy*." He laughed. "This way new year start off in very good style."

Snow began falling, large, heavy flakes. Pop and I inched the refrigerator off the curb and onto the dolly positioned in the gutter, the wet snow acting as a lubricant. "Does this thing work?" I asked.

"It has to work," he said. "It's all mine now! Good machine better than money. Money you spend—no more, all gone. Paper turn into air. Nothing. But a machine like this refrigerator is different. If I keep it full up, it always give you plenty good food to eat."

Following my father's directions, I backed the car inches shy of the Frigidaire. Pop lashed the refrigerator to the car's bumper, then twined a bedsheet over it. "Chinese people don't like to show off," he said, addressing the look of disapprobation on my face. "We don't want to call attention to ourselves. I don't want people to say, 'Oh, look at that big shot, he must have won that nice refrigerator'."

Even from my sixteen-year-old's perspective I was dubious about his scheme. Such an opinion was fully consistent with others I held for whatever Pop did or put his mind to doing. His intentions and deeds arrived in my brain like the sight of a man who tips his hat and reveals a head of blue hair: The man is a whole human being, bearing all the requisite parts, but at the same time everything about him feels wrong, patently untrustworthy.

I put the car in drive. The tug at my rear made me feel important, heroic. The enormous weight, the mystery beneath the white sheet, my father's winnings and how he would not brag about it to the world; the big snow and hard wind, the wipers barely keeping pace with the storm, the wheels' flimsy contact with the road.

My father was smoking, more relaxed now, and when I reached for a cigarette, fully expecting my hand would be slapped away he tilted the package to facilitate the maneuver.

"One time," he said, snapping his steel lighter in my direction, as if the Lucky were a cigar in celebration of the birth of a son, the sheet-swathed baby riding in back.

I turned my head to catch the flame, my eyes momentarily leaving the road. As I sucked in the first big smoke and coughed into my hand, the traffic light changed without my noticing from yellow to red. I slammed on the brakes in this winter world with its white cars and white roads and white headlight beams. The snow-slick road itself seemed to move, and I honked the horn. All I could see in my panic was the black word "Stop!" like soot stamped on my mind's eye, and all I could feel was shame, building like a fire under my collar, a heat as mean as hardware on a burning door, and all around I could smell it: the tobacco, the metal, the vinyl, the heater, the sudden aging of the man and the boy within the compartment.

Everywhere cars were honking. Ours had skidded nearly perpendicular to the traffic flow. When I started driving again I felt a lightness. A release, my opponent in the tug-of-war letting go. In the rearview mirror the Frigidaire was free between lanes of traffic. A snowman adrift on wheels, but stuck in its place. Cars swerved to avoid it. One driver sped up until our cars were rolling side by side. He honked impatiently, and I motioned for Pop to lower his window. The driver and his buddy, men with blue eyes who seemed to own the road, stared into our car. "Oh, it's just some crazy chinks," the driver sneered, and as they laughed at Pop—they couldn't have been laughing at me—I came to the quick conclusion that those two thugs were right, there was something unerringly Chinese about hauling this useless machine, a won-at-cards, slant-eyed prize, garbage-picker special, tethered to the car like

Gregory Peck on the back of the Great White Whale; I couldn't imagine my friends and their dads doing likewise in their Electras or Continentals. But as the other car peeled away in the slickness, my father stuck his orange-hunting-capped head out the window, bracing himself with his Lucky Strike hand, and shouted, "Fuck you!" without a trace of accent, and flipped them off with his free hand, the right one, the one that lit matches and in anger struck blows. It was all too much. At that moment Pop was Superman. If he'd gotten hold of the thugs' car he would have torn loose the hood and tossed the engine into their laps. Instead he had a firm hold of me, his hot words ripping a hole in my chest as fresh and smoky as the one those men had just shot through my boy soul.

WE PARKED AND RESCUED the refrigerator. While I held off traffic, Pop pushed his prize to the curb. He told me to telephone a taxi. He brought out a palmful of change and let me pick my own coins for the call. This was unexpected, something new—letting me dip into his personal till must've been like having blood drawn for him, and yet he didn't flinch. I could smell the coins' metal, warmed by the heat of my father's leg. I drew twice, two nickels.

I struggled through the storm and found a pay phone. I dreaded having to talk to adults, strangers who would look at us funny once they saw we were Chinese. When I returned to where I had left my father, he was still standing beside the Frigidaire. Both were covered with snow. I wondered why he hadn't taken shelter inside the car but decided not to ask. I wanted to remember my father's imitation of a real man, the man with the dangerous voice, the man with a palm of silver.

We sat in the car. I suggested we wait at Uncle Law's place, Pop's friend's laundry up the block. Warm and steamy, fragrant with pressed cotton. Maybe we'd even score a cup of hot tea. But Pop wouldn't bite. He had lost face, and his only son had failed him.

When the taxi arrived, Pop stuffed a five-dollar bill in my jacket pocket and zipped it. A surprise reward. Perhaps he wasn't so disappointed after all. He went home in the taxi, leaving me to guard the refrigerator. Fortified by the money he'd given me, by the love the cash signified, I never strayed from my post. Even as day darkened and cold cut crosswise against my cheeks, I didn't budge: I would impress him with my stamina, obedience, and devotion.

When Pop returned with the upholstery-man neighbor and his pickup truck, he said I was *saw-saw* for waiting outside by the refrigerator rather than in the car. "Did you think it was going to run away?" he asked. After a protracted struggle they loaded the refrigerator onto the truck. As Pop was about to climb into the cab, he grabbed my sleeve. Pop would give thanks now, I thought, for a job well done, mission accomplished. Pin a medal on my chest, plant a kiss on my cheek, shake my hand firmly, tousle my hair. Robert Young and Fred MacMurray, slippered and piped, their depthless compassion and broad streaks of sanity, as white as their starched shirts. Right then, in the exhilarating moment of anticipation, the upholstery truck's idling motor was music, its blue burning oil, perfume. But what Pop did was unzip my pocket and filch the five-dollar bill—a tip for the upholstery man.

Later that night, after the New Year's Eve feast and the chores and the homework, when we were all washing our feet before sleeping into the next year, and all the sinks and pails were occupied, Pop filled his new refrigerator's vegetable drawers with hot soapy water and rolled up his pants and plunged his blue-white feet in and said, "Who said it's good for nothing?" He had cleaned his prize with Comet, scrubbing away paint as well as dirt, and defended it against my sisters' wisecracks, and by now had shed whatever diffidence he felt when he introduced this newest member of the clan. Then he plugged the Frigidaire in and sat there, with the door open, soaking his feet, wiping down its insides, using a rag and soapy water from one of the vegetable bins. Nobody could see his face, but I was onto him. Cut off from the rest of the family, my father basked in the refrigerator's chilled air, its silvery vapors, its measly light's glow. What I saw in my father's gentle cleaning of each egg holder's deep dimple was kindness, and the pang I felt, like fingers fanning in my throat, was envy, and the motor's hums were murmurings of love. And I wondered then if I would ever be so brave as to love like that. A machine or the man.

Chapter 5

"DIDN'T YOU EAT rice yet?" Zsa Zsa says. She comes over and shuts the refrigerator doors. "What are you looking for? What you want is your bride, and she's not in there.

"Here's some tea," she says, dropping the lid, *chink,* on the teapot. I shake my head. "I don't want any of that."

"Yuk likes a cup at night." A self-satisfied look comes over Zsa Zsa's face. "She has such a clever tongue. 'One teaspoon of tea leaves for each cup of tea brewed,' she says. So fastidious. The correct balance. Very scientific. Who ever heard of such a thing?"

"I said I don't want any tea."

"No matter," she says. "Just bring some to Yuk."

She has set two cups and the teapot on one of her orchid trays. It's just painted tin, but formerly, in the pre-Yuk era, the tray and its mates were reserved for special occasions.

I pick the tray up roughly. I can't unravel the nature of the agitation stirring inside. The taxonomy of emotion is nowhere as precise as that of cooking. Cuisines, food groups, methodologies. Easy. Take smells: Potatoes smell like potatoes, oranges like oranges. But emotions tend to blur. Hard to put a name on what you feel sometimes. At best, I can only approximate the nature of the passion boiling in my gut: jealousy. But jealous of who, what?

Zsa Zsa says, "Pour yourself a cup of tea. Keep her company. You don't have to drink tea if you don't want to. Nobody's forcing you." And as I turn to go, she adds, "I'm glad you got a haircut for Yuk. Finally you show some respect for your father. And your bride. You should've been ashamed, a grown man looking like that. Yuk would've laughed at you. She has a sharp palate and sharp eyes. She might have decided not to marry you."

"Ma, I'm not marrying her!"

She looks at me as if I'd just slapped her across the face. "Are you still fooling around with that *lo-fahn* girl?" She's referring to Bliss, of course, but she's run that same question at me dozens of times over the years, making no distinction between one girlfriend and the next. I don't answer her. And even if I were inclined to answer, I'm not sure what I'd say. This morning I sent Bliss a postcard of Picasso's *The Man with the Blue Guitar,* a favorite because the central figure's misery inside shows in his twisted posture of improbable angles outside, sadness breaking through like that shoulder bone of his about to shoot through his skin. I sent him as my personal messenger: his misery a visual shorthand for my own. My message: "How can you be ready? I'm not ready. Let's take things nice and slow. We have plenty of time." Plenty of time in the distant future to have a child, if we have a future together.

"You won't marry Yuk-girl?" Zsa Zsa says, dumbstruck. She is in her going-to-Chinatown dress, a floral print with a smart little belt at the waist, her lips colored red, her jet-black hair tightly curled by Yuk. She busies herself with the dirty bowls in the sink, then abruptly turns off the water and stares at me, her face collapsed around her mouth. When that mouth opens she hisses, as cats spit at other cats. "If you don't want her," she says, with more conviction than I've ever heard from her, "I'll keep her."

They already have kept her, moving her from my sisters' room and installing her in the basement. Cool and damp, grow mildew in her bones. Isn't it a little mean-spirited, cruel even, to treat their prized Sizzler buddy so shabbily? My sisters' room might be small, but at least it's not underground; I fear Genius is so fond of this newest, dearest, and most Chinese of daughters that he's moved her downstairs in anticipation of her eventual departure: her exile to the basement will mitigate the enormity of my parents' heartbreak once she's married and gone.

She opens the door when I knock. The room is dark, except at its far end, where a lamp reveals an orange couch that's been folded out into a bed. At the foot of the bed, the Hitachi television chatters. Between the door and the couch the place is its usual mess. Scraps of linoleum. Carpet remnants. Boxes stacked shoulder-high. My sisters' old bikes, bicycle parts, old-fashioned laundry equipment, sacks of unclaimed clothes, books of upholstery samples, junked cathode ray tubes. And then there are Genius's ubiquitous automobile hubcaps, stacked on the floor, strung together with rope, mounted on the wall, which he collected over the years, seeds he hoped would germinate into cars.

From the clutter I watch Yuk walk into the more orderly half of the room, lit by the lamp and the TV set. Her movements are loose and languid, not the mincing steps Zsa Zsa takes in her cork-soled soles; her creamy skin as twenty-four carat as the flesh of the ripest peach. She glances my way, her eyes dark and fluid, as if she wants to make sure I am watching. Everywhere the light touches bears her imprint, an oasis of tranquillity she has created in the chaos of our lives. She sits at the edge of the sofa bed, the corners of its wafer-thin mattress springing into the air.

I set the tray down on the nightstand, under the lamp, a piece of junk that Genius found and repaired. "Thank you, Mr. Sterling," she says. It's the first time she has used my name. "*Starsky Hutch* is my favorite. Very enjoyable. You watch too?"

I sit down next to her. She jumps to her feet. "Mr. Sterling!" I realize too late that "You watch too?" was not an invitation to join her on the mattress but an inquiry into my prime-time viewing habits.

"Sorry!" Now I jump to my feet. "You sit."

"No, Mr. Sterling, you sit."

"I didn't mean to sit when I sat. I mean, I didn't sit the way I think you thought I sat." I'm talking rapidly, with a quiver in my throat, my heart pounding in my ears.

"Please, you sit. You are my guest in my home."

I do as she says, feeling stupid, staring up at her. "See? I'm sitting. Everything's okay."

But it's not. This is her bed, and I've made her a refugee in her own room. Dislodged, she leans against the wall, a few feet to my left, her arms crossed under her bosom; the gathered material of her blouse, billowing like bread dough rising, crowds in on her. She's watching the TV, her gaze so intense it can be plucked like a guitar string. On the screen, Starsky and Hutch drive through a wall of flames. It's hard to say what is on fire, but I love the stunt—a chance gas leak and the whole thing blows.

At the instant of the explosion Yuk sucks in air, a rough gasp that breaks off, as if her throat had been cut. Her delicate Chinese sensibilities are shaken: fragile Yuk shocked by American violence, just as she was offended by my immodest move onto her bed. "Wow!" she says. "That was good one!"

How much more wrong can I be? When I look her way, her eyes are glued to the screen, where another car has taken up the chase. "Tea?" I say, standing and pouring two cups. But she isn't listening. The car slams into an electric tower and the television screen erupts in a massive fireball, and she gasps again, holds her breath. When the program fades to a commercial she bubbles: "*Ai-yah! Starsky Hutch* perpetrate best explosion every week!"

I put in my time, sitting on the edge of her bed, hands gripping kneecaps, back as straight as it was during my admissions interview at the CIA. My heart is pounding like a cardiologist's dream, but this turbulence inside my body isn't in response to what's happening on the screen. What I'm feeling is my fourteen-year-old heart careening through my chest at midnight while I'm seated on a terribly uncomfortable chair also occupied by Brenda Bloom, the girl I liked, who liked me; her mother's sleeping inside, we've been sitting like this, on her porch, stone silent for the past hour, Brenda waiting for me to make the first move, to finally kiss her. But I just can't do it, no matter how much I want to.

The show ends. Right then, our good-bye scene is upon us. I dread the moment, teary-eyed Yuk begging me to rescue her from her life in a basement under a store on Long Island, her brain cells filled with exploding cars and having to pretend she digs it. And here I am, mobile, educated, twice-degreed, a holder of civilization, my shoulder set firmly against the gate, pushing back the savages, her ideal mate, express ticket out of her misery.

But I can't rescue her. Now or anytime soon. I wish I could erase from Yuk's memory this horrific misadventure, I wish she had never stepped from the photograph and had stayed forever in her turquoise-and-tangerine-colored Hong Kong dress, forever celebrating births or weddings. While Lisa Lee was snoring in my bed, Bliss accused me of being undisciplined, my desires running over me like the Germans through France. Genius holds a similar opinion. In his view my lack of discipline shows in my embrace of what he calls the "America way": my alleged tendency to indulge my whims and fancies over more pressing matters such as family, tradition, nation, culture, blood, race, face, shame, pride, honor, dishonor. He fingers my interest in Bliss and her kind as evidence in support of his contention. Quite frankly, my purest desires are in the kitchen: for the exact flavor, the clearest consommé, the perfect meringue, precise paysanne-cut potatoes, one-half by one-half by one-quarter inch. My greatest desire, the one that inspires the others, is to please my diners, that they love my food and love to take me into their bodies, into their hearts. Outside the kitchen, contrary to popular opinion, my desires go largely unrealized. This is why Brenda Bloom went unkissed that night; why Bliss remains a giant blip on my personal radar screen; why leaving Yuk is so difficult now; and why, if I have to get married, it won't be to her.

The show's credits are still rolling when Yuk drops to her knees at my feet. I keep my eyes on the TV and anticipate the desperate embrace of my legs, her arms clinging, begging me to stay.

"Before you go, Mr. Sterling, this is for you," Yuk says, reaching for something under the fold-out bed. She stands, and on her dewy palm is a small box wrapped in sultry gold paper. To judge from its size, the box might hold a ring, cuff links, a biggish ball of hashish. Zsa Zsa had warned me, I know, "A Chinese always brings a gift when visiting." I did try to find Yuk something. Not that that matters, of course, but I still do feel upstaged, caught empty-handed, exposed for the uncouth boor I am, thoughtless, ignorant of custom.

"Wait! I have something for you too! Close your eyes until I get back." I remember Fuchs's salami; that yard of beef by-products, fat, and sodium nitrite has saved my life. I head out to the car. See, I'm not so crass after all. But when I open the trunk, I discover the real gift.

STAGGERING, I OPEN the basement door a crack and ask Yuk if her eyes are closed. When I see her sitting on the edge of the bed, arms folded across her belly, eyes shut so tight her face pinches as if tasting lemon, I am seduced by her innocence, by the faith that has brought her so far down into this hole.

Slowly, carefully, I set the David next to the Hitachi. What more can she hope for? American TV, and now a Michelangelo! I imagine she doesn't see much High Art in Hong Kong. Besides, it's a personal gift, coming directly from my Valiant (where I recently relocated the statue for safer keeping), more substantial than her little present, and infinitely more classy than salami. I tell her to open her eyes.

One look and she drops her face in her hands and weeps. I certainly didn't expect she'd be this overjoyed. She looks up from her hands, her face red and moist, and when my heart is split wide to receive her gratitude, she laughs. The back of my neck burns: She is laughing at me! My store of goodwill quickly evaporates. What's eating her? I note the David's chipped nose and broken curls. (It's not easy riding around in the trunk of a car.) Is that so funny? I can see her in Italy or Greece touring the classical ruins, laughing her ignorant head off. Finally she gathers herself and looks me dead in the eyes. "In Hong Kong," she says, "my uncle's factory produces object of beauties in mass quantity. Chinese pagoda, Chinese sage mans, no-arm Venus. British buy for their garden. Look."

She gets off the bed, onto her knees, and with my help tips over the statue. There it is, stamped into the bottom of the plaster base: "Made in Hong Kong."

I stand the statue upright again. I couldn't bear seeing him down on the floor, a fallen hero, defeated by Yip Yuk Hing. She is good enough this time not to laugh too hard. The words pour out of her: mostly she marvels at the small-world aspect of the fact that her uncle's statuary has followed her to the United States. Then she tells me how much she loves Italian Renaissance art and names the Italian city where the David is displayed. She tells me she's seen the original in person. "He's really big," she says. I am overcome by a feeling of inevitability. As if I were standing in the ocean and watching a fierce wave that's about to knock me over. I had the same feeling once before, when Genius was informed that one of his kidneys had to go, that the growth was not a harmless sac of water or an aggregate of minerals, but a living, spiteful thing. There was no choice then. There isn't one now. I have to marry her. She's been to Florence, she's been to Rome; she knows Michelangelo and Paul Michael Glaser; she's not even remotely beaded slippers, kung fu shoes, electric rice cooker, or ginseng root. She's not

Genius or Zsa Zsa Chinese. That's why I have to have her: she's my parents' darling, she has been to the Vatican, she speaks English, she's beautiful, she's not pregnant.

She presses the little gold-wrapped box into my hand. My guess is this: The box holds an engagement ring, from prospective bride to prospective groom, a Chinese custom that Zsa Zsa hasn't told me about. When I unwrap my present my fingers can't work fast enough. In those slow seconds I sense Bliss out there in the Milky Way, like a spy satellite. I can't see her, but she's riding her own orbit, infrared camera focused down on my head.

Beneath the gold wrapping paper is a hinged velvet box. In the moments before I open the lid I imagine Bliss smiling benevolently, hoping I'll reject the engagement ring, send it and the girl back to the Orient.

"Is this a joke?" Inside, on a bed of white satin, are two small blue-gray rocks, dimpled, with rusty lichenous shadings. Common-looking rocks.

"Not joke. Moon rock," Yuk says, pointing to the ceiling, indicating the heavens. "I purchase in Kowloon from highly reputable merchant. Specialist in gemology."

"This is the moon?" Pieces of the moon for sale? Lunar real estate. How much is a standard-sized lot in the Sea of Tranquillity? Location, location, location. Did Neil Armstrong scoop these two rocks off the lunar surface himself? What would he think of his mission if he knew the fruits of his labor have wound up in a gift box, in the hands of the son of a Chinese laundryman, in a basement on Long Island? A decade hasn't passed since the moon walk and already mineral merchants in Hong Kong are selling the rocks, once quarantined because politicians feared they might harbor killer viruses or new strains of radiation. I remember my disappointment after all the buildup: We put a man on the fucking moon, and find little but dust and holes and rocks more inert than the rocks here on earth. I felt toyed with, and these many years later I don't know what to make of the gap between expectations and reality. As I had expected *something* from the moon, I expected Yip Yuk Hing to be a Hong Kong hick, I expected this beautifully wrapped package would contain an engagement ring.

"Don't you like, Mr. Sterling? You give Yuk ideal masculine beauty. Now I am afraid you don't like my humble gift."

"No. I do. Thank you. Did you pick these out yourself?"

"How can that be? Only American man visit moon."

Had Genius or Zsa Zsa made the same mistake, I would've scolded them. "No, I meant at the store where these came from."

"My mother says don't buy moon rock. Just rock, she says, like rock on earth. What kind of insult is to give rock for present? What will he think of you? But I tell my mother in America Americans have everything. What to get for man who is from the land of everything? I see advertisement in newspaper. I go to gemologist. He say this is not top-quality specimens of moon rock. But I buy because you know why?"

I look into the little box, at the two small rocks. When I was in college, a few years after the moon walk, I cut class one day and went to New York to view the moon rocks, on display at the UN. I waited in line for hours with people from around the world. Back then, Yuk was just the girl in the photograph, snapped, oblivious to the fact that at that very instant Neil Armstrong was taking that first step on her behalf.

"Mr. Sterling?"

"I'm sorry. You were saying?"

"For American man who has everything, I must bring something not from earth. A piece of the moon! Out of the world!"

"BYE-BYE NOW!" she says. "Tea is cold already." She spreads a baby-blue blanket over the sheets. She fluffs her pillows, in unmatching pillowcases, one pale green and one white. When she notices that I'm watching her she hides the pillows, unconvincingly, behind her back. Too personal. Is she afraid I might see, projected on the fabric, the very dreams she has dreamed there? "Before you go, I have question," she begins, holding the same posture, pillows behind her, breasts thrust forward, as if her arms were forcefully tied behind her back. "In America is it not true that you do not have to marry someone you do not wish to marry?"

"Freedom of choice, I guess."

"Good!" She sounds relieved.

What is she talking about? Who doesn't want to marry whom? What have Zsa Zsa and Genius told her about their reluctant son? Has Genius, the original reluctant groom, poisoned her with his history, a cautionary tale of life with an unwilling partner?

"Freedom of choice really good," she says. "Just like sometime I choose Starsky and sometime I choose Hutch. Now this time I choose to go to sleep." She puts the teacups on the white orchids painted on the tray. Her breasts tumble forward beneath the peasant blouse's cotton. "Tea is really cold already."

I see what she's doing. She's throwing me out. I can't believe she's throwing me out. And worse, I can't believe I don't want to leave. An invisible electrical fence keeps me in bounds.

IN THE VALIANT, the tiny box of moon rocks, lid open, rides in the passenger seat. Its contents glow in the dark compartment. She has given me the moon. The rocks emit deadly radiation. They are charmed. They are magic. They are as beautiful as diamonds. As precious as jade.

Chapter 6

IN THE LIGHT of day, away from the glare of Yuk's blinding brilliance, the moon rocks come down to earth: they are just a pair of rusty stones in a velvet box. No matter what type of light I subject them to—direct sunshine, the sixty-watt bulb of the rickshaw driver lamp, the darkness inside a closet—they stubbornly hold their new-found ordinariness. I'm not sure what has happened overnight. Has their glow dissipated, as odors will naturally thin in the air, or have I imagined the whole thing, the radiant rocks, the heat of our meeting?

I am sitting at my kitchen table, taking my second mug of morning coffee. French roast. I don't imagine a tenth mug will change the moon rocks' nagging dullness. As it is, I am already too awake.

Since the time I rolled out of bed I have been trying to plan the next lunch menus. I have my Julia Child and my recipe binder from the CIA splayed open in front of me. Usually when I flip these wonderful pages I hear Julia and my professors speaking directly to me, their voices familiar and comforting as they guide me through each dish so that I feel safe, centered, and loved. I have come to think of it as my equivalent to the happiness some people, including Bliss, claim is theirs upon hearing the voice of a loved one, a parent, for instance, or in her case, a grandmother. But today, as has been true since the day I received the pig postcard and the day Yuk's imminent North American arrival was announced, my cooking heart has turned to stone. I look over some favorite recipes—*blanquette de veau, boudin blanc, gigot d'agneau, saumon unilatéral, rognons de mouton au gratin.* Nothing sings in my heart. Only the *filet aux moelles* elicits a whistle, but a feeble one at that. A minute later I come across a recipe for a *lièvre rôti en saugrenée,* which I've never tried or tasted, just a mimeographed sheet passed out in class. At this moment, though, it seems just the thing to shake me out of my doldrums, a dish with a ruthlessly French soul, and yet one that will challenge the Richfield Ladies' Club palate. Now, if only Fuchs has a hare.

I momentarily lose myself in the recipe's exotica (I'm thinking especially of the blood sauce, of course, from the ladies' point of view). This version, adapted from Alain Chapel's classic, begins as do most CIA teaching recipes with the *mise en place*, literally the "putting in place" of the ingredients and flavorings, equipment and tools, necessary for the orderly preparation of the dish. This is one of the first concepts we learned in cooking school. Each session of Culinary Skills Development I and II started with the same tedious ritual of chopping onions, celery, and carrots for fine- and then coarse-cut mirepoix that would eventually be used to flavor soup, stews, or stock. So much endless repetition, until each act became second nature. We learned hundreds of skills and techniques—separating eggs, clarifying butter, pounding cutlets for paillards, deboning chickens. But what is all this knowledge without *mise en place*? As futile as the lungs or stomach, kidneys or bowels laboring outside the human body. *Mise en place* is more than just what one does with one's hands and a knife, it is a state of mind. A chef orchestrating a meal, juggling several tasks at once, assigning value to each, setting priorities, anticipating contingencies. In a metaphysical sense it is being attuned to the order of things in the universe.

I realize then I have to attend to my personal *mise en place*. Once that's been accomplished, my cooking heart will beat strongly again.

I push Julia and my CIA binder aside. I retrieve the velvet box from the periphery of the table. I am giving the moon rocks another chance: If there's magic, show me! I remove the aspirin-sized moon rocks from their satin bed and set each on the yellow Formica table. Forget the surface sheen. I lean in close, go eyeball to eyeball with the moon rocks, search for signs of life within.

Nothing.

I sit upright and grab my recipe binder, and hold it propped between the edge of the table and my lap. With intense concentration I study the hare with blood sauce recipe, in hopes of obliterating my disappointment. I try to imagine the dish taking shape. But I get no further than skinned hares hanging from the ceiling of the Ladies' Club kitchen. It's useless, I can't stay focused, am distracted, as if someone's watching me.

I peer over the top of the blue binder. And there, blazing up from the yellow surface, is Bliss's dead-eye stare. Then I see the full-moon shine of her baby belly.

I call Bliss. She doesn't answer. Either she's never there or she's stonewalling me. It's been this way since I sent her Picasso. Just pick up the damn phone! What does she expect me to do, drop everything and drive to Iowa, show up on her doorstep? A few weeks ago, I was packed and ready to go. But she said she wasn't willing to see me yet. It's ten forty-five in the morning. She must be in class. What if she isn't in class? The school of dentistry is on the same campus as the hospital. She rubs shoulders with medical types every day. Between classes she could easily stop by the family planning clinic, and who knows?

A few minutes later I call the laundry. I refuse to accept my eyes' verdict on the moon rocks. I want to appeal to the sanity of my ears. Hear Yuk's voice. The fun she had last night, the sleepless hours following my departure. As expected, Genius answers and teases me about Yuk: Weren't they right? Isn't she great? Wasn't I stupid for putting up such a fuss? Then it's Zsa Zsa's turn, and she abuses me anew, adding a pitch for grandchildren. When I remind her they already have three (Patty's two, Lily's toddler), she fires back, "We want yours!" My genetic material more highly valued because I'm their lone male child, passer-on of the vaunted Lung family name. Finally, without warning, she puts Yuk on the phone. Our conversation is courteous and brief. I ask a question, she answers; I ask another, she answers. In the combination of our two voices I hear as little as I've seen in the moon rocks. By the time we hang up, a hammer of disappointment has blunted my anxious heart.

I look out my window and draw inspiration from the big white house. I park myself at the table, grab the recipe binder. Thank God for work! I turn to the first page of my Julia Child, on which I have written: "You can't eat eight hours a day nor drink for eight hours a day nor make love for eight hours—all you can do for eight hours is work. Which is the reason why man makes himself and everybody else so miserable and unhappy. William Faulkner." But he's wrong. Obviously Faulkner never had a pregnant girlfriend in Iowa, and a picture-bride in New York, and a houseful of club ladies in Connecticut dissatisfied with their chef's distracted lunches. All at the same time. If he did, he'd eat his words. All there is is work.

I call the butcher shop. At least Fuchs answers his telephone, and when I ask him a question he doesn't just mutter a few monosyllables. "Four hairs, you want? You want the last four on my head, or four from my nose? What is this, some kind of joke?" he says. "You're the guy who sells hair."

"Hares, Fuchs. H-A-R-E, hare, not H-A-I-R. You know, like a rabbit, only bigger."

"Call 'em what you want, hares and rabbits, I don't carry. They don't move fast enough." He laughs. "You're better off chasing down a few in that yard at the club. Maybe you can get your ladies to help you hunt. You've got as good a chance of that happening as getting that crowd to eat Bugs Bunny."

I return to the table. I slap the moon rocks off the Formica. I rip the *lièvre rôti en saugrenée* recipe from the binder and tear it into little pieces. What was I thinking? Hare in blood sauce for the ladies? Love between me and a Hong Kong girl? Genius and Zsa Zsa making an enlightened decision? Bliss doing the right thing?

I go to the bedroom, jump into bed, and hold a pillow over my face as if trying to smother myself. My *mise en place* is one big mess.

FORTY-EIGHT HOURS LATER the moon rocks show no sign of improvement—if anything, whatever luster I might've imagined into their bland, dimpled surfaces has seriously degraded.

As I CLEAN UP after the ladies' lunch, Libby Drake enters the kitchen and asks if I'm feeling okay. I ask what she means. "Well, Sterling, you seem different since you cut your hair. You don't have your heart in our lunches. Now, don't get me wrong, everybody likes tuna salad, but not three days in a row. Let's face it, even Millie Boggs is capable of making a tuna salad sandwich."

Good, I think, I'll leave the can opener and mayonnaise out for her. "I'm sorry. I'm just in a little slump. I didn't realize it's been three days."

"It's been three days, all right." As she's leaving she suggests ways I might pull out of my slump: "Try something new, Sterling. Something you've never done before." She flashes a flirty smile. "We'd love some Chinese," she says. "And I personally want to try that new French food." She snaps her fingers, trying to remember its name.

"*Cuisine minceur,*" I say.

"Yes, that's the one!"

"You won't like it. It's so boring. With an emphasis on all the wrong things—simple treatments, low fat, thin sauces. It's hardly cooking at all."

"Sounds like tuna fish. It shouldn't be problem for you, then, should it?"

I BUNDLE UP in a heavy sweater and lie in the narrow space between the rosebushes in the garden. It is dusk, the air fragrant with burning leaves. I watch the breeze blow tree limbs bare. I feel like these oak, elm, sycamore, and maple: not so very long ago I was in my full glory, a graduate of the nation's finest cooking school, with an excellent first job, access to rich and powerful palates, and now I'm buffeted on all sides. My last stitch of dignity blasted off by Libby Drake's assault on my very essence, who I am, what I cook.

I lie here until I'm buried in leaves and night. Under the early November sky's stars and crescent moon, I try not to think of anything. Not the chill in the air, not the glorious wind, not the music in the dueling branches. I am quiet. For brief lovely moments I forget myself. All I am is what I sense, an invertebrate existence, floating in the sea, unaware of destination or danger, of past or pain, every act involuntary. That's what's so sweet: I cannot do wrong; no one can think ill of me, because I don't have a will, even eating, I don't choose when or what to eat, I just ingest the good with the bad, all day long. The thought that breaks the surface of my calm: "The discovery of a new dish does more for the happiness of mankind than the discovery of a star." Brillat-Savarin. Whenever I feel like an emulsion, that is, easily destabilized by inner turmoil, and my cooking legs go wobbly, and my faith is challenged, I read a passage or two from *The Philosopher in the Kitchen* and feel restored.

I scramble to my feet, egged on by this inspiration: I'll make a new dish of myself. I am seized by the urge to cook, to take what already exists and do something to it, then take that and do something to it. I stride toward the carriage house. In the distance, underneath the lingering scent of smoldering leaves, I catch the sweet fragrance of pot roast, meatloaf, chicken noodle soup in the neighborhood.

I will deglaze my soul, scrape that pan until I cry. Escoffier, my French father, must be smiling.

I CLIMB the stairs to my apartment. The phone is ringing.

"Of course you're not ready!"

"Huh?"

"I'm not ready either! How can anyone be ready?"

"Bliss?"

"It's such an adventure. And we're just at the beginning!"

It's been a month or so since I received the pig postcard. I have to put an end to this. Scrape the pan like crazy. "I'm not ready. I mean what I say, and I meant what I wrote." Slowly I go through my sane, rational argument—her career, my career, the relatively short time we've really known each other, my lack of confidence in my abilities as a parent, and money. "I'm just not ready."

"Yeah, like I was ready for the nausea, the fatigue, the swelling. I couldn't get out of bed yesterday it was so bad."

Ah, so she was at home and didn't answer the call.

"And I didn't answer the phone because I had a feeling it was you. And I was miserable, and since you're the reason I was feeling so miserable, if I'd picked up, I would've chewed your head off. I didn't want to do that."

"Bliss, I don't want you to be miserable. And I certainly don't want you pissed at me the rest of your life. We live in enlightened times. You're a liberated woman. I think you know what I'm talking about."

"I've already been a liberated woman twice and I don't plan on being liberated again. I'm closing in on thirty, Sterling. What're you, twenty-six?"

"I'm closing in on twenty-seven."

"Okay, basically three years younger, and male." She says this as if she's talking to herself. "It's a known fact that at the same age men are emotionally slower than women. You obviously don't understand where I'm at. But I'm going to do this, with or without you. Ready or not, you're going to be a father. Now you can be a father or—" She chokes back tears.

I hate this. She's threatening me, and she can't spit the threat out. "Or *what*?"

"You won't ever get within ten feet of my child."

MORE THAN TWO WEEKS have gone by since I was at the laundry last. It isn't the official start of winter yet, but already quite cold. I take Genius to the doctor tomorrow. He has lost his appetite, and complains of aches but can't pinpoint their precise location in his body. He works in the laundry, of course, but is listless. Zsa Zsa reports that he smokes his cigarettes but without his usual conviction. This worries her. "He used to smoke each cigarette to the very end. Now he leaves half." (In Chinese, the verb for "smoke" is "to eat," so "smoking to death," to me, sounds like "eating to death.") She asks me what I think is wrong, as if I were the physician they've always wanted me to be. I tell her, "He looks fine." What am I going to say? She's already out of her mind with worry.

I step into their bedroom and stand over Genius napping. He is pale, and thinner than usual. His jagged breaths vibrate through my body. I'm about to leave, when he says something, I assume from inside a dream. Soon I realize he is talking to me, and I think I'm the one who's dreaming. Yuk, he mumbles, has left the country.

In the kitchen Zsa Zsa confirms what I have just heard. Her voice is edgy, as though reporting an accident. Their dutiful imported daughter is visiting relations in Montreal, which from Zsa Zsa's mouth comes out sounding like "Monty Hall." I ask her when Yuk is coming back. "Why? Do you care?" she says.

The pump in my chest: *Yes, of course! Yes, of course!* But I can't tell her that, nor should I be having such a thought. Into my silence Zsa Zsa shakes her head, then adds, "Yuk's a good girl. *She* knows family comes first." And this she says while I'm standing in her kitchen, having driven all the way from Connecticut to take Genius to the hospital tomorrow.

Zsa Zsa is cooking dinner as if it were her husband's last supper. Four dishes, plus soup and rice. For the three of us. And she already knows Genius isn't eating. She's in red-alert mother mode. Here's her chance to load her two boys up with her goodness. Her superior food, the only worthy edibles in the universe, nutritious and delicious, the antithesis of the impotent dishes I cook and favor. In every bowl she'll set in front of me will be a rebuke of what I've made of myself; in each mouthful of rice I'll take a self-criticism.

While she cooks I inspect one refrigerator, then the other. Standing at the first, the Frigidaire, I'm munching on dried anchovies steamed in soy sauce and peanut oil, leftovers from some distant night before. These are grim little fish, bitter as tobacco, eaten whole, fins, head, guts, and gills. I'm after the wisp of protein lingering in the cardboard flesh. I imagine the outrage at the club if I granted the ladies' wish for Chinese food with a saucer of steamed dried anchovies. Now *that's* Chinese! I wonder how they'd take to the famous French dish *ortolans en brochette,* bite-sized birds (buntings, to be exact) roasted and eaten whole, everything in your mouth but the feathers—beak, skull, bone, intestines (full of partially digested millet, berries, bugs, buds), and pinhole anus. So which is worse, which more uncivilized, ingesting whole fishes or whole birds?

As she goes about her business she has the segmented movements of a row of ants. "Shut the refrigerator door," she says. "Why are you staring? Are you afraid I'm going to poison you?" The lid of the rice pot trembles. It's a huge pot: the more rice she cooks, the more bowls I might eat; the more I eat, the better a mother she is. Uncooked rice *is* the color of mother's milk. In another pot, chicken gizzards, liver, neck, and carcass roll into stock. At her cutting board near the sink she slices flank steak with a cleaver, then marinates the beef in soy sauce and cornstarch. She cuts broccoli, onions, scallions, and reconstituted black mushrooms; she smashes ginger root under the blade and minces cloves of garlic. Then it occurs to me that, improbable as it may seem, I'm

watching Zsa Zsa perform the meal's *mise en place*. To think such similarities exist between her casual, capricious, undisciplined style of cooking and what I learned at a cost of thousands of dollars in student loans.
But what about the bigger picture: Is it possible that things are in place
in her life? Genius's too? That my parents want what they've got? That
they have a plan and have set priorities? That in the manual labor, the
hard life, the creepy children, the sputtering English, the days without
grace, they are closing in on a particular goal? You come from China, I
guess, you better have a plan.

I still can't get over the amount of food she has planned for us.
Crazy. But I say nothing. The wok is smoking. The air tingles with the
healing vapors of garlic and ginger hissing in hot peanut oil. She adds a
pinch of salt, stirs the oil with a spatula, then lowers in a bluefish, one
half at a time. A great commotion, oil splattering, crackling, popping.
She flips the fish, the skin beautifully crisped and blistered, and once
the other side is fried she sprinkles matchsticks of ginger on top, then
water and dark soy and salt, and reduces the flame and covers the fish
to braise. She's in constant motion. When she grabs a small pot and goes
to the *mi-gong*, a thirty-five-gallon garbage can that holds a hundred
pounds of rice, I ask why she's making more rice when there's already
a huge pot on the stove. She ignores me. Lost in concentration, she taps
grains into the pot from the scooper, an old Campbell's soup can, its
label pink with age and talc; she's measuring out her worth with the
precision of an apothecary measuring drams of opium. "What are you
making so much rice for?" I repeat.

"If you come home you have to eat rice. Rice is the only thing that
fills a person's stomach. Only your mother makes sure you get the rice
you need." She tosses the soup can back in, then as an afterthought
reaches for an extra handful of love. She says, "That *lo-fahn* food you
cook, don't tell me that's what you eat too! I worry for you." When she
passes I grab at the pot—enough with the rice already!—but I accidentally hook her arm, and the rice spills out, each grain crashing on
the linoleum, crackling like static. "Are you crazy?" she says. She kneels.

I kneel, and we nearly knock heads. When I try to help her clean up, she pushes my hands away and sweeps the grains herself, banking the rice against her knees. "Dead boy, who would've guessed you'd resent your mother so, you the youngest, the great son." With that, I leave her to her work, her hands swift and frantic, as if she were expecting a baby and her water broke and she were ashamed and trying to scoop it back inside. "I never would've guessed when you were little you'd grow up to be this way. Why do you think your father's sick?" It's a rhetorical question. She's shoveling the blame once again on my head. Then, without missing a beat, she wants to know what my intentions are for Yuk.

"How should I know? I only saw her once, Ma." That's all I risk saying; I don't want her getting more nuts on me.

"Are you blind? It doesn't take five minutes to see she's too good for you." She leaves the pot of rice on the lid of the *mi-gong*, and returns to her cutting board and viciously hacks at a hunk of pork. In no time the meat is reduced to a pink patty. A childhood favorite of mine. Add some minced Smithfield ham for flavor and water chestnuts for texture. Steam. But she doesn't get this far. She slams the cleaver down. "You don't want to eat, don't eat!" Her voice so loud, I'm afraid she'll wake Genius. She sits at the kitchen table, in Genius's seat. It's strange to see someone else there. She crosses her arms and sulks. "Your father refuses to eat, you don't want to eat, and Yuk isn't here to eat."

"I never said I wasn't going to eat. I ate those little fishes, didn't I?"

"Good. If you're hungry, you cook. My appetite just ran away." She plants one elbow on the table, locks her hand over her mouth, averts her gaze.

I check under the lid of the wok. All of the liquid has been cooked off, and the fish itself looks dry. I keep expecting Zsa Zsa to jump out of her seat and wrestle the spatula from me, reclaiming her kitchen, but she is welded in place. I plate the bluefish and arrange the pieces so that the halves are aligned and the fish looks whole again. I put it on the table and sprinkle on scallion curls to camouflage the cut. Zsa Zsa peeks at my handiwork but doesn't say a thing. I know she thinks presentation is a waste of time that I learned from stupid white people. I've heard her and Genius plenty enough: Americans don't know how to eat; they're more concerned with how the food looks than how it tastes.

When I see she's not going to budge, I take over. Someone has to act adult around here. Genius might not eat much, but he has to eat. And besides, she's given me a chance to show her my stuff, show them both my worth. This is the first time I've cooked for my parents since I graduated from the CIA! I take up her cleaver and whack at the pork patty. I've never liked using a cleaver, too Chinese-cloddish and heavy and medieval, but for this task it feels perfect in my hands. With the blade's broad face I scrape the pork patty off the cutting board and set it in a dish for steaming. This is the surprise: How much I absorbed of Zsa Zsa's methods, her "little bit of this, little bit that" style, while I sat at the table doing my homework and she prepared the family dinner. I don't remember paying much attention to her, but clearly I must have. It was the same at the CIA. No matter how many lectures we attended or books we read, nothing was as useful as the cooking demonstrations. We were shown how to sweat onions and leeks, taught their desired look and smell when properly cooked; the professor would pass the pan among us to sample the aromas, and I'd scoop the vapors from the air with my hand and inhale until they became permanently imprinted in my memory.

I wash the wok, and I know I'm doing something wrong because she's clucking her tongue and making snorting sounds. Her eyes cling to me like a bad memory.

I slap the wok onto the stove and fire up a burner. I look down at the empty wok and it stares back like a big black hole. From the table Zsa Zsa keeps serenading me. I wish she would stop fooling around and take over. I'd hate having an amateur clowning around *my* kitchen—I don't see how she can stand it.

From Genius's chair she scrutinizes everything I do. I feel more edgy now than during the practical examination before graduation, when I prepared an entire menu on demand while the professor observed my every move and interrogated me: "What is the difference between a blond roux and a dark roux?" "In your preparation of a *sauce espagnole,* why is it important to let the tomato 'cut out'?" I heat peanut oil, throw in the beef, broccoli, and onions she has sliced. But there's no sizzle, pop, explosion of fragrances in my head. Something's wrong. I turn up the heat. Finally she stirs from her seat at the table and comes up behind me. Now she'll take over, reclaim her rightful place: *I am your mother; I will feed you; we told you you can't cook; you want to be a good boy, marry Yuk.* She's rocking back and forth on the gold-mesh wedges that Yuk brought from Hong Kong, her soles sticking to the shoes, making more noise than the food in the wok. "You afraid I'm going to poison you?" I say.

"You call yourself a chef? Look, the beef's done," she says, "but the broccoli's going to be hard as wood."

I push the spatula through the limp, hissing pile of ingredients. The beef has turned from ruby red to brown. Broccoli pieces ping against the wok metal.

"Didn't they teach you anything at that school?" She clucks her tongue, and goes to the refrigerators and returns with a bottle. "Oyster sauce is always good." The store-bought sauce is against everything I've ever learned about gastronomy. Sauces are the supreme test of a chef's skill. Often, cooking is the sauce. But sauce out of a bottle, some anonymous committee of tongues in a laboratory determining the proper blend of flavors for *my* palate, *my* dishes? I read the label: "Oyster extractives, sugar, water, monosodium glutamate, salt, cornstarch, caramel color." Why not ketchup? Why not Drano?

"What are you waiting for?" says Zsa Zsa. She wants *me* to dump it in, to sin against all I believe in, sin against myself.

"I don't use oyster sauce."

She takes the bottle and unscrews the cap. "This is the best brand money can buy. You're crazy. All you believe is what the *fahn gee lo* tells you."

"That's enough, that's enough."

"Oh! Is this how you cook for those white women?"

"They wouldn't eat this," I say, knowing all too well how much they want to.

"Sure they would. They don't know what's good Chinese."

"Yep, they don't know how to eat, right?"

"Well, they hired you."

No one will eat. I've been waiting for Genius to break ranks. But no. He says he's lost his appetite. "Let's go find it," I joke in English. He doesn't laugh. Zsa Zsa then says she's lost her appetite. Where are they, on vacation? After I was certain Genius wasn't going to exercise his patriarchal right, I take a shot of her watercress soup, another favorite. No one follows my lead, though, which leaves me feeling guilty, a greedy child who can't wait his turn.

Zsa Zsa tells Genius that I cooked the meal. Genius quickly snaps his head, as if a mosquito had just bitten him, and looks over at me. "Not really," I say. "I helped her." Zsa Zsa sighs, annoyed, the slow exhalation carrying with it the color in her cheeks. I see her game: She's trying to entice her husband, sell the meal as something new and exotic, trick a few bites of rice into his mouth.

"Eat," she implores.

"I'm not hungry."

"You must eat. Just a little bit. How about this fish? *Bluefishy.* So fresh and sweet, I warn you, you might swallow your tongue." She chopsticks a hunk of fish, leans over the table, and reaches for his rice bowl. My body tenses, anticipating Genius's blow-up. But he disappoints. He just sits, not quite staring, not quite not there, but there.

"You eat," she tells me.

"You eat too."

"I've lost my appetite," she says again, staring at her husband.

My eyes dash between the two. They both look wretched to the point that I'm tempted to act on the crazy thought that then bursts in my head: Tell them I'm pregnant. That'll leave Zsa Zsa and Genius so happy they'll be deaf and blind to the fact it's Bliss's womb in which their genetic material once removed has taken up residence.

But I chicken out. "I don't feel like eating either," I say. There's a fullness in my chest, a foreign growth inside pressing up against my heart and lungs. I pack my appetite off to join theirs on holiday.

I try not to dwell too much on the possible reasons for their refusal to eat. My father isn't well and can't eat; Zsa Zsa is brimming with worry. Or to look on the bright side, all is well, Genius has simply slipped into his usual mode of spitefulness, in protest of my profession, reasserting his unequivocal refusal to eat what I cook.

"Eat," Zsa Zsa orders me. She sells the different dishes. "The pork biscuit was one of your favorites when you were little. Where are you going to get pork biscuit but here? You're not going to make it for yourself." She loads up my bowl with the pork. Then, sensing I've lowered my defenses, she exploits the opening and piles on fish, beef, and vegetables. I hold my tongue and let her have her way. "Eat," she says, as she brings to my lips a spoon laden with her soup and her rice. "Show your father how it's done."

WHILE ZSA ZSA WASHES the dishes I go to work in the front of the store. I start by firing up the shirt presses; they're set in the display window so that customers driving by can be assured by the sight of their Chinese toiling on their behalf, twenty-eight cents a shirt. I am a real pro at this, having worked the equipment more than half my life. Three machines: (1) collar and cuff, shoulders and cuff; (2) right front panel, the back in two steps, left front panel; (3) sleeves. All the equipment going at the same time. A twelve-step process that ends with the shirts thrown across a simple steel rack. The sweet, burnt-toast fragrance of the moist cotton! I'll press a hundred or so shirts before I leave. This is the currency of love. My sweaty labor at this triangle of electricity and steel is the truest gauge of my worth. I put in five hours or so, and I'm a good son. For as long as it takes them to fold the shirts I've pressed I can bask in their goodwill, the aura of family harmony.

After I've racked a dozen or so shirts, Genius comes out front, his black eyeglasses low on his nose, his spine apparently bent by the droopy sides of his unbuttoned vest. He puts on a Chinese opera tape and starts folding shirts at his ironing board. I have a head start but he soon cuts into my lead. Before I know it, there are only three shirts left, and for a short time we run neck-and-neck, Genius plucking off the freshly pressed shirt as soon as I'm done with it. Then his energy sags, and the shirts start piling up. He is taking frequent breaks, standing immobile at his station, arms at his sides, as though startled by the music, putting all else on hold while he listens. He must really be suffering. Not eating, lazy on the job. I'm thinking I ought to lead him to the machines, lay him down on the middle one, and press the badness from his body. That's what I used to do as a kid when I was sick with a fever, shivering with chills: I would cozy up to the machines, soak in their intense moist heat, lay my hands directly on the hot pads of canvas. Cook illness from my cells.

LATER, AFTER I'VE DONE my hundred shirts, another installment of my debt paid, I catch Genius at the kitchen table, his eyeglasses slanting across his face, cheeks studded with stubble. An ash snake dangles from the end of the cigarette at the edge of his mouth. A cotton tourniquet is tied around his bicep. A needle in his arm. "What are you doing?" I ask. He looks up, and then without comment goes back to his business. He injects into his vein a clear brown liquid, the color of diluted soy sauce. Genius getting whacked on Kikkoman! He moves his trigger hand off the syringe and reaches for the cigarette, but it sticks to his lips. "Here. Let me." When I touch the Lucky the old guy jerks his head away, and the glasses fly off his face. Through all this his arm stays cemented to the tabletop, the needle firmly in place like a nail in wood. I pick the glasses up off the floor. "Sorry," I say. "What is that stuff?"

"It's good for me."

"Yeah, like the cigarettes."

"Ah, you don't know. Give me." He means the glasses. "I have to see what I'm doing."

I put them on his face.

He withdraws the needle, sighs, swabs the puncture with a cotton ball. He shrugs in response to my question. "What do stupid doctors know, anyway?" He stores his kit in a wooden cigar box and tells me to go to bed. But he looks so pathetic I find it hard to leave him like that. "You should have some soup," I say. "I'll heat it up for you." Genius nods, but says he'll warm the soup later himself. Of course, he's lying. "You already did a lot of work tonight," he says. "Go to bed. You have a long day tomorrow."

A few steps down to the basement I feel terrible. Genius is going to get worked over by the doctors, and he's warning *me* about tomorrow. Someone should've hugged the poor guy, kissed his rough cheek, spooned soup into his mouth. Someone should have told him not to worry.

T HE DOCTORS DECIDE to keep Genius in the hospital. Preliminary tests and past medical history necessitate such a move. His "bloods" and "markers" are depressed, his "counts" elevated; these are anomalies; he has had renal cancer, the "internist's tumor," in the not too distant past. All the signs are there for more trouble. They call his case "mysterious" and "very exciting," and upon hearing these words I am initially flattered. My father! Spoken of in such terms by men of learning, whose opinions count. But soon I come to my senses. As far as I can tell, the doctors are tantalized by what they don't know, by what's beyond the reach of their expertise. They revel in the fact that Genius isn't a case study. I know now their professional enthusiasms aren't in our best interest.

GENIUS IS ADMITTED into the hospital on Sunday afternoon, and by Tuesday the doctors are ready to send him home. Since they aren't sure what's wrong, they don't know what to do for him. Throughout his hospital stay he has slept extravagantly. Around the clock, heavy snores, coming to only long enough to complain about pain, or get poked by the IV nurse, or be wheeled to Radiology. Zsa Zsa doesn't want him home. She's afraid of so much sleep: it's unnatural, something's wrong but no one's saying so, and she wants her husband in the hospital, where he's safe. Right now they're running an IV drip of salt water into his veins. I'm comforted by the fact he looks about the same as he did the last time he was in the hospital, and this despite being one kidney and ten pounds of his stringy flesh lighter, a decade or so older. Genius stirs, first kneeing the sheet taut, then kicking his leg free. I straighten the bedding, holding the covers aloft for a moment, and stare at his bare, ineloquent rump, his salt-and-pepper pubes, puckered scrotum, walnut-sized balls. Genius is tripping on sexy dreams: poking out from the womanly gown, powder blue with royal-blue diamonds, his dark, ponderous prick stands fully erect, its thick, belled tip pointing skyward, like the nose of a pup, eager and expectant. Here's one thing of my father's I would've wanted to inherit, but of course, I didn't. As I lower the sheet I shiver, thinking I have come from that and will one day come to be that too.

A doctor yanks me into the hallway just outside Genius's room. He is tall, hair shining like a trophy, lab coat unbuttoned and starched, dark blue dress shirt immaculately laundered and pressed, silk tie shimmering like a tongue of mercury. He's talking at the speed of light, explaining Genius's condition, but in the end he has no diagnosis, only a prognosis: "Your father has six months to live." As he says this I lock my eyes on the Band-Aid on the bridge of his nose, finding a flaw—a raging red zit beneath the cotton pad—in someone delivering a life sentence at that moment so irresistible.

"What're you talking about? You just finished telling me you don't know what's wrong with him!" Afterward, I hold my lips in my fist, between thumb and forefinger, as if they'd just been cut off, a medieval punishment for speaking out of turn. I'm trembling, though he can't see, in my thighs and shoulders—the world is balanced on my forehead. The doctor wants me to break the news to my parents, citing the language barrier as the reason he can't do the deed himself. "I don't get it. Yesterday you said it could be weeks before you knew anything. And now you're saying he's going to die."

"We did tell you renal cancer's very difficult to diagnose."

"So you do have a diagnosis?"

"Did we say that?"

I try to imagine divulging this horrible news to my parents. If our usual conversation is a paper plane, what the doctor's proposing is an SST. The best Chinese sentence I can muster is: "Six months you die." Very smooth, like trying to whip up a meringue with a chisel. "I think he'd rather hear the news from you," I say. "My parents will believe you."

"Have it your way. But most regular people like to take matters into their own hands."

ONCE BACK AT THE LAUNDRY, I enter the bathroom, shut the door, turn on the light. I stare at myself in the mirror. I practice what I have to say, the bomb I've agreed to drop on their heads. How stupid I look, like a character in a Hong Kong film whose voice is dubbed—the words don't fit my mouth. Then—I'm not sure what is in operation, sadness for my father's plight, or self-pity—I start to cry, the tears rising from my chest like an electrical charge. I weep and weep and weep.

I splash cold water on my face.

I flush the toilet for effect.

Once I exit I'm returned, I'm myself again.

LATER THAT NIGHT, I'm talking to my sister Lucy. "Well, you're the son," she says. What she means is that I've benefited disproportionately from my status as first and only male; I am Genius's presumed favorite, and now I have to take the bad with the good. It's my job to tell Genius about his condition. Still, I'm stunned as to where she gets her ideas. My father has never played favorites. He has been scrupulously even-handed in his indifference toward each of his children. Maybe what she remembers is seeing me hovering around him, and assumes it was the man who wanted the boy close by. But it wasn't like that. I was very young, two or so, and I was drawn to him: I didn't know better. During breaks in his work I tried to get him to play. At these times Genius's face brightened as soon as he replaced his drab everyday eyeglasses with the gold-framed model he used for reading. He would then cross his legs at the knees, light a cigarette, and vanish behind his newspaper. I'd stand close by, just shy of his twitching foot, shod in brown leather, screened off by the Great Wall of Chinese newsprint, simply to take in the bit-tersweet mix of smoke, ink, sweat, and paper. Sometimes, sensing my proximity, Genius, in his distracted, miserly fashion, for a moment would play. His eyes never relinquishing the precious pages, he would release his left hand from the newspaper and dangle it dead in the air, and when I came near he would snap his fingers at my boy flesh. But if I hung around long enough—that is, if he hadn't already shooed me away—I might carry off some of that burnt-honey smell on my clothes, hair, and skin, and when alone I'd savor the molecules I had stolen.

Even now I don't understand what the big attraction was, the mag-netic field that seemed to surround the man and hold the boy. If, for once, my father had freed one of his hands and absentmindedly petted my hair or caressed the queer curves of my ears, then I'd have reason enough. Or if he had offered his lap, or handed me his cigarette, so I might tip its long, curling ashes into the sardine-tin ashtray, I'd have an explanation for the blood dancing wildly in my scrawny chest. But he didn't trouble himself over me: no smoke rings for my amusement; no reading out loud in a singsong voice; no invitation to lean into his chest, nestle my head under his chin, the stubble tickling my scalp; no request I hold the cig-arette to his dark lips and watch the embers fire up orange-red, until he gave the signal—a sly, faint gesture only I, through often repeated intimacy, could detect—and I pulled the cigarette away, a smear of paper sticking to his lips. What contentment I would've felt at a moment such as this, just knowing that I was of some use to the man, that I had secured a place in his life! The galaxy settling into a perfect spin.

THE NEXT DAY, while driving Genius home from the hospital, I decide against telling him anything about his prognosis. Why worry him, when the doctors aren't even sure what the problem is? Who knows, they might be wrong; then he would have wasted all that fretting.

It is raining, the road slippery with sodden maple leaves. I watch the windshield wipers work. They are my favorite part of any automobile. One moment you're blinded by heavy rain or snow, and in the next you can see again—each swipe an epiphany. Genius has his eyes closed, head bowed, his glasses barely clinging to the tip of his nose. I switch on the radio, and before the initial burst of static gives way to the deejay's patter, Genius jerks to life and motions for silence.

His head is bobbing at the end of his neck, ripe grapes on the vine. Like that, he's gone. Snoozing. I wouldn't want to know I had only six months to live. I'm not one of those people who'd try to wring every drop of experience, meaning, pleasure from their last days. Jet to France and gorge at La Côte d'Or? Climb Everest? Parachute from a plane? Who'd be in the mood for any of that? For me, in this case, ignorance surely is bliss. Slap blinders over my eyes. I look over at Genius, his eyes shut—he's got the right idea.

Once I park the car behind the laundry and the engine stops cranking, Genius starts talking, as if in his sleep. He tells me about Yuk, the letter she wrote him from the Canadian tundra; she has had a change in plans; she is taking a part-time job as a waitress at a restaurant (sounds like a deli) there. And long range, she's contemplating going to school for her degree, or a career as an airline stewardess.

"What's with her, anyway?" I say. "She came to this country to marry me, but now she's running wild in Canada." I'm trying to be lighthearted, but it doesn't find the mark with Genius. He stares at me. Puzzlement or anger? Rain beats against the roof of the car, rolls down the windshield like a liquid curtain. Genius is spotted like a bad case of measles: the parking-lot light silhouettes raindrops all over him.

"Are you going to marry Yuk?" he asks, lurching forward in his seat, eyes pried open. I nod. Then shake my head. Marry her? I think. The world has gone marriage happy. Finally I shrug. "What's the matter with you?" he says. Then, with more energy than seems possible, he tells me, "You're a *juk-sing,* okay? You don't know anything about Chinese ways. Nobody blames you. You're not stupid, you're just born in America." The rain shadows crawl over him as he speaks. Chinese parents are duty-bound to see that their children are set up in life, se- cure in good jobs and married; only then are their lives complete. I am their last obligation. He says Zsa Zsa wants grandchildren, and while Patty's and Lily's kids are fine and loved, my sisters technically are no longer members of the Lung family, and only I, the son, am left and can carry on the line. Once they have put my life in order, they can go peacefully to their graves. When he says that, I wonder whether he already knows about his prognosis. "Nobody's dying, okay?" I blurt out, with a suddenness and fervor that must arouse his suspicions. In a calmer, softer tone, I add as a point of clarification, "Nobody's dying. Not you, not Ma."

But he abruptly pushes his way out of the car and into the rain. "Everybody has a day!" he says, slamming the door, and when it doesn't properly engage he slams it again. Good riddance! I spank the steering wheel. Why does he have to be that way, especially now when he has so little time left? I have a good mind to tell Genius the news just to get back at him. Then I catch myself. He does have only six months. It might be too late for him to learn new tricks. But I can still pull myself from the wreckage. He is standing in the rain, trying to find the right key to open the metal door. I give the ignition a half-turn, and the headlights come on, bathing him in a bright, watery beam. I switch on the windshield wipers: I see him, and then I don't.

EARLY THE NEXT MORNING I'm on my way back to Connecticut. On the Merritt Parkway snow starts falling. Unusual for this time of the season, mid-November, so rare, in fact, it feels like a bad omen. But I love the snow, the flakes' gentle fall, peace descending on the world. And calm. How long has it been since I felt calm, even in the kitchen? Probably not since Lisa Lee came bearing the news of Bliss's pregnancy.

I love this road, especially when I'm headed north, back to Richfield and my own life. I love its beautiful overpasses, its bare trees, their limbs lightly dusted with snow. *My father is dying.* My body tightens at the thought, as if in anticipation of a blow. Half a year. Six months more of hitting the Sizzler with Yuk, if she comes back. Smoking Luckys. Pressing and ironing shirts. First and last there's work. He'll breathe his final breath at the ironing board. Site of his life's greatest moment: In advance of a whistle-stop in Lynbrook, during the 1960 presidential campaign, Secret Service agents came to the laundry with two of John F. Kennedy's shirts. What big face for Genius, the future president, who one day would strong-arm the Russians and put a man into outer space, had chosen him, out of all the launderers and cleaners on Long Island, to wash and iron his shirts.

Six months. I count them off on my fingers: December, January, February, March, April, May. In May, I inherit Zsa Zsa! My sister Patty is married, living in Chicago. Lily is married and going to school in Boston. Lucy is in her usual state of transition, from husband to boyfriend, from career to career, from state to state, most recently Texas. I'm the logical candidate, the closest geographically, the youngest, the least encumbered. Ideally, I'll marry Yip Yuk Hing, and we'll live at Ma's in the love basement.

I slam on the brakes. The Valiant skids onto the road's narrow shoulder. Six months! May! June if Genius is late! What a thought! On time. Late. The way people talk about impending births. I count again, this time starting with September, and reel off nine months. May, if Bliss is on time. April, if she's early. June, if she's late. I lean forward in my seat, my forehead coming to rest on the steering wheel. Passing drivers, when they see me, might be put in mind of a suicide keeled over from carbon monoxide in his car.

AS SOON AS I step into my apartment I telephone Bliss. She'll tell me what to do. But when I hear her voice, springy with expectancy, as if she's been waiting for my call, I hang up. I put on my overcoat and walk to Fuchs's.

"You've got six months to live," I begin. "What do you do?"

"Nice to see you too," says Fuchs. He's cutting steaks from the rib.

"Fuchs, please. Let me ask the questions, okay?"

"I just made a fresh pot," Fuchs says, tipping his head in the direction of his back room.

I rinse the mugs in the sink. They are cheap, permanently stained with coffee, with little handles that hurt my finger when I drink. Woolworth's specials. My folks have the same ones. I pour two cups of his weak, tea-colored brew.

"Let's try this again. You're told you have six months to live—"

"Who's telling?"

"Fuchs!"

"Hey, if the mailman's talking, I tell him to go to hell. If you tell me it's a doctor, I go get a second opinion. You got a problem with that—sue me."

"Forget it. Just give me three pounds of flank steak, and I won't bother you anymore." I scan the refrigerated meat case. "If you don't have flank steak, I'll settle for skirt."

"Sterling," Fuchs says, stepping away from the butcher's block. "Why're you acting so meshugge?"

"Me? It's you! I asked a simple question and you—"

"Say it in plain English, then."

It feels like I'm talking to Zsa Zsa or Genius. I repeat the hypothetical. Fuchs answers now. "This is a toughie. A complex braintwister that encompasses personal ethics, morality, philosophy. Whatever I say will tell the world if Fuchs is a mensch or a horse's ass."

I am sorry I ever started the conversation. I can't tell if he is especially crazy today or if I am especially edgy, impatient, distressed. I feel pieces of my mind have been pared away. "I want serious, Fuchs. Be straight with me."

He takes some coffee. He's leaning against the tile wall, arms crossed against his bloody apron, ten-inch knife pressed to his cheek, salamis hanging over both shoulders. "I sure wouldn't keep cutting meat. There's not a worse job under God's creation. These damn carcasses. Dead flesh. That's my life, all day long. And so cold! Meat locker like Siberia."

"So what do you do, then?"

"That's not enough? It's plenty enough for me."

"Okay, you stop working. But there are a hundred seventy-nine more days after that."

"You make it sound like there's so many left. It's me, Fuchs, dying here."

"At least you know." Genius in the dark, facing the grave.

"Yeah, thanks to you I know. You handed down the death sentence."

"What if I didn't tell you?"

"You'd come in here six months from now and find me dead along with all the other dead things. But that won't happen, because you told me, and because you told me, I'm hanging up my apron. And then I'm going to rob a bank. Then claim my birthright as a Jew in America: find me a shiksa, one of those who wouldn't know a yarmulke from a bialy, and buy us a Caddy and head for Miami, winter at the Fontainebleau. And when I die, Sterling, bury me on the beach inside a cabana."

It pisses me off to no end that Fuchs is making light of my father's situation. I switch gears and abruptly ask for the meat I ordered.

"What's the matter with you?" he says. "What do you want me to say? You asked, I answered."

"Just get me the beef. I have to make lunch."

Fuchs prepares the package.

As I button my overcoat, Fuchs says, "Seriously, Sterling, this is what I'd do. I'd make sure my father's set up good."

"You have a father?" This seems incredible. Fuchs being born, ever being small or cute or dependent.

"That's right. I'm one of those. Pappy is strong as a bull. He lives in Cleveland. He plays golf. He putzes around the garden. He's okay. I'd just set him up. You know, lay in a supply of steaks, even though he's not supposed to eat too much meat because of his heart. But with steaks in the freezer he knows I'm thinking of him."

I leave, guilt-ridden. It's not so much about telling or not telling him what the doctors said, but the way Fuchs had on the tip of his tongue his plan for his father.

By the time I return to the club I'm satisfied as to how to proceed. My job now is to give Genius his equivalent of the freezer full of steaks: a grandchild and a Chinese daughter-in-law. That's what he wants, he said as much last night in the car. But that's crazy, right? Get tied down with a lifelong mistake just so Genius can go in peace? What happens after he's gone?

GENIUS HAS BEEN HOME for a week. Zsa Zsa plies him daily with her medicinal brews—teas and soups. *"Bu sin,"* she says of her concoctions, *"bu hwoot."* Strengthen the body, fortify the blood. An overall tonic effect. My sister Lucy calls Zsa Zsa "the witch doctor." Ingredients from mountain, forest, jungle, and sea. Squab, quail, black hen, beef shank; seaweed, seahorse, shark's fin; deer antler, bear gall, snake gland floating in rice wine; countless twigs, roots, berries, and leaves. Over the years she has stockpiled the ingredients; whenever someone was coming over from Hong Kong or China, she would place an order, making smugglers of them all. Even Yuk sneaked in a box of contraband for her. Twice daily Zsa Zsa seeks to heal him—double-boiled brews in the mornings, slow-cooked stews in the evenings. She claims Genius has started to gain weight.

"I thought he'd lost his appetite," I say.

"Who has an appetite for medicine?" she says. "You just open your mouth and pour it in."

And those mysterious injections? According to Zsa Zsa he's still shooting up. But she hasn't a clue what the medicine he self-administers is.

FINALLY I GET HOLD of Bliss. I start with Genius and we never stray from the topic. We actually have a pleasant conversation. It's great to have ready access to a medical care professional, even if she's only in training. Her guess on the Kikkomanish fluid he pumps into his veins (I hear her flip through several reference books): Vitamin B or male hormones.

"Male hormones?"

"Testosterone."

"What for?"

"It's hard to say. Feel better? Enhanced sexual performance?"

"Come on, Bliss. Sex at his age?"

"Hey, we both know how potent you Lung men can be."

DAYS PASS, and Zsa Zsa's medicine seems to have beaten back the doctors' prognosis for Genius, and I am cooking brilliantly again, when she calls one night from the hospital. I'm amazed. Zsa Zsa operating a pay phone. Long-distance, no less. An operator in her ear, telling her how many coins to drop in the chute. That's the first clue that the situation is serious. Genius has pains in his abdomen. (I'm not surprised, after the brews she's been stuffing him with.) "Dead boy! Come to the hospital before it's too late."

"Are you all right?"

"What are you asking? Your father's the one who's sick." She orders me to Long Island. She needs help in the laundry, she doesn't know how long Genius will be kept, she has no idea what the doctors and nurses say.

"Isn't Yuk back yet?"

"Why are you always worrying about her? She's not his child, you are. If you have to know where she is all the time, marry her and keep her at your side."

THE NEXT DAY I drive home to Long Island, after the ladies have had their lunch. Before I leave Richfield, Libby Drake and I hold a high-level executive meeting on her plans for the upcoming weeks, the holiday season. Of special note: As a gift to the "Jewish people," the club plans a Hanukkah luncheon, so I should start thinking of "appropriate cuisine" for the occasion. Then there's the annual club Christmas party, perhaps even a Christmas dinner; also, might I be interested in catering a dinner party for the Drakes at their house?

It's snowing again. Bleak season. Cold and snowy. I'm exhausted by the unseasonable temperatures, the constant threat of storms and black ice on the roads.

When I arrive at the store, Zsa Zsa immediately unplugs her iron, grabs her red coat, and slips on her galoshes. No concerns over keeping business hours. No note or sign for the customers. And we're off to the hospital.

I confer with a new doctor. He looks as if he's slept all night in his clothes. He's a kid, about my age, and as I listen to him I can't imagine being in his shoes, making life-and-death decisions. I just couldn't do it. Genius, he tells me, doesn't have appendicitis. His abdominal distress might be something as worrisome as an inflamed liver or as simple as spastic colon or gas. "I don't understand," I begin. "Why can't I get any answers in this hospital?"

"Under the circumstances we're doing the best we can."

"In a professional kitchen you can't get away with all this guesswork."

"A laparotomy would answer the questions. We can open him up and take a look inside at what's wrong. But with a man your father's age, you don't want us to do that."

When I ask if he and his colleagues have established a diagnosis, a reason for the grim forecast the other doctors have hung on Genius's head, this doctor says, "I really can't say. I'm too new to really know anything."

WE LEAVE GENIUS in his bed, dozing, waking, watching TV, seemingly all at once. We are sitting in the waiting room, waiting for someone to tell us we can split. The doctors want to keep him for observation one more night, then he can go home. "What am I going to do with him by myself?" Zsa Zsa says. "I'm no doctor. Who's going to be there with me?" I shrug. She won't say it outright, but she wants me to stay at the laundry with her and Genius. I immediately volunteer Yuk for the task, that is, if she ever returns from Canada. To which Zsa Zsa brusquely responds, "She's not my child. You are." All I know is, I'm glad I had the wisdom to keep Genius's prognosis a secret. She would be so miserable now. But the secret gnaws at my insides. It never leaves me. I don't have to think, and it's there. The waiting room's soundproof tiles, its fluorescent lighting tubes, the residual stench of disinfectant and coffee and hair spray grind down on me. On the TV set, bolted high on the ceiling—Walter Cronkite, just pictures, no sound— Boat People are landing in Malaysia; Jonestown revisited, the bodies, the washtub of Kool-Aid. This is what I mean, I can't escape it. Everyone running from death, running to death. Genius is not running to or from, and one day he'll be snatched by death, and only I could've warned him.

Zsa Zsa asks about the mass suicide, the bodies strewn across every inch of the screen. "I've seen this for days," she says. "What's going on? Your father won't tell me. You tell me."

I don't answer. A minute later Zsa Zsa points at the TV again. She wants to return to Jonestown. "What am I going to do?" she says, grabbing my arm.

"He just has a big stomachache." That's as close as I'll ever get to translating "spastic colon." Not surprisingly, she doesn't believe me.

Then she speculates about Genius's imminent demise, the miserable future awaiting her. Her talk drives me crazy. How dare she bury the poor guy, when she has no idea of his prognosis. She careens into ground Genius recently covered: Parental duty. Family obligation. Old stuff, ground so well trampled there's a bald path blazed across my heart. "You can't let him die before he's fulfilled his responsibilities to the ancestors," she says, and then she unleashes alarming, gut-wrenching wails.

My ribs tremble. My eyes sting. The waiting room's drab pastel greenness presses in on me. A poster of the Bee Gees on the wall. Their freakishly huge teeth bring Bliss to mind. "You can have your damn grandchild," I almost say, then don't. I stare at Zsa Zsa. She is no longer crying, though tears hang in her lashes. She is no longer fearful or sad; she seethes. I've stared at her a thousand times before, but now a peculiar thing happens. It's as if I'd stepped free of my body, I were not her son, and my gaze poured from someone else's eyes. I see her as others would, the red lips that match her coat, her eyes tricky and bright. She's pretty and still youthful, hardly the object of pity, the prospective widow she casts herself as, or the mother and laborer I condemn her to be. I want to touch her, the girl who never wanted to marry him, never wanted America, never desired the man or the nation, and yet she is bound. To work and childbearing, to a long, quiet, furious sorrow.

"*Ai-yah,*" she finally says, "who'd believe you'd turn into such a bad son? Why don't you settle down? Always one girl, then another. You pick them up like other people pick cabbages at the market." She sighs and reaches up, grabs a handful of my ear and, like when I was a kid, twists, putting a lifetime of disappointment into it.

"Ow!" I can't explain why, but I start crying, my sadness lodged high in my throat, then escaping in a single violent surge. I pity Genius,

I pity her having Genius, now losing Genius, and most of all I pity myself for the mess I've made of the little corner I've backed my life into, for the knowledge I have to hold of the imminent death and birth that consume me like hungry mouths from the inside out. Then the sadness passes, floating away as silver-edged clouds do after a summer storm, though my breath remains coarse and my vision moist.

I WALK BACK to Genius's room to see what's holding things up. I peek in, his bed is empty. Where have they taken him? I ask a nurse, and she says he's downstairs having a test done in Radiology. I ride the elevator to the first floor. The doors open in front of the cafeteria. Immediately I'm struck by the harsh, generic food smell, overcooked broccoli and hot deep-fryer grease and meat products. The diners shovel the stuff into their faces. They eat neither for nutrition nor for pleasure. This is their waiting room, and the food is time. They eat to make time pass, or else to hold it as long as possible. What is eating but a hedge against our mortality? Our place at the top of the food chain only underscores our dependence on the deaths of others to sustain us. What am I but someone whose job is to prolong the wait or make the wait more bearable? And one day the wait ends.

I RETURN to the waiting room. Genius wasn't in Radiology and he still isn't in his room. When I enter, a nurse is sitting with Zsa Zsa, their backs to me. Oh, my God! I think, something must've gone seriously wrong with Genius. I feel so ill equipped for this. I have no wisdom, no reserves of tenderness or compassion to draw on. "What's the matter, what's the matter?"

"Where have you been?" my mother says, standing, turning to face me. "This crazy nurse has been talking to me, and I don't understand a word she says. She seems to think she knows who I am."

She must've planned the next few seconds in our lives for dramatic effect. Because from behind, in her white lab coat, she does look like a nurse, and because she has chosen to wait for me to come to her, perfectly content to let the confusion ride, rather than simply unmask the mystery. I should've recognized her hair, the ultrapale crescent of jawbone that she is willing to show, with the stingy quarter-turn of her head toward me. But I am in a hospital, my father, a patient here, has disappeared, is dying, my mother is panicked by a nurse who quite possibly is breaking the worst news to her. Sure, on the surface, I might seem as emotional as a loaf of bread, but inside I am bubbling grief and despair. "Is something wrong?" I ask the nurse, dreading her reply.

"Of course not! Your mother's adorable," says Bliss. "Now I see where you get it from."

My first instinct is to bark at her, "Why are you here? What do you want now?" But when she rises out of her chair awkwardly—because she's pregnant, or because she's scared of which me she's going to get?— I open my arms, hungry to catch her. Her wide face shines, her pupils flare like little Fourth of Julys. I melt into her, losing myself in her soft, fluffy hair that's like a faceful of spider web. And when her big padded hand cradles the back of my head and presses me deeper into her smell, of salt and iron, lime and quinine, and she says hot into my ear, "Oh baby, my poor baby," I crumble, a knife plunged into my side and the sawdust running out. I hold on tighter, lengthen my arms by inches and hold her more. The heat of her blood envelops me like the hot haze of a sauna, and every place we touch, in the crook of my elbows, the caps of my knees, I feel the vibrations of her sturdy pulse, which echo in cartilage, bone, sinews. I've been rescued. I am overwhelmed by a sense of relief, my body sighs, *It is over, it is over,* and I have to believe it. And for a few seconds we pulsate together, she the star at the beginning of all things.

ZSA ZSA SUSPECTS the worst: My father has passed away, and the nurse is consoling me. "What is it? Tell me," she begs, slapping me between the shoulder blades.

We hustle over to his room, and though he's still not back in his bed, a real nurse there assures us he's okay. I introduce Zsa Zsa to Bliss, whom I refer to as "my friend," same as what I called all my other girl-friends. Zsa Zsa now mistakes her for a doctor. Why is she running around in a lab coat? Is she covering up her figure? I don't ask, but it looks impressive on her and imparts an air of authority. And I am grate-ful for the way she has taken control of the situation. "She's learning to fix teeth," I correct Zsa Zsa, which dazzles her even more. "Wah, she must be very smart!" Bliss repeats that Zsa Zsa is "adorable"; she declares her love for her and her utter "delight" they have finally met. She grabs my mother's hand and steps right into her face. "Ma," she says— *"Ma!"*—holding her hand provocatively flush against her belly, squeezing her hand like a bar of soap. "Mr. Lung's going to be all right. I'm here to make sure he gets the best medical care possible."

"Bliss, she doesn't understand you."

"What is she saying?" Zsa Zsa asks.

"She understands," Bliss says. Then repeats what she just said. "Okay, Ma?"

Zsa Zsa puts on her worried look, eyes, nose, lips sagging slightly. Before her face completely falls off, I serve up a spotty translation of Bliss's overly optimistic prognosis. Zsa Zsa grabs Bliss's hand and tells her, "Thank you, very much."

"I don't know why I translated what you said. How can you make promises like that? You're not a doctor, you're a dental student. I don't think a teeth cleaning is going to extend his life too long."

"Sterling, I'm on your side, okay? Hope is good medicine."

Right after the phone conversation in which I told Bliss that Genius was seriously ill, she apparently contacted her advisor about her "father-in-law's" condition. (She claimed she had to put it that way in order to underscore the urgency of the situation.) Her advisor called a college buddy, a researcher at the top-shelf cancer hospital in Manhattan. "I've made all the arrangements," she says. "We can't leave your father in this hospital. This place is Tad's Steakhouse. Sloan-Kettering is Le Cirque."

BLISS! That night she sends Zsa Zsa and me home; she will stay in Genius's room overnight. "That's absurd!" I tell her. "I never did that. He doesn't need someone at his bedside."

"Well, if you haven't been there, how would you know?"

WHEN I ARRIVE at the hospital the next day, Bliss isn't there. "This is for you," Genius says, handing me a scrupulously folded piece of paper that he has apparently kept hidden under the bed sheet. "From your nice girlfriend. She loves to talk. And she looks like a nurse."

"I know."

I unwrap the thick triangle-shaped note. It looks like a mini bikini-bottom. She writes that my father is "adorable," that she has explained the plan to Genius, that he understands everything she said. We are to meet her later in the morning at Mount Sinai Hospital for a consultation with her advisor's friend Dr. Zimmer, who will refer "us" to the proper subspecialist.

Bliss has taken matters into her capable hands. Who am I to argue with her? She has the connections to open doors (Zimmer's nurse tells us how lucky we are, otherwise he's booked into the new year); she is wise to the medical lingo and talks easily to the doctors; and she holds Genius's hand throughout the many interviews and tests. I admire the way she smiles reassuringly at him, and shoots the doctors skeptical "Don't fuck with me" stares. Frankly, I can't do any of these things for him. But with Bliss present, they're getting done. Zimmer refers Genius to Sloan-Kettering in Manhattan. A battery of diagnostic tests and physical evaluations brings no good news, but there's no really bad news either. After a closed-door meeting between Bliss and the doctors, she says that once the results are in and the pathologists have done their jobs, "we'll put our heads together and come up with a game plan."

Bliss was right about the hospitals being different. The waiting rooms cleaner and more commodious, the doctors smarter and more handsome, the nurses prettier and more plentiful. What a place this is! Like the kitchen of a four-star restaurant! Big and bright, an atmosphere buzzing with excitement and high expectation—so many talented people exerting massive watts of brain power toward a single goal. Genius has machines and specialists for every piece of his body. I'm so proud. *We* have accomplished so much, in so little time. My chest rises like buttery sheets of puff pastry and the weightiness of the possible diagnosis lifts off my brow.

I am signing the discharge papers. Genius's ordeal in Sloan-Kettering is over, at least this round. Seated next to me at the desk, he is squeezing Bliss's hand to bits. He doesn't want to let her go. I understand how he feels; when she isn't comforting Genius, I find myself grabbing her hand or rubbing her back: I want everyone to know this smart cookie is with me. While she batters the paper-pusher with questions about how we should proceed from this point, I remember last night, when Bliss came to the laundry and spent the night in the basement, on Yuk's sofa bed. The first thing she noticed was the David, and was impressed with my parents' good taste. Later she exposed her belly to me, and though she insisted she was really showing, I saw only the subtlest change—a dash of salt in a five-gallon stew. Before I went upstairs for the night, we made love briskly, my passion fueled, no doubt, by my gratitude for all she had done.

From the hospital Genius and I drive Bliss to Grand Central. She's taking the train to New Canaan to visit her folks before returning to Iowa. As she says good-bye to Genius she administers the first and only hug I've seen put on him. He accepts it and reciprocates without any of the awkwardness I would've expected of someone with so little practice.

On our drive back to the laundry Genius is silent, his eyes closed, head loose on its stem, rocking to shifts in the traffic. I'm fine with him sleeping. We both need the break after so much activity at the hospital. And I welcome the unasked questions about Bliss (not that there's any real threat of that happening). I'm annoyed, though, that once Bliss left us, he suddenly turned mineral. When she was with us he bobbed his head to the things she said, the nonstop chatter that rolled from the backseat. She was nosy. *When did you come here? Why? How did you and Ma meet? Was it love at first sight? Why'd you wait so long before you sent for Ma? Were you always drawn to laundry work? Was that what you did back in China?* Then a barrage of questions about China. Weather, geography, language, and the Lung family history. I couldn't believe her balls. Where Genius comes from, such probing is considered disrespectful, even rude. But he didn't seem to mind. If he could answer yes or no, and he was moved to, he nodded or shook his head. Other questions he ignored completely. Which didn't discourage her.

I ache with resentment when I recall her ease with him, as if they had known each other a lifetime. I could never ask those questions, even though, over the years, they've bloomed a hundred times in my head. But not once did I think it a good idea to loose them into the barbed-wire air between us. I try to put everything in its proper place—he is sick, I am indebted to her—but I can't hold both in my heart at the same time. It comes apart. And I'm left with neither one inside.

Part Two

Cooking is like love. It should be entered into with abandon or not at all.

— HARRIET VAN HORNE

Chapter 7

A S I'M CLOSING IN on the junction of Routes 7 and
106, near the town of Wilton, the halfway point
to New Canaan, home of the Sasses and site of this year's Thanksgiving
feast, the Valiant loses power, struggling up even the most casual rise in
the road. I notice this happening just as I notice the trees are barer here
than in my part of the state, a mere twenty winding miles away, their
branches colliding like knife blades to sharpening steels against a pale
gray sky. I try the radio again. A minute ago the reception suddenly
soured. It's not much better now—a thick icing of static over a faintly
audible "Just the Way You Are."

I am going to the Sasses' because Bliss asked, because I owe Bliss
for all she's done for Genius, because we agreed my presence there
would signify nothing other than that it's Thanksgiving, a festive time.

The car hesitates and sputters but finally conquers a mildly steep
hill. At the top I pull onto the shoulder of the road. From here I gaze
out at an impressive estate, enormous acres of white fences and

manicured lawn, with pond, tennis court, horses, and huge stone house, black-shuttered, slate-roofed, smoke curling from its many chimneys. The scene outside has me by the throat. I exit the Valiant. I sit on the hood, inhaling the same lush burning-wood fragrance as the people in the house enjoy. I try not to think about anything, and without thinking, I'm thinking about Genius and Zsa Zsa: No Sterling, no Thanksgiving. They are as pathetic as the Pilgrims without their Indian friends that first Massachusetts winter. For years I have cooked Thanksgiving dinner. Even when I was away at college I returned home to do the holiday, despite their protests (Genius: "Turkey is bad-eating, turkey meat is coarse and dry"). Without me there, they won't bother. Tonight, a few bitter grains of rice and some dried sardines.

It just never was in their bones. No turkeys in China. No Pilgrims. No Indians. No *Mayflower*. But for all the years of elementary school, my teachers inculcated me with the holiday. Already a veteran in the construction of paper-plate turkeys, I was doomed to yet another fall without thanks or salvation, when the Chins, enlightened friends of my parents', folks Zsa Zsa had met at the Ellis Island detention center, invited us to our first-ever Thanksgiving feast.

They served all manner of poultry. Huge poached hens. Deep-fried squab. A mallard stew. But no turkey. Our host, the hunter who bagged the ducks, claimed that *fuo gai* wasn't a good-eating bird, its flesh coarse and dry. I was skeptical of his appraisal: once a year the entire nation came to a standstill for the sake of turkey, so why wasn't it good enough for us?

As the next Thanksgiving approached, my sisters and I lobbied hard for a proper celebration. In response, my father simply parroted his friend's low opinion of *fuo gai ngook*. "Only stupid Americans eat turkey." No further explanation was forthcoming, nor did I expect one. Back then I saw this as the supreme advantage of being Pop. He got away with saying as much or, as was usually the case, as little as he wanted, in Chinese or English, his own ideas or those stolen from others, and no one in the family dared to question his pronouncements, large or small. That year and for the next several, our family celebrated with other families, only now someone brought a turkey roasted in Chinatown. No thought was given to home-cooked turkey because Chinese didn't use their home ovens for anything but storage; they prepared everything—boiled, steamed, fried—on the stovetop. Pop often was the self-appointed head chef at the Thanksgiving gatherings, even though at home all he did in the kitchen was eat. But on these special occasions, he seemed larger than life. White apron tied around his waist, brown paper bag on his head like a chef's toque, he manned the stove, surrounded by steam, his brow gleaming with sweat, flames reflecting off his glasses as if his eyes were on fire. With his shirtsleeves rolled to his elbows, exposing his long, bulging, shiny forearm muscles, he banged spatula to wok, steel against steel, like some Oriental instrument he had mastered. Broth rolling, oil crackling, smoke twisting from Pop's cigarette, his buddies stopped to watch and chat, refilling his cup of Scotch whiskey and their own, which made them loud and bold and wise about everything: the Japanese bombing of their village; John F. Kennedy; how best to iron nylon and Orlon and Dacron; the cost of starch and sugar; fishing; the taste and texture of turkey relative to other fowl; and a long line of other "gotdamsonuvabitchee" subjects.

But these Thanksgiving meals he cooked were still Chinese. Served in grand Chinese style, on makeshift plywood tables, the brown paper used to package customers' laundry doubling as tablecloths. Rice bowls and chopsticks. The turkey, chopped into inch-by-two-inch chunks, was parked next to bird's-nest soup, mung bean threads, sautéed abalone. The spread looked nothing like it was supposed to, nothing like Thanksgiving on TV, the turkey brought whole to the table, drumsticks wearing paper crowns, keeping company with stuffing, canned yams, celery sticks, cranberry sauce, pumpkin pie. In the end, I blamed my father for ruining Thanksgiving. The meat *was* coarse and dry.

Not this year. I begged my sisters to take my place—invite the folks to their homes or spend Thanksgiving with them on Long Island. But no one bit: prior commitment, too broke to travel, not celebrating any longer. And where's Yuk when I need her? If she had returned from Canada they would gorge at Sizzler, and who would need me then? Now Zsa Zsa will miss her annual hit of the mashed potatoes and gravy she's come to love. Genius will be spared another encounter with the dreaded bird. I remind myself that by saving him from the stressful meal, I'm adding days to his life. And while he didn't seem to care that I wasn't going to prepare Thanksgiving this year, he might feel different if he knew how sick he supposedly is. Since I'm the only person, besides Bliss, who does know this is likely his last turkey day, I probably should spend it with him.

My eyes are bone. I have stared so long and hard at the estate my vision blurs. Bliss's neighborhood. Not exactly, but it's her general neck of the woods. Who can argue with any of this? When you wake up in the morning, don't you hope that during the course of the day you'll do something that will bring you inches closer to this manner of life? Isn't that why Genius came to this country in the first place? Isn't that the purpose of every shirt he's pressed? Without Genius, I could never have arrived here, on top of this hill, on the verge of gaining a foothold in the genteel culture below. It was Genius who put these eyes in my head, planted my feet on this land. What am I thinking? I should get my ass immediately down to Long Island, give him my thanks.

I get back into the Valiant, open the glove compartment, and find a New York map. I determine the best route from here to Genius, and when I drop the map in the passenger seat and gaze at the real road outside the car, I'm seized once more by the beautiful landscape that says *Bliss* to me, *America* to me. To love this is natural for the person I am.

These contortions are my struggle to fit the two together in my heart. I don't know why one always pushes the other out, why I can't hold Genius and Bliss (or whoever it is I'm dating) at the same time. I don't know if it's the size of my heart, if it's too small to hold them or too niggardly to welcome them or too weak to keep them in its grasp.

I start driving. When I reach the intersection where I should turn left and point the Valiant south toward Genius, I speed through, quietly persuaded by the riches that surround me. Continuing its course toward New Canaan, the car—nervous and hesitant—struggles up another hill. The open glove compartment rattles noisily, and when I reach to shut the gaping mouth I notice the velvet box that holds Yuk's moon rocks, which I banished to the car back in the days they commandeered my attention like an addiction. I open the box and wedge the moon rocks between the windshield and the dash, directly under the rearview mirror. As I roll down the hill and close in on the Sasses', I see in the rearview the road that has brought me this far recede, and at the same time the moon rocks, like distant headlights, rapidly approach.

I FINALLY FIND the Sass property. I steer the Valiant through the opening in the low stone fence, and immediately my eyes are filled with the bright whiteness of the vast groves of birches on both sides of the asphalt drive. The trees are so densely packed in the endless acreage that the moment is dazzling: it's like tearing through clouds at thirty thousand feet. All I see are the tall, papery-barked trees and the long black drive that cuts through them to oblivion. I blink, inhale deeply, set and reset my jaw: I'm adjusting my body to the new light, air, and sounds.

The road narrows and winds, five-mile-an-hour curves as tight as fish hooks, to the right, to the left, tortuously luring me in. Here the birches have been cleared back from the narrow road, opening my sight-lines. In the distance a lightless corona of dark-limbed elms and oaks rises above the tips of the birches. At last, I see the house plainly—a giant tease, like gold littered on American streets, set among somber centuries-old trees, the ultramodern glass-and-steel jewel Bliss calls home. I am in love! My body flutters as it did the first time I laid eyes on the Ladies' Club.

But the more I drive, the farther I seem to be from reaching my destination. Bliss had warned me. Her father, Morton Sass, designed the looping drive to make access and getaway more difficult for trespassers and thieves.

It works beautifully.

Bliss calls her father paranoid. "Remember one thing, Sterling. He trusts no one," she said, after I agreed to come for Thanksgiving and meet her parents. "In his imagination, everyone's after what's his." The winding road is less a product of the terrain than evidence of his "warped mind." When I said, "He just wants to protect his family," she fired back, "*Ha!* You don't know!" Okay, I don't. But once Morton Sass crept onto her brain, her voice changed as if at the onset of migraine. Even I, no stranger to tensions between parent and child, was left breathless and singed by how candidly she displayed the spectacular quantities of hatred her body seemed to hold for her own father. And not because of any cruelties he had perpetrated against her personally, but because his parents, as survivors of the camps, gave him—in Bliss's view—the "moral justification" to fashion himself into a bigot. "He trusts no one but another Jew."

I don't blame him. "With that behind me, I'd be suspicious too."

"That's fine. But everyone who's not like him isn't worthless. You're not worthless, are you, Sterling? I know my brother isn't worthless."

"What's wrong with Lester? Did he convert?"

"He's gay. Disowned, until he comes to his senses."

Bliss also disapproves of how her father makes his living. Morton Sass acquires things—land, lakes, stocks, bonds, buildings, airwaves (an AM radio station and, recently, a cable TV station)—then resells them at a profit. "He doesn't make anything, he doesn't provide a service. How does he benefit society? Genius is a thousand times more productive than Morty'll ever be. He just makes money. And do you know why?"

"Pay the mortgage? Buy groceries?"

"No. So he can say, 'Fuck you! You put my family in death camps, but I am better than you. Look at my Cadillacs, look at my gigantic house, look at my children's straight teeth.' "

For these reasons she has contemplated, since senior year in high school, legally changing her last name: put some bite behind her opinions. I asked if her parents knew of her plans. "Of course I told them. There'd be no point in even thinking about getting rid of their name if they didn't know."

"Why'd you change your mind?"

"I haven't. Trust me, Silvy, I'll do it someday soon."

Was she talking marriage? As in changing her name to mine? Bliss Lung? If what she said about her father was true, that would be a punch between his eyes.

I PARK between Cadillacs. On my left a pair of matching his-and-hers gold DeVilles, and a funeral-black Fleetwood to my right. That one must belong to Morton Sass's mother, Tessie.

Outside the Valiant the crisp air stings my lungs. I barely reach the imposing oak door, when it opens. Bliss and the smell of roasting turkey rush at me. Her hair, the soft brown of calf liver in this light, is piled on her head, loose strands falling prettily around her smiling face. She's in a see-through white blouse with a prissy little schoolgirl collar, pearl buttons, and pleats down the front; a camisole underneath has the skinniest straps. In the instant I catch an eyeful of her, I think it's impossible she's pregnant. She looks too good, better than ever. Her usually frail white skin, preternaturally slack to the touch, shines pink, burning blood just below the surface. We kiss, our bodies collapse into an embrace. My arms feel for a change in her girth; if anything, she seems thinner than she was a week ago. "You look nice," I whisper.

"I told them." Her breath tickles my ear. A giddiness in her voice.

"Told them what?"

"I told them I'm pregnant."

I stagger back from her as if she were a hot wire and I badly burnt. My body slips into a numbness equal to that when I was told Genius was dying fast: Pins and needles, each tipped with the doctor's words, now replaced by Bliss's simple announcement. "What'd you do that for?"

"Because I am?"

"Well, who exactly did you tell?"

"Is that you, Sterling?" a man calls from somewhere behind me. "I've been waiting for you."

MORTON SASS, a daunting figure in chinos, desert boots, and plaid flannel shirt, takes me on a tour of the grounds, specifically to show off his new anti-deer fence. Deer have been coming up to the house, he notes, spring and summer, to eat Selma Sass's lettuce and petunias. The fence isn't much, just three bands of heavy-gauge wire, strung at foot-wide intervals from evenly spaced metal posts along the entire perimeter of the property. Smart deer will step right through, between the wires. But how smart can a deer be? When I reach out to test the wires' tension, to see what those woodland creatures are up against, I am jolted back by a sharp electrical charge that brings tears to my eyes. "Hey!" I shout, shaking, then inspecting, my fried hand. Morton Sass laughs. In a dark corner of my mind I register the moment as a milestone in our brand-new relationship: I have made Morton Sass laugh; the man will come to associate me with pleasure, good, but will that be enough to make him forgive me for knocking up his daughter? That's not to say I forgive him for letting me grab the fence when he knew the electricity was flowing. "You're all right," he says, a few feet ahead of me. "It should take a lot more than that to hurt you."

He comes closer and examines my hand with the appraising gaze of a shrewd shopper or middleman. "You'll live," he says. There are bags under his eyes, like small dumplings, and tufts of gray hair blooming from his ears, and I wonder if I am to blame for these, keeping him up nights fretting about his Bliss big with a Chinaman's baby. Imagine the man's shock at hearing such news. How he has suffered weighing his dismal options. Toast the bastard on the deer fence? Take him in as a son-in-law? Lose his daughter—the snappy sizzle and hiss of Bliss Sass—to a Chinese guy and his ugly tampon plug of a name. I feel wretched, and only just now realize what I have done.

But then consider this: A switching of names is, in a certain light, like the trading of fathers. Trading hers for mine, Sass for Lung. Anyone can see what a swindle that is. I would gladly accept such a one-for-one swap. And why not? Look at this land, this house, those fine automobiles! He makes tons of money without having to press a single shirt, without having to kiss a single customer's starch-or-no-starch ass. What's so bad about that? Change my name, slip free of the old yoke, refathered, reborn, Sterling Sass? Absolutely.

He slaps my shoulder, a surprising but fatherly gesture, one Genius has never attempted, and then we walk the property, the fence marking its boundary, tall brown grasses in the clearings, otherwise a thick cushion of leaves underfoot. The terrain at times is strenuous, steep downhills, brisk rises, gigantic outcroppings of granite to climb. Canada geese fly overhead; oak logs burning in fireplaces, perfume the air. Morton Sass knows the name of everything.

It is cold out here; my nose is running. At last we approach the end of the circuit. We come within sight of the big white house. Honey light pours from its many windows. It looks like a furnace inside. Morton Sass carries on about football. College, pro. Gibberish to me. But I listen to every word, awash in the man's smell (mothballs, moss, and twigs), his voice whining on about sports, his endless land, countless trees, elegant home, brutal fence, four-hundred-volt deer. The thought comes upon me fully formed: Until now, I have been an orphan; my father has never talked with me this way.

As we hike uphill to the house I spot a deer. Majestic, with a full rack of antlers. Morton Sass is in front, his khaki butt at the level of my face. I breathe heavily, concentrating on the climb. The deer stands twenty feet away, steady as a tree. I've never seen anything so beautiful and dignified in nature. "Look!" I whisper. "Look, on your left!"

"Jesus fucking Christ! Look at the size of that bastard. He can eat through all of Thanksgiving in a single bite." He abruptly bends and picks up a stick. He brings it behind his head and fires at the dumb-founded deer. "Here, eat this!" he shouts. "Get off my property."

His voice thumps off my heart and echoes in my chest, as if the anger were really meant for me. When the deer bounds away, part of me runs with him.

"I paid good money for that fence. It's supposed to keep deer out, not draw them in close so you can stare at them. They're nothing but vermin. Long-legged rats."

It's a deer, I want to say, not a rodent with a thyroid condition. It stood respectfully on the other side of the electric fence, minding its own business, a head as wide as my chest, antlers as broad as I am tall, its glistening nose a thumping black heart. Why is this man so upset? Suddenly he isn't the successful businessman in command of the staff of a hundred employees whom I've imagined, spending his days in an office tower. Being in his presence feels undeniably less substantial. It's like a fallen soufflé, which still tastes good, even though you know it's not all it should be.

I say nothing. And this seems to suit Morton Sass, because he's silent too, until we reach the front door. "A couple of things," he says, "before we go inside." He slaps me on the shoulder again and huddles close, about to offer up secrets he doesn't want anyone else to hear. My heart races, we are so cozy, so fast, Morton Sass all over me, the way the burr-covered husk of a chestnut surrounds the edible meat inside. His breath, a steamy creamed-corn scent, heats my nose, and his eyes cling to me like sap from these trees. "In ascending degree of importance," he says: "One, Blissy loves you to get my goat—I can't prove it but I know it's true. Two, good move cutting that hair of yours—Blissy had warned us you kept it sissy-long, but I'm glad to see you're a man now. And three—" He has us moving toward the door and brings his mouth closer to my ear. "You're a cook. Selma's not. Maybe you can find your way into the kitchen and show me something."

WHAT A MAGNIFICENT HOUSE INSIDE! The first floor is almost entirely glass, ten-foot-tall windows looking out at acres of prime Connecticut real estate. The floors are slate. On the few solid walls are pieces of modern art, hanging objects, disks that resemble painted garbage can covers, copper and tin projectile sculptures like phalluses in repose. Every flat surface holds a craftsy bowl or vase or antique knickknack.

Morton Sass leads me to the kitchen, where Selma Sass is peeling potatoes behind a peninsula counter jutting from a wall. She has the thick, big-boned amplitude of a horse. Nothing in her face or figure suggests an earlier stage of life—she entered this existence an adequately developed adult, with a Dorothy Hamill cut and lots of bosom and hip, and eyeglasses as big as shop windows, though no one has gone window-shopping there recently. Under a "Kiss the Cook" apron she's wearing a lumpy brown turtleneck sweater and a skirt I've seen on Bliss before, milk-chocolate brown, coarsely woolly, with a llama woven into the fabric. I immediately like this woman, who is every inch Bliss, except she won't ask anything of me.

Morton Sass does the introductions.

"Oysters," I say, sniffing the bivalves' leathery brine, mingled with turkey fat and an overdose of nutmeg in the pies.

"Bliss told us you were clever," she says, stepping away from the counter and toward me. "Nothing gets past you, am I right?"

"At the CIA I was famous for my nose." I extend my hand to her.

She says, "What's the matter? Can't you read?" With her chin she points to the "Kiss the Cook" apron. So I kiss her warm, puffy Jean Naté cheek.

Morton Sass leaves the kitchen. Selma Sass and I chat. When the conversation slows I go back to my strong suit: food. "I thought Jews didn't eat shellfish."

"That might be true, but we're not your average Jewish family, are we?" She wags her eyebrows and smiles conspiratorially at me, as if to say, *You're* here, aren't you? Then, in the next beat, comes the inevitable, dreaded question. "Is it true that your parents work in a laundry?"

"They own the business."

"That must make it nicer for them."

I change the subject, nothing gained stumbling along that path. It's guilt by association, and I'll only be linked that much more closely to them. Instead, I offer to help cook. "You're my guest," she says. "I'm doing Thanksgiving, though I have to admit I'm a little intimidated cooking for a professional chef."

Morton Sass returns, fixes himself a vodka on ice, and announces that Bliss is upstairs holding a dental clinic for all comers. "She won't get me," he says. "I took a rain check. But I volunteered your teeth, Sterling. You're up after she's through with her grandmother and Randi." Then Morton Sass glances at his wife, then at me. Get in there, his face says, work for your supper. Show us what you can do besides impregnate our little girl.

I watch Selma Sass do everything wrong. Take how she peels potatoes. She whittles the spud like a block of wood, her technique dangerous and wasteful, producing potatoes with more facets than a disco ball. I look over at Morton Sass, and his eyes meet mine. I get the message. "Let me do that," I say, and this time I bully her, swiping the potato and peeler from her hands. "I'm such a klutz with a knife anyway," she says.

I tell her she was doing fine.

"Don't lie to me," she snaps.

I don't need this, lady. I came here as your guest, but so far I've been electrocuted and tossed into the middle of a long-simmering dispute over your cooking skills. I hesitate before I start peeling. I'm getting crushed between the Sasses. I wow him with my estimable skills, she'll be pissed I'm trying to make her look bad. It's a test, I know. It has everything to do with the activities inside their daughter's womb. I wish they'd say what they think about the situation. Whether they're with me or with Bliss. Or, I suppose it's possible, languishing somewhere in between.

I ROTATE THE LAST POTATO, the utility knife held just under its skin, generating a foot-long ribbon of peel and a flawlessly smooth spud.

When I'm through, Selma Sass says, "Is there a special way for rinsing potatoes too?" My mind goes blank. I see stars in front of my eyes. Suddenly I long for the old Thanksgivings. Food from cans and boxes. For the company of Genius and Zsa Zsa, who didn't criticize, because they were without standards. Then Selma Sass laughs. "I was just joking, Sterling. You did a beautiful job. I can see why those club ladies like you so much."

She knows several of the members, and is especially friendly with Millie Boggs, the two having gone to Wellesley together. Selma would be a perfect fit, except that in two weeks' time the ladies managed to drive away Barbara Cohen, the only Jewish woman ever admitted to the club. Bliss had told me in anticipation of my coming to dinner that her parents weren't too thrilled that I was cozying up to "that pack of anti-Semites."

"How are *those* ladies treating you?"

In other words, am I embraced by the Jew-haters? Don't they say the company you keep reflects who you are? But what if I lie, and tell her they're not as pleased as she's heard through the grapevine (*their* young chef, with his silky hair and beautiful hands, his sly, quiet, "mysterious" demeanor, his warrior's gaze and angelic food)? I don't want the Sasses thinking that I'm a failure, that I can't satisfy a houseful of female appetites. So I say I aim to give the ladies what they seem to want—more wine, less salt, more pastries, less butter, less cream, no garlic, mushrooms, or sweetbreads. "And they keep after me for Chinese food."

"Bliss told us you won't cook Chinese."

"It's not that I refuse. I just don't. It's not my thing. But they're getting more insistent. The club president—"

"That Drake woman."

I can hear the bitterness in Selma Sass's voice. I decide to exploit my position as an insider and Selma Sass's as a nose-pressed-up-against-the-glass outsider. "Yes, well, *Libby*. She's gotten so insistent. You know what she said to me? 'We don't expect anything elaborate. Whatever you cook back there in your apartment will be just fine.' " Libby Drake's words had the ring of an ultimatum. She said I'm a Chinese; I said I'm a chef, one who specializes in continental not communist cuisine. I feel myself relaxing a little; I tell Selma Sass how Libby Drake pushed the sherry cart into the kitchen, and on the cart were four aluminum Chinese-restaurant-style serving dishes, the lids topped with nipples for handles. "Aren't they darling?" she said. My brain was spinning in my skull like a marble in one of her metal food receptacles. She wanted me to use those things. If not chow mein, then Swedish meatballs. How insulting! Here I had studied at the premier cooking school this side of the Atlantic; an informal poll of my classmates voted me "Most Likely to Serve." When three-star chef Gérard Maré came to the CIA to give a master class, I was his handpicked sous-chef. (As a token of the master's high regard for me, I was given an autographed whisk, which he claimed he had used to whip the meringue that topped off his fabled 1963 dinner at the White House, just weeks before the Kennedy assassination.) Now Libby Drake expected me to throw my pedigree away? At graduation the dean had concluded his remarks in this way: "Cook not what you want to feed your diners, but what your diners want to eat." That's fine. But sometimes the people one serves don't know what's good for them.

While I'm talking I boil the potatoes and tinker with the creamed onion casserole (which looks as medieval as blancmange), candied yams, string beans, and pumpkin soup. I add salt and pepper, dried sage and thyme, canned chicken stock and Gold Medal flour, cloves and chopped chives. Selma Sass has the kitchen of death, great equipment that far outstrips her technique. I do as much as possible to heal the dishes, trying for the perfect balance of flavors, the exact chemistry. "Some sherry might neutralize the cinnamon," I suggest, and she pours, pinches, sprinkles, minces. Whatever I tell her.

"Sterling," she says, "let me tell you something. As a collection of human beings those ladies aren't my favorites. But there's no question, Morty and I love Chinese food. Every Sunday night."

When I hear this my stomach twists, like sauce wrung through cheesecloth, and I flinch, as I did when Morton Sass lost his head and attacked the beautiful deer. In her profession of love for Chinese food I hear: They both have forgiven me for what I've done to Bliss. I know I'm right, just as I know I'm standing at a Viking six-burner professional range, in the fabulous Sass house, before a casserole of creamed onions, the whitest dish I've ever seen, its steam and stench rising to blister my brow.

Behind the stove, bathed in cooking's moist heat, I feel at peace, at home here. I look at Morton Sass: I love this man, his open heart, his willingness to bend my way, the vodka in his hand shimmers like silver. I look at Selma Sass in her apron, her liberalism reflected in the riches of the kitchen she keeps: the bulging bowls of fruit, Golden Delicious, Red Delicious, Granny Smith, Pippin, Empire, Jonathan, McIntosh, Cortland apples; Bartlett, Bosc, Anjou, Comice pears; expensive out-of-season peaches, cherries, plums, and nectarines; crystal dishes brimming with walnuts, pecans, almonds, hazelnuts, brazil nuts, chestnuts; pumpkin, spaghetti, hubbard, acorn, turban squash for show; loaves of white, rye, challah, and pumpernickel that Bliss's sister, Randi, brought from New York City; twenty pounds of turkey, and the best ingredients money can buy for sides, blue point oysters, Iowa pork sausage, Idaho russets, Carolina yams, Long Island corn, Cape Cod cranberries, Florida oranges. I can hardly recognize myself, an emergent madness surfaces on my face, lost as I am in such a magnificent jungle of goodness.

Selma Sass comes to the stove and stares into the onion casserole. "Can it be saved?" she says. I pour canned chicken broth in to cut the cream. The dish is a bad car wreck, but I lie. She spoons some and tastes. "You're such a genius!" she says. "My creamed onions never tasted this good." After another taste, she adds, "I wonder about that Libby Drake, making those demands on you. If she's so crazy for Chinese food, she should hire herself a real Chinese cook."

"Wait a minute, Sel. You better get your eyes checked," Morton Sass says. "He looks Chinese to me."

Looks can be deceiving. America's a great nation because its people are judged for who they are, not what they are. Who Morton Sass is is a real estate developer / communications magnate / business-man. What he is is a Jew. And what I am is a chef. Damn it, Morton Sass should know better than to label me Chinese. This is America.

BLISS'S LITTLE SISTER RANDI and her grandmother Tessie come downstairs. They show Selma Sass their teeth. "Selma, dear," the grand-mother says, "that daughter of yours has a touch. Not once did I mind her fingers in my mouth. That's such a talented girl Mort has raised." Turning her wrinkly palm up, she says, "Tell me, dear, why is she doing this?" By "this" she means me. Selma Sass pretends she doesn't hear. I glance at the old woman, my eyes narrowed so only the smallest dose of her gets in. Selma Sass introduces us, and I force out a hello. "Sure, sure!" she says back, then shakes her little head, topped by permed white curls that resemble cauliflower.

I reach for her small hand. She wears a ring with a diamond as big as her knuckle. I see the row of numbers tattooed on her wrist.

WHY DID YOU TELL THEM?" I'm seated on a swivel chair, its back to a pink writing desk that anchors two lamps, their hot light trained on my face. I'm surrounded by scraps of her adolescence on the walls—posters of Degas ballerinas, Monet water lilies, Beatles Sgt. Pepper's Lonely Hearts Club Band, Che Guevara *¡Viva la Revolución!*, McCarthy for President, and National Turn in Your Draft Card Day November 14.

"Thanks for dressing up," she says.

I'm wearing my navy blue wool gabardine slacks and the shoes I stole from the bottom of Genius's wardrobe. Very serious adult leather shoes, too costly for me to justify buying, too fancy for my father's life.

"*What* did you tell them?"

"Why're you so paranoid? I told them I'm pregnant—"

"And?"

"You're the father."

"Great. That's just great."

"Why are you so upset? What was I supposed to do, lie?"

"Well. Maybe. I don't know."

"I'm not going to hide. I can't pretend for the next six months I'm not pregnant, when I'm blowing up like a giant balloon."

"Forget it, forget it. Okay? But you have to tell me, what do they think?"

"Why does that matter? You just met them."

I slap my forehead out of frustration. "They're your parents!"

"That's right. They're *my* parents. And the baby is in *my* body. Why are you so hysterical?"

"I don't want them to hate me."

"Why would they hate you? You're the father of their first grandchild. Is that so bad? Just mellow out."

"Mellow out, she says. Okay, I'm mellow." I pound my chest with my fist. "See, I'm mellow. Shit, what am I going to do?"

"Marry me."

I shake my head, just the slightest back-and-forth, a leaf trembling after a breeze has passed. Mine is a knee-jerk reaction: she talks marriage, I tell her no. But this time my head feels as empty as a bobble-head doll's; missing is the grease fire of fear and indignation that at these moments I normally substitute for brains. No vinegar boiling in my chest, no temper bleaching my vision. I close my eyes and savor the weight of my skull pulling taut my throat. One picture trips under my lids: my initial glimpse of the fabulous house, its dazzling glass and steel, high atop a hill.

From behind, her hands clasp me, like forceps, at each temple. "Stop shaking your head," she says. "How can I work on you if you keep moving around?" There's no mistaking the antiseptic smell of the fresh set of dental instruments she's unrolling—picks, probes, scalers, files—which clatter in that metallic, threatening dentist's-office way. My heart beats wildly; my head fills with the stench of ground enamel. She sharpens her tools against an emery board.

She asks me to open my mouth. I pry back my lids and stare at the needle-sharp tip of the probe poised in her hand. "I'm not going to hurt you. Haven't you been to a dentist lately?"

"Not one without a degree," I say. "Or who's pregnant."

"Do you think you can say that a little more disdainfully?"

"Sorry."

"You owe me now. Let me work on you."

"What do they want?"

"Who?"

"Your parents. Where're they at? Especially your father, he fried me on his new fence before."

"I warned you. Charming, isn't he?"

But my first response is defensive—I remember Morton Sass affectionately slapping my shoulder, then huddling close like a TV father with serious things to say. "He's okay. I mean, you told him you're pregnant, and he knows I'm the father, but he didn't try to kill me."

"You just told me he tried to electrocute you!"

"It was an accident. I touched the wire—" Of course, he could've stopped my hand. "It's not like he threw me against the fence."

"Morty wouldn't do *that*, Sterling. But he didn't warn you that the electricity was on, either." Bliss steps from behind me, and stares into my eyes. "Don't you see, he was testing his new toy. You're the unsuspecting deer, get it?" She shrugs, rolling palms to ceiling: I told you he's a creep!

She pats my cheek and disappears behind me. I hear her dental tools clink against one another. She gently tips my head back until it nestles against her soft body, between her breasts. "Why worry about him, when he's obviously not worried about you? He's out for himself."

"Who isn't?" I say, looking up at her. "You're going to tell me you're not out for yourself?"

She clenches her lips, as if restraining her tongue. She bats her eyes, fighting back the tears that form and hang there. I have no doubt she knows my mind's full of her insistence on having the baby.

"I never said I wasn't," she says. Then the tone of her voice changes. It is the good Bliss, the hand holder, the rescuer of teeth. "Look, Sterling, I know you don't love me. It shows in everything you do. Or don't do."

"That's not true—" I begin, in my cook mode, the nurturer, the pleasure giver. But before I can finish my denials, she tips my head back again. "Don't trouble yourself. It's okay. I'm not stupid." She leans over me, her face eclipsing the desk lamp's light. I don't know why, but I think she's going to kiss me: The fight's over. Pretend the discussion never happened. I close my eyes, the soft ends of her hair tickling my cheeks.

She taps my chin. Tender love tap. Automatically, my jaw drops, I tilt my face to her, like a hungry hatchling, expectant, all mouth and hope.

She touches a nerve. My eyes mist; I force them open: one of her scalers, a long and dangerous piece of metal, extends from her fist to my gum line. I raise my hand: *Stop!* I stare up at her topsy-turvy face. Just admit it, Bliss, say: *Oh baby, it's all on me. I'm the one who's out for herself. Keeping the baby, insisting on our marriage.*

"I know, I know. I know you don't love me," she goes on. "Whether you like it or not, whether I like it or not, I'm carrying your baby. Our baby! Isn't that crazy?"

She starts to laugh, but it's forced. And soon she's crying and laughing, or laughing and crying (I'm not sure which engenders the other). Then I see her stampeding into the hospital in her lab coat, comforting my mother, loving my father, saving me endless self-doubt, indecision, self-loathing. I think of Genius that night before I took him in for his tests, watching the old guy shoot up, scared and resigned, and how I couldn't hug him, couldn't even pat his hairless forearm and say, It's going to be okay, you're fine, you're strong, you've survived a son like me. And I think of what he wants, because despite my deception he must know the end is nearing: he's yearning not for a Michelin three-star meal or a freezer full of beef, but to see me established in a family, even as the only one I've known dissolves.

Bliss says, "You don't love me, but that's okay." Her voice soft, pulling like undertow. "But he is your son, and while you might never love me, Sterling, any better than what you've shown so far, at least love your son."

My eyes are moist but burn. Fire on water. "A son, really?"

"I'm positive he's a he," she says, hugging me from behind. I lean into the chair. I can't see her and she can't see me, and this is fine, this seems appropriate for us. She kisses my cheek but I can't kiss her back, and this too is fine. "A baby Sterling!" she says. "We'll name him after your father!"

For the last five minutes my life has felt as if it had been shot numb with novocaine, the drug's effect getting stronger each passing second. More kisses. My body is wound tight, every muscle from toe to brow rigid, the overlying skin as taut as glass, so the kisses will just slough off me, long before they have a chance to sink and tickle nerves and blood, as they're supposed to.

"We should get married, Silvy. If love's too hard for you, then for his sake."

I HEAR FOOTSTEPS. We watch the door, as someone knocks. It's Randi. "Hey, lovebirds," she says sarcastically. "It's turkey time!"

WHAT ARE YOU thankful for, Bliss?"
She looks across the table at her grandmother Tessie. Her eyes hop from person to person, until they stop on me. "Well, I'd have to say Silvy!"

Tessie stares me down. The lenses of her giant Jackie O glasses squint; it's like we're at Cape Canaveral and she's expecting me to blast off. "Mort," she says, turning to her son, "why this?"

"Oh, Grandma!" Bliss says. Clutching my arm and leaning her cheek against my shoulder, she nearly tumbles out of her chair.

"I'll tell you what I'm really thankful for," she begins. "I'm thankful I don't have to take Gross Anatomy again. That's where we dissected a human cadaver last year."

"In dental school?" her sister asks.

"A dentist is an M.D. And it was disgusting. I had a defective corpse. It seems at the morgue my guy was left lying facedown. You know what happens when that happens?"

"Tell us, Blissy," Tessie says.

"Bodily fluids—blood, lymph, urine—pool in the organs, and they engorge. Given the chance, they'll explode. That's why sleeping on your stomach isn't the best thing for you."

Tessie says, "Isn't she clever. Mort, your daughter. Such things she knows!"

"When I was in cooking school—" I try to break in, let everyone know I'm there.

"Just a second." Bliss cuts me off.

"She's not done yet," Tessie says, too loud for the table, as if she had just caught my hand in her purse.

Bliss continues with her story. "My body had a bullet hole right here." She taps her brow. Then reaches over and claps her hands around my face: "I could pick up his head and see clear through to the other side."

"You can look right into a guy's head," her father says. "A regular mind-reader, you are."

"I said she was clever. Even when she was little, Mort. I saw."

"What did you want to say, Silvy?" Bliss kisses my forehead, on the spot where the bullet hole presumably would be.

"It's not important."

"Please? I'm sure we'd all love to hear what you had to say."

I stare into her bright, expectant face. I relent: "In cooking school," I offer, addressing the old woman directly, thinking that's the respectful thing to do, "we had to butcher a lamb and a cow. That's how we learned about the different cuts of meat, your chops from your saddle, porterhouse from your brisket, and separated the edible offal from the nonedible—"

"Mort," Tessie says loudly, her face collapsing around her prunish mouth, "why does he have to do that? How are we going to eat Thanksgiving after that? Thank God Grandpa's not here to hear this."

"Look!" says Randi, pushing back from the table, pointing at me.

"Son of a bitch," Morton Sass spits. "How'd he get in here?" He springs from his seat, hands balled into fists.

I grip the edge of the table, as I did at home when Genius was in a terrible fury.

I turn in my chair. Framed in the sheet of glass is the same magnificent deer, its antlers spanning the window. He stands inches from the pane, his ears cocked and wary, eyes bright, tender, gleaming like oil in a cast-iron pan. At the table no one moves. We recognize we are in the presence of a force we are not going to understand. As he absorbs our abrasive stares he stares back at us: his dark eternal gaze, bulging with longing, eats right through me, and I feel undressed, dissected, unsexed.

I know then, in my most honest heart, that I don't belong here, absorbing their heat, eating their food, getting high on their good fortune. I've earned none of this. New Canaan is mine because of their charity. Bliss is my pipeline to this bounty, and I don't even love her. Upstairs she accused and accused, and I didn't even contradict her once. But wait! Isn't this love I feel? I find it in a crease inside me like a utility bill I've lost, sandwiched between other papers, and neglected to pay. My unworthiness of this bounty explains my vague love. What in my history allows for such presumption? It's my back-of-the-laundry soul clanging inside her beautiful house; it's my bigoted immigrant parents who'll remain, until their death days, bottom-feeders, washing and ironing for others, while her bigoted immigrant grandparents ran a tailor shop into a chain of department stores.

The deer shifts its position slightly, showing more of its bountiful flanks; the reflection of my face is superimposed on the deer's body.

"Look at the son of a bitch standing on my property," Morton Sass says, each successive word burning with more anger. Finally he jumps out of his chair, on fire himself: "My five-thousand-dollar fence!"

The deer bumps his big wet nose against the glass, antlers scratching against the pane. His eyes jump, hardening in astonishment, and take in each face at the table, before they lock directly with mine. He rocks back on his haunches, rising tall as a tree, showing off his smoky belly, his startling prick; his hooves like large black plums clack the glass. The window wobbles. The noise startles him. He turns and bounds off, carrying my heart away like a tick, flourishing his erect tail and salt-white ass.

Chapter 8

YOU ARE in the men's room. When you're finished here, you and your bride will cut the cake. By the laws of the State of Connecticut you are now officially a good son! Look at the immediate fruits of your newly arrived-at station in life: Your father's health, which has steadily improved since you announced your brief engagement, is now a nonissue; on the receiving line and here at the reception he's a transformed being, pumping hands, laughing out loud, puffing on cigars. And should his health decline, he'll have peace of mind knowing his parental duty's done. Just like that, you're married. In a few head-turning months, a grandchild. Maybe even a son. Heavens rejoice your kindness and sacrifice!

But now, finally, a minute alone. You can't believe your good fortune. This reception must cost a ton. And all done in your honor. How far you have come! When people tell you "Congratulations!" they have no idea how truly deserving you are. As a kid you would've killed to be in a place like this. You would've proudly taken this rest room as your home, claimed any one of these spacious stalls as your own, and pillowed your head on the twin rolls of toilet tissue. Savor the moment. Check out the marble wall in front of you, the solid brass fixtures, the urinal wiped to antibacterial high gloss. Dig the Mozart, the pine-forest air freshener, the attendant who'll stand all night by the sinks and bottles of cologne, while men shit and pee. For you.

The door opens. Your hope of getting out of there without having to meet another of her uncles crumbles. Curse yourself for wasting so much time in self-congratulatory reverie: you're still unzipped and your champagne-sodden bladder unrelieved.

"Where else would I find the man but in the men's room!" You want to die. You want to hop into the sparkling white urinal, kick aside the deodorizer disk, and flush your tuxedoed ass into Long Island Sound. Your father-in-law of a few hours parks his sizable self in the urinal next door, so close your elbows bump. His body radiates moist heat. He says he's been looking for you. Wonder: How can he miss you in this crowd, the groom, the lone Chinese guy of marrying age? You fuss with your recalcitrant fly because that will signal you want privacy, and he should do his business as you do yours. But when you finally succeed with the zipper, nothing comes. No vivid, mind-numbing, near-orgasmic gush. Stage fright. He tells you he wants to talk, as he unhooks, unbuttons, unzips, spreads his pants, his shirttails and boxer shorts blooming forth. He fishes for his prick through the slit in his shorts, and it seems to leap forward to meet his hand. While you nestle your body as tight as a cork in a bottle within the urinal's porcelain flanks, afraid the scantiest fleck of light might expose some dread secret of yours to this man, Morton Sass stands an unsettling distance from his target, hands on hips, waiting for his friend to finish its business.

Your prick starts to get the idea. The power of suggestion, the raucous noise of liquid landing, Morton Sass pissing like a garden hose, like a waterfall, tickles your own bladder into action. A trickle, then a knee-shaking stream. "Ahhh!" he says. "There's only one thing better in life." You realize then that he wants you to look at him down there: this is why he insists on talking at you, makes no attempt to cover up, to nod in modesty's direction. You don't look but can easily imagine that such prodigious output must have at its source a stupendously sized sex, form following function, and that's what he wants you to take account of. That, and his stupendously sized house on thirty prime acres, his Cadillacs, his gardeners and cleaning ladies, his winter getaway in Florida, his checkbook that will swallow this party in a single gulp, his fertile daughter who sprang from his loins. He has charitably taken you into the fold, into his personal bounty, his piss stream arching like a rainbow, landing in a splash of gold. Bright hopes, uncompromising futures.

Your father-in-law finally runs dry. He shakes himself, stuffs himself into his trousers. Now, once he's zipped, put back together again, you should take his hand, be it sticky or wet, let him know how much you appreciate all he's done, what he stands for, let him know that nothing can come between you, not ceremony, civility, or germs.

Morton Sass complains to the marble wall inches from his nose: The champagne isn't chilled enough; the band, a jazz quintet his wife hired—a move he claims has turned his wedding reception into a Great Society program—is overpaid and lazy; your new mother-in-law is drunk and flirting with the help.

You nod. What are you going to say to your benefactor?

You move in tandem to the sinks. With a flourish the attendant adjusts the hot and cold faucets for you. You're grooving on the soap, its luxurious lather. You take peeks at your father-in-law's reflection in the gilt-framed mirror. At once you are beaten down by the worry that you'll soon be found out: You've pulled one over on him, and it's just a matter of time before he'll come to his senses and show you the door. You wonder if he knows what a shit you've been to his daughter. And that there's nothing storybook, inevitable, fated about your entanglement with Bliss.

The attendant fluffs towels for both of you. "How do you plan to keep my Bliss happy?" The question comes so unexpectedly you are dazed, unsure of the ground on which you stand. What kills you is how reasonable his question is. You trespass into this good man's life and steal his daughter. He throws this party in your honor. Of course you owe him an answer.

He gives you permission to call him Dad, and you want to weep. As usual your emotions are too complicated to sort out: while you're flattered by the invitation, thrilled at the prospect of Morton Sass's being a father to you, you are also suspicious and saddened because this substantial man, possessor of the equine member stabled in his trousers, has run out of luck. You, of course, aren't the reason for the bad luck, just a succinct sign of its arrival.

You are heading for the exit, following six respectful paces behind Morton Sass, when he stops and reaches for your hands. These Americans love to touch. How many times today have you touched his large hands, meaty, with freckles and knuckle hair like wires in a transistor radio? Good morning. Good luck. Congratulations. And now, Excellent peeing!

"You are one lucky man," he says, as if reading your palms. "Since you're what my daughter's picked, out of the whole wide world of possibilities, I have no choice but to arrange for something good to come your way."

Weird world! Weird, weird world! You glance skyward and think of your father: What a mixed blessing it is that he is dying, thereby making all this necessary. Up from the ashes new life blooms. Imagine, springing from Genius and landing in this man's hands. Twist of fate? You've wrung the hell out of fate. Think on it: Morton Sass says it's okay if you call him Dad, even though his mother hates your guts.

"Bliss says you've got good hands," he says, and wants to have a look. There's reason for all this scrutiny. He anoints your hands "telegenic," and tells you you're going to star in your own cooking show on cable TV. "Cable's the next big thing," he assures you. As he sees it, food programming lacks a real male presence; the greatest chefs in the world are men, but on TV "all you get is Julia Child and that fruity Galloping Gourmet."

That simple gold band on your left hand binds you to this man. You accept the offer. You don't need to hear the details. You extend your hand, you want to shake on the deal.

The men's room door opens and Teddy walks in. Teddy is one of your wife's exes; he was the guy who immediately preceded you, and if the stars were aligned differently Teddy might now be standing in your place, holding hands with Morton Sass. In actuality, though, that is highly improbable. After a lifetime of denial and two years with Bliss, Teddy—and this is from the horse's mouth—realized he prefers men. "Oops! Excuse me," he says, backing away from you and your father-in-law, his hands raised in front of his chest. "I didn't mean to disturb you two. I mean, this *is* the boy's room."

"Hey, come back. It's okay," you say, glad for the interruption.

Teddy halts his retreat and says, with feigned hurt in his voice, "Silvy, you promised you'd call *me* first, if you ever came to your senses." He disappears into a stall. "Nobody's listening, okay?"

Your father-in-law whispers in your ear: "Selma says Bliss says she made that one go fruity. Do you think she can do that?"

Apparently he does. And this sets off a burglar alarm in your head: He loves you, and already fears he might lose you one day. Think Thanksgiving Day, you and this man at the threshold of his fabulous house; he tells you his daughter loves you only because she wants to get at him. Now his concern is that she'll try to wound him by turning you, a perfectly good heterosexual, gay.

Finally you say, "Bliss is capable of making a lot of things happen, but I don't think we can give her credit for Teddy."

Teddy flushes. Waves, washes, tips, waves, leaves.

Morton Sass sighs and shakes his enormous head. To you he opens his heart about his exiled son, Lester. You can't believe this; he has been your American father for just a few hours and he's already seeking solace in you, confiding in you, saying more to you than your real father has in a lifetime. Lester is not here, because Morton Sass wouldn't allow him to come. (You know this, and Bliss is furious with her father but won't

show it. Marrying you, you see, is revenge enough.) He says that in high
school Lester had his name legally changed. From Sass to Sinclair. "A
slap in the face," he says, and you feel the slap too. It is not just anger in
his voice but trembly pain: "Can he get a more goyishe-sounding name?
Why stop at changing his name? Why not change into a dress? Go all
the way, baby. Change so I don't even recognize you one bit. Then I
don't feel so bad."

You feel awful. Poor Morton Sass. His disappointment with his son.
You realize that your initials are Lester's, only inverted: S.L. and L.S.
You're mirror images. In your father-in-law's eyes you're an improve-
ment on his other son.

The men's room door flies open, and Fuchs calls, "Sterling, you in
there?" He can't see you because Morton Sass completely shields you,
a total eclipse.

"Fuchs! Fuchs!" you say, grateful for the intrusion.

"Sterling. What're you doing? It's too late to hide—you're married
already. Your bride's got everybody looking for you."

You do the introductions. It's strange to see Fuchs in a suit. You want
to tie a bloody apron around his waist. "It's cake time," he says.

Fuchs goes to the door and holds it open, waiting for you. Morton
Sass says, "Tell his wife he's coming."

After Fuchs leaves, Morton Sass tells the attendant to go on break.

Once again you're standing face to face, perhaps two feet apart.
"Now, Sterling, I want you to show me what you got."

He wants to see your sex. Wants to see if you measure up. He's going
to whip out his prodigious horse and you your wee birdie. Assert his
dominant position in the family. More than ever, you wish your real
father had passed on some of his size. Then you think that perhaps the
reason for the inspection is not about inches or girth but whether you've
been circumcised. You're not one of them, but at least you can look like
one of them.

"Give me your best shot," your father-in-law says, holding his
hands open and high at his lapels. "Selma's boy won't do it. Come on."

You're not sure you're willing to do this. You were right the first time, his purpose isn't biblical but urological. "Show me what you got." He jiggles his hand. That's what this is, a test of your worthiness, your virility, and it's going to take quite a shot, slightly uphill, across a span no sperm under normal reproductive conditions would ever have to cover.

You beg out. Lose nerve. Can't get it up. No balls. "The cake," you say. "Time to cut the cake."

"You serious? That whole cake-cutting business is girlie stuff. Lester would be all over that damn cake."

You don't want to get lumped in with that crowd. He puts his hands up to his lapels again, like a bad guy surrendering in a cop movie. "Come on, show me your knockout punch."

You're so relieved you don't have to ejaculate into his hand that you want to kiss him.

Without hesitation you launch your best punch. Your fist slams into his meaty paw with an ear-splitting clap. Such violence nesting inside you, now rushing out through your arm like electricity from Morton Sass's fence.

There's no doubt about what you're feeling: You enjoy hitting him.

On demand, you let fly with your left. The blow lands low on the heel of the man's hand. *"Ow!"* you say.

"It's your wedding band against your bone."

He wants you to throw more punches, but this time with the ring off.

You hesitate and wonder if you should. What are you without the ring, the amulet that makes you visible to Morton Sass and star of your own TV show? The ring protects your stake in this good family; it nudges the brother further into oblivion, and you securely into his place as son.

The wedding band is hot. All that blood underneath, rushing to soothe the trauma, heats the gold. When you try to take it off, the ring resists, and you sense that some force in the universe is inhibiting its removal, the breaking of its spell, the onset of new dangers. Once the ring comes off, Morton Sass shows you how to jab. You pepper his hand with jabs. You savor each impact. You feel you had wanted to hit him your entire life. When you're through, your hand is on fire. He slaps you on the back. You have passed the test. When you go to put on the ring, it slips through your fingers and strikes the marble floor *ching!* Before you can, Morton Sass kneels and retrieves the ring. Still kneeling, he hands it to you on his pudgy palm, as the rabbi had presented you the bride's band hours ago.

Those jabs you threw have slightly swollen your hand. The ring won't fit. Morton Sass comes with a squirt of bubble-gum-pink soap on his palm. He smooths it on your finger like a lubricant before sex, an ointment on a newborn's bottom, a ritual oil applied at the time of death.

With his hand supporting yours, Morton Sass slides the wedding ring on your finger.

THE SASSES PULLED the wedding together in short order. A date was set, and within the span of a week, arrangements were made for the hall, music, flowers, invitations, photographer. Selma Sass must've been planning for the eventuality. She seemed to have all the vendors on standby, waiting for her call.

WE'RE ON THE DANCE FLOOR. "I Can't Help Falling in Love with You," the Elvis song. Bliss's idea. I had argued for "You've Lost That Lovin' Feeling." It's a great song, and I reasoned since Selma Sass had hired a jazz quintet, and the musicians were black, and the Righteous Brothers who originally recorded the song tried to sound black, it was like a perfect match. But Bliss was hung up about the lyrics, which made no sense because the quintet didn't have a vocalist. This is our first dance, the whole world watching, all of human history having led us here.

Halfway through the song Morton and Selma Sass hit the dance floor. Instantaneously I fear some know-nothing will urge Genius and Zsa Zsa to dance, and in the spirit of the occasion they'll drag their wooden bodies to the middle of the floor and shake their booties. Can there be an uglier sight under a disco ball than the dumb feet that gave birth to my klutzy feet?

As expected, Morton Sass is a champion dancer, a regular middle-aged Jewish Travolta, and Selma Sass, her big-boned self jacked up on trim high heels, is smooth and slick on her feet. They impress with their interlocking fingers, as natural as can be, their bodies casually making contact, moving breezily across the floor. Physical familiarity I've never seen between my parents.

From Elvis the quintet segues to "The Girl from Ipanema." Lisa Lee, in a purple halter dress, hair piled high on her head, is singing with the band. "I didn't know she had such a good voice," I say. Bliss and I struggle with our dancing, terribly out of synch but getting by, like lovers out of love.

Then it happens. My sister Lucy pushes Genius and Zsa Zsa onto the dance floor. Fortunately they don't venture very far from the edge, and stay confined to a three-by-three-foot corner. They move side to side, stiff as rocking chairs, their movements no more elaborate than the ticks of a watch. How did they manage to rub together enough times to produce my sisters and me? Zsa Zsa is so pretty, dressed up, big corsage pinned on her chest like a wreath. ("They must've spent a lot of money," she said, when I pinned it on her.) They hardly move, and touch demurely, hand to hip, hand to shoulder, their contact as functional as grabbing a doorknob.

"They look like they're having fun," Bliss says.

"I guess so."

"They look happy. Your dad looks good."

I nod. She is right. There's nothing wrong with the picture. But I can't trust that others will see what Bliss sees. I fear exposure, my parents' inarticulate feet giving me away.

The Sasses glide to the edge of the dance floor, dangerously close to my parents. Morton Sass steps away from Selma Sass. He wants to swap partners. But Zsa Zsa refuses, shaking her head so hard her curls loosen and an earring flies off. The threat is averted. Morton Sass gallantly goes after the earring. Zsa Zsa stutters after him. But then Genius flings open his arms to Selma Sass, as if he's been waiting for this chance, waiting for Zsa Zsa to turn her back. Selma Sass, the bigger of the two, envelops him. She's going to discover the hole the surgeon cut in Genius, put her hand right through it, and then everyone will see how little there really is inside.

Wedding Pictures

He is a slightly built man, and the tuxedo suits his body, broadening his shoulders, accenting his waist. He looks legitimate. As he dances with Selma Sass he appears to have grown. This even though his chin barely clears her shoulder—she is big in the magnificent way of trees, and extra tall in her special-occasion high-heel shoes. But for those three minutes he appears younger and taller and more substantial. His pant legs flutter. His hair shines. For those long three minutes, as slow as an eclipse, I think I'm watching a movie. It seems impossible this is my father, with his two left feet and bum tongue, dancing, not Fred Astaire, not Morton Sass, but respectably. And Selma Sass, a woman an ocean and a continent and an alphabet removed from Genius's own wife, with jewels and perfume and bosom that populate daydreams, smiles and laughs easily at the things he says. My father is suddenly handsome, Hollywood sexy in the gangster mode, the tux, the hair, the cigarette in his hand that puts gentle pressure to the small of the lady's back, controlling her every move.

———

I sit next to Zsa Zsa. I ask if she knows how to dance. She stares at her husband moving like the Americans, his feet flashing, on fire. Her eyes are riveted to his expert hand squirreled against the large white woman's back. They turn: we catch eyefuls of the woman's tight buttons, my father's handsome false teeth. The corsage pinned to my mother's chest looks tired. Usually a sturdy woman, Zsa Zsa now seems frail, all the water drained from her body. The drops of perspiration rolling from her 7-Up, off her hands, are tears. Seeing her this way, I'm so glad I didn't tell her Genius's prognosis. For her sake I want the song to end. But I also want the music to go on indefinitely, so I can watch this new and improved father, a sight more wondrous than a dancing bear.

———

A man with a goatee comes to the table. He winks as he takes my mother's hand. "Congratulations, madam," he says. "Your son's done himself a big favor." He's talking about my establishing a beachhead in the Sass family. "Tell her," he commands, nodding in her direction. "Tell her what I just said. Tell her you're the lucky son of a bitch you know you are." He leaves. I'm grateful my mother suspects nothing. That man is just another one of them.

———

Genius never asks Zsa Zsa to dance. An hour after I question her about her dancing abilities she's holding the same glass of 7-Up. "Of course I can dance," she says unexpectedly.

I wrestle the glass from her and try to pull her onto the dance floor. But she fights me off. "Are you crazy?"

———

"She doesn't know he's sick."

"How can she not know that?"

"What I mean is she doesn't realize how sick."

"You should tell her."

"I will. Right after I tell Genius."

"Sterling, this is incredible. How can they still not know? They're people, after all."

———

"Sterling," Bliss says, "*I'm* leading. And don't you forget it."

———

"Hold me tighter."
"Okay?"
"Tighter!"
Pulling her by the small of her back, I crush her against me.
"Did you feel that kick?"

———

Genius keeps bugging the musicians, five older black guys in tuxedos on their break. Cigarette in the corner of his mouth, face flushed with Hennessy, he runs drinks from the bar to the quintet. He says things and they break up in laughter. I've never seen him so animated. Must be the cognac. Maybe it's seeing him in a tuxedo.

———

I overhear a conversation Zsa Zsa is having with one of her Chinatown friends. The subject is Lucy's date, a man she met on the plane from Texas.

"What are you saying?" my mother says. "Of course that's her husband."

"Is that so? I met her man at her wedding banquet. And that's not the same man."

Zsa Zsa's friend, of course, is correct. While the new guy, at least in his general outlines, bears a vague resemblance to Lucy's ex—tall, lanky, non-Chinese—a person with average to below-average eyesight should not confuse the two.

"It's the truth. Why would I lie to you? I know my son-in-law."

"The man I met had yellow hair. This one has brown."

"What do you expect? In America you have freedom of choice."

I imagine Zsa Zsa saying this of Bliss: "Of course she's a Chinese. She's just not from our village, she's from up north. Who can understand the way they talk? They almost aren't Chinese, but they are."

—

The photographer has an idea for a pose. He wants Bliss and me to part the gold-and-scarlet curtains just a crack, and let the slip of light silhouette us for a "very romantic shot." He orders us to tilt our heads slightly and to look at each other. Over her headpiece I see a wooded highway and the competing Shell and Texaco stations at the corner. I see hills in the distance covered with bare trees, and a solid gray sky above. I can almost smell the lung-freezing air, feel the breezes tousling the branches. A bird, then an airliner, enter my field of vision; I can feel the jet roar. I am gripped by the unshakable belief that Yuk is on board that flight. Days before the wedding, Genius told me she was planning to fly from Canada for the ceremony. Since then, I've imagined her in every plane I've seen in the sky.

—

Genius and Morton Sass stand together at the edge of the dance floor. Dad's head is bowed, nodding at whatever my father's saying. From Dad's expression I can't tell if he's deeply interested in the conversation or just struggling to understand Genius's English. Whom should I feel worse for? Dad, having to work so hard when the payoff's that small; Genius, so grossly overmatched, intimidated, lost in the other's shadow; or me, my fall from that good man's graces already beginning. I go to police the situation. If necessary, rescue Morton Sass.

"Sterling!" he says. "How's the man?"

"Hi, Dad." It's the first time I've called him that, though I've played with it in my head as many times as a teenager thinks about sex. But surprisingly, when I deliver the word into the world, it snags in my throat like a bone. Genius is the cause of my suffering: my giant slug of a tongue wilts under the hot killing glare of his presence. By the time I say, "Pop," to Genius, he is already stomping away, arms stiff at his sides, body tilted forward cartoonishly, as if led by the cigarette pinched in his lips. I shouldn't have said it in his presence. In hindsight I see how, to his ears, my "Dad" must've sounded premature.

Chapter 9

MY PARENTS ARE SHOCKED when they see Bliss. She has gained weight during our ten-day honeymoon at the Sasses' condominium in Fort Lauderdale. Stopping at the laundry for a two-night visit in order to "check up on your father" was her idea. The day after tomorrow we fly to Iowa for the start of her new semester, and then forty-eight hours later I'll return to Connecticut and the ladies. (We have agreed that she should finish her second year of dental school, and I need to continue my cooking career at the club). "Is she having a baby already?" Zsa Zsa asks, in giggly Chinese. "No, no, no!" I say, shaking my head. Bliss and I are seated at the kitchen table, while Genius is out front with a customer and Zsa Zsa is flitting among her stove, refrigerators, and sink. She steams her egg cake, boils water for instant coffee. After she sets the sugar bowl on the table she pats Bliss's cheeks and teases that the hollows there are gone. Bliss wants to know what Zsa Zsa's saying. I shrug, then tell her, "Nothing. She says you're getting fat. That's a compliment."

During the honeymoon I cooked for Bliss, three meals a day, and in return she ate everything—conch, skate, periwinkles, pompano, mussels, flying fish; she gnawed on the fins, sucked out the cheek meat, licked the shells clean. After each meal her plate was immaculate, every morsel, every drop of sauce swept or sopped up with a chunk of my homemade bread. In short, she ate prodigiously, an orgy of food, sexy ingestion. She was, as she said, "eating for two." For the sake of appearances, she had repressed her appetite until after we were married, at which time she said, "I couldn't care less what shows and who knows now." And before my eyes, she grew, more nose, cheeks, hands, hips, breasts, feet—every part of her thicker, broader, chunkier. By the end of the honeymoon, I was amazed by her body's elasticity and flattered by its outward expansion, the cells multiplying at an inconceivable rate, all in the name of nurturing and protecting the bits of my DNA in her womb.

Bliss is tanned and healthy-looking, her brown frizzy hair falling loose over the front of a teal-green sweater of mine that she's wearing. Zsa Zsa jokes about her darker complexion. About how "Americans" hate black people, but love to lie in the sun to make themselves look black. "Crazy," she says.

"She's not so dark."

"And you're crazy too, always copying Americans. We Chinese hate being in the sun."

"What's she saying?" asks Bliss.

"Trust me. It doesn't matter."

Bliss shrugs, then motions for me to cut her a slice of my mother's pastel-yellow throw pillow of an egg cake. When Bliss refuses a cup of Taster's Choice, Zsa Zsa wants to know what's wrong: "Americans always drink coffee!" I don't tell her Bliss isn't taking any caffeinated drinks nowadays because of the baby.

Genius joins us at the table; he's in his usual white shirt with sleeves rolled halfway up his forearms, gray slacks, brown leather belt, and olive-green quilted vest. Where's the man in the tuxedo, my father the dancing bear? After Bliss cuts him a wedge of the spongy egg cake, I can't resist asking in English, "Danced lately?"

He stops chewing, and his black eyeglass frames slide to the tip of his nose. "Why are you always fooling around?" he says in Chinese. "What are you going to do about Yuk and your wife?"

I glance at Bliss—does she suspect he's talking about her? Luckily, she's busy with the cake. "Why are you talking about Yuk?" I ask him. And with a slight tilt of my head in Bliss's direction, I say, "I married *her*," and I'm tempted to add, "for your sake." He tells me that Yuk is back from Canada, that at this very second she is under our feet, in the basement napping. She returned a couple of days after the wedding, and is in the process of applying for a job as an airline stewardess—a long-standing ambition of hers—with Pan American, which is staffing a new route to mainland China. Her plan is to first win the job, then get the green card. Here I feel a brilliant stab of guilt: I was her most direct route to a permanent resident alien status.

Bliss asks what he's talking about, but she does so casually, to be polite, to show Genius she's interested—her heart's really on the egg cake. I hold a finger up to her, Wait, I'm trying to figure this out myself. Is Genius trying to make me feel guilty about Yuk, or is he letting me know I'm off the hook, she's landed on her feet? But I tell Bliss: "My cousin's here. She's visiting from Hong Kong by way of Canada."

"Oh, that's great! Where is she? I didn't know you had cousins! You never mentioned any of them before."

What's the harm? In high school she was my "cousin." Bliss doesn't need to hear the truth now. Why rock the boat? She doesn't need to know that she's sharing a laundry with the woman my parents would've preferred to be their daughter-in-law. For better or for worse, we're married. She's carrying a grandchild for Genius and Zsa Zsa. I have no interest in reawakening the old "You don't love me" demons.

Out of nowhere Zsa Zsa says with a knowing smile, "There's the two of you now. The basement is perfect for a married couple. That was our plan all along. Now that our plans change, Yuk-girl can sleep in your sisters' room again." Then she addresses Bliss directly in Chinese. "You'd like the extra space and the privacy, wouldn't you?"

I translate as well as I can.

"No, no, no, no!" says Bliss, grabbing Zsa Zsa by the wrist. "We're all family now! She shouldn't have to move her bed. She was there first."

"Bliss, you don't know what you're saying."

She looks my way; her brows thicken, lips curl.

"I meant, she doesn't know what you're saying."

"Then tell her," Bliss says, with an elaborate swing of her hand. "She's going to think I have no manners. I don't want her to think I expect special treatment like I'm some kind of JAP. Just tell her I'm not for it, even though you know she's going to do what she's going to do because"—she leans closer and whispers—"I'm pregnant and she knows firsthand what that's all about." Bliss unglues her lips from my cheek. "Why am I whispering?"

"What now?"

"I just realized I don't know if they know that I'm you-know-what. What've you told them?"

I glare at her as if she had just accused me of murder, and it were true. "Keep your voice down. I don't know what they know."

"You haven't told them yet?"

"You don't understand. I was thinking I'd just spring it on them one day."

"Which day is that?"

"How about when we have a kid to show them?"

She squints, flattens her lips, and pushes away from me. In an inappropriately loud voice she says, "I need a glass of milk."

Genius leaps from his chair and goes to the refrigerators, checking each one. I know there's no chance of his finding a single drop. Zsa Zsa says, "What are you doing?"

Right then, the front door's brass bell sounds, and Genius goes to help the customer. "The milk's already on the table," Zsa Zsa says, pointing at the jar of Coffee-mate. "See, I told you," she says at me. "Americans have to have coffee." She stands to boil her water.

"No, no, no, no!" I wave Zsa Zsa back into her seat. "She's wants milk to drink."

Zsa Zsa looks at Bliss, then at the jar of Coffee-mate. She shakes her head. "Crazy American," she says, amused by this curious creature, her daughter-in-law. "I don't know how they drink the powder. You're the *lo-fahn* cook, you make your wife a cup of milk."

I GO TO FOOD FAIR for a quart of milk, and return from a wet driving snow onto this scene: Yuk, in bell-bottom jeans and beaded slippers, her hair in braids, peeking over Zsa Zsa's shoulder, while Zsa Zsa, pinching Bliss's sweater off her body, pats her daughter-in-law's tummy. "Mr. Sterling, you are father so fast!" says Yuk, with a mischievous smile. Zsa Zsa scolds, showing her teeth, "Wah, you didn't say a thing!"

"What did you tell them?" I ask Bliss.

"After your father introduced me to your lovely *cousin,*" Bliss answers. "I thought it was appropriate to introduce her to the truth."

TWENTY MINUTES LATER Genius returns from his errand to the supermarket. He has bought for Bliss pig tails and chicken. He's planning to cook them with medicinal herbs. According to Yuk, the former will strengthen the baby's back, the latter will fortify Bliss's general constitution. To save him the effort, I say, "She's not going to eat that Chinese stuff!"

But Bliss does, pleasing Zsa Zsa and Genius to no end. She expertly nibbles the stringy meat off the pig tails and sips the husky chicken brew from a porcelain spoon. We are home from dinner at Sizzler (typical mass-cooked cuisine, with emphasis on low-grade beef and approximate flavors), and Zsa Zsa has reheated the concoctions she cooked for Bliss and the future Lung. I'm flipping through an old newspaper, keeping Bliss company, while my parents are working and Yuk is preparing her basement room for us. Time and again, one of the three drifts through the kitchen, Genius and Zsa Zsa coming to admire how obedient and dutiful their daughter-in-law is, Yuk carrying her belongings from the basement to my sisters' room. Whenever Yuk walks by, she either minds her own business and smiles in an unfocused manner, or quickly offers Bliss encouragement, "Good! Eat a lot." In return Bliss stretches wide her eyes, on the lookout for danger, her gaze pouncing on Yuk, riding her until she's out of sight. Then she turns it on me until she bends mine from her like a Uri Geller spoon. I don't know why, but Bliss doesn't care for Yuk. I've noticed how she has to force a "Yes" or a "Thank you" from her body in response to Yuk's small acts of kindness.

Later, lying in bed, I ask what's eating her. We're married; we're having a kid; for all she knows, Yuk *is* my cousin. But she says nothing, though the sinews in her neck are popping with barely contained rage and her bottom lip is quivering. She's as tight as she was the Lisa Lee night. I wonder if I've given myself away. Betrayed my own lie. Have I looked at Yuk in uncousinlike ways? Did I hover too close to her at dinner? Do I mention her name, enumerate her virtues, when she isn't around? Does my mood change when I'm in her presence? Tonight, I hope, I won't talk in my sleep.

I slip into bed, and as I switch off the lamp the last thing I notice is the David's white flash. How strange it is to see Yuk again, especially from this end, married and a father-to-be. Wasn't that the reason for her coming here in the first place—to make a good son of me? But even though I've been welcomed into the mainstream bosom of the Sass family, and my parents for the time being are pleased with something I've done, and as a result Genius is in apparent good health (though his doctors scratch their heads and warn his health might go south at any moment), I feel the same agitation I felt when I first met Yuk, heart pumping in my throat, my brain emptying like air from a balloon.

I can't tell if Bliss is asleep or not. But I cuddle up to her, front to back, and as I had hoped, her body's oven heat, her ever-blooming size obliterates my earlier thoughts; and in this moment I feel I've caught up with her, no longer a straggler along the path she's chosen for herself, confident in her judgment of where we ought to go.

I am approaching sleep when she shifts, jerking her body free of mine, and this lost contact, a plug yanked from a socket, shocks me to wakefulness, a white light popping in my head, the brightness then coalescing into the shape of the David, the statue dissolving to Yuk. She slaps my heart, and I won't sleep tonight.

THE FOLLOWING DAY Genius accompanies Yuk to New York for a second round of interviews with Pan Am. When I suggest he drop her off at the station and have her ride the train in, he almost loses his mind: "Wah! I don't do family that way! She's new to this country, and since you did not marry her as we promised, we have to help her." Zsa Zsa and I work the laundry, and Bliss tags along with Yuk and Genius; she's going to meet her mother for lunch and a museum, then she'll catch a train back.

I pick her up at the train station later that afternoon. She is tired, cranky, and hungry. "Are they back?" she asks, before we've left the parking lot.

"Who?"

"Your father and your cousin."

"They returned hours ago."

"How'd your cousin do? She get the job?"

I'm uncomfortable with this line of questioning and change the subject. "How's your mother? Have a good time?"

"You haven't answered me yet. Did your cousin get the job?"

"She has a call-back tomorrow. Some kind of physical examination." I wait two beats, then add, "Genius wants me to take her."

"Why you?"

"He says he can't go two days in a row."

"She can't take a train? I'm pregnant and I took the train. What did you say?"

"I have to do it, I guess. Family obligation. It's a Chinese thing. She's family, and Genius's duty is to help her. For whatever reason, he claims he can't do it, so he wants me to step in. I'm doing the guy a favor. Trying to be a good son. Left to me, I agree, I'd just put her on the train."

"But instead you're going to put me on the plane by myself."

"Shit, that's tomorrow!"

"Like you didn't know, Sterling. Don't act so surprised. Remember, this morning, your mother making more pig-tail stuff for us to take to Iowa? You were watching her when we left."

"I'm sorry. I forgot." She doesn't believe me, but our departure date did slip my mind. It was a stupid plan anyway, flying all those miles, at a cost of several hundred dollars, only to turn around a couple of days later. "Bliss, I'm really, really sorry. I'll just tell Genius to take her."

She doesn't say anything. We drive in silence. I'm satisfied I got in the last word, but the spoils of my victory aren't obvious.

We are almost at the laundry when she says, "Sterling, I want you to quit that job at the club and move to Iowa. We're married and we should act that way."

"That's not possible."

"Why not? You can cook anywhere. Didn't they tell you that when you graduated?"

"The farmers won't understand me."

"You can cook for us."

"Who's us?"

"Us is me and your baby. I guess you *are* forgetful today."

O N OUR WAY to the city for Yuk's physical with Pan Am, I drop Bliss off at JFK. I leave Yuk with the car at curbside and accompany Bliss to the check-in. In her plaid muffler, bulky fisherman's sweater, brown wool overcoat, and boots, and with a piece of luggage in each hand (she won't let me help her, since I insist on helping "her") and a shoulder bag slung across her chest, she is a walking, human Everest.

At the departure gate I take her hand, but she doesn't squeeze back. I'm dazed she can behave so badly. So selfish! She'd have Genius negotiate those winter roads, have Yuk shipped back to Hong Kong.

When it's time for Bliss to board, I give a big hug. I want to feel myself melt into her as I did last night, but there's too much between us. I try to kiss her; she averts her lips. Naturally, I pull away. Then she cups the back of my head with her big hand, her fingers weaving in my hair. I'm dumb enough to think she's yielding, coming to her senses. She says, "She's not your cousin, she's no twig on the Lung family tree. Your father told me—his family obligation to me."

EARLIER THIS MORNING Yuk's all-consuming worry was with weight. She has to demonstrate she can lift a forty-five-pound box, and she herself must meet the weight minimum for stewardesses. At forty-six kilograms, she is about nine pounds shy of the mark. I went out and bought bacon, eggs, bread, butter, and cooked her breakfast. Genius had posited that the airline's weight and height restrictions were meant to screen out Chinese girls. Zsa Zsa added, "Who is that big? Only stinky American girls."

As I drive from the airport, Yuk now in the front passenger seat, I ask, "How's your bladder?"

"Pardon?"

I clear my throat, getting revved to reveal my delicate plan. "A pound is sixteen ounces. Sixteen ounces is a pint. You with me?"

"No problem."

"Okay. Two pints to a quart. A quart is thirty-two ounces. Four quarts in a gallon. That's a gallon. One gallon equals one hundred twenty-eight ounces, or eight pounds."

"Your recitation very enjoyable," she says. "But Mr. Sterling surely is not speaking in earnest."

At a red light I hurry to the trunk and retrieve a gallon jug of distilled water. I set the eight pounds on Yuk's lap. "You drink, I drive."

She saturates herself, taking long, lung-emptying drinks. I hear the water splash in her belly. I see how desperately she wants the job. I'm glad I never was in her place, a newcomer to a completely different country. Too often I have speculated how my life would've evolved had Genius and Zsa Zsa stayed in China. In those educational-TV documentaries, the Chinese peasants—that's what my parents are, after all, old peasant stock—seem so content with their modest lives, no one complaining about working sunrise to sunset for next to nothing, wearing shoes they'd sewn from rags, walking miles up sides of mountains to collect firewood.

"Go slow," I advise Yuk. "You want to fly to China, not swim there. You have plenty of time, just sip the water, you won't fill up as fast."

By the time we cross the Queensboro Bridge she's drained more than half of the first jug. "Don't stop now," I say.

"I already drink entire ocean, Mr. Sterling."

"Good." I point at the second jug. "Now drink another."

IN THE WAITING ROOM Yuk is beyond bursting. "When flood come, Mr. Sterling, you swim, save self. Don't worry about Yuk." Tears hang in her eyes. She grabs my hand and squeezes. I hate myself for doing so, but I want the gesture to mean more than I know it does, a stark show of affection, a sexual advance, even. But let's face it, she is simply trying to ease the tension caused by a gallon of water in her bladder, the dam about to break. She holds on and on and on, so not a drop, not an ounce, goes to waste. Her knees clap hard together. She can crack nuts.

IN CORPORATE AMERICA deception pays. Cheating is a sign of commitment. Yuk is hired. She will be in training for weeks. And if all goes as planned, she will work the first-class cabin on Pan Am's inaugural flight, Los Angeles to Shanghai. To the non-Chinese, she'll speak English; to the Chinese, either her native Cantonese or Mandarin. America to China, China to America, six miles high, in first class, proud of the dainty hot hand towels she dispenses, of the cognac she serves in precious little glasses, of how she cheats time, losing a day on the outbound leg, gaining two on the trip home. Her new home will be Los Angeles now, much to my parents' dismay. And so she will soar out of my life.

I FLY OUT TO IOWA for Valentine's Day. Once I arrive in Iowa City, I have the taxi driver take me to a florist, and I buy roses, not carnations.

She comes to the door of her apartment on Dubuque, and around her head is a halo. She wears her hair brushed back from her face, the two inches closest to her scalp a solid bar of silver.

"Are those roses for me, or your cousin?"

"Oh, come on, Bliss. I came all this way."

"Just joking."

What allegedly happened is this: After she returned to Iowa for the start of the semester, Bliss was so distraught I had chosen to accompany "your cousin," rather than her, "your wife," she drank "several" glasses of wine and fell into a deep, dreamless sleep. In the morning, after her shower, she noticed her hair was silver at the roots. A full inch of new growth overnight! She went to her doctor, and while he had never seen a woman's hair so transformed in such a short period of time, he assured her that with pregnancy came all manner of strangeness. What is strange, as she tells the story, is the humorous bounce in her voice, which leaves me with the impression she has detached herself from the incident, a thing of the past to have a laugh over. "Thanks to you," she says, "I look like a fucking skunk!" She speculates on the broader meaning of her "follicular outcroppings," the link between the sterling-silver color and, of course, me. She says the silver hair pushing out of her skull symbolizes one of two radically different phenomena: Either I am leaving her, or she is ridding herself of me.

"Can't you just dye it?"

"Why, and cover it up, like nothing happened?"

"Nothing happened except what happened to your hair. You can't pin that on me. I wasn't even here."

"That's my point exactly!"

AT THE BEGINNING of May, Bliss is so uncomfortable with her and the baby's stupendous size that she decides not to finish the semester, not to take final exams. She comes home to Connecticut huge, a grand, glorious sight, shining good health, the creature inside kicking up little ripples across the front of her sundress. But what commands my longest attention is her hair, now cut short, the ends skimming her jawline, a shimmering saintly ring that caresses her face, a crown of silver radiance. I love her new look, the Giottoesque halo, and its dramatic contrast to her darker earthy brows.

When we visit my parents for an overnight they are shocked by the change in her appearance. "Wah," Zsa Zsa says, "she looks more like a grandmother!"

"I like her new hair."

"What do you know? Crazy *juk-sing*, always fooling around. You're going to be a father soon."

"Why are you yelling at me? What's wrong with my hair?"

"Not your hair, your brain. Why did you make her dye her hair that way? She looks like an old sow."

Bliss asks me what the matter is. "Nothing," I tell her. "It's under control." To my mother I say, "She woke up one morning and her hair had changed color while she was sleeping."

"That's crazy talk. How's that possible?"

What am I going tell Bliss? She is glowingly ripe, just weeks shy of delivery, but they can't get past her hair; and now, suddenly, I can't either. It is so there, out in the open, no hat, no babushka covering up the billboard that screams, *Look what your son's done to me!*

WE MEET for the first time as parents. Her silver locks shoot out from her scalp like strands of electrified tinsel. She knows I'm here, but she's lost in a postoperative haze, eyes lead-lidded, head hanging heavily. I'm full of pity and gratitude for all she has done, carrying the baby, then, after a long labor, enduring a C-section. Finally she fights through the drugs and the exhaustion, and in a cottonmouth voice mutters, "Moses," as if it were her astonished last gasp on earth. It's the name she chose in accordance with some "Jewish cultural tradition"; why she's suddenly upholding anything that involves religion, especially her own, is a mystery. But as the birthdate neared, whatever name she wanted was good enough for me. Now, hearing the name and knowing there's an actual baby boy attached to it, indeed, my own son's, a charge of pure feeling rips through me, the outrage of a victim of theft. She's snatched my baby from me! Back when the child was still inside and making her huge, to be perfectly honest, I felt he was all hers. Against my wishes she kept the baby, doing what she thought was best for both of us. But now that he's here, his eight and a half pounds of roiling pink flesh, how can I not think he's mine too, especially since Sass gene is so evident in the child. How far I've come! His reddish hair, if I'm to believe the stories, is the color of Morton Sass's in his early youth. They share too-big ears, and a withering look of disdain in their dark eyes. I'm relieved that the baby, at least in his first hours of life, has chosen to resemble Morton Sass, and not Genius or some mutty blend of the two. He is my child, precisely because he is loaded with Sass genetic material.

I caress her pale, slack cheek. I tell her I've seen the baby. I tell her he's beautiful. I tell her I love her, mother of my son! I kiss her brow; she sighs, throws back her head, and says that name again. Moses. Morton. This is what confuses me, her sudden tilt toward her father, her incomprehensible desire to honor Morton Sass. Why the shifting allegiances? We were like the superpowers, China, the United States, and the USSR, playing one against the other. I didn't make this up. It was Morton Sass who said Bliss went for me to get at him, and she said he embraced me to get back at her. Now that they're all over each other, and she's glorified his DNA with "Moses," where does that leave me?

I can't help it, but I feel the name ricochet between us, multiplying in intensity like words of anger. I fight myself, and lay my head on her shoulder, seeking shelter, solace, salvation there, as I've done in the past. She grunts, dips her shoulder, seeking perhaps a more comfortable place for my cheek. "I'm just being stupid. Jealous maybe. I don't know," I say, talking more to myself than to her. "This is not the time for doubts." Then, to her, I plainly say, "I'm glad we're doing what we're doing." She moans, then shrugs, and my head slips off its perch like a boulder when the ground underneath gives way. I stand up and take her in. Has she intentionally pushed me off? I put her to the test, and nestle against her breasts, then low on her thighs, and each time she moans, "No! No!" opening her eyes to slits, then shutting them like steel curtains: the sight of me is too bright, too much to bear.

W E ARE at the Red Dragon Restaurant in Chinatown for Moses's one-month haircut party. Genius chose this place for its name: Red for luck; Dragon because that's our family name in English. He also chose the banquet menu, negotiated the price, and invited most of the guests. The party is the baby's public unveiling, a celebration that he's survived the perilous first month of life; now it's time for more trivial matters, grooming, a ritual snipping of the baby's pate, which Zsa Zsa performs. Bliss and I are the official hosts, though almost all of the guests are my parents' friends. At first Bliss was keen on the idea, always happy to accommodate my parents, show off what a gem of a daughter-in-law she is. But her enthusiasm for the banquet dwindled when they demanded she dye her hair back to brown for the party. Which she did in the end, after a hundred refusals, but she wasn't happy, covering up, as she put it, "the truth."

GENIUS AND ZSA ZSA are making the rounds, going from table to table, ten in all, showing off their son's son, their only male grandchild, passing out White Owl cigars, picking up red envelopes of lucky money from the guests. From a distance, just as my professors used to assess my handiwork, the crests of my meringue, the crown on my brioche, I scrutinize Moses' face, his grapefruit-sized head, his pomegranate cheeks. It doesn't matter how many times I blink, how wide I stretch my pupils, how near or distant I focus my gaze: My baby boy looks like a little old Chinese man. How did he ever pop out of Bliss? He started life logically, a miniature Morton Sass. But after the first seventy-two hours he started losing his red hairs, until he was almost bald; then, in the days and weeks leading up to his party, Moses' hair grew back, black. His ears unfolded from his skull like the petals of an artichoke peeled away from the heart; now they are identical to the wings that adorn the sides of Genius's head. Cradled in his grandfather's arms, among this mass of Chinese people, Moses has taken on a decidedly Chinese cast. I want to believe it's nothing more than a case of guilt by association, but in my heart I know I'm wrong.

"DOUBLE HAPPINESS," I tell Bliss, referring to the gold Chinese characters mounted on the red walls. I'm trying to bolster her. She is bored. She hates her hair. Her family left early, Grandma Tessie unhappy with the food: "A nice brisket they got, Morty?" She claimed she had a headache during the squab course, deep-fried pigeons, their smooth bald heads as round as the tip of a cock. With her family gone, Bliss is alone among the Chinese. She has had enough of the grannies with their taut skin, jade-braceleted wrists, blunt-cut gray hair, germy hands, and crooked lipstick as they come over to see the Chinese baby that has sprung from the white demon's womb. They love to yak Chinese at the baby as they wrap his sleepy fingers around their crooked joints. Bliss is worn out after absorbing the amazed stares all night long, the exclusionary bursts of Chinese, people laughing and no one explaining why.

A waiter brings a platter of noodles to the table. "Can we go now, Silvy?" she says, trying to sound patient.

"We can't," I say. "We're the hosts."

"Fine," she says, folding her arms under her milk-laden breasts. I offer her some noodles.

"When're they going to stop with the food already?" she says.

"You've hardly eaten." I put noodles on her plate.

"I don't want any. I'm tired. I just want to go."

"But you have to eat." I pat my chest. "For Moses. You have to make milk for the little guy." I chopstick a bunch of noodles and lift them high off my plate. "Long noodles," I say, "for long life."

"Why can't you just call noodles noodles? Why does everything on this table have to mean something? The shark's-fin soup, the chicken, even a simple hard-boiled egg." As each dish comes, Zsa Zsa gives the tour. No detailed explications, just basics. The white egg equals a head of white hair; the red eggs, abundance; the ginger wards off sickness. "To Moses," I say, again making an offering of the noodles. "To a long, long life."

Bliss takes the noodles between her fingers. "Okay, okay. I'm eating. Long life, long life!" She takes a bite.

"Hey, I'm only passing on what they tell me. If you don't want to eat, don't eat. Do whatever you want to do."

"I will."

Chapter 10

A YEAR AGO I was driving to the Sass house for the first time. What a state my life was in! Bliss was pregnant and bitter. Genius had only months to live. Yuk had arrived, was unexpectedly magnetic. I was flailing and fearful. I went for a bite of Thanksgiving turkey, and ended up meeting my new family. Now all is good! I'm one of them, baby Moses my permanent membership card. Morton Sass has summoned me to his office, Dad's office, over in Stamford, about a half-hour from his place in New Canaan. I'm sure he wants to discuss the proposed cable show, he wants to put me and my telegenic hands on the air; such faith he has in me, Sterling Lung, the male Julia Child, the lean James Beard! What chef wouldn't kill for this? In the morning I can push forward my cooking career at the Ladies' Club, and in the afternoon cultivate my TV stardom.

I finally locate Morton Sass's building, an ugly two-story steel-and-glass box, sandwiched between a dilapidated hamburger stand and a Shell station at the corner. I double-check the address. My heart sinks:

given Dad's fabulous house, his many and varied holdings, I have every reason to expect more than this piece-of-crap edifice.

Upstairs, his office, at least, is spacious, with gray carpeting, a leather couch in the waiting area, fluorescent lighting tubes in the ceiling, paneling on the walls, and a young secretary who's stringing beads at her desk when I enter. She has on cat-eye glasses and introduces herself to me as if I were someone worth knowing. Heidi. Her hair is egg-yolk yellow, perfectly straight, long bangs falling over the tops of her eyes like drapes. She gives the impression of milk-fed veal. "You're Morty's famous son-in-law!"

"I don't know about the famous, but I am his son-in-law."

"Oh, you're famous around here. Morty loves you," she says. I'm pleased to hear this. Dad! She reaches for the door—an oddly substantial hunk of wood in this oppressively unimpressive, dare I say, cheaply appointed environment—that opens to Morton Sass's office.

He sits at his heavy oak desk like the Wizard of Oz behind his curtain. Arrayed on the desk facing me are framed black-and-white photos of Morton Sass with Sid Caesar, with Jerry Lewis, with Lainie Kazan. Heavyweights: that's the message. "I know what you're thinking," Morton Sass begins. "You're thinking, Why the low rent, the cheap digs? I'm doing what your people do. I saw it on TV. You eat modestly at home, and for fancy you go out to restaurants. Same here. No fancy in the office. For the real business we do outside."

Heidi brings in two mugs of coffee.

"And speaking of fancy. That banquet you threw was terrific." He tells me how much he enjoyed the meal in Chinatown. What am I in, a time warp? The haircut party took place back in July, and he's talking as if it happened yesterday.

"Thank you."

"I'm telling you, I never tasted anything like it."

"I'm glad you—"

"No problem. It was my pleasure."

"Thank you—"

"For what?"

"Enjoying?"

"Hey, don't do that. Why're you thanking me? You're the guy who did me the favor. I'm supposed to thank you."

"I'm sorry."

"Don't say you're sorry. What're you sorry for?"

"I don't know."

"Don't say I don't know. Only babies are allowed to be that ignorant. What's Moses going to think of you?"

"Moses?"

"Yeah, my little Moses."

Sweat boils on my brow. I'm startled by his claim on the little boy's body. He is my son. He is my blood. I ball my hands into fists. I salivate remembering the impact my flesh made against his flesh. Something about this man, the stubble that pierces his cheeks, the pits and scars in his skin that pulse and creep. He is distinctly old-world: fleshy-headed birds, blind faith, and leeches; pickled meat, blood sacrifice, ritual bones, salt-in-wounds retribution.

Morton Sass leans closer, hanging over his desk. He questions my family's future, my financial outlook, my career plans. "You can't play houseboy the rest of your life," he says. "What will Moses think of you?"

"That's a long way off. He's just a baby."

"Believe me. He's watching and he's measuring you already. He hasn't missed a thing."

"What hasn't he missed?"

"He sees it on your face. In your body. Your posture. His little brain is soaking you up. He's forming opinions about you that will turn your heart to chopped liver one day."

I imagine he's talking from experience. Bliss and Lester. I try to remember taking Genius in through my infant eyes and infant pores. I draw a blank. But I'm sure Morton Sass must be right.

"Do as I say, Sterling," he says, his elbows planted on the desktop, chin perched on his hands, one layered on top of the other, like cuts of pork. "Stop taking orders from those damn ladies. You've got too many bosses. A bunch of females telling you what to do. You think Moses doesn't see that? This one wants something, that one wants something. Every want-something is like a blow to your head. The kid sees that. Punch-drunk daddy. It's all over you. Do yourself a favor. Quit the club. Do it for Moses."

He looks me in the eyes. I shy from his gaze, I can't meet it dead-on. Too intense, too harsh, and to stare back I might lose myself, be immolated like bugs in fire. Not the bushy gray brow, the seething facial hair, the black nostrils like windows on the afterlife.

"Breathe, Sterling."

I've been holding my breath, as I had inside the temple when they circumcised the poor kid, making him eternally one of their tribe. Standing next to Morton Sass, I felt queasy and lost, and wanted to evaporate from the musty room, its smell of sweet wine, leather-bound pages, bloody inked scrolls of sheepskin, from the baby's pain and the vast vacuum that is my lack of faith. Sitting across from this man who would take from me my son and my livelihood, I am a little boy craning his neck, shattering his eyes on gold-robed authority. Thou shalt not toil any longer at that goyishe ladies' club!

BLISS IS OUTRAGED her father wants me to quit my job: "It's obvious Morty's pissed his son-in-law slaves for a house full of Wasps who won't have Selma for a member." Bliss wants me to sit tight. "Don't you dare give in to him."

I'm surprised by her anti-Morty stance. After all, since Moses' birth, she has drawn closer to her family, honoring them with the name she gave our son, the many hours she and Moses log in their house, and her newborn religiosity, her weekly attendance at Sabbath services. Taking all that into consideration, I don't get her icy rejection of her father's wishes. She's not as concerned about my career as she claims she is; she's trapped in her decade-old habit of automatically vilifying Morton Sass.

Underneath their gaudy displays of civility, a guerrilla conflict is still being waged—through me.

T HE BABY BUMPS against my feet. Again and again. His pediatrician says Moses has precocious motor skills: a kid with places to go. Finally I open my eyes, my lids cracking with sleep. As I suspect, it's still the light-stingy part of the morning. I feel the few drops of patience draining from my body, but how can I get mad at him? It's not his fault he sleeps with us. This arrangement is what Bliss calls "a family bed." I call it suicide. Any intimacy between the two of us is impossible now. Every night she parks the baby in the middle of the mattress; then we flank him like slices of bread and engage in a queer semi-embrace, a hand touches the other's ribs or hip, arms flung over the baby, but this gesture is more for Moses' benefit, our limbs forming a shelter or shield, and that is why—I assume—we go through the trouble. I think we both know it.

At this early hour Moses has crawled countless times up and down the alley formed by our bodies, like a guard patrolling the Berlin Wall. Moving south, toward our feet, he travels in reverse, then comes charging up. I lie here, as still as possible, and watch his performance. We do this every day, and every day without thinking I examine my son's face, wondering if overnight he has grown out of his Genius stage, just as he suddenly lost his Sassian features, his fine red hair, for instance. His Chinese looks have hardened, and this morning the last remnant of his link to Morton Sass, his high-altitude nose, seems to have come down to sea level, flattening and broadening.

Bliss clears her throat and flips onto her side, showing me her back. This is her signal. She's tired of faking sleep and wants the real thing. Now I'm supposed to take the baby from the bed. Division of labor. My job these first months of parenthood is to respect her sacrifice; she has given her body to making a son for me and sustaining him now that he's here. In the middle of the night, Moses nurses, and while Bliss has mastered the maneuver of latching lips to breasts without fully rousing herself, she assures me milk production is serious, exhausting work.

I wait until he creeps up to my face, then I grab him by surprise. "Let's go, let's go, let's go! Mommy's gotta sleep!"

We rush to the kitchen. I make coffee. Eat toast. I leave Moses on a blanket on the floor. He's content there, putting everything he gets his hands on into his mouth. After breakfast I join him on the floor, and we look at books and play with blocks. I build towers, and he knocks them down. His favorite new trick is to crawl—technically, according to the books, he doesn't crawl, but scuttles along like a crab—into the blocks, like a four-legged bowling ball. To make this happen I pick him up and deposit him in a far corner of the room; then I hurry back to the blocks and quickly erect as tall a tower as possible, as he sprints toward me, destruction burning in his eyes.

Today's tower is exceptionally tall, the last teetering block at the height of my collarbone. "Eiffel Tower, Moses! Come and get it!"

He charges at full speed, which is not fast. His desires far exceed his physical ability to satisfy them. He stumbles, tripping on the very blocks that fill his eyes. His strong legs drive him forward, but his arms are the laggards: planted stiff on the floor, they are plowed under by his fat, onrushing body. I can smell his frustration, hear in his panting breath an adult-sized anger too big for his chest to contain. But I egg him on, "Eiffel Tower!" I say, pointing to the prize. He stumbles again, this time his chin grazing the carpet; he lies there on his belly, quiet, stunned like a baby seal. I consider rescuing Moses, bringing him closer to the tower. But I let him be. No one ever picked me up, made my life ten, fifteen feet easier.

Finally he rams the tower, leading with his head, like a bull. An avalanche of blocks comes toppling down. I laugh. Nothing mean-spirited. If anything, I want to run for the camera. A picture for the ages: A baby in a bath of blocks, the stunned look on his face, one of absolute bewilderment. His world shaken to pieces. The blood seems to drain from his face. "Oh, Moses, Moses!" I pick him up, and instantly he bursts into tears, cranky ear-splitting wails. I walk him around the apartment, bouncing on the balls of my feet. No luck. I cover the four corners of the room, but the boy is inconsolable. Bliss will be so pissed if she doesn't get her extra hours of milk-making sleep. I'd love to take Moses outside, walk him until my legs fall off in the ladies' infinite yard, but unfortunately that's not an option, at least in the daylight.

Which is why I'm trapped in here, the four already close walls of the carriage house apartment cozying in on us, with each of Moses' long, lingering blasts, which start in his toes and rage up through the roof of his head, like lava in a volcano. I'm positive he isn't seriously injured. He has no cuts or bruises. He's just spooked, as well he might be, having flattened the Eiffel Tower. At least, that's how it looks to me. But then, the sky didn't fall on my head.

What is my little man thinking? On his moist, red face, an angry knot grows on his brow; tears carve his skin like new rivers over virgin lands; and his huge, high-wattage black eyes accuse: How could you let that happen to me?

I won't look at him. I stare straight ahead and do all the tricks I know to calm and comfort: bounce on the balls of my feet, rock in the rocking chair, sing "You Are My Sunshine," distract him from his misery with toys, books, a tour of the kitchen cabinets.

BLISS BURSTS from the bedroom and grabs the baby from my arms. I feel terrible I woke her up. Her glare says, What's wrong with you? You bad father. You bad husband. She yanks open the top of her shapeless nightgown and docks Moses to one of her ripe, milk-hard breasts. She sits down in the rocking chair. Moses quiets immediately, tit-lust satisfied. He devours her. They conspire to an odd balance: the more he drains from her, the less that's left for me. At this moment in our lives, this narrow slot of time, for this and the next few seconds—or perhaps minutes—as she shifts the baby from one breast to the other, she hates me. The hate is pure, intense, and piercing. It shows in each of her parts, the bloodless cheeks, the formless legs, even the dense silver hair, bunched this morning against her sleep-humid head. It accumulates around her interrupted slumbers, her vanished woman's body, her strangled freedom, as a pearl buds around a grain of sand. In her heart, she knows she chose all this for herself, she knows she could've walked away, earned her degree, and be laying root canals by now. Her heart's sealed. Why not hate me instead? I would. But I don't hate her back—we'd be at a standstill then. Love needs two people to make love happen. Hate is a colossal solo act, whether or not it hits its target.

I walk over to Bliss and Moses. His eyes are shut, his mouth clamped over her nipple, lips working furiously. From his tiny nose fitful exhalations beat against her breast. My head tilts, as my concentration settles on the two of them. At once they are my heart and my blood, and both fine strangers. I am jealous of the boy. Not at the beginning, but I am now. I reach down and hook a finger on the opening of Bliss's nightgown and lightly tug at the material, so more of her whiteness shows past the whiteness of the heavy cotton. Her breast pops free, preternaturally round and plump, at its moon-glow milkiest, rising past the edge of her nightgown. I gasp: It's so erotic! Beauty unmarred by baby.

"What's with you?" She doesn't even look at me, but stares straight ahead.

This has been happening more and more often: I look at her as a woman, as my wife, not just as Moses' mother. And she gets mad. We got married, for good reasons and bad reasons, but I did it, and I'm in it. And I intend to make it work. This is where the fight usually starts, the same fight: I don't love her, or I just want her for sex, or I just want her to raise Moses. Then the fight flares in several directions—money (my not so grand salary), careers (should she go back to school?), sleep (its scarcity in our lives); then it might limb to such matters as living space (physical and psychic), living together (a tricky adjustment after our thousand-mile postcard-writing courtship), and living with a stranger (who demands many meals a day and doesn't clean up after himself). At our worst we become so devoted to the task at hand that we squander opportunities to catch up on our sleep, and late into the night I find I've circled back to the beginning, back to *I don't love her; I never loved her; we are married only because of Moses.* Eternal return.

Moses cries out against her breast. He's not really crying, just making noise, testing his vocal cords. His eyes are open and twinkle like a bird's. Because of him I resist her invitation to fight. I pity Moses, tumbling from contentment like that, cast out into the cold-world sight of me. He stabs me with a queer, one-eyed fish stare, even as he sucks the life from her. In a certain light I see how he's killing both of us. What is Moses thinking? I wonder only because Morton Sass has planted that seed in my head. A six-month-old human being thinking? But when his fish eye finds me again, I see my toddler self looking up at Genius, standing at his knee while he smoked his Luckys and worshipped the newspaper—Moses and I are staring at our fathers, disbelief on our pupils.

I AM PREPARING the ladies' lunch. The kitchen air is thick with the musk of peaches and honeydew. It is that time of year, the days hum with humidity, the grass and trees sweat their greenness. Yesterday we went to the Sass house for Father's Day. A celebration of me and Morton Sass! The "two dads," as we were called by Selma Sass. I loved how she lumped us together. I brought steaks from Fuchs's, and the two dads grilled, like real men.

Today the ladies are getting shrimp quenelles. I adore working with shrimp. I know a lot of chefs who hate the bother. But I enjoy peeling the shell segments, which seem designed for the labor of the human hand, and finding the nimble flesh underneath. The way the gray-brown flesh in a sauté pan of hot butter quickly turns pearly white and tropical orange. I love that: the hardness laid bare, the vulnerable made beautiful. It is my hands' work—my heart's work—that gets me through my days. So I cook like crazy. More food than the ladies can ever consume.

Yes, perhaps, I am secretly competing with Bliss. Her ample breasts versus the bounty of my dishes. I am grateful for the tireless work of her glands, but at the same time I am useless to my son. And to my wife. So I feed my ladies. I put mountains of food on their table: I'm not useful? I can't nurture? I can't provide? Says who? And Morton Sass will have me give all this up?

Libby Drake enters my kitchen. As usual, she's here earlier than the rest. Today she looks cross-eyed. On her bleached blue jeans is sewn a patch that says "I'm Okay, You're Okay."

"You and your little family living in that apartment," she says, after the expected preliminaries, "that's not a good situation for anyone. You must be at each other's throats by now." She fears our being cramped in the carriage house apartment might ultimately force us to move.

"We don't mind."

"Of course. That's what I expected you'd say."

"We really don't."

"I've heard you're weighing other career options. Who can blame you?"

"What options?"

"Well, the man at the butcher shop, he seems to think you're destined to become a television star."

"It's just talk. I'm not serious about—"

"And can you blame us for doing the same? Watching our backs. Weighing *our* options?"

"I'm not following you."

"Sterling, we can't have you leaving us in the lurch. As president of the Richfield Ladies' Club, I can't be caught cookless."

"But I'm not going anywhere. I promise."

"Sterling, you can't make me promises—you're a father now."

"That doesn't change a thing. I swear."

"Things have changed. The salads aren't as crisp, the coffee isn't as strong, the fish usually comes from cans, and the cottage cheese—what can I say? And look at those shrimp."

"What? I just bought them. What's wrong now?"

She shakes her head. "If you can't see what's wrong, that only confirms my point."

T HERE ARE RULES of the house," I say, as Bliss puts the final touches on the invitation she's making for what she calls Moses' "eyeglasses debut party." Each invitation consists of a photograph of our man sitting in a sandbox, a pair of orange-grease-pencil glasses drawn around his eyes. Moses has to start wearing corrective lenses because of an astigmatism in his right eye, and Bliss's thinking is that the party will make his ordeal a "positive experience." I'm all for her plan, except for the party's locale. She wants to have it at the apartment—well, she wants it to sprawl across the great lawn that separates us from the main house. But the club has its rules. "I'm an employee," I tell Bliss, "not a member."

"I'm not an employee," she says, "and neither is Moses."

"Why can't we have the party in New Canaan? Your parents and Tessie are coming."

"We can't do everything there!"

"Why not? You're always there, anyway."

"Well, if there was a little more space here, if we were more welcomed here—"

"Forget it. Do whatever you're going to do, but this is not my gig." I have to cede ground; since Moses' birth—more than a year ago now!—Bliss and I have swapped premarriage positions. I want her, but she's Moses' mother and gravitates to the Sassness she once rejected. I can't risk losing more of her; besides, it's my son's eyeglasses-debut party.

SHE HAS INVITED virtually everyone who has a baby in the tristate area, school friends, cousins, Moses' play-group friends and their families. Kids are crawling and running and sliding all over the lawn. The grown-ups are drinking, eating, crushing their cigarette butts out on the beloved grass carpet. I had begged Bliss to keep the guests inside the apartment, but after I saw the masses arriving, even I knew that was impossible.

Worse, because of the sheer numbers, she insists I give her access to the kitchen in the main house. Again, I surrender to her wishes. What am I going to do? Professionally, I can't allow her in there, but maritally, how can I say no? It's not as if I didn't know about the demands on a kitchen a party of this magnitude makes.

Bliss is removing a baking sheet of hors d'oeuvres from the oven. This is her party, and she's doing the cooking and won't let me help. I'm just here to guard the appliances and other equipment (it's my livelihood, after all). When she kicks the oven door shut, I can no longer suppress the distress that's tensed my body ever since Bliss commandeered the kitchen. "They're wrecking the lawn!" I say, throwing my arms in the air for emphasis, a gulp of Chardonnay sloshing from my glass onto the floor.

"Shit!" She drops the cookie sheet of pigs-in-a-blanket (kosher pigs, of course). "Look what you made me do!"

I'm on my hands and knees, cursing Bliss's clumsiness, herding the runaway piggies, when I see Libby Drake's slender ankles and Bass Weejuns on the linoleum in front of me.

I follow Libby Drake out of the kitchen. On the concrete patio, she pulls over her eyes the sunglasses she's been wearing as a hair accessory. She looks out at the lawn, at all the partygoers, as she says, "You've changed, Sterling. Ever since you've been a father. That's all I'm saying." She crosses her arms. In the old days, when my hair was long and fatherhood was absolutely unfathomable, she would've seized upon a moment like this and caressed my ponytail, and I would've felt welcome and wanted.

I try to appeal to whatever maternal feelings she might hold in her body. "I'm sorry. It was my wife's idea." I look back into the kitchen at Bliss, and she nods. "My son has to wear glasses, and it's been hard on his mother, so she had to throw a party. I'm sorry, it was a mistake in judgment."

"I can't tell you how right you are."

A WEEK LATER, as I'm finishing my post-luncheon cleanup, Libby Drake enters the kitchen. "Sterling," she says, "this is a stressful time for any new father. You have to feed your young family, and you have to be responsible for feeding all of us. You know what I mean, don't you?"

"Sure."

"Good. Because there's someone here I want you to meet." She hurries to the swinging kitchen door. "Come on, come on," she says to someone I can't see.

Several paces behind Libby Drake is a Chinese guy. He is the same height as she, in regulation Chinese white shirt and black slacks and kung fu shoes.

"What is this?" I say.

"Sterling, I'd like you to meet Mr. —"

"Wong Chuck Ting," the Chinese guy says. Then, without solicitation, he adds, "I cook."

"I found him at First Wok. You know, the new place on Atlantic?"

My jaw hangs loose, my mouth as dry as phyllo baked to a crisp. The world is closing in on me. I'm withering, like Moses' weakening sight. I am desperate. "Whatever he can do, I can do better."

"I don't think so. He's Chinese."

"So am I!"

"But he's from China. He's authentic."

BACK AT THE APARTMENT Bliss is making applesauce. She has made her own baby food ever since Moses started taking solids; she grinds apples and pears, mashes bananas, beets, zucchini, and mills rice into cereal. Her exclusive domain. I think—I know—the boy can eat adult food, but she's crushing the apples in a food mill, which produces a loud rasping noise each time she turns the handle. I start telling her about what Libby Drake said about the Chinese dishwasher she wants to cook for the club, but Bliss shushes me—Moses is napping; she points to our bedroom. Why is it that I can't talk about matters that are life and death to me, but she can keep turning that brain-splitting crank? I stand in the kitchen, a few feet from her, watching her work. Waiting to see if she will come to me. Daring her to ignore me completely, as she does each night in bed. We lie on opposite ends of the mattress, Moses between us, Bliss perpetually exhausted, drained by her cunning son. I remember how, early on, I used to try to make love to her. I'd scoot onto her side of the bed and touch her, in attempts to bring her back to the days when she was pregnant with Moses, probably the most sex-filled time in our life together. But she would gently repel me, offering her cheek to kiss, turning her back, and in the tenderest voice saying, "Good night, baby!" Later, she'd snap, "Stop it! Act like an adult!" I think of how nowadays I don't bother. How, while mother's and child's lungs fill with each other's breath, I toss and turn, waiting for her to come around, make the move toward me.

She acts as if I weren't even here now, and just ladles more boiled apple into the mill and turns the crank, oblivious to the conversation we were having.

Standing there, waiting: once again I fall into the old habit of waiting for Bliss to come rescue me. I see then my own culpability in our shared drowning. We've let ourselves drift, Bliss in her Moses-induced haze, and me stonily watching to see how far she'll dare slip away. When we're deep into it, I never feel I'm doing any wrong—in bed, at night, I'm blame-free, while she's off in her own outer space, tripping in her personal Milky Way. But standing here now, my gaze falls on my own head, on my brutal listlessness, like a witness to Kitty Genovese's murder who doesn't scream, lift a finger, call for help.

"Stop it!" I shout, stepping heavily over to her. I check her apple-saucing hand. "He's not a baby! You can act like an adult again."

"Are you crazy? You'll wake him."

"What is he doing in our bedroom? In our fucking bed?"

She blinks. And blinks. Her bottom lip trembles.

A chef is one who finds beauty where others might not. In truffles, for instance, offal, rennet, dandelion greens. But I don't see beauty anymore. Within the walls of this marriage, inside the wrinkling skin of family, I am sick with apathy. Only the baby and our wedding rings bind us together.

EACH MONDAY MORNING, I find myself peeking from the carriage house apartment and watching Wong Chuck Ting traverse the vast lawn in his black-and-white outfit, his fleshy pink cranium in the sun shining in my eyes like diamonds. That pathetic figure, and I'm losing the ladies to him. I can no longer bear entering the kitchen on Tuesday mornings, after the much-praised Wong Chuck Ting has perpetrated his particular brand of culinary heresy. The rancid peanut oil, greasy steam, rotting garlic collecting, moldering on the walls are nothing less than insults he leaves me. This is not my kitchen anymore; it's as if he'd worn my gloves and stretched them out of shape. When I cook now, my nose is full of him. And this throws me off balance, compromises my sense of taste, and the rest of me along with it.

I walk into town to do some shopping, but go immediately to Fuchs's. "What's the word on the Chinese guy at the club? How's our dishwasher-turned-cook doing?"

"You don't want to know, Sterling." Fuchs is wearing a Yankees baseball cap and pulls the brim lower, hiding his eyes.

"Sure I do. Why do you think I asked?"

Fuchs stares at me with enough heat to fry bacon. Finally he says, "They love him." My insides collapse like a fallen cake. Fuchs must see it on my face. He reaches across the counter and puts a consoling hand on my shoulder: "Hey, it's still early, they'll get over him. It can't last. We both know you're the real thing."

"Who's your source? You have to tell me." My body is shaking, rattled by the fervor that propels my words. It's so close to the surface, the feeling of betrayal at being so easily and, now I hear, joyfully replaced. "It's not him, is it?"

"No, the ladies come in here. They talk."

"What exactly do they say? Do they ever mention me anymore?"

"Well, it's hard to say. My memory's not so good. Maybe they do, maybe they don't." Now Fuchs won't look at me at all.

"They turn so quickly on you." I drop my head in my hands. "Fuchs, Fuchs, Fuchs!" My fingers rake my scalp, my elbow stabs the refrigerated case. "As a friend, I want you to answer me straight." I look him in the eye: "Does he . . . does he?" I'm ashamed I feel the need to air such a question.

"Does he, who? What, what?"

I inhale roughly. Exhale. "Fuchs, you have to tell me, does the new guy buy from you? And what does he buy?"

"Sterling, come on. Why you putting Fuchs in such a tough spot? You wouldn't like it if I told folks the kind of meat you buy, just because they asked. You should understand this better than anyone, we're talking a very intimate matter here, best left between a man and his butcher."

"So he does shop here!"

"I didn't say that."

I shrug. I can't look at Fuchs right now. I can't tell if I've lost him too, if he's part of a cover-up. "They don't leave any leftovers. I go in Tuesday morning and the refrigerator's got nothing he's cooked. They lick their dishes clean for him."

"Sterling, what gives? That crowd, they don't know what's good. Just because they love his cooking doesn't mean he's any good. You're better off without those ladies. You don't need that gig."

"Why are you protecting him? You're putting the blame on the ladies. Don't you realize the kind of person he is? Every Monday he wears my apron, he uses my pots and pans."

"Sterling, get a grip of yourself. The guy's in your kitchen, not your bedroom."

"Is there a difference?"

"For your sake, I hope there is."

I CROSS THE STREET in front of the store, and I haven't gone very far when I see the usurper coming toward me in his usual garb, his fashion sense stolen from Genius. I duck into the entryway of a dress shop, and once I do so, Wong Chuck Ting crosses the street I crossed a few seconds ago. The home-wrecker enters the butcher shop, without hesitation—he knows this ground, and has been here plenty of times before. I can't believe Fuchs's deception.

I imagine bursting into his shop and catching them red-handed. A block of meat passing between the two. But I decide not to press matters. What's the point? To Fuchs we're just two Chinese guys. Look at how he must see things: he'll sell his rump roast to just about anybody.

A few days later Libby Drake asks me to teach Wong Chuck Ting how to cook other cuisines besides Chinese. "You don't expect us to eat Chinese food all the time," she says. I tell her she doesn't. Only on Mondays. Then I shut up. I understand what she's asking. Wong Chuck Ting is being groomed to replace me full-time. I'm supposed to teach him Western cooking. I'm supposed to make myself eminently dispensable.

I tell her I'll devise a series of lessons for her man Wong Chuck Ting. In two months I will have imparted all the knowledge I learned in two years at the CIA. I tell her I am glad to help her out.

"Fuck Chuck!" I shout, when the coast is clear.

That weekend I move Bliss and Moses permanently out of the apartment and into the Sass house. They spend so much time there as it is, and now should the ladies dump me they won't have those two to justify their cruelty. I stay behind in the carriage house apartment, a last-ditch attempt to appease the goddesses—things are back to normal, and more than ever I'm devoted to their appetites.

LIBBY DRAKE WANTS ME to start the cooking lessons. Time to make good on my promises. "Why are you being so immature?" she says. "I've never heard Chuck complain about sharing the kitchen with you."

Fuck Chuck! He doesn't speak English, that's why.

That night I telephone Morton Sass; I tell him I'm quitting the ladies.

He says, "It was just a matter of time."

I can see his face crack with pleasure, the persistent stubble on his cheeks like a battalion of worms pushing through dirt during a storm.

I MOVE MY BELONGINGS from the carriage house apartment to the Sass residence, and a week later Bliss and Moses move out. Temporarily. Monday I'm in, and Wednesday they are flying to California to visit her brother, who hasn't seen his nephew yet. It's more of the *Roots* quest she's been on since she's become a mother: first, her return to family, religion, "culture," her roosting in New Canaan, the inevitable dash to the nest, and now reclaiming the lost sibling. The trip itself I'm fine with. Morton Sass, in fact, bought the airline ticket. I'll never figure these Americans out! He says one thing, and he does another, subverting his own wishes. It runs in the family; his daughter wanted commitment, and since the marriage—well, actually, since Moses—she's drifted, in love with her child, too tired or busy for me, uninterested in my food.

One night I'm sitting up with Morton Sass. We're in the living room, I'm doing the *Times* crossword puzzle while he is reading the business section. Once in a while I read clues to him, just to break the

uncomfortable silence, just so it feels as if we were friends doing something together. Earlier, at the dinner table (hey, I'm the new resident
chef at the Sass house!) over a meal of *champignons à blanc, champignons
sautés au beurre,* and *champignons sous cloche,* dishes I had watched Julia
prepare this morning, an episode devoted totally to mushrooms, Selma
Sass, Morton Sass, and I discussed my cable show. Morton Sass unveiled
the name he's come up with: "Enter the Dragon Kitchen," a takeoff
on the Bruce Lee film title, and an unequivocal pronouncement of
the show's basic theme: Chinese cooking. I was pissed that Morton
Sass would do me this way. His impulse was the ladies all over again.
In our planning discussion I had respectfully argued—that might
too strong a verb—I had vehemently suggested that Chinese cooking
wasn't my strong suit, that he should exploit my best talents and schooling, especially in the art of French cooking. About the show's title,
though, I had to keep quiet. How was someone in my position
supposed to argue with the man who owned the studio, the broadcast tower, the show itself, and who moments earlier had sampled
and despised my lovely mushrooms, prepared in the French style? When
I told him the recipes were Julia's, he wasn't impressed. "This is why TV
needs you," he said, playing hockey with his fork and a mushroom cap.
"She calls this dinner?"

"Morty, I've seen you eat mushrooms."

"Yeah, but a fungus smorgasbord like this?"

I felt crushed; Morton Sass had never rejected my food before.

The night is speeding away from me. Morton Sass is headed for bed
soon. I can't bear the thought of going to sleep knowing he is unhappy
with me. I decide to ask for his help with the crossword, lob him an
easy clue, one he'll nail quickly, then he'll feel good about himself and
about the time he's spent with me. "Dad," I say. " 'Apples and oranges,
for example.' Five letters."

" 'Fruit'!" he answers, swiftly and bluntly, a verbal slap that says,
Idiot! Don't tell me you didn't know that.

He gets up from his easy chair. "I'm turning in." He walks to the stairs, and when his foot lands on the first step, he asks, "What does Bliss say about me?"

The question is a surprise. Which is true of most things that Morton Sass says. "About you? She doesn't say all that much, really."

"Sterling, she's kidnapped your son, my grandson, and taken him to fairyland. Do you know what that means? She wants Moses to come under Lester's influence. And you know why, don't you?"

"Honestly, Dad, I don't think she's doing that."

"Sterling, wake up! She lives to piss me off. Why else is she in San Francisco? Why else is she exposing my grandson to Lester?"

"They'll be back soon." I say this, and then pause. I absorb this moment in my life, taking it in as I might the bouquet of a rare wine, the acids standing my taste buds on end, the vapors ruffling my thoughts: After Morton Sass, I am the man of the house, and one day all of this will be mine; I only need to behave himself.

He rises. "Remember what I told you," he says. "Don't come crying to me one day, saying I didn't warn you."

"She's in California on a little vacation. I'm not worried."

"Suit yourself." As Morton Sass stalks out of the living room his shoulders seem to bear a great offense, his legs massively burdened.

THE LEAVES ARE beginning to turn when Bliss and Moses come back from California. I meet them at JFK. They are the last to deplane. They come down the red-carpeted jet-bridge alone. In the time away, Moses has grown, noticeable increases in height and muscle mass. He is sturdy on his legs now and walks like a human. From this distance, with the black frames on his face and his speedy gait, more than ever he's a miniature Genius. Bliss waves; she's tanned, her skin contrasting sharply with her bright silver locks. "Look, it's Daddy! Wave!" she calls, but Moses doesn't seem to hear.

He nearly walks right past me. "Where're you going, mister?" I say, as I grab him under the arms and hoist him high in the air and, with pleasure, feel his newfound solidity. He laughs, digging his sudden rise in elevation, the air under his feet. But then something happens, and he squirms, his face twists the way it did when he was a baby and had to pass gas. I set him down, and once he touches the ground he's gone.

I take Bliss's shoulder bag and canvas tote, and during the exchange we quickly kiss.

Moses walks a few feet ahead of us. I am utterly charmed by his newest tricks, by how unfragile and fearless he now appears. I have a constant urge to touch him, squeeze his powerful little legs with both my hands. But I resist temptation. I'm hoping for a fresh start; maybe this new Moses has forgotten the Eiffel Tower of blocks that crashed on his head, or whatever it is that holds us apart.

In the car he demonstrates his most amazing and transformative trick: from his mouth flows the most amusing chatter, some actual words, "ball," "more," "dog," "cat," "apple," "egg," and wonderfully eloquent nonsense. He pulls off an impressive "Mama!" and almost a "Lester," though he drops the *l*. I'm disappointed there's no "Dada" or "Papa" in his vocabulary, but what can I expect—I wasn't around when he made his linguistic breakthroughs.

"MOSES LOVES LESTER," Bliss says to everyone seated around the kitchen table. "Remember Uncle Lester?"

Standing on Morton Sass's lap, Moses twists toward his mother's voice and laughs. His face is turned from me as he listens to his mother recount a story about him and Lester. My ears fill with his happy cackle, his attempts at his uncle's name; I stare at the back of his head, the black hair and the red elastic band that secures his glasses to his face. Then, as in the airport, in the car, and in the house, I want what the others have so easily with him, the touching, the chatter. Again and again I have resisted, but now I reach out and pat his head, then run my hand down and squeeze his sweat-sticky neck. I feel his voice vibrate through his vertebrae and into my fingers. At first, my sense is that I'm stealing from him, taking what he would not readily give, but the thought comes to me: He lets me, he wants this. Then, without provocation, he whips his head around. He recognizes my face, my smell, my way of metabolizing the air; he swipes furiously at his glasses, and when I try to stop his hand—"What is it?"—he bursts into tears.

Chapter 11

I T IS THE LAST WEEK in September. A hot evening, after another hot "Indian summer" day. The weather has been like this since Bliss and Moses' return, as if their presence has sent temperatures soaring. Had Bliss gone back to dental school, she'd be a month deep into the semester by now. We are dining at First Wok, that's right, First Fuck Chuck Wok! Bliss has lusted after this joint since it opened, but because she was nursing she stayed away, afraid of passing spicy, greasy milk to the baby. Against my own wishes I've acquiesced to hers; since she came back from California, Bliss and I have been on an inexplicable roll as a couple. In the past week alone we've dined at Randazzo's, The Canal House, and Chez Jules et Moby. These outings mark the first time we've both been away from Moses for more than an hour. The first time she would allow it. The key is the boy's sturdiness, his bipedal mobility, his freedom from the breast, his hunger for solid foods, his ability to articulate desire. Physically he's a new man, an entirely different species. Less dependent, his own person. Like Moses,

Bliss has changed. For one thing, she's shed her pregnancy pounds, having taken up jogging in San Francisco while her brother watched Moses. Her legs are lean and muscular, her tummy flat, her eyes, bright and rested. She polishes her fingernails and toenails, and her hair, while still silver (and therefore full of biting accusation), seems lightened further by the California sun. She is different, and she's not. Different because she's no longer as joined at the hip to Moses, and not different because she's essentially reinhabited her pre-Moses body. In short, she has emerged from her baby haze as spectacularly as Renaissance Europe emerged from the Middle Ages in high school history books.

First Wok is packed. It's the Studio 54 of chop-suey-jointdom. I keep my eyes out for Wong Chuck Ting; I can't bear the possibility of his spotting me in here among the flock that craves the greasy goodness he dishes out.

Our waiter asks whether I speak Chinese, then says a few words in Chinese at me—the same dialect Libby Drake's husband speaks. I shake my head. Why bother trying to explain I know a little bit of another dialect, when every Chinese-Chinese ever created thinks his dialect is the only dialect, and those who babble another are, in some measure, barbarians? I just let him hate me for being American-born, for having an American wife. I don't need to add, for not being the right kind of Chinese.

After she orders, I ask, "What about your career? What are you going to do after Moses goes to school? You wanted to serve humanity, fix every cavity, Bliss the missionary of teeth. What's happened to her?"

"You sound worried."

"No, I'm just looking at the long view, the big picture."

"Do you want me to go back to school?"

"Only if that's what you want."

"Would you like us to live apart? Is that why you're asking?"

"Absolutely not. I never want to be apart again."

The meal—Orange Chicken, Twice-Cooked Meat, Spicy Tofu—passes without further incident. For the first fifteen minutes after the food arrives, my heart rears like a startled horse each time a white-shirted Chinese guy bursts through the kitchen door, but I finally relax and find my appetite. Bliss is crazy about the food. She declares it the best meal she's ever had.

"Can I ask you something? If you're on a diet, why're you eating this stuff but not my cooking?"

"Isn't it obvious? This is Chinese!"

BACK AT THE SASS HOUSE we neck in the Valiant.

On our way inside, I stop, then lead Bliss around to the rear of the house. And there, on the hottest night of the month, on the cusp between seasons, in full sight of pots of Selma Sass's petunias, we make love on Morton Sass's late-summer grass, the first fallen leaves beneath, while on the sidelines a herd of deer watch.

A T LONG LAST, Morton Sass and I successfully develop the cooking show. It is scheduled to air Sunday mornings opposite preachers, cartoons, and *Face the Nation*. He figures I should clean up, knockout the competition. I'm encouraged by his optimism but can't help thinking we're not going to pull any of the viewers who turn on their sets looking for Daffy Duck or spiritual salvation. Still, I am less nervous about the show, now that it's been revamped and renamed *Enter the Dragon French Kitchen*. I warned Morton Sass my repertoire of Chinese dishes was limited, and proposed an alternative plan, a combination platter, a smorgasbord of a show, blending the aristocratic cuisine in which I was schooled with sprinklings of the plebeian fare that the masses apparently want. "You don't want the best of me to go to waste, do you?" I argued. At first, Morton Sass dismissed my proposal. "Why do you want to compete with that crowd already cooking normal food? Look, imagine you're a housewife, and you're looking to improve yourself, and you want to be more than just macaroni and cheese, more than just pot roast, boiled chicken. You aspire to, I don't know, crêpes suzette, whatever that is, so you flip on the TV set for help. Who do you want to teach you to crêpe suzette, that fat James Beard or some Chinese guy?"

"The Chinese guy who went to the CIA?"

"No, Sterling. Not the Chinese guy," Morton Sass said. "But do you know what? That Chinese guy is where you go if you want to egg foo yung. And do you understand who that Chinese guy will be?"

"Me?"

"You. And do you know why you?"

"Because I'm a Chinese guy?"

"Exactly! The only Chinese guy on the airwaves. You'll be a pioneer, Sterling. Like Columbus! Neil Armstrong! Hey, what am I thinking. You'll be the new Marco Polo!"

I stared at my father-in-law in amazement.

Twenty-four hours later I got up the courage to whine to Bliss, who lobbied Selma Sass on my behalf, and she got results. I was amazed. Morton Sass, the famously immovable object. He agreed to a compromise. I cook Chinese every fourth Sunday, the rest of the month I cook my French specialties. Which explains the show's peculiar name.

In celebration of my victory and to prove to Morton Sass the wisdom of his decision, I prepared a heavenly meal for everyone, a ragoût of wild mushrooms with veal stock and red wine; confit of duck; watercress salad; poached pears and figs with cassis cream.

"That was good, Sterling," Morton Sass said, pushing away from the table. "But who's to say this food'll make good TV?"

EARLY ON THE MORNING of my first show, Bliss wakes up feeling sick. She goes to the bathroom, and by the time she returns I've fallen back to sleep.

"I'm pregnant. Sterling, do you hear me? I'm pregnant!"

Moses! She's talking about Moses, I think. My mind drifts to the show later in the day, to the dishes I will prepare, a repeat of the duck confit menu I cooked for the Sasses. I panic: Even after I've prepared parts of each recipe in advance of the broadcast, can I possibly assemble four dishes in a half-hour?

My eyes open. Bliss is standing at the foot of the bed, Moses in her arms; they are looking in my direction, as if waiting for me to wake.

"Did you hear what I said?"

"I don't know if I can do it. How many can I possibly take on?"

"For me, one's plenty."

"One's not enough. I have to do at least two. Maybe even three."

THE TV STUDIO is in a building that looks like a mobile home, only bigger and made of brick. To say I'm bummed out by the low-end digs is a gross understatement. Would Morton Sass put Julia in this dive?

No one has come with me for moral support. Bliss and her father were supposed to accompany me, but at the last minute Morton Sass decided he wanted to see the product on TV. And Bliss is sick. How can she be pregnant again? It must've been the romp in the garden after the meal at First Wok. The warm evening air, Wong Chuck Ting's cooking, and my overly virile sperm. What a strange combination!

The show's crew—well, there is no crew, really—consists of Nick the cameraman, who doubles as director, and an intern who handles the lighting and sound. I have brought my own ingredients and my favorite knife.

I'm dazed with exhaustion, nerves, and the early-morning revelations. "Are you sure?" I asked her. "Sure, I'm sure. Unlike you, I was there at the beginning when I was pregnant with Moses. This is morning sickness, not stomach flu."

"When are you due?"

"I don't know. You do the math."

"June? July?"

"Well, we might never get there. I just finally lost all those pounds,

I got my body back, and now I'm getting my life together. Why would I want to do this again?"

"Because we're married. Because things are good between us."

"Are they?"

"They're not?" Doesn't she have everything she wanted? "I think it's all worked out pretty well," I said. I have my own TV show, and Morton Sass loves me. All the craziness surrounding Moses' birth is behind us. And on Long Island I'm thought of as a good son. "From the beginning, you were right and I was wrong about us."

"I'm not so sure about that."

"What does that mean?"

"Nothing. I'm just upset. I didn't expect to wake up pregnant when I went to sleep last night."

"I didn't either, but don't you think I'm handling this pretty well?"

"Compared to the last time, I'd say so. You're like a new man. I can hardly recognize you."

THE CAMERA'S STARE is one hundred times worse than anything Genius has ever dished out. I am so tired and thrown off balance by Bliss's news I have made a bunch of mistakes during the first dish. I didn't realize trying to narrate my cooking moves while I'm cooking would be such an unnatural activity. At the start of the duck confit recipe, instead of saying, "Melt six cups of duck fat in a pan that can hold the duck pieces in a single layer. The fat should cover the duck . . ." I hear myself blabber, "Melt six cups fuck fat . . . the fuck should cover the duck. . . ."

I survive the first show; I do okay. It'll take time getting used to the nonstop talking. There is almost no occasion to think: my hands and mouth have to keep moving. I drive home depressed. It's unsatisfying doing all that cooking for the camera, all those people out there watching but in the end no one eating my food.

At the house, Morton Sass greets me at the door with a glass of champagne. I wonder what he's celebrating—my inaugural show, or the news of a second grandchild? Morton Sass pats me on the shoulder.

"You gotta remember you're live, son," he says, laughing. "Good thing nobody's watching!"

I walk into the house. "Where's Bliss?" Moses is running with a big red ball in his arms, under his chin. Selma Sass says, "She said she had to go out. That's all I know. I was hoping she went to the studio to watch you."

"Did she see the show?"

Selma Sass shrugs. "Not here. I'm sure she did, wherever she went."

WHEN I ASK, Bliss says, "Tending to my mental health." I give her space; I know in the mornings she doesn't feel well. She's contemplating the commotion inside her womb, *my* baby. Moses is hers. This one's mine. Ours. He—I know it's a boy—will have a better start. Bliss and I were more together as a couple at the time of his conception. "I need space," she says. "I need my life back. You're a man. You can't understand what the last two years have been like for me."

"Okay," I say. "Do whatever you have to do."

We don't go out together anymore. Often, she simply disappears. No one knows where she goes. Fearing I might set her against me, I don't ask. She usually leaves Moses with her mother or me. And if she vanishes while I'm out of the house, how often has it happened that upon my return, when I ask her mother or a baby-sitter or the cleaning lady where Bliss has gone, they answer in umpirelike fashion, "Out!" Sometimes they say she's having tea or cocktails with friends, she's shopping, she's taking a walk, but none of them ever sounds convinced. At night, I lie there in the dark, knowing nothing of her but her coarse breaths, the child between us, his brother whose days on earth she plays God to, and I think she must be feeling like her pre-baby self again, stepping into the world she left behind to become a mother. That has to be the answer among all the answers. But as I struggle after sleep, my hand rubbing Moses' sweaty little head, I don't truly believe it.

"H EY," Bliss says, "I don't feel nauseous." It is morning. Moses is sitting up, in the space between our pillows. Outside the bedroom's small window the world is storming,
whipping winds, sporadic downpours, huge, distinct raindrops pinging
against the glass and Morton Sass's roof. "I think it's over," she says. "I
can't believe it."

"That's really great." I'm still sleepy, eyes sticky-shut. Resting on
my side, I reach over and touch her. Squeeze her thigh, then run my
hand up to her belly, and with a swirling motion massage the epicen-
ter of her two-month-long unhappiness. As I do this, I expect at any
moment she will shift her body, ending the contact, or brush my hand
off her. But it doesn't happen.

"I want to move M-O-S-E-S into his own room," she says. "It's time.
He can stay in Lester's bed."

"Won't he escape? Shouldn't he be in a crib? Behind bars?"

"Maybe. I haven't thought this through. The idea just came to me."

Finally. "What brought this on?"

"Then by the time number two's here, we can move M-O-S-E-S to
Lester's bed and give the baby the crib."

"Okay." I don't dare venture much else. She's talking to me, but she
might just as easily be talking in her sleep. I'm listening, though it feels
more like eavesdropping, and I don't want to disturb her until she's
reached whatever end she might eventually come to.

T HE LAST SIX MONTHS of the pregnancy are the best time
of the marriage. We are in step, moving in unison through
a single life together. Without Moses in bed with us, we've reclaimed
the nights. Moses, indeed, all but disappears; he spends part of January
and February with Morton and Selma Sass in Israel; after that, he stays
a month at the laundry.

I cook, and Bliss eats; she and I inspire each other to greater heights of, respectively, culinary creativity and consumption. Whatever her appetite, she tells me, and I do everything in my power to satisfy her. (Except for her too frequent hankering for Chinese food, which I handle with takeout from First Wok. Chinese food—that is the only rough spot.) No one knows how many people are watching the French Dragon, but I've gotten the hang of talking nonstop while I cook. What simplifies matters is that I steal from my loose-leaf binder of CIA recipes and snippets of my professors' lectures. But the every-fourth-Sunday Chinese shows are a strain. For those, there are no notes, no intellectual underpinnings, no schooled methodology; all I have is instinct, and what I thieve weekly from Zsa Zsa.

Chapter 12

A MONTH BEFORE Moses' second birthday his brother, Ira, was born. He was big and healthy, and in the hospital, the first forty-eight hours of life, he looked, to my disappointment, like a Lung. But I was happy, Bliss was happy. And I was happier still when, in advance of his first-month, first-haircut party, a small affair held at the house in New Canaan, Ira, like his brother, only in the opposite direction, metamorphosed from Lung into Sass. No sign of Lung chromosomes remained. Natural selection. We had finally done something good together. The result was perfect Ira.

For the first three months, Bliss let Ira monopolize her every waking minute. She did nothing without considering her sons' needs first; one was her head, the other her heart, and she could not go two feet without both boys in tow. Friends and strangers alike were awed by her love, sacrifice, and devotion. I felt nothing but gratitude, though I was— I hate to admit it—jealous of an infant and a toddler. They were getting it all. Sleep-deprived, milk-making-exhausted, Bliss slipped into the all-too-familiar baby haze, mind and body fixed on nothing but sustaining her boys, especially Ira. She was used up by them ("my darling little cannibals," she once said). Which left little of her for me. While I believed—she kept arguing this point—her biology had changed her, and what I felt was denied me was given to my sons, I still longed for the way things had been between us the last six months of the pregnancy. When I complained, she said, "Would you rather we had not had Ira?"

She was right. There was Ira, his delicate head of sparse reddish-blond curls, his slightly upturned nose, his blistering eyes. Perfect creation! So I resigned myself to waiting. We emptied ourselves, pouring our love into Ira, then lapped up the overflow. A few times she joked about taking a trip to California. She would come back, she said, as she had before, a changed woman. Her miraculous transformation fresh in my head, I wanted the same to happen. A tempting proposition, but a logistic impossibility—she couldn't leave Ira, and I didn't want her to take the little guy away.

SOON AFTER Ira's six-month birthday, Bliss stopped breastfeeding him. She sent her parents and Moses out of the house for the night, put Ira in the crib in his brother's room, and let him wail. She didn't say so, but she was doing this for us. She wanted to strip away the haze, reclaim her life, our life, before the demands of motherhood abducted her. So I was behind her. For two hours, we left Ira, hungry and scared, screaming in the darkness. I tried to sleep, pillow over my face, while she gripped the edge of the mattress closest to the door, and wept her own tears. Each time I moved to console her, I felt her body stiffen under my hand. I lay there helpless, listening to both their suffering. I slid across the bed, moved to comfort Ira as much as I was to comfort Bliss. She seemed lost in the deepest grief. I pressed my cheek between her shoulder blades, my hand smoothing her sweaty hair. "Not now!" she yelped, shrugging me off.

"Why are we doing this?" I said.

I couldn't stand to hear Ira so miserable. I went to his crib and picked him up. Downstairs, I heated a bottle of formula, and he quieted immediately. As he drank he stared at my face, his eyes dark and floating in pools of cooling tears. This is my love. Moments, I might've thought it was Bliss, but no, it's Ira I'm in love with.

WE LOVED EACH OTHER through Ira. But after he drained the bottle and I returned to bed, after I had settled in for the night, she said, "We're even now. You have yours."

Ira knew better than not to be weaned. Once that happened, she drifted into an orbit of her own. Her own space. She started running, often leaving the house for hours. She went on diets, restricting intake of my cooking in particular. She made noises about returning to dentistry school, or getting a dental hygienist's license, or starting any career. I watched her in silence, respecting her "space," as she ran and starved her body into a new shape, her mother's-milk-melon breasts flattening into pear halves, her complexion shining from hours exercising in winter's cold. I saw what was happening, and while I hoped it wasn't true, I knew she wasn't in training for my sake, getting herself into tip-top condition so she might better please me.

I told myself I had Ira (and my show, and my place under Morton Sass's roof), but still I wanted more from her than just the leftovers that glanced off her sons. After giving my love to Ira—I fed him, the bottles of formula and purees of my milder dishes; I walked him in the snow, in a harness under my coat, warm against my body—I needed her to replenish me, as a stockpot needs fresh celery, more soup bones, more love, if it's going to keep giving. Did she expect tiny Ira to fill me up, he so vulnerable and needy himself? Of course not, we were the adults here. But her needs were the opposite of mine; after her long days, she wanted to be left alone. In bed, my caresses, my kisses—oh, she met my lips with a clenched jaw—she was chaste, modest, immaculate-conceptional.

ON MY WEEKLY TRIPS to Long Island to steal recipe ideas from Zsa Zsa for the Dragon portion of my show, I bring Moses with me. He loves going there, and I owe my parents a chance to see at least one of their grandsons. When Moses was younger, Bliss used to insist we visit them once a week; when I balked—I had lots of excuses—she would make the trip without me, arguing that he needed to come under their influence, get an early jump on his schooling in "the Chinese culture," as she put it. But she's been different about Ira. I don't know why. Maybe because he doesn't look Chinese, and therefore has no need for the exposure? In any case, she insists it's too much for me to have both kids in the car at the same time. There might be some truth to that. Moses used to climb out of his crib and beat his fists against our bedroom door because he knew Ira was in there with us, taking his former place between us. These trips together without Ira are probably good for Moses and me. At the Sass house, things have gotten worse since Ira's been around; I try to hide, but probably not too successfully, my preference for Moses' younger brother. But when we're in the Valiant together, heading for Long Island, Moses is perfectly content to be with me because he knows what awaits him on the other end: the Chinese culture, namely, the language and Zsa Zsa's cooking. During the drive we practice our baby Chinese, "Ah-Yeah," Grandpa, "Ah-Ngin," Grandma and "Baba," Dad. Moses loves rice, and he will eat everything Zsa Zsa puts in front of him, no matter how Chinese; he loves even the funkiest of her concoctions, the meanest specimens of a base cuisine, elemental forms born of lean times and coarse palates, sodium-rich, designed for the simple purpose of helping ease the grains of rice, as Zsa Zsa would say, past the tongue:

salted fish, shrimp paste, black beans, preserved turnip. For my part, after
the first few months of the show, I've run out of Chinese recipes and
need to leech off Zsa Zsa for new ideas. Yes, I've bought a cookbook, I
have my culinary instincts and my education, but I'm walking on foreign soil, and it's my duty to my fans to be as authentic as possible, and
to that end I come to learn from the native.

MOMENTS AFTER WE ARRIVE, Moses beelines for Genius, and
Genius is all over him. They are like fraternal twins born sixty-odd years
apart: the short legs, round heads, peaked eyebrows, black eyeglass
frames fluttering, twitching; and today, to compound their resemblance,
I unconsciously dressed Moses in Genius colors, white turtleneck top
and gray sweatpants. They play peek-a-boo; Genius tickles Moses, tosses
the kid in the air; Moses chases the old guy around. Both of them laughing. It's hard for me to watch. I don't remember Genius playing with
me. In fact, I know he never bothered. Each time I witness this scene
my insides clinch, every muscle, every cell contracting around the envy,
pulsing through my body. I am jealous of Moses, of the magnets in his
tiny being that attract my father so.

One day Zsa Zsa is preparing stuffed bitter melon, canoes full of
minced meat. I make mental notes. I ask her the name of the dish. "Bitter
melon stuffed with beef," she says incredulously. Morton Sass has been
bugging me about jazzing up the names of the dishes on the program.
"You wouldn't happen to know any chicken dishes named after gener-
als, would you?" he once asked. "How about something with 'nest' in
it?" Or Crispy Phoenix? Or Seven Stars of the South Lake? He had
pulled those from the menu at First Wok. Or Happy Family? "Don't
you know how to make a Happy Family?"

I wonder if I can build a half-hour show around Bitter Melon
Stuffed with Beef (or how about Beef Stuffed Bittermelon? No, this:
Happy Oxen in Sampans on Zsa Zsa River). It's a simple dish, but I fig-
ure I can complicate the directions for my audience, and no one will

suspect being played with. Zsa Zsa throws together another peasant dish: a base of beaten chicken eggs, with minced dried shrimp, salted duck egg, and mung bean noodles steamed in the wok. The viewers will never believe that one.

BUT MOSES DIGS the dish. Behind the lenses of his black-framed glasses, his eyeballs bloom with excitement when Genius chopsticks the bright orange yolk of the duck egg and plops it at the center of his plate of rice. Moses doesn't hesitate, he isn't concerned about what Ah-Yeah has given him, he's all trust, and he spears it with his spoon and pops the whole thing into his mouth. "Waaaah!" my mother says. "Such a big bite!" She tells me to feed him some rice to cut the egg's saltiness. But Moses scoops the rice himself. He blows on it, then snaps at the spoon. Zsa Zsa and Genius laugh. Isn't he clever! When he's here his spoon skills are far more advanced than they are at the Sass house. As if he's motivated to achieve when Zsa Zsa's food is in front of him. My parents teach Moses the Chinese words for all the ingredients in the egg dish. He picks up the Chinese effortlessly. With his every Chinese utterance, whether at their prompting or his own spontaneous ejaculation, Genius and Zsa Zsa crow about his blossoming linguistic talents, comparing his development favorably with mine at the same age. I hear in their praise of their grandchild censure of me, their deficient, less talented son. Never do they say, "He's a chip off the old block. At his age you were already pressing shirts, making our lives more tolerable." I do not understand why it happens this way; the bitterness I feel now like the sourest thing in my mouth isn't directed at my parents, but is heaped on my son's little, spectacled head. Under that grimy film of feeling, I know that the boy is blameless, that he's caught in the line of fire. But holding this in my head doesn't alter how I maintain my emotional ledgers: Genius's playfulness, his and Zsa Zsa's swooning over their grandson's appreciation of their world, his appetite for their food and language are registered as trespasses Moses has perpetrated against me.

This is why Ira is so important; I won't let this happen again; I will see to it that Ira remains pure.

AFTER DINNER Genius is sitting in the forward part of the store, where business is conducted. He is smoking a cigarette, blowing smoke rings at Moses every time he approaches. Then Moses turns, an awkward maneuver, too slow and too many steps for an efficient escape, and runs, chased by the smoke. He flops headlong onto a pile of unwashed sheets on the floor. "Hey, that's unsanitary," I say, though I remember doing the same when I was a kid. But Genius says it's okay. "They're clean. Those devils sleep on them once, then it's time for washing. You should know that." Moses scrambles to his feet, stomps back to Genius, who blows more smoke, and the boy cartoonishly reverses direction and collapses onto the mound of dirty bed linens again, arms closing around the swirls of cotton as I've seen them close around Bliss's long skirts. Genius laughs—another rarity, he laughs only when he's with his buddies—and the smoke seems to catch in his throat, and he starts coughing fiercely, roughly, something lodged inside that he needs to get out.

Moses runs to the man; I follow, bending, my hands on my knees, to look in his face. "What's the matter?" Genius is slumped on the milk crate, his head bowed, still coughing into his chest. He looks at me over the tops of his eyeglass frames. His eyes are moist, the whites screaming red. Moses senses something, as an animal senses a storm well before the first raindrop. He tugs at Genius's pant leg, grabs fistfuls of his shirt front—he looks like a ventriloquist's dummy that has fallen and is trying to climb onto his partner's lap. For his efforts he might pull his grandfather back, shape this stranger into the playful Genius. But Genius stays put. He's stuck in the world of biology gone bad. Coughs, hard breaths, an old heart draped in stillness, and furious lungs. Moses sticks his hand in Genius's face. How grown-up and dexterous he is at the table, but now his hands are bats, flying out of control, his fingers coming away tangled in his grandfather's glasses. Just then Genius looks abruptly youthful: coughing has flushed his cheeks, thousands of capillaries bursting there. "It's no good," he says in Chinese, then packs his lips with his Lucky Strike. Moses immediately reaches for the bright ember—he must think his grandfather's playing again, about to blow a smoke ring. I thrust my hand forward to bend Moses' back, but seeing this sudden snatch at his face Genius jerks his head away, which causes the very mishap I was hoping to prevent. Embers fly. Moses yelps and seems to jump a yard in the air—I see myself soaring from the electric deer fence. And just before his eyes melt to tears, behind those lenses, they are Genius's, staring me down when I was small, Moses-sized, unwanted, sent away.

Zsa Zsa comes running. Moses cries, clutching his wounded hand. I try to help, try to get him to unfold his fingers; I imagine the shallow bright orange hole the cigarette has left in his skin. But he wants to show Genius, not me.

As his grandson slowly peels away his finger to reveal the wound, Genius taps his chest with his fist, a gentle *tap tap tap*. I have no idea what he means by this. He coughs, as Zsa Zsa arrives on the scene, and keeps tapping. Then stops. He appears to deflate, his chin drops to his chest, his shoulders fall.

In the brief moment before recognition, when one has yet to comprehend what has happened, before the helping hands, the screams, the settling in of helplessness, Zsa Zsa and I are frozen, and in the still silence, all I hear is Moses, recovered from his own hurt, tapping his own chest.

Part Three

On earth no feast lasts forever.

— CHINESE PROVERB

Part Three

Chapter 13

A MONTH HAS PASSED since Lung lost his wind and his wife and son thought he was dead. When he came to, he was in a police car, the siren blaring, a mask over his mouth. In the inky corner of the backseat, the boy sat mute, his eyes as big and bright as full moons of fear. After three nights in the hospital, Lung would be sent home, a doctor telling him to stop smoking and to return for more testing the following week.

In the hospital, Lung bangs the call button, clutched in his fist like a dagger held against his chest. He groans. From the bedside chair his wife leaps to her feet. "What's the matter? Where does it hurt?" With her soft, pudgy palm she rubs the front of his hospital gown, just over his bony heart.

"I'm fine, I'm fine," he says. "Leave me alone." He pushes her away. His eyes are embedded in the TV screen as deeply as the cancer is in his kidney, his gaze locked on his son, the monster in the box, the source of his pain.

The shiny cleaver chases the knuckles along the stalk of cabbage, a blur of a blade that slams hard against the cutting board, just shy of his hand. Where did this technique come from? All for show. Americans eat this crap up. And what are they really after? They want to see him slip, see the chink lop off a digit. If he had any real balls, he'd drop his trousers, hoist his dickie bird onto the chopping block and give them a real thrill, something to remember. Lung tries to laugh. But it hurts too much to be funny. Look at him, out for everyone to see. Shameless. Making a fool of himself. Like his dick's already been cut off.

His son finishes the last stalk of cabbage with an emphatic *whomp* of the cleaver. "Wow!" he says, smiling into the camera, eyes as big as Ping-Pong balls. "Velly, velly fast!"

Lung groans again. He reaches for the ache in his side. It screams deep within the walls of his body, then rises to the surface and runs along the dark scar on his flank, the X that marks the spot. The TV screen is the scab of his heart's pain.

"What's wrong? What is it?" his wife pleads. But he knows what she's thinking: He played too roughly with his grandson, a man his age chasing a child and letting the child chase him. No wonder something broke, and that started the terrible coughing, and the coughing shook and tore at the parts that make a man.

What's really wrong is that Sterling, her excellent son, who appears harmless in black-and-white, a nonthreatening few inches tall inside that box, is killing him. To someone glancing in from the hallway, Lung's already a goner, with his gaze stubbornly stuck on the ceiling-mounted set, his eyes like a dead man's rolled to the top of his skull. In a sense he is dead. One can witness only so much ugliness in a lifetime. Then the eyes give out, as anything will, especially if you treat it badly. Eventually a whole body shuts down from the accumulated abuse. Lung has seen his share: This hospital bed is well deserved. But does he deserve that son of his? Why does he have to act that way? Disgrace himself and, worse, his family name. At what age, into what depth of despair must one sink before one realizes life's simplest truth—that it ends, and because it ends, one should live out one's days with as much dignity as possible. For Lung it wasn't until they took the kidney, years ago; he was in the recovery room, speeding back from dark anesthesia, too bright consciousness funneling in, and as he started to comprehend the flood of shadows and smudges of color that lit his head, he was seized by an enormous pain that seemed to levitate his body, and when he came down he was nothing but that body cut in half, sewn together, sutures pulsing beneath pounds of gauze. All around him were his insides, and a strange comfort it was to see his insides on the outside, being able to monitor their work, his blood and urine and food, precious life hanging from clear plastic bags and inching through transparent tubes.

Now this, his flesh and blood on display like a rare zoo creature for everyone to gawk at. He groans yet again at the sight of his son. His greatest discomfort at this moment is not physical, nothing a doctor can cure, unless a doctor cuts his son open and transplants into his chest a pound of dignity.

His wife leaves in a rush to find help. She calls for a doctor in her English, and it occurs to him to stop her; this is a hospital, not an open-air market.

A nurse leads his wife into the room. She glances at the TV set to see what he's watching. "My son," his wife says, thumping her chest.

"No! Really? You're kidding?" Then, patting his knee, the nurse says in that nurse's voice meant to cheer, "Your son? Are you sure?"

He snags the nurse's eyes with his and, turning down the corners of his mouth, shakes his head no, closing his eyes for emphasis.

A NEW DOCTOR enters the room. He is young and neckless. An intern, new meat making the rounds on a Sunday morning. He nods and smiles but doesn't say a thing. He keeps smiling, as he listens to Lung's chest, abdomen, groin. Next he touches him all over, his short, pink fingers typing on his skin. Soon he is joined by a nurse and another new doctor, another kid, this one with lots of shaggy hair and a mustache like the son-in-law in *All in the Family*. He mans the other side of the bed, and together they run their hands over his body; as they work, one doctor grunts, the other hums. Lung keeps his eyes on the TV screen, watching what his life has come to. He pays the doctors little mind—he knows if the hospital is spending two doctors and a nurse on him there's nothing but bad news. They pass Lung's chart back and forth over his body. They exchange sneaky glances. One nods, the other blinks his agreement. Then the nurse says, "You know, he hardly understands any English." Lung understands perfectly what she means: Feel free to talk; without his son here to translate for him, the old guy is as good as under general anesthesia.

The doctors are unmuzzled. The intravenous pyelogram, the blood studies, the urinalysis, the renal arteriography, the films and scans show signs of trouble but are ultimately inconclusive. High sedimentation rate; mild anemia; traces of blood in his urine; a grape-sized mass in his remaining kidney that could be a stone or more disease. "Shouldn't Grandpa be dead?" one of the young doctors says. They rule out exploratory surgery. Too risky and stressful. And what if it is a malignancy, they're not going to remove the kidney and leave him with nothing. The young doctors finally agree on a plan; they will give Lung a drug that might dissolve the stone, if it is a stone, and enable him to pass the mass out with his urine.

Because he is at that age of easy worry, and possesses a dangerous history, and because good news is never delivered by two doctors, Lung doesn't expect that something passing through his dick will save him, change his luck.

A N ESCORT in a flimsy mustard-colored jacket wheels Lung to the hospital lobby, and he is left parked next to a white-haired woman also in a wheelchair, also on her way out. She has her baby-blue ID bracelet on, and from the looks of her, she'd better not take it off, because she'll need it again soon enough, a fellow cancer case sent home to die.

"You're kidding me. Nobody's here for you?" the escort asks.

Hospital policy doesn't allow patients to leave unaccompanied. He didn't want his wife to close the store, and he hated the idea of her roaming the streets alone, unable to read or speak, the little heart in her chest pounding, while she waited for her bus to stop, fearing the ultimate nightmare, getting off too early or too late. So she had to call Sterling. He agreed to bring Lung home, but not without kicking up a fuss. He was too busy, he had his family, they had a second child, and he had to prepare for his stupid TV show. Lung has come all the way from China only to raise a servant for the barbarians. First he cooks for those stinky ladies; now he serves his beloved Jew. It is bad enough Lung has spent his American life a servant, but at least he has a valid excuse, at least according to his children: He's stupid. What's Sterling's excuse? College boy, fancy school. Top pedigree. He likes to point to his head and proclaim how smart he is. How smart is eating shit? That's why he's too busy to come pick up his father. Aren't sons supposed to serve their fathers?

The escort wheels Lung outside, into a patch of sun. Lung hates being in the sun. That's for peasants, their skin toasted brown, work in the fields, eyes sweating, bugs circling their heads. He is thinking he ought to wheel himself into some shade or back inside, but doesn't. The greater his discomfort, the more justified his annoyance toward his son.

STERLING FINALLY DRIVES UP, in his new car. Bright red like the communist flag. Father-in-law's purchase. Wonderful father-in-law! "Sorry, I'm late," he says, popping out from the car. Then he stands there, holding the driver's-side door as if it were the lifeline to his very existence.

"Where's your first son?" Lung asks. "I thought you'd bring Modoy."

Sterling shakes his head. "I didn't say he was coming with me."

Lung rubs his hand across his face. "I know. But I wanted you to bring him."

"You should've said so."

"Since when do you listen to what I tell you to do?"

Like an astronaut leaving the safety of his ship to walk in space, Sterling reluctantly breaks his contact with the car and helps Lung out of the wheelchair, a hand jabbed in his father's armpit. The boy, like his oldest sister, has a hardness to him, but unlike Lucy he is too much of a coward to let it shine through all the time. Of his four children, Sterling has always been the one who would do what was asked of him, but afterward he would hate you for having asked and hate himself for doing something he didn't want to do. Wasn't that how the boy found himself married? Didn't he know he was going to be a father long before he ever considered being a husband? A long time ago Lung warned the boy that fooling around with girls was trouble. Didn't Mo-doy leap from his mother's belly too soon after the wedding? And what a shock that was, the boy's getting married. Especially after he turned down a fine girl like Yuk. Did he think he had found someone better? His wife is a nice girl, but she's no Yuk.

WHEN HE LEFT the hospital the time they took his kidney, he was in far worse shape. He was drugged, barely conscious, his body was yards of gauze and plastic tubing. But once outside, the air was delicious, and once in the laundry he was hungry to work again. What is he, in this country, but work? Without it, he's worthless, he is even more a nobody than he already is: he goes from laundryman to Chinaman. A few days after his return he operated the pressing machines, even though the long scar had not yet closed. Sweat trickled down his ribs, along the red channel of his scar, then over his hip, and down his leg, the thick, white-blood-cell-heavy liquor collecting in his cotton sock, so when he moved, from machine to machine, he would feel a tug at his foot, like an ocean current dragging him in deeper. When he worked, the wound seemed alive, each stitch the leg of an insect crawling within him. He wondered if he had made a mistake, going back to work so soon, letting his body's own acids and waste eat away at the tender cut. But when all you know is work, you work, no matter how difficult or distasteful it is. He has always said that life is good as long as your body is strong and you're able to work. The day to dread is when his usefulness goes. He is nothing once he loses his appetite for work.

LUNG TELLS STERLING to turn left out of the hospital parking lot. The boy looks at his father as if the doctor had cut out his brains. "That's not the way home!" he says in English. Lung taps the dashboard. "Go, go, go!" he says, flicking his fingers. How satisfying, throwing shit back at him. Lung's plan is simple: All he wants to do is see, for one last time, the places of his decade-long American life before his wife's arrival. He does not trust himself behind the wheel anymore, so why not exploit the boy while he has him and his new car.

Sterling straightens his spine, grips the steering wheel with both hands; the hairs at the back of his neck are standing on end: he can dish it out, but he can't take it; he doesn't like his stupid father getting snappish, especially in his fancy car. Sterling speeds out of the parking lot, deliberately forcing his tires to squeal, just to show Lung his irritation. Behind them a car honks, the boy stares at the rearview, his palms pounding the steering wheel, the nose of the red car running up the tail of the black car ahead.

"Big shot," Lung says.

"What?"

"Watch the road!"

The boy swerves, abruptly changing lanes, drawing honks from another car.

"You almost killed us!"

NICE CAR," Lung says. Great father-in-law's car. Not his son's money. But he acts like it's his. Why not? Lung wouldn't mind getting behind the wheel himself. He has never driven such a fancy car. Lung caresses the dashboard. "How long have you had it?"

"You know already!"

Exactly, that's the point of asking. Lung was in the hospital and his son was buying a European luxury car. Weeks have passed, perhaps a whole month, and this is the first time Lung gets a ride in the new car. What a fine son!

The car reeks of self-congratulation; in Sterling's mind it substantiates how far he has traveled from his beginnings. This is why he has resisted letting his father ride in his new car and share in his good fortune—he might drag him back to where he once belonged. He is feeling good about himself, as if his marriage and family were the rarest of things. As if he had invented marriage. As if he were the only man who could have had that wife of his. As if he were no longer the brat Lung used to lift high over his head or the one he smacked until both their souls melded with the ache in the world. Once the boy screamed, his face tear-wet, "You don't love me!" He seemed truly to believe the love he saw on TV existed and to expect the same from Lung. Stupid boy!

Lung brings out a cigar, a White Owl, his new habit since doctors forced him to quit cigarettes. He strips off the cellophane wrapper, twirls the cigar between his lips, and depresses the lighter, and just as he is about to take his first puff, the boy shouts, "Don't do that! Bliss will kill me if she smells smoke in the car."

And that's why Lung lights the cigar: His son frets more about his car and his American wife's delicate nose than his father's health.

"WHERE ARE WE GOING?"

Lung doesn't answer. Why is the boy so nosy all of a sudden? He usually waits for his silver-headed wife to ask the questions. "Just go where I tell you to go." Sterling shakes his head. Why is he so easily irritated? Where did he learn such impatience? Where is the boy in the boy? His pint-sized cute self murdered by the odd person he's become. Look at his brooding, blank eyes. They remind Lung of Sterling as a teenager, at the age when lives are made, leaning against the laundry's plate-glass window, his knee bent, the sole of his sneaker flush to the pane, the building's tons apparently supported by his single standing leg. Shoulders droopy, hand playing with his hair, he would occasionally look up and gaze longingly at the street, perhaps wishing he could hitch a ride in every car streaking past. Out of there.

They are on a road that runs through two counties, a straight line linking town to town. This was the way to Lucy's. Back then, thirty-some years ago, when Lung first took the bus to her place, this was the potato road the farmers took to market. Later, the commuter railroad was built, paralleling its path. The train used to deliver the family into New York, Penn Station, and from there they rode a taxicab to Chinatown. He would treat everyone to noodles and dumplings. Then they would part ways, the boy and Lung to take care of his business, while his wife and the girls visited friends, or got their hair done at a beauty salon. Lung would meet his buddies on the street and they would go for coffee; the men would buy Sterling egg-custard tarts and sponge cake, and Lung would share his coffee with the boy, adding lots of sugar to make it extra sweet for him. On several occasions he took his son on secret trips, to the Empire State Building, the Central Park Zoo, the Statue of Liberty. But he doubts Sterling remembers. Once, on the ferry, he pointed out Ellis Island and told him his mother used to live there. The boy probably thought that island was China itself.

They cover parts of Long Island Lung hasn't seen in decades, not since Sterling was an infant. So much is new. Entire towns. The road is wider. The woods are less dense. Stretches of farmland are now punctuated by gas stations, car dealerships, nurseries, water tanks. In the incorporated areas there are streetlights and telephone poles. When he used to ride the bus to her house, he wondered where the other passengers were going: there was so little life on this land.

Lung tells the boy to pull into a Wesson's hamburger stand on the side of the road and offers to treat him. "That's bad food, you don't want that," his son says, and drives by. Lung doesn't answer, but he remembers that when the boy was little he loved going to the Wesson's a few blocks behind the laundry. Lung used to take him there on the sly, usually after they had run an errand together; they would get off the bus at the hamburger stand, then walk the rest of the way home eating their treats. How does he think he got his taste for American food? But now he is too good for Wesson's. Big chef, big shot.

Lung closes his eyes and imagines he is riding the bus again along this very road. He sees himself as a young man, no older than Sterling, walking (skipping, perhaps), from the bus stop to the slit in the wall of hedges that opens to her house. He sees himself lying in her arms, his cheeks caressed in the cool fabric of her dress, the heat of her thighs rising through it. He hears her humming—so free she and her race are with their voices—songs he would later hear on his radio at home, as if she never left.

"Sorry, Pop! I'm in a hurry. I have to go home. I have to get ready for my TV show. And I'm supposed to take Bliss to the doctor."

Lung pries his lids open. "Doctor? What's wrong? Is she having another baby so soon?"

His eyes are flooded with the boy's full face turned his way. What has Lung done to earn that look of insult that Sterling always wears around him, as though the sky, the trees, the buildings had wronged him?

The car closes in on the row of cars stopped at a red light. Sterling brakes at the very last moment.

"Why are you so distracted?" Lung says. "If you don't want to drive, let me drive. You go where you have to go. Take care of your family."

Which is what Lung has done. At the end of his life, when his body is in the grave, no one can accuse Lung of not having taken care of his family. His work was his love. If he didn't love in other ways, he will have to be forgiven. He has lived three lives. As a boy and son in China; as a husband and father; and in between, as a man in America.

T HE ROAD they are driving used to dead-end. That was how Lung knew he had reached his destination. Where it all ended. He is getting worried he might not be able to find her house again. He keeps a lookout for familiar landmarks—the farms, the farm-stands, the field of weeds, the mounds of gravel and sand, the runaway woods, the tall hedges. He doesn't want to send the boy on the wrong turnoff and give him reason to scold.

Houses. Cultivated fields. Lots of supermarkets and gas stations. Everything has to be fed. He remembers riding the bus to Lucy's, how he always brought her a bag of groceries, which he would keep on the seat next to his, and assess whether she would like what he had bought. He wonders if the boy and his wife are having another baby. He'd just better be careful. The kids start piling up, and before he knows it, he'll be left wondering how life has run away from him.

"Turn here!" he says. There's a large housing development on the right. Back then this was a vast emptiness. What he recognizes now is the fence. Americans are in love with fences. Keeping things in, keeping things out. He used to marvel that someone had gone through the expense and bother of erecting the fence around the vacant lot.

"NOW WHAT?" asks Sterling.

From inside the boy's father-in-law's European car, idling in the driveway, Lung stares at Lucy's house. First of all, he's amazed and impressed he was clever enough to lead them here. "How old are you?" he asks the boy.

"Is that why we're here?" he says, talking in English. "Okay, I'm almost thirty. Why don't you tell me how old you are, and then we can go."

He is surprised by the number of years, though, of course, he shouldn't be. He glances quickly at the boy, shakes his head: Lung has lived this life so long.

Now, in the late afternoon of the day that doctors have said his life should be over, he has come to the house expecting to find her standing once more, in her egg-print dress, pitiless among strangling nature and the ruins of human neglect, the wind blowing through the trees, the sun burning their eyes, as it was that day she stole the baby, when the rain clouds lifted and no one's lashes were dry. He wanted to see her one last time, to take the measure of his life, to calculate the breadth of his regret, and to let her see Sterling, the child she had run off with, and see how little she was actually denied.

Lucy's house has been remodeled. A second story added. The place painted a dark blue, with white trim. Most startling are the two modern-style houses that have been built on the property, two stories high, modest homes, nothing like the fancier ones his customers lived in. Lucy must've sold off some of the land.

Lung pushes out of the car and cuts around the front end. The boy calls after him. "Where're you going?" he asks. "You can't go knocking on people's doors."

"Good idea. You knock for me," says Lung, waving at Sterling to leave the car. "Stranger come to door, you talk best English. You say, My father live here thirty year ago."

"I can't lie. Who'd believe that?"

He knows the boy's mind. Who will believe that this old Chinese guy, whose natural habitat is the back of stores, ever lived in a genuine house?

Lung slides into the car. "See if someone is home," he says. "Then I won't bother you anymore, okay?"

He is surprised when the boy actually obeys. He exits the car in a huff, and he's shaking his head, a bug buzzing inside his skull. Watching the boy drag his feet toward Lucy's house, Lung remembers the first time he was here, how his feet were slow, his heart brimming with pride. To be an immigrant, and to have come so far, so soon. He had arrived.

Chapter 14

A T THE AGE of twenty-six Lung came to America, alone. Before he could leave China, he had to bury his old life. He took care of his filial duty. He first married the girl of his parents' choice, and next left her big-bellied with a grandchild. Once he was gone, he sent home money every month, almost half the American gold he earned heading salmon, picking cotton, rolling cigars, sewing shoes, washing dishes, ironing shirts. He begrudged his parents nothing, their daughter-in-law nothing, their grandchild nothing. His discomforts, humiliations, and bad luck seemed fair exchange for his freedom. Having satisfied his obligations, he was beyond reproach. Not from the dead or the gods. No one could question the integrity of his deeds, the rectitude of the arrangement. His parents could say: Our son is in America, making us all rich; he has given us a splendid daughter, and a grandchild, perhaps even a grandson, is already on the way. We can now die in peace, our duties done.

For nearly a decade he and his bride lived apart. She was not as easily satisfied as his parents or his ancestors. No matter how many years separated the two, she still expected he would honor his promise, and she would join him in America one day. In her letters she reminded him that she alone in all the world called him "husband." At the detention center on Angel Island, off the Pacific coast, he sat in his cell, and because he was scared, he longed for her, missed her; he wondered why he had ever left his month-old marriage. He had bought another man's life, his birth papers, and his brains were crammed with details of that other man's life story, which was now supposed to be his own: He was born in Redlands, California; his father sold pots and pans, hardware and dry goods to miners; in the courtyard of the family home in China there is a fountain with eight goldfish; he was married to the daughter of a dye factory owner. His wife wrote letters addressed to his paper self, a Mr. Wong, the identity of the man whose citizenship papers he had bought, and she signed the letters with the name of his pretend wife. In his cell, after two long months had passed, he would read the latest letter from China, and he would believe he was the paper man and the fake wife was his wife, and at other times he would wonder who was this strange woman who was writing to him. Day and night he watched the land, and decided he would keep his promise and bring her over as soon as he could. He slept poorly, his rest coming during brief naps, his dreams always vivid, his real and fake selves making love to his real and fake wives.

Even more, he craved the land, though its hills seemed no gentler, its air no softer, its trees throwing no more shade than their counterparts at home. He came to love the cold, daily fog of San Francisco Bay, the certainty of its coming and going, its temporary obliteration of the unattainable world. He loved the night, the fog lifting, when he could stare at the lights onshore, pieces of gold.

When he was finally released from Angel Island, his feet set firmly on American soil, he put his pledges and resolutions aside. He was Lung, a new man! But she still wrote letters to her fake husband, to Mr. Wong, in the hand of the fake wife. In these letters she urged him to return home. She was no longer eager for America, not after what he had told her about the long journey and the things he had encountered at its end—the long faces on the people, the long vowels they uttered, their long, enervating stares, the long hours of toil. Why should she leave home and raise her child away from her brand of sanity—the familiar smells, sounds, looks, and flavors; why deny herself an old age surrounded by grandchildren who spoke the language, cooked the food, honored and feared her in equal parts? Why would he go back, after all the trouble of getting here in the first place? And she was right not to want to come. Her fears were justified. He had no intention of taking her away from his parents—she was technically theirs now—but if she had to leave, why not opt for a softer landing, a life in Hong Kong, Malaysia, Singapore, Hawaii, even Cuba?

I N 1943, WHILE THE WORLD was consumed in war, he opened his first laundry business. It was a loser from the start, planted in a bad location. He had walked the streets in the area, the south end of Freeport, on Long Island, and counted the houses. He had hundreds of reasons to believe the laundry would be a success. What he did not realize was that most of these people were also immigrants, saving their pennies, housewives scrubbing their clothes against washboards and ironing their sheets, while tubs of tomato sauce simmered in the yard.

Still, as a one-man operation, he was busy enough. He worked ten hours a day and slept in the rear of the store. He rarely left the premises, except to buy groceries or cigarettes, or to make excursions to Chinatown. Most of his time was spent in the front of the store, in a fifteen-by-fifteen-foot work area. Over the years he wore a triangular traffic pattern on the dark green linoleum-tile floor: from ironing board to linoleum-topped counter—where the transactions with his customers were conducted—to the pine shelves where bundles of clean laundry were stored.

The most demanding chore was ironing. For hours each day he was tethered to the ironing board, and as he swept the hot iron over shirts and sheets, he would stare out the shop window, daydreaming about the world on the other side of the glass. Often he saw himself driving a car, in his suit and hat, honking the horn as he drove past. This particular daydream was so pleasurable he would scorch whatever he was ironing, waking himself to the aroma of burnt cotton.

IT WAS A GLORIOUS AFTERNOON, the sky as blue as the blue of the flag, the clouds as white as its stars, the temperature in the low eighties, the leaves on the trees showing no sign of turning, the car windows down, the women bare-armed and in ankle straps, the servicemen with their cuffs unbuttoned and folded above their wrists. Lung was inside, of course, surrounded by the familiar smells of his sweat, ironed cotton, and cigarette smoke. He was ironing, as usual, his movements automatic, etched deep in his bones, a Lucky smoldering in the glass ashtray at his right hand, when she first cut across his line of sight. He had no reason to notice her out of all the passersby, rare as they were. But he did: her shimmering yellow hair, her dress with the eggs.

He forgot her, until she returned the next day. And the next. Always at the same hour, the shop window's row of red backward letters hitting her across the cheek, partially blocking his view of her, the woman coming to him in pieces. Her hair flew off her shoulders, catching the sun; her mouth gleamed like a freshly skinned knee. With each passing day he noticed more that her gait slowed as soon as she reached the H in

YRDNUAL DNAH SGNUL

and she would turn her head slightly and peer inside. What was catching her eye? The sight of a man ironing another man's shirt? Or the man himself, separate from his work? Was she looking at him because he was Chinese, as others had stared, or because he was something good to look at?

He set a trap to draw her closer, give her a reason to come to a full stop. Then he could steal a full-face look at her. With the first few dollars he had earned with the laundry, he purchased a handsome tea set in Chinatown, plum-red glaze, flowers, and gilt edges, made in Japan. He was planning to ship the set home, as a gift for his wife, but one of his buddies suggested he hold off—perhaps someday he would have the opportunity to give it to her in person, either when he returned to China or when she came to America.

He arranged the teapot and its companion teacups on a wooden milk crate just outside his front door. On that first attempt and again on subsequent days, she stopped and greedily took the bait.

She was different from the other women who came to his store— uniformed servants from the good homes, red-eyed and impatient, smelling of milk and fire. She wore a pretty dress, dark blue with eggs, and he could see her hair was clean from the way it held the sun. She would bring her round, puffy face to within inches of the tea set for the closest possible look. At these moments, with her hand gingerly securing the little white hat she wore tipped at an odd angle, she reminded Lung of actresses he had seen in movies.

He threw open his front door to catch the year's last warmth. September was never like this in China. It was never like this in his earlier years in America. The difference was the work. What work he did now was his. He owned his labor. That was why this season's rains were milder, why sparrows roosted in his store, why the war was winding down in far-off Europe and Asia, why his wife and her daughter had found refuge in the relative safety of Hong Kong. That was why whenever this woman stopped at his open door, she invited his glances and let the breeze carry her scent to him.

THEN SHE STOPPED COMING. And the heavy autumn rains fell, stripping bare the trees. The reason for her absence was probably the rain, but he did not allow himself the luxury of such a simple explanation. As he ironed or sorted the dirty laundry or sat in front of his evening bowl of rice, he wondered what had gone wrong. At the end of these long, wet days he felt wearier, lonelier than ever. In the not-too-distant past he had had work buddies and bunkmates to fill the hours, too much company, in fact no privacy at all; with the opening of Lungs Hand Laundry, he had been too busy and self-satisfied to notice the solitary life he was living. She was just enough companion to satisfy his needs. But he never realized how much he had looked forward to the daily collision of their lives.

ONE NIGHT as he brought in the tea set, the cups brimming with cold rainwater, he thought, She is as invisible as the tea in these cups. Right then, he decided to change his luck. If his bait had real substance, if the cups were filled with tea, she would appear.

The next day he brewed a pot of tea. He would use tea leaves that legend alleged the poet Lu Yu favored—at least that was what the tea merchant had told him. It was a husky, smoky black tea, which yielded a brilliant orange color, reminiscent of the freshest egg yolks. He carefully carried the tea set outside, steam rising from the spout, while drizzling rain rippled against the surface of the golden disks in each cup.

The rain fell harder. The accompanying winds crashed the droplets against the shop window. Lung's plan was a failure. He went to the door, and was about to bring the tea set in, when he changed his mind abruptly. He emptied the cups overflowing with tea and rain, then refilled each with more of the hot tea.

It was a typical fall storm—brooding and black, but over by late afternoon. The sun burned through the heavy clouds and warmed the sidewalk, steam rising off the pavement like threads of fog. In the wake of the clouds, she suddenly appeared. Under a blood-red umbrella, her orange legs slashing through the flaps of her raincoat, she slowed and, as before, took inventory of the items on the milk crate: the sodden white handkerchief, the teapot, the twin teacups holding miniature liquid suns.

Without hesitation she pinched a teacup between her fingers and brought it to her nose and sniffed. When she tasted the tea her face closed like a fan. She then emptied the rest of the cup on the sidewalk, her expression radiant with insult.

She glanced into the store. In that instant, just as the long curls of her shoulder-length hair settled back into place, the yellow framed against the umbrella's red, their eyes locked like chain links, and into her face, as round and pink as a chrysanthemum, he stumbled. A smile split his face, and feeling the corner of his mouth stretch and burn, he flushed with shame for forgetting himself in this way, showing his teeth—how foolish he must look. And as if she knew he was too flustered to see her clearly, she dropped the teacup nonchalantly into her purse and walked away.

Lung hurried to the door. She rushed down the block, umbrella open across her back, her feet, which barely touched the ground (so tall were her shoes), kicking up the hem of her egg dress. He gave no thought to the stolen cup, his wife's tea set broken up. He did not see a thief making her getaway.

ON THE FOLLOWING DAY he replaced the stolen teacup with another. There had been eight in the set. She came again, on that breezy afternoon, and he watched as she pinched, sniffed, drank, then emptied a teacup on the pavement. As she stole another cup, she waved, and when she made her escape, he rushed to the door; his first thought was that her dress was made of cotton: with its simple lines it would be easy to iron, and he was undaunted by the long row of buttons that ran from between her shoulder blades to the bottom of her spine, each button as white and big and round as the flesh of lichee fruit.

For five more days she came and stole a cup, one each day. He was down to his last teacup. And once that teacup disappeared, so would she. On that final day he was determined to take her in fully, the other teacups payment for this privilege, the price for one last lingering look at her downy arms, chunky calves, flamboyant hair, and the purple birthmark on her arm like China on a map. Lying on his cot some nights, he imagined touching her, not on the soft, white, elastic skin, but there on the dark, chaste spot, a button that once pressed would spring open a trapdoor to oblivion.

Unaware of the significance of the occasion, she arrived, filched the teacup, and left. As was his habit, he ran to the door once she departed. By now, she had to know he did this; she must have felt his eyes swarm her. Their time together was dwindling. Tomorrow she would come looking for more; she would snatch the teapot, and after that he would have nothing left that could hold her.

LUNG SET THE TEAPOT alone on the milk crate. He did not bother filling it with tea. Having to lift and empty a full pot of tea would only annoy her.

She arrived wearing a light tan coat over her dress. She raised the teapot to her face, appraising it in the same way she did each of the teacups, as if she were going to buy. Just as the teapot was on the verge of vanishing inside her coat, she found his eyes on her. And now she stared back. Their gazes bumped. She smiled and looked down at the teapot cradled in her arms like a baby, and left.

But she was no more than ten paces removed from his life when he saw his way back in: a tear at the back of her dress, a clean right-angle rip, the fabric snagged on a nail, leaving a triangle of air through which, as through a keyhole, he spied otherwise hidden inches of her legs. Lung hurried into the store, and from behind the counter retrieved his sewing kit in the red tobacco tin.

Outside again. She was nowhere in sight, and while lost hope at first froze his legs in mid-stride, he quickly recovered, remembering from her other departures that she always turned left at the end of the block. He ran, reached the corner, and sped after her with the softest of steps. She must have heard him, his hard breaths catching her from behind, because she spun around, squealed, "No!" and quickened her gait.

Even though she could not see him, he waved for her to stop. Let him close the hole in her hem and prove his worth to her. "How you?" he said finally. He was so amazed words had tumbled past his lips that he came to an immediate halt.

She seemed equally stunned by his voice, its sudden emergence, as if from the jaws of a dog. She looked over her shoulder at him, twisting her neck at an impossible angle that showed her freshly bloodless face full-on.

She tried to escape, twisting her body violently, but with the forceful first stride forward she burst the ankle strap of her shoe. She stumbled, and like a heavenly chicken, the teapot leapt from her arms and soared through the air.

WHILE SHE KNELT near the broken pieces, he came up behind her and took a handful of the dress's hem, fanned on the sidewalk. Touching her skin could not be any more exciting than touching her dress just then.

He carefully searched for the hole, his fingers prying open the smooth folds of the fabric. She seemed indifferent to his proximity, to his hands, to his impudence, which surprised him even more than it apparently surprised her.

When he found the rip in her dress, he pushed his hand through the hole, so she could plainly see what the matter was, why this strange man was latched to her dress. Lung opened the tobacco tin, and as he fumbled for a needle he realized he needed to iron the fabric before he could properly mend it. He wanted to tell her to stand and follow him back to the laundry and let him sew the hole closed. But when he summoned his tongue this time, it was stuck in his throat, and when he finally did manage to speak, it came out in rapid-fire Chinese, his scarce English the language of commerce and daily survival, and this was love and lust, desperation and desire that shaped these words. Of course, she did not understand. All she knew was that she was a thief, and that the man detaining her was the man she had stolen from.

A WEEK PASSED before she showed up at the store again. This time she walked in and onto the countertop unloaded pounds of brilliantly white mother-of-pearl buttons, a slippery pile of polished rice. Then she left. For the next seven days the same thing happened, her appearance, the cascade of buttons, the wordless departure. By the weekend he had an impressive stash, which he kept stuffed in mismatched socks, a dozen lumpy feet piled in an empty starch crate.

When she showed up next, she came empty-handed. She stood opposite the cash register, leaning her elbows on the counter, as if with the buttons she had bought herself that spot.

He ironed, sorted, marked, wrapped, shelved, and paused only to refill her cup or offer her a light. He was afraid to stop work, because she might leave if there was nothing for her to watch. She said her name was Lucy, and she drank his tea (with spoonfuls of sugar), smoked his cigarettes, and talked incessantly. When she talked she used her hands, pointing at things, gesturing, pantomiming actions, to help Lung understand. She liked to comment on the things she saw him do, and named the parts of a shirt or each action of his hands. He was shy about looking at her directly, but she demanded that he do so, constantly teasing his eyes up to her lips, in order to watch words form. Hers was a loud, sonorous voice that made his hands tremble; once he wasted nearly an hour ironing a tuxedo shirt because her voice made the complicated ruffles and pleats on the front impossible to manage. When she wasn't there he found himself reciting the nouns and verbs she had put to the objects and deeds. Soon he was practicing diligently, unaware of the silliness of the repetitions, touching a shelf and saying, "Shelf," a bundle of laundry and saying, "Bundle." Doing so made his chores seem less arduous; a newness permeated the familiar. Work felt worthwhile, of a piece.

One day Lucy did not appear. And he was utterly surprised by the chaos that overran him like fever. He couldn't work. He stood by the door smoking, staring in the direction from which she came. He felt the door against his spine and thought "Door," the cigarette between his lips and thought "Lucky," but he could not name the riot inside. Until then she had not named what she could not put a finger on, what a person could not see. "Fold," he thought, as in "Now you're folding a sleeve." His insides were folding onto themselves like paper, crease after crease, one sharper than the last, and the deeper her absence the tighter the folds, and if he did not slow the folding soon, his insides would fold into a dense dice-sized cube. Without her he would shrink into something no bigger than that.

L UCY HAD A JOB at the button factory not far from Lung's store. She worked as a sorter, picking through button lots for imperfections—missing holes, odd shapes, off colors. On her way home she had to pass the laundry in order to reach her bus stop. But the button factory had laid her off, which explained her weeklong absence from the store. The country did not need as many buttons, she would later claim, now that the war was coming to an end. Lung was dubious of this. He had not seen an increase in business; the men and their dirty shirts were still away at war. After picking up her last paycheck, she came to Lung's store. She insisted she did not care about losing the job. It was "stupid people's work." She would miss the money, but "not as much as you think, because I wasn't pulling that check that long enough to get used to it being there."

She leaned across the counter, reaching for Lung's Luckys. He handed her the pack. He did not mind her smoking his cigarettes, but wondered whose she was smoking when she wasn't smoking his.

Lung was hungry. Usually Lucy left after a half-hour, forty-five minutes, and he could retire to the back of the store and fix something to eat. But today she lingered, talking, naming things, singing. When she ran out of things to say, she liked to sing along with the radio. He loved when she did this, her voice so confident, so firmly American, and in that way, so starkly different from his.

"Change it, change it!" she said, waving her cigaretted hand. The song had ended, the news had come on, and she hated the news.

Another time he might have jumped to satisfy her. Most days he did. But he was hungry, and daydreaming about what to eat. Steak, pork chops. A friend in Chinatown had set him up with extra rations. And she was all that stood between him and his supper. He wanted her to leave, but feared she might never come again.

Without asking if he minded, she stomped past the counter and into the private area where he worked and lived, and turned the radio dial until she found satisfaction. In this case, Frank Sinatra, whom Lung liked because she liked him and because she had shown him his picture in a magazine, and Lung was pleased the singer was as skinny as he.

She was standing next to the shelves of laundry, her ear close to the radio, nodding, the little red hat bobbing in her yellow hair like a pomegranate on water. She sang, tapping her foot, swinging her hand in time to the music. It was strange having her there, where she wasn't supposed to be. His feelings now were the same as those that raged inside him when he had first touched her dress, let its silkiness melt through his fingers, and again when he had ironed the torn fabric, with her sitting on the ironing board, smoking a cigarette, legs crossed, the hem held high, exposing the seams someone had drawn up her calves to the backs of her knees. As he ironed and sewed, how his hands had trembled; he had to hold his breath to steady himself, to make himself as inconspicuous as possible.

Now she snapped her fingers to a new song coming through the radio. He was astounded by the little explosions, like firecrackers, and stirred, awakened from the spell. She must have seen a change in his face, because she then took two quick steps toward him, and pulled him away from the ironing board.

In the middle of the work area, on the floor covered with piles of dirty laundry, they danced. Lung did not move his feet, just held her hand, the tips of her fingers up to the second knuckle gripped in his sweaty fingers. While he was paralyzed, though everything inside him was furiously in motion, Lucy was the dance: singing along, wagging her head, kicking her legs, tossing her skirt, like an actress in a movie musical.

A slow song came on the radio, a woman singing. Something in the music softened Lucy's face, the lines filling in, her lemon hair falling, each strand seemingly weighted down with sadness. She reached for his hand and pressed it to her hip. In the next breath she stepped into his arms. She started to rock from side to side, slowly.

He moved as she moved, not thinking about what he was doing. All that was left of him was his violent heart. Otherwise, his consciousness was the heat of her body, the soft flesh on her hip, her staggering size. She was not much taller than he, but she was such plenty. He could press and press against her body and never meet resistance. Their dance, while covering very little of the floor, was to Lung like driving in a car of his own. And most certainly he was going places.

ONCE THE SONG ENDED, Lung locked the shop and led her to the rear, into his kitchen, where he cooked them something to eat—a pot of rice, fried steak, cabbage with dried shrimp. Again, she watched him work. When the steaming dishes were spread out on the table, and she was seated at his right elbow, he was no longer hungry. Or at least his appetite was not for food.

He was an excellent host. He cut the steak into bite-sized pieces and poured ketchup on top. She asked for a fork and, with it, piled her bowl of rice high with the meat. He resisted thinking she was greedy;

she was what she was, and this was the way Americans ate. He tried to educate her, teach her proper etiquette, taking only as much as he could eat in each bite.

She did not seem surprised to be sitting in a kitchen, at the rear of a Chinese hand laundry, adjacent to a Chinaman at his steel table, which any patriotic American would have donated to the war effort as scrap metal. Lung could not get over the sight of her in his living quarters; he told himself she wanted to be here—not that she had no better place to go. Lung chewed but had difficulty swallowing, and eventually stopped trying. He brought her a cup of water, then whiskey in a shot glass, then coconut candies and fruit jellies in rice paper. When she saw he was in a generous mood, she pointed behind him at the Henry VIII roasted chicken on the shelf that served as his pantry. When he turned, following her hand, he immediately saw what she wanted. He had bought the can because he saw other shoppers at the market doing so, and his plan was to send it as part of a package to China. Without hesitation he swept it off the shelf, and was about to pierce the lid with an opener, when she stopped his hand: She wanted to take the Henry VIII back home with her. She motioned for the can and set it on the floor at her feet, between her legs. "Thank you," she said. Then she instructed him to say, "You're welcome." But he knew this. When he first set foot in this country he already knew not to speak unless spoken to, and to be polite to Americans, and that the only sentiment he should show them was gratitude.

"You are welcome," he said.

LATER HE WAS GRATEFUL when she claimed she had missed the last bus home. She wanted to go into the village to see a movie. *One Body Too Many.* He loved the possibility of being seen with her, walking the twenty minutes to the theater, buying two tickets, and finding seats next to each other. Everyone would stare, just as he stared at drivers and their cars outside his shop window. But who would look on him as an object of envy except someone as needy as himself? He knew it was not wise for them to be seen in public together.

So she went alone. Minutes after she left, he regretted not having gone. He had turned his back on good fortune. If it never found him again, he could blame no one but himself; he had unlocked the door and let her get away.

His hand burned now with the heat of the iron, not the skin beneath her dress. He kept seeing her escape down the street, never looking back. She said she would return, but he tried not to believe her. What reason did she have to come around anymore? She no longer worked nearby, and she had her last paycheck. She had even taken the stupidly precious can of chicken with her.

HE WAS SLEEPING when she tapped at the plate-glass window. His dream was chaste—he was counting the eggs on her dress, pressing each with the tip of his finger—and yet when he woke, he was terribly excited. He let her in. On the street out front was a car with two men inside, its engine running. When she walked past him into the store, she smelled of beer. A man called from the passenger-side window, "What's in *there,* honey?" Lung put his shoulder to the door and turned the key. As the tires spun noisily from the curb, a large object was thrown from the car in the direction of the store. Lung flinched. It thudded on the sidewalk, the can of Henry VIII roasted chicken, then rolled into the gutter.

"Where can I sleep?" she said. "I just want to sleep, okay?"

He let her have his cot, and he would sleep on the ironing board. When she used his bathroom he stood outside the door and listened to the sounds she made, marveling at the differences—the male and female difference, the American and Chinese difference. When she exited from the bathroom, he was standing so close to the door that he was certain she knew he had been spying on her. Yet she did not appear flustered or angry when she stepped around him and nodded with a nonchalance that told him she had expected him to be there, like a dog left to wait at a designated spot.

THE STORE WAS DARK. He lay wide awake, not because the ironing board was uncomfortable—in fact, it was more commodious than the cot—but because he was uncomfortable inside his body. He kept returning to the dream he had had earlier in the night. The more he thought about the dream, the more he came to realize that he was counting the eggs on her dress in his parents' home in China. That meant the bed he had dreamed she was lying on was his marital bed. Who, then, was under the dress? Whose body had he felt through the flimsy cloth, so warm and forgiving to the touch? He had assumed the woman was Lucy, but perhaps he had arrived at that opinion because hers was the face he saw upon waking. Could it be he was dreaming of his wife then? Was it her body underneath the eggs that excited him so?

He had to find out. He tiptoed to the kitchen and retrieved a memorial candle, the kind lit to illuminate the way to the spirit world (even in America he could not escape his obligation to remember his ancestors with food, wine, and incense). The yellow flame and red wax guided him to Lucy. He knelt beside the cot, and gently folded back the blanket, and counted the eggs.

Though his fingertip barely grazed the fabric, he could clearly discern the textures in the rayon's fine weave, the fire in the eggs' ash-white glow. She was sleeping on her back, her arm slashed awkwardly across her face, her wrist bone resting in the well of her eye. In the candlelight her skin glowed golden yellow, her hair spread on his pillow flaring like an orange crown. He started with the eggs on her shoulder. On one short sleeve he counted nineteen. He touched the eggs across the square neckline, left to right, then counted the next row the other way. In this fashion he slowly zigzagged down the front of her dress, but he kept losing count, his concentration evaporating the farther south his finger traveled.

When they had danced earlier, her scent was sweat and cigarettes. Now she smelled strongly of beer and perfume. His buddies said American women perfumed their bodies because they hated themselves. He could not believe that of her. Counting and recounting the eggs lying over her softest parts, he was frightened when she rolled her neck and her hand fell off her face, and she momentarily pried open her lids and looked at him. Even in that dim light, all things shimmered. And as crusty reality shivered into her just-opened eyes, she blinked once, then replaced her hand and succumbed to sleep. She had to believe she was dreaming. Just as he, in these minutes too precious to count, was living a dream.

Chapter 15

FROM THAT DAY ON, she stopped coming to the store. Lung had to go to her.

She lived far from men, at the end of the line, her house invisible from the road, set among a stand of towering oaks (he thought *ook,* the Chinese for "allergy," when she pointed out the trees), in a lot overrun by uncut grasses and untended weeds. The house was cocooned in vines. Inside, it was musty and dark, the paint on the walls peeling, the floor-boards warped, the chairs missing backs and nails. But he liked being there because hers was the first American house he had entered, with its pitched roof and windows that opened and closed. Years later he would find insult in a drawing his six-year-old son made when asked by his teacher to draw a picture of where he lived: an American house, a box with a triangle on top, not the flat-roofed square in which the boy and his family lived and worked. So young, and the poor boob was already making distinctions, staking out what he wanted and what he wanted to deny. Although Lung understood the boy's instincts, he tweaked his ear and led him outside, to the middle of the street, and forced him to face the truth, the harsh reality that was life inside a store, and forget the home of his imagination.

He felt special inside her house, even though he preferred his solid milk crates to her rickety chairs, and was frightened to death of her crazy dog, as blond as a mourning suit, the beast barking and snarling every time Lung stood up.

HE WAS ON THE BUS to Lucy's. It was a month since she had stayed the night at the store. He visited her on Mondays, his work somehow lighter those nights. But from the start she did not seem as happy as she had seemed in the laundry. He could not tell why. She smiled less, she no longer wore the flattering dresses, the tall shoes, she did not talk as much, whereas in the past words floated out with her every exhalation. Often he brought a bag of groceries, roast pork, soy sauce chicken, bok choy, things he purchased on his Sunday excursions to Chinatown. Before long she started telling him to buy her soap, beer, Quick Soup, Colgate toothpaste. He might cook for her, wash and iron her clothes. Lucy loved having her things ironed; she said it was "luxurious." And he would try to please her, standing for hours pressing her bed linens and blouses. It was work on top of work, but he lost himself in the challenge of her garments, maneuvering the tip of the iron up and down tight pleats, along darts in bodices, with the ultimate goal of a dress or blouse that on a hanger looked as if a woman were inside, pushing at the seams. Or as he had done the week before, he might cut her weeds and grass, on his hands and knees, with the scythe he found in a shed in her yard. Or he might repair her chairs.

On the seat next to him were today's two shopping bags. In one, a wedge of winter melon, some meat, and a quarter of a roasted duck; in the other, a gallon of paint and two paintbrushes for her walls (though she would have preferred a gift of stockings, which she had asked for in nylon or rayon, not cotton).

As the day's last light filtered through the bus's dirty window, he reread the letter he had received from China that morning. She was hoping to join her sister in Hong Kong soon. She regretted leaving his parents, but they were determined to stay in their village, they were not afraid of the communists. Didn't he fear for her safety, for his daughter Oi Ling's safety? Wouldn't they be safer farther from the communists? Why stop in Hong Kong, why not continue on to America? He looked away from the letter. He did not need to read another word. He remembered too well what she wrote next: "Why did you have to marry me?" This made him angry. What more did she want? He already mailed money to her every month in an envelope. He spent his days in stiff, hard-soled leather shoes, standing for hours on an incomprehensibly hard floor to support her. He hardly drank or gambled. His lusts were few. In polite, respectful terms, she had once written that he was a man without passion. Perhaps he was. Perhaps she was right when she accused that that was the reason he had refused to bring her to the Beautiful Country. Her idea of passion was the body, making more babies. It was different for him, but he had no way of explaining it to her. If she could only see him on this bus, speeding through the distances, or better yet, see all the cars on the roads, then she might begin to understand. He was passionate about dominion, admiring the cage that holds the bird more than the bird itself, the tractor that levels the land rather than the land.

He returned to the letter and read to the end. As he folded it his eyes snagged on the salutation at the top of the blue paper. The letter wasn't addressed to him anyway. How should he know why "Mr. Wong" married her?

HE PICKED HIS WAY through the hedges and trees, and inside the house her insane dog barked. That meant she knew he was here, and would be expecting him. So he hurried to the car. After a month of weekly visits he hated to admit to himself that what he liked most about coming here was the 1936 model Ford. It belonged to a friend, she said, and it stopped running the day after he went away to war, in the Pacific. She was vehement Lung keep his distance from the car. But how could he? It was love at first sight. That was how it had been since he first saw a car, in China, an ancient heap of metal, noisy and slow, but it sped through his boy eyes and into his boy body and rolled up his veins, its thumping engine force that drove his desire for America. He hurried to the car, its broken locks, and sat in the driver's seat and pretended he had just driven up in it. He loved getting behind the steering wheel, his body barely fitting the wells his predecessor had rubbed into the leather. He turned the wheel, hand over hand, all the way to the right, taking pleasure in its rubbery resistance. His favorite was letting go, the wheel spinning briskly, in lovely release.

THEY WERE SITTING on the porch, at the rear of the house. He loved the old couch; he owned nothing so big and luxurious. Those dimensions and materials, all in the name of comfort! It did not matter that the cotton batting billowed from the upholstery, that the springs dug into the backs of his legs. This was the best part of the evening. In the darkness, listening to the sound of her voice, the cars racing past on unseen roadways. It was warmer tonight than it had been all week. But cold weather would be upon them soon enough, and their hours on the porch over. His first time on the porch she pointed at a wall of trees, to the source of a noise in the distance. "That's the ocean," she said. His eyes were fixed on her finger. "No, genius, listen," she said, touching her ear. He heard nothing. "That! Don't you hear? The ocean!" A faint swishing sound, then another, and another, then silence. He nodded, touched his ear, I got it! *"Ai hoy,"* he said, "big sea," though it didn't sound like any ocean he was familiar with. But then, most things were somewhat different here—the cattle, the taste of the pork, the behavior of the children. Why not the sea? He was excited, he wanted to see the ocean. He asked her to show him the way. She laughed, and did not stop until she was choking on her tears. "You *are* a real genius, aren't you?" She laughed again. "And the salt air you smell? Well, that's gasoline." They were more than twenty miles from the closest beach. Car tires on an invisible highway were the breaking waves. "Boy, you're a genius, all right." When he learned what *genius* meant, he was so fond of its definition he wanted her to call him that all the time. His American name, one he could grow into.

She was not talking much tonight, except at dinner, because she loved the duck, and did not tire of telling him so. Now he wished she would say something or, better yet, sing. That would make all the difference. He could think that she was happy, and that she wanted him here, and that it was all right to keep close in his heart the night he counted two hundred seventy-nine eggs on her dress.

He watched her smoke a cigarette. The sight of her smoking made him not want to smoke. Her feet were up on the sofa, and she was hugging her knees to her chest and staring straight ahead. He also looked out at the yard. Even at night he could see (and she too had to see) how much he had transformed the place. The tidy lawn, the trimmed trees, the patched shed roof, the porch itself, rescued from vines. There were holes on the roof to find and patch, windows to repair, walls to scrape and paint. He glanced at her, wondering if she saw what he saw, his hand everywhere. Look at her! Did she notice that she also had changed? Her face and arms and hands appeared plumper, thanks to the groceries he brought and the meals he cooked for her.

"I think you should leave," she said, her eyes searching for his reaction, though she barely turned her head.

Where was he supposed to go at this hour? He had taken the last outbound bus here, and the next bus back in wouldn't be until morning, six-thirty. Daylight was a bright, abrupt accusation. No matter how many times he told himself during the previous sleepless nights that she was his American wife, and what they did or he did were things that any wife could expect and respect, the bus ride home was torture. The sun pouring through the window, the bus driver's casual rearview glance, each new passenger's bleary-eyed stare was filled with hatred. On his first visit to her house, he accepted her invitation to her bed. It seemed right that she would ask and that he go to her. He was a nervous bridegroom. Her dog barked and whimpered just outside the bedroom. It threw itself against the door, a loud thump that sent his heart racing and hot sweat pouring over his skin. This did not help matters. He was so excited. He had never thought he would be horizontal in her house, with his eyes closed, his brains swimming in the soapy fragrance that floated just above her skin and then in the stinging perspiration underneath. Everything happened and ended quickly. At the start, she gasped and told him, "No, no." Then, "Come on, come on." Some moments he wasn't sure if he was inside her. He was certain he was still himself and he had not exited, but amid the barking, the thumping against the door, his nerves, her words, he felt nothing. Either he had shrunk to a little boy, or she was as open as a canyon is wide. Different anatomy, he thought, on this side of the world. It was over, yet in his mind he was not sure if he was—the climax, in the general agitation of the moment, was more like a cough in a stream of dry sneezes. Afterward he did not sleep. He lay in the dark listening to his heart crashing in his chest, her rapid, mechanical breaths, the click-clack of the dog's nails, its damp lapping of its private parts, the walls creaking, the wind in the trees, and the noise inside his head. He was awed at the size of his nonexistence. How he was nowhere, barely noticed in the solid world, unpresent in the world of sleep. Governments did not know him, his own daughter did not know him, his own wife addressed him by another's name, his presumptive wife hardly felt his presence.

On subsequent nights under her roof, Lucy insisted he and the dog swap places, Lung on the couch, the dog in the bedroom. Lung still could not sleep, even though he no longer had to listen to her frenzied breaths or the dog's licks or its pacing in front of the door. The noise inside his head was as loud as ever.

For this reason, had it not been for the lack of transportation, he would not have minded leaving, as she seemed to desire for him to do. "You're fooling with the car again," she said. "Don't even try to tell me you're not. Lying'll only make matters worse."

"I fix for you."

"Oh, you're a mechanic now! Is that it, Genius?"

He did not know what *mechanic* meant, and assumed it was a good thing. How was it that she always spoke in such rough tones when she was conferring good words on him?

"Too bad you're not a doctor too," she said, looking straight ahead at the moon in the yard. "Too bad you're not Jesus Christ raising the dead. Too bad you're not Danny, back from the dead." She took a long puff on her cigarette. "Too bad you are only what you are, and not anybody's daddy."

HE WAS ON HIS WAY HOME. He wasn't afraid of walking. In the past he had walked, it seemed, the length of entire states. The only thing he feared along the dark, desolate road was the solitary passing car, because he knew that unless he was useful to Americans, he was hated.

His toes were damp and cold. Dew had soaked through the shoe leather. After the first hour, his legs tired, and every step he took was another step closer to China, the strides he had made in America undone. He felt his body flush with his exertions, a mild coat of sweat lubricating joints, extremities, even his brain. He was thinking about what she had said. At least, that is, the words he had understood. *Daddy.* There was one he recognized. Another of the ways they said *baba.* Why was she putting that good word on him? Why the tears once she did? Why the explosion that followed the tears? "Go, go!" she had shouted, and stomped into the house, as if admonishing herself to leave.

It was dark in front of him, on his left the damp road, on his right an empty field. The air behind was graying with soft dawn light. A car headed in the direction from which he had just come passed him, its tires swishing on the blacktop. As he did with every passing car, he turned and looked, just to make sure he was safe: the round red tail-lights receded into the unlit distance. But this car's shone brighter than the others, and this car slowed. And before he had fully comprehended what was happening, the car reversed direction, its headlights suddenly flooding his eyes.

He was walking faster than he had ever walked, ignoring the bright new sores on the soles of his feet. His breath was in his way, the steam from his lungs blocking his view of the road. The car pulled up along-side him, its driver slowing to match the speed of his gait. Out of the corner of his eye, through the thickening puffs of steam, Lung saw the passenger-side window lowered, a bare-headed man framed in the open-ing. "Where you coming from?" the man said. Lung would not look at the car or the men inside. But they were at once familiar and anony-mous, which was how Lung processed most Americans, especially the men. These could easily have been the same men who had dropped off Lucy at the laundry, or they could be an entirely different pair of trou-blemakers. "Hey, didn't you hear me? Where you coming from? What's the matter, no speakee English?" From the far side of the car the driver made ching-chong noises, those embarrassing, inept approximations of Chinese that signaled danger. Lung quickened his pace and resisted the temptation to show himself to the men, stare at them full-on, and spit in their faces. Which was exactly what they would do, if given the chance.

The passenger door opened, and a man stumbled out and landed hard at Lung's feet, blocking his flight. The man scrambled to his knees, grabbing Lung's slacks, fighting to find his balance. "Don't you ever . . ." he said, and yanked brutally at the loose fabric. As he pulled Lung toward him, the man rose and rammed his skull into the soft meat between Lung's belly and his sex. Lung fell backward, as if propelled by the wind knocked out of him. His head bounced off the packed-dirt shoulder of the road. The man's smooth leather shoe smacked, loud and wet, against Lung's side, over and over, each collision punctuated by a fierce exhalation, "Jap! Jap! Jap!" Stupid man, Lung thought, and the last thing he heard, just as the shiny black shoe met the side of his face,

"Go back to where you came from." Then a flash of whiteness exploded in his eyes.

W HEN HE CAME TO, he struggled to his feet, his side aching, as if something sharp and metallic were embedded there, and with each step he took, his muscles and organs seemed to close around it. He was not far from a bus stop, and when he arrived he sat on the ground and waited, his head in his hands, a mouth-watering pain at the back of his eyes. It was bound to happen, he thought. Their children throwing stones and rotten eggs at his windows, rapping on the glass for his attention, showing their tongues, pulling their eyes into slits. Their fathers no different. Unwilling to share the sidewalk, always cursing, spitting, wagging their fingers at him. Only worse since the start of the war. Those Americans, always mistaking him for a Japanese. And those damn Japanese, killing Chinese no matter what continent they're on. Whom should he hate more?

Chapter 16

H E WAS FITTED for eyeglasses in three months' time. Even before the beating he had been worried about his vision, the long view having become blurry. But since the incident the opposite was true. He had difficulty seeing what was right in front of his face—shirt seams, the outline of pockets. He was leaving wrinkles and, worse, pressing unwanted creases into the fabric. Customers complained.

The eyeglass frames were heavy and black. While they obscured the tips of his steeply pitched brows—in his opinion, his face's most striking feature—they enhanced the already intense darkness and density of his hair. How strange he looked. He was, in such small ways, a new man. In the weeks before he finally visited the optometrist, he could not see himself clearly in the shaving mirror anymore. Morning after morning his reflection grew cloudier, and soon he was content to let that man fade away. What good was he? It was best to start his American life over. Now, with his new eyes, in a vastly different sense, he did not recognize himself. During this period he rarely thought about Lucy. Fear had blunted desire. The less his body ached, the less she occupied his mind. By the time he corrected his damaged vision and was seeing clearly again, she was, literally and figuratively, nowhere in sight.

THE WINDOWS WERE LAYERED with dense condensation, the frigid air on the outside of the thick pane meeting the lovely warmth within. If it was snowing outside, Lung wouldn't know it. He was listening to one of his Chinese opera records, *The Bride with the Purple Hair:* the betrayed wife was about to disguise herself as a man in order to spy on her unfaithful husband. The brass bell above the door rang. Even where he stood at the rear of the work area, sorting and marking dirty laundry, he braced for the inrush of cold air, as he did whenever someone entered the store. He clutched again when he heard her voice, the muscles in his chest and throat gripping. He did not quite believe his ears, and he did not believe his eyes, but when he took off his glasses, he saw plainly it was she.

"You look funny," Lucy said.

AT THE TIME, he had been wearing glasses for only about a month, so he had every reason not to trust his sight. A little later, he did not trust his hearing, his ability to understand English. Under a fur hat, worn low on her brow, with cheeks burnt as bright as tangerines by wind, and lips purple with cold, she did not look like herself. She looked even less herself when she said she was carrying a baby in her belly, for four months now. She opened her brown overcoat and patted her sweatered midsection; he removed his glasses and blew on the lenses. What was he supposed to see? Why was she here? Except for aches that were the by-product of his labor, his body was feeling no pain. He had survived, but she was trying to pull him back in.

When he did not respond, or respond in the manner she was hoping for—at least, this was how things appeared to him—she added, "You better care. It's your baby."

It was impossible. Their intimacy was passionate but brief. How could he have given her a baby? Didn't he need to be inside the whole time? He no longer remembered her smell, her taste. The sweet pressure. He refused to believe her.

"Take those glasses off," she said. "You look silly. I liked you better the other way." She approached; she was going to do it for him. But he would not let her. When she reached for his eyes he jerked his head from her gloved hand. He waved at her: "No more, no more!" He retreated to the back of the store, and in the kitchen picked canned goods off his pantry shelf and filled a brown paper bag with them.

When he returned to the front, he found that she had turned off the phonograph and switched on the radio, replacing his Chinese opera with one of her singers. He showed her the contents of the bag. "For you," he said.

"That's not what I came for," she said.

He shook his head and hurried to the ironing board, then wrapped white twine around the bag, transforming it into a more manageable bundle for her to carry.

"Okay," he said. "You go." He turned off the radio and put the package in her hands, and pushed her toward the door. "Go, go! I have too much work!"

"Don't touch me!" she said, shrugging his hand off her shoulder. "Yellow bastard! I'll call the cops on you. I'll tell them what you did to me."

H E BEGAN a new regimen. On Mondays and Fridays he closed the shop early and went to her, and later caught the last bus home. While she bathed, looked at magazines he brought, or sat on the couch smoking and "thinking" (as she called her habitual staring off into space), Lung cooked for her and the baby. Thick porterhouse steaks, roasted pork, poached chicken, boiled eggs, pig knuckles stewed with white vinegar. Foods that supposedly would fortify the female body.

As the months passed, her body swelled and her face thickened. She rarely left the house. Sunlight, she claimed, dizzied her. She preferred the perpetual dusk inside, winter's slanting rays, the clouds of cigarette smoke, the hunger for sleep. He had to bring her more supplies each time he came, and so he was increasingly worried about money. His extra expenditures, of course, did not mean he could send less money back to China. Her paper husband had to return and, once every month, pulse in her palm.

HE HAD TO DO with less. No more records, no more movies, no more meat when he cooked for himself.

By the first days of spring his good deeds started to pay dividends. His love for the abandoned car had never died, and once the weather changed, and as long as she insisted that she needed to stay housebound during daylight hours, he had easy access to the car. Sitting in its interior again after the time away, he was intoxicated anew by the aromas, animal and industrial, grease and gasoline, sweat and leather, sealed within the metal, frozen all winter, then thawed in the March afternoon sun.

One evening he left her earlier than usual. She did not seem surprised, nor did she seem to care. She was large in the belly, but not nearly as big as he imagined for this many months. Toward Lung she was the same as before—she needed him to be there—but once she had him, caught and committed, she seemed befuddled by the Chinese man's presence in her house. He was tolerated, eyed suspiciously. She would sit on the couch, next to her Bing Crosby ashtray, which she always kept within reach, thinking, picking tufts of cotton stuffing from the torn upholstery. When he said he was leaving, all she did was ask for the package of cigarettes in his shirt pocket.

He walked toward the road, and once out of sight of the house, he circled back around to the car. He got inside and sat in the leather seat and turned the steering wheel. He wanted to sound the horn but had to settle for pretending. He rolled down the window, tapped the smooth domed disk at the center of the wheel, wagged his finger at an imaginary figure, and mouthed, "Fuck you!" He laughed, delighted with his antics.

He was so good, so impressed by his performance. You see something often enough, you pick it up; it becomes part of you. He went through the same motions again and again. But he stopped playing when he realized the object of the others' honking and cursing was, indeed, himself.

He rolled out of the car. That was enough of that. He wanted more. He wanted to cut to the heart of things. He tried to get under the hood, put his hands on the engine. Numerous times before, he had tried to lift the hood and caught his finger on the latch and pulled, without results, except once, when the hood bit back and ironing was impossible the next day. But, this time he willed a miracle.

He touched everything, blackening his hands. His agitation exceeded that when he had first touched her, when he had lain in her bed. He unscrewed, uncapped, unplugged, and disconnected; then he replaced all he had undone, only now more securely than before. When his fun was almost finished, he accidentally touched two loose wires together, and the engine belched, farted, chugged. It was the happiest moment of his life.

THE NEXT TIME he came to her house, he toyed with the stem that protruded from one of the wheels, and the tire hissed, and the air streaming out cooled the blood underneath his fingernails. He loved the air's rubbery odor, the way it left him lightheaded.

Eventually he learned that if he touched wire to wire and maintained their contact, while he was behind the steering wheel and the engine was belching, farting, chugging, and he depressed the proper mix of pedals, and pushed this black lever, that black button, and he held his breath, the car would jump to life. Before dying, just as precipitately.

At those moments, over the span of a yard or two, he was actually driving!

LUNG VISITED HER more and more often. Yes, she was getting bigger with each week, and he was obliged to take care of her, even if he did not believe the baby was his. There was no one else to help. But increasingly he came for the car. At the store he could barely contain his excitement, anticipating the next time he would get his hands on it. His head swam in hood smells: grease, soot, gasoline, rubber, steel. The iron in his hand was a car, speeding across vast white roads. When cars passed on the street in front of the store, he no longer yearned to be the driver. He was one of them now; even if he was just a baby driver, he was one of them.

In early May the Germans surrendered, the soldiers' imminent return was on everyone's mind, and Lucy rarely left her bedroom. She seemed unmoved by the news of the world, as if the only news that mattered was that which emanated from her womb. She complained of backaches, headaches, nosebleeds, and incessant hunger. When he was visiting he served her, hand and foot. What she did when he wasn't around, he had no idea. Perhaps the dog brought her things. In any case, she somehow managed. She often grumbled about the size of her belly, her swollen feet. The only thing Lung noticed growing was the pile of cigarette butts on Bing Crosby's face.

He brought tools from the store to supplement those he found in the shed. In two weeks of visits he had disassembled the engine, as much as he dared, cleaned and polished the parts; he stripped worn wires, tightened screws and bolts, replaced belts, hammered the fan blade back into shape. He went about his business boldly. "I know what you're doing out there," she said. "You touch his car once more, you won't set foot inside this house again. I swear, I mean it." What was she going to do? She was like a fisherman scolding the waters that bring the fish. He nodded and returned to the car. He dropped to his knees, released air from the tires, and inhaled deeply.

SHE WAS EIGHT MONTHS pregnant, and the car was repaired to the best of his abilities; Lung spent his private time now keeping it clean and polished. One day he arrived with three pounds of fresh pig tails, for a soup with black beans. Good for the baby's backbone. He headed first for the car. He sat behind the wheel and pretended he had just driven up. He stayed inside long enough to smoke a cigarette, the driver-side window cranked low, his bony elbow sticking out. The last time he was here he had put on the finishing touches, running a rag across every inch of the interior, spit-shining the knobs and handles. It was like a giant jewel box inside, even the nonmetallic surfaces caught the sun.

His pride doubled once he was outside. As he stepped back from the car he took in his work, his baby, his labor of love these months. That he felt he had built the car himself, gathered the necessary raw materials and produced this miracle, was justified. The car was dead and dull before he laid his hands on it.

He would do now what he always did: enter the house through the kitchen, unpack the groceries he had brought, then start the meal, before going to see her. But today she was standing in the middle of the kitchen, her hand gripping a yellow chair back for support. She was paler than he had ever seen her, pale as waxy jade. Her hair hung loose and limp, like blinders over her eyes. Between strands, her pupils peeked through, fully dilated by fear, a luminous blackness. After long seconds, she finally recognized he was there. Her jaw dropped.

His gaze fell to her anemic legs, spread and quivering, poking out from underneath her white cotton nightgown. Then, as if the heat of his eyes were the cue she had been waiting for, the waters fell. In no time she was standing in a puddle, her feet, in some man's black socks, soaked. Lung reached with both hands and pushed back her hair. He spread his arms: What's the matter? From the bedroom the dog came running. Lung backed away from its mistress and raised his foot, ready to kick. But the dog ignored him and went directly for the water. It lapped the water, and when, disgusted, Lung nudged it with his foot, the dog staggered but sprang back, licking the water's edge insistently.

She was going to have her baby, even though it was not her time yet. "Baby come! Baby come!" he said, clasping her by the shoulders and shaking her.

She shook her head, then averted her face, avoiding terrible medicine. She looked tired and amazed, her features floating on the surface of her face, her sockets shallow, lips barely anchored.

IN PAIN, SHE SQUATTED in a corner of the bedroom, her eyes shot into her head, her lungs torn. She did not want him near, after he helped her from the kitchen to the bedroom. Banished from her sight, he smoked a cigarette just outside the door.

An hour later, she had not moved from the corner, and was shivering. Her whole body shook, and with increasing violence. Her jaws clacked, her teeth smacked together, the sound of breaking glass. She rubbed her face, her belly, she bit the top of her hand, the tips of her fingers.

She screamed. A short, breathless blast. Then clamped shut her jaws, with such a furious force he saw tiny shards of teeth fly through the heavy air, and tap the floor—two delicate tinks! She was silent and still, and that was enough inspiration to drive Lung outside. He ran to the car, touched the wires together, depressed the gas pedal, and the car coughed to life.

She said she did not want to leave the house. But she did not resist him either. He lifted her from the bed by her armpits. She was surprisingly light and pliable; her body, her fate surrendered to his machinations.

He had no plan in mind. When he saw her frozen as if she had breathed her last, his instinct was to run; he turned, and his legs carried him directly to the car. Now, next to him in the passenger seat, she stared out the windshield, her hands braced against the dashboard. He hated having her in his car. It seemed wrong, especially at that moment, but he couldn't suppress the feeling. He pushed every button, yanked every lever. When the car finally lurched forward, she sucked in a long, coarse breath that nearly choked her. The car rocked and stalled. "Oh my God! Oh my God!" she cried. Then groaned in pain, inhaling and exhaling through clenched teeth.

His hands shaking as he reached for the wires under the dashboard. The engine moaned, coughed, and at last started.

He joyfully slapped and kicked the car. It began to roll. Then he felt gasoline surge from the tips of his toes into the engine, then its vibrations rush back through him like a transfusion of blood. The car was covering ground, crushing grass and flowers. At the edge of the driver's seat, steering wheel under his chin, forehead bouncing off the windshield, glasses jumping on his nose, every organ inside hopping, on fire, he was driving, going places. He was American, as American as he was going to be.

But driving wasn't as easy as it looked. So many obstacles in his path: gopher holes, trees, garden tools, bushes, and Lucy in the passenger seat. "Oh my God," she said, "he can't drive!" Over and over she said this, in the rhythm of waves, steady and cresting, at odds with the dips and swerves of the slow, bumpy ride. His hands and arms were weary from gripping and jerking the wheel. Didn't she see he was trying his best to maneuver the car off the property, onto the street, to a midwife or a doctor, to the hospital on the way back to his place? Then she stopped saying things, her breaths quick, blunt again. Her exhalations were moans and sighs. He was afraid she might explode before the baby burst out of her.

He managed to navigate the lurching car to the rear of the house. Up ahead he saw an opening in the hedges. Weeds had overgrown it, but with the power at his command he was confident, if not excited that he might plow the car through and out into the world. "Oh my God! Oh my God!" He fed the engine more gasoline, tapping the pedal, small drinks. The car rolled easily over the crabgrass, picking up speed. With one hand she grabbed her abdomen, hoping to steady the baby inside, and with the other she reached for the dashboard to brace herself against the ride. "Baby not come yet, okay?" he said. He was in control of the situation. He would soon deliver her to the hospital. With every passing second, every revolution of the wheels, he was a more masterly driver. She just had to make the baby wait.

He forced the car forward. It was running more smoothly—he had better command of the gas pedal, and the ground was flatter here. At that moment he was so proud of his achievement, his mechanical genius, his driving genius. Yes, Lucy was in distress, moaning, panting, in a panic, but he knew it was just a matter of time before she was out of his hands and in someone else's care. Though he had not relaxed his stern grip on the wheel, and his forehead still bumped against the windshield, and his glasses still bounced on his nose, he was feeling so good he lost himself. He turned his head, and said out the window, "Fuck you!" That felt good. He giggled. He said it again. And again. And by then, with the car moving at his command, he was feeling so good he thrust his hand out the window, and wagging his finger at the world at large, he stuck his head out and shouted, "Fuck you! Fuck you!"

As he delivered his fourth "Fuck you!" and gathered his spirits for a fifth, the car hit a dip in the earth. His head smacked into the window frame, and out of instinct his foot flattened the gas pedal, and the car surged forward, and she screamed, "Oh my God! Oh my God!"

The car plowed into the hole, its front end crowning through the hedges, and he flew forward, face first into the top of the steering wheel, a sharp, sour pain between his eyes. Next to him, she was moaning, unaffected, it appeared, by the crash. His glasses had snapped in two, down the middle, from the impact. But he held the pieces to his face. He saw the main road. He had made it, to the world outside.

H E WAS WIDENING the opening, pulling branches back from the car. It was stuck like a giant plug, half in, half out. As he clawed at the leaves and limbs his face burned. Through the deep scratch between his eyes all of the jagged world seemed to drain.

When he opened the car door he was greeted by the smells of salt and iron, and air rippling with the violent rise and fall of her chest. The baby was the ugliest thing he had ever seen. It was about the size of a large pigeon, and writhed at her breasts like a worm. He heard the creature suckle, its mother wincing in pain, even as she slept. He held the pieces of his broken glasses to his face. Her legs leered at him, wild patches of blood on her thighs. How was this his baby? He thought of photographs of his daughter, Oi Ling. When each one arrived in the mail he had glanced at it, then quickly stuffed it back into the envelope. She did not start life like this one, amphibious, violet-skinned. After glimpsing the photographs only once and briefly, he was surprised how well he remembered them now: Oi Ling's healthy round face, burning eyes, and shiny black hair. With its swirl of dark hair, its thin, black streaks for eyes, this baby looked vaguely Chinese. He had an irresistible urge to touch the baby, who had transformed Lucy into milk. But armed with its smallness, its nakedness, its nakedness dressed in sticky blood, it seemed to have sprung from her body as a reproach from his own child: Why haven't you come home to see me?

He picked delicately at the baby's hair. It was a thick scab, viscid with blood and purplish muck. Lucy stirred momentarily, then fell back to sleep. He pinched a glob of the baby's gummy hair, pulling it through his fingers, squeezing the strands clean. Even without his glasses, right away he saw its hair was not black. *His* child's hair was black. He reached for another bunch of hair—a second test. Now he felt a sudden tenderness, as if this were his child, and he were touching her for the first time. He pulled gently; he did so as a parent; he wanted to clean her, pretty her. He gently massaged the baby's scalp, her little head moving this way and that, in response to the pressure. When he sensed the softness of her skull, he trembled, its vulnerability staggering through his fingertips. Oi Ling! he thought. He wanted to see her better.

But the baby's face was buried in Lucy's chest. When he tried to turn the baby toward him, he had no luck—the little head was glued to her bosom. After he rearranged the halves of the broken glasses, he tried again, this time with a firm twist of his wrist. The baby's cheek peeled away from its mother's skin, blood from blood, like a bandage from a wound. Its ugly puckered purple face stared back at him, tiny mouth locked in a waiting O, minutes-old life screaming out.

Chapter 17

IN AUGUST the United States dropped two atom bombs on the Japanese. The war was finally over. Lung had already seen a noticeable increase in the amount of business with the end of fighting in Europe, the soldiers gradually coming home, and now he expected more of the same. Besides the money earned from extra shirts he laundered, he was saving money because he was no longer buying Lucy groceries. That was over. And on the day after Lucy's baby died he took his daughter's photographs out of hiding; he propped all four on the cash register keys—Oi Ling as a baby, as a toddler playing with stones, in her first dress, under a parasol—and each time he completed a transaction, he saw her again. By the time the new year arrived—the Year of the Dog—though he still felt a pang of longing when he watched cars drive by the store, he knew the feeling would pass. That was over too.

Now he enlisted the help of Gok Pan, his friend the apothecary on Mott Street who read and wrote English well, and who for years had advocated that Lung bring his family over to the relative safety of America. It was time. They filled out the forms together. Lung filed the applications, paid the fees, and waited. A year went by, and finally he was going to see his daughter. Seven years old! Which meant he had been away for just under eight. When she arrived, he thought, then he would see the true measure of his American days.

O I LING HATED HIM from the start. At Ellis Island, among the hordes of the newly arrived, stinking of months in steerage, tagged and herded like pack animals, dazed with hunger and fear, Lung stood out as a lucky man, handsome in his suit and hat, his freshly laundered shirt that he had starched and ironed himself. In that crowd, in that giant hall, in all the commotion, he spotted her immediately—yes, her mother was wearing a dress made from the fabric he had sent, but he would have picked her out regardless, so familiar was he by now with her photographs. He went directly to her and opened his arms, acting out a scene he had watched happen for hours while he waited: families reuniting, hugs and cries of joy. "Hello! Hello!" he said in English, with a big voice, to impress both daughter and mother. But Oi Ling, in a white cotton dress and with red ribbons in her hair, hid behind her mother's skirts. She would not greet him or let herself be touched by him. He tried again, this time lowering his voice, speaking in Chinese. "Don't be shy," her mother said. But Lung could see right away she was not shy. Even as she clung to her mother, not once did she take her eyes off him. Peeking around her mother's hip, she glared at him, until her eyes smoked.

He lost patience and lit a cigarette. He was on the verge of scolding her mother: Why had she raised her to be so ungrateful? Look at how fat she was, healthy and well clothed, even after their three-month-long detention. How could she not know her own father? Yet he held his tongue. He grabbed their suitcases, wedged a bulky, green-paper-wrapped bundle under each arm, and led the two through the crowds and outside to the start of their new life together.

FOR MONTHS OI LING and her father were rarely in the same room at the same time, the girl fleeing whenever he entered. How often he watched the tip of her ponytail and soles of her feet as she sped from him. She usually ate with her mother, after Lung had dined alone and returned to work. When he spoke to her or called her name, she pretended not to hear him and did not answer. His wife was embarrassed by Oi Ling's behavior, and begged him for patience, while privately she reprimanded the girl. "She treats me like I'm a stranger," he said one night in bed. "I'm her father!"

"You are her father."

"But she acts like I'm nobody, like I don't exist."

"You two just met two months ago. She's not used to having a father."

"How can you say that? She's always had a father. Me!"

"Let's be truthful now, for all her life you didn't exist."

"I sent money. Who does she think sent the money?"

"It's not the same as your being there," she said. "Believe me, I know from experience." Her face seemed to go blank, and she got out of bed. Why was his wife behaving so badly? Lung thought. I brought her over; she got what she wanted.

LUNG PUT OI LING in school. Except for the painful daily separation from her mother, she adapted well to leaving home and picked up English effortlessly. Lung had his theory about her learning so well: Her plan was to distance herself from the man who claimed to be her father. At school she did not have to be on the lookout for him, and she believed the teacher's propaganda—personal betterment through education. The more English she picked up, the greater the distance she was putting between them.

Soon Oi Ling pestered her mother for an American-sounding name, because the other students were making fun of her real name. This desire offended her mother, who scolded the girl for letting trivial matters bother her, for being silly, for needing to be reminded that she had a Chinese name because she was Chinese and part of a five-thousand-year-old civilization. But Lung stepped in and announced he thought a new name was a splendid idea. And without hesitation he sent a name soaring into the air, as if it had been perched on his tongue, waiting for release: Lucy. Oi Ling was astonished at how resolutely he had spoken the name, at the authenticity of its pronunciation. She told her mother other girls at her school had the same name. But her mother was busy laughing: she thought he had said *lo-see,* their word for "mouse," and was as pleased as she had ever been with her husband for siding with her on the matter.

Days later, after she realized that she was mistaken, that her husband wasn't teasing the silly girl but had actually pinned an American name on her, she asked what the funny-sounding name meant. "Trust me," he snapped, "it's a good word." For the next few weeks no one had an ally. His wife would not call the girl Lucy, and Lucy would not answer when she was called Oi Ling. And while she still did not talk to her father beyond yes and no, she no longer dodged his presence, at least not as aggressively as before. She did not hide her eyes, and on occasion she held him with her gaze. Between Lung and his wife a gap opened that in shape and feel recalled Oi Ling's hatred. At night they slept like death, their rare bouts of lovemaking dark and dutiful. His wife stormed through the hours of the day, acting as though he had taken something precious from her.

A YEAR AFTER HIS WIFE and daughter arrived, his second child, another daughter, was born. Eleven months later, on the day the communists took power in China, a third daughter was born. With each birth, Lung died a little, so fearful was he the child might enter the world, only to exit quickly with its mouth frozen open, drinking eternity.

THE YOUNGEST WAS TWO when Sterling was born.

Several months after his arrival, on an unusually hot spring day, Lucy appeared at the store. Lung would not have been any more surprised if he had seen his mother and father there. She was like a person rising from the dead. She was standing outside, at the edge of the plate-glass window, watching, little different from those who came at the beginning to gawk at the new Chinese bride. After seven years, he recognized her immediately. He could not say which apprehended her first, his eyes or his heart, but fires flamed under his skin. What did she want? She waved hello.

"Who is she?" said his wife.

He had forgotten she was there, behind him, at her ironing board. "What is she looking at?" she continued. "Do you know her?"

He shook his head. "Get back to work," he said.

A few days later Lucy entered the store. Up close he saw she had aged, the bones in her face dissolved to fat, puffiness in her cheeks, her eyes swimming in flesh. She had with her two men's shirts she wanted washed and ironed. "How's your baby?" she asked, addressing Lung's wife, stationed at the ironing board farthest from the counter. To her left Sterling was sleeping in a bassinette. She asked again, and this time Lung's wife wanted to know what she was saying. He translated for her, and his wife said, "What business is it of hers?"

This was none of her business. "It's just the way these barbarians are," he said. "They're very nosy."

Week after week she came, and every time swapped two shirts for those she had dropped off the week before. The shirts did not need his attention; they had not even been worn, the sleeves were still pressed flat, the creases still sharp in the fabric. She had simply shaken out the folded shirts and brought them back in. "What demon is spanking her?"

his wife said. Each week she would stay a little longer, staring at his wife, talking to Lung. The pennies she spent gave her the right to stay, just as a nickel bought you a cup of coffee and a seat at the luncheonette. She stood at the same place she used to stand, behind the cash register, across the counter from Lung, and smoked a cigarette, which she always waited for him to light.

"I don't like her," his wife said at last. "Something is wrong with her. She's always looking at me. Like she's looking for something, lost something."

"That's enough," he said. "She's a customer. You don't like her. But you like her money."

"Two shirts! What do two shirts buy? I don't want her business if she's going to stand there talking to someone who doesn't exist. Who can understand the things she says?"

About a month after she first returned to the store she showed up wearing the egg dress. Lung looked up from his ironing when he heard a customer's footsteps approach, and turned his body to face the counter—ready to serve. But when he saw her in the dress he froze, and did not move until after she had unfurled the two shirts from her bag and waved her ticket insistently at him. He was not sure whether in the years since he had seen her in the dress she had grown or his memory of her had deteriorated, but her bosom was enormous, unrestrained by the silky fabric, and her arms and neck burst from their openings. He might have been even more in awe of its fit, but he remembered his wife was wearing her own version of the egg dress, the one cut and sewn from fabric he had sent her in Hong Kong, the one he told her was his favorite, the one he had been urging her to wear again. Nobody said a thing. Perhaps Lucy and his wife did not notice the similarities in their dresses, but the eggs were like hundreds of pairs of eyes staring each other down, Lung caught in the middle.

"I never questioned whether you missed me, Genius," she said, leaning forward over the counter. "But I never guessed you missed me this much!" Her voice, made bumpy by smoke, touched places deep inside his body; her red lips shriveled into a mischievous smile. He felt his wife's stare boring into the back of his head. He wanted to rush Lucy out of the store. He wanted to tell her, in his very best English, to leave him alone. But he was afraid he might arouse his wife's suspicions. Who taught you to speak like that? All he could do was pretend things were as they should be. She was his customer, and he would treat her accordingly. And surely his wife would not jump to the same conclusion as Lucy; surely she would respect the possibility of coincidence in this world. "I don't understand her. I don't know what she wants," he said to his wife.

He wanted to be the center of a miracle: to shield his wife from Lucy's coarse scrutiny and Lucy from his wife's, and at the same time be invisible, as insubstantial as smoke.

"So this is what you were waiting for, all those years?" Lucy said. "I'm surprised. It's not like she's some Chinese Zsa Zsa Gabor. Do you think your little wife is pretty?"

She was trying to sting him. And had succeeded. It was evident in the way he snatched the ticket from her and went to retrieve her bundle of laundry.

"Not for one second," she said, "do I believe you go for her looks." He peered quickly over his shoulder at her; she was staring at his wife.

"Who does she think she is?" his wife said, shaking her head, her red face like a bruise blazing at her twin. "What are you saying?" she said directly to Lucy. "Why don't you talk Chinese like a real person?"

He returned with her bundle of shirts, coming between the two wives. "How's my baby today?" Lucy asked, her words ripping through his chest, her eyes looking past him, searching for his wife and the baby in the bassinette. She seemed to know his wife understood what "my baby" meant; when Lucy saw the bewildered look in Lung's wife's eyes, seeking out Lung for protection against the barbarian attack, her face blossomed, as if nourished by the other's discomfort. He made change for the dollar bill she had given in payment for the laundered shirts. "Okay," he said. "Thank you. Bye-bye."

But she would not leave yet. "Do you like being a father, Genius?" She cleared her throat, a cigarette in her fingers. She wanted Lung to light her Lucky. His wife was familiar with the signal. "Don't," she said sharply. "Let her go." She stared at Lucy, then into the bassinette, then again at the woman. With her eyes fixed hard on Lucy she picked up the sleeping baby and disappeared into the family quarters.

"I can't explain her," Lucy said. "She's your little wife." She cleared her throat again. He had no choice but to light her cigarette: she was who she was; and he feared her more than he did his wife, because she was a daughter of the nation, capable of inflicting greater pain because he and his wife were just guests in her house. But once he flicked his lighter and she blew smoke in his face, he could feel his fingernails growing, his teeth decaying. He knew his wife was watching, and he knew, in her heart, he was dead.

L UCY CAME, AS USUAL, on a Monday afternoon. It had already been hectic and noisy enough. Lily was sick, Patty a reluctant napper in bed. All day his wife had shuttled between her chores and the children. Lucy arrived just as his wife hurried out from the living quarters holding Lily and baby Sterling in her arms, both in tears. Behind her there was a thud, followed by a scream of Patty's—she had probably fallen climbing out of her bunk bed again. His wife—she knew he had no talent with babies—stuffed Sterling in his arms, and rushed, with a quick look over her shoulder at Lucy, to tend to Patty wailing.

Another customer entered, and immediately started in on Lung, complaining in a voice louder and more wicked than Sterling's crying about tiny creases ironed into the tips of his shirt collar. "Sorry, sorry," Lung said, over and over, with bows of his head, the baby hot and kicking. But the man continued to scold Lung.

"Hey," said Lucy, "didn't you hear the guy say he's sorry?"

"Who you think you are, lady?"

"Guess," she said, extending her long white arms toward Lung and his boy.

What choice did he have but to surrender the baby to her? Or did she snatch the baby from his hold, as if Sterling were her own flesh?

In her arms, against her bosom, the baby instantaneously seemed content, eerily quiet, serene.

He heard his wife's footsteps, Lily weeping, Patty staggering in front, impeding her mother's progress. The angry customer heard too, and did not say another word. Lucy heard the same and reached across the counter, the baby at the end of her hands. Lung stretched out his arms, fully expecting the soft pressure of the baby lowered onto his palms. And for an instant that seemed her intention: she offered the baby's perfect pounds to him, but before he could wrap his fingers around the soft, forgiving flesh, she turned on her heels and ran out the door.

HE STOOD on the sidewalk, watching her shoulder blades, as articulate as the cheeks of fish; he believed he was losing his son forever. He had traveled so far to come to this country and over mind-numbing distances across the continent he had seen many troubling things, but nothing had prepared him for the place where he had just arrived and its sights: his baby boy looking at him over his kidnapper's shoulder, while his father stared into the face of the chaos of his own design.

HIS LEGS would not move. This was like watching a movie, Lucy walking down the street with quick, purposeful steps, stealing what was his, withdrawing from the same account as she had in the past. But when she turned the corner, vanishing from view, he started after her, his hard soles pounding the pavement, sending shocks up both legs.

He took the corner, and when he did not see any sign of her and the baby, he was sure he had reached the end of life. He stopped running, colliding into an invisible wall, his heart falling from his chest, and through the resultant hole crazy thoughts rushed in: Why would his wife care if he donated the baby, when she had more than she could handle already? Why not let Lucy keep the baby, replace the one she had lost? Why not join her and the baby, and live a life like that?

He closed his eyes, and inside his lids saw her holding his baby, but it was her baby in her arms, violet, mouth frozen in an O. When he opened his eyes, he was already running, past the row of storefronts, toward the bus stop.

Well short of the bus stop he saw she was not there, and turned and ran back to the laundry. He would tell his wife that he planned to telephone the police, that the police would be on their side. Beyond that, he had no answer for the disorder awaiting his return, the small-girl hatred, a wife's blinding anger. He ran harder to get there.

"GENIUS!" She was seated in the entryway of an abandoned beauty shop, the baby lying contentedly on her lap. Her face hung over him, and she seemed poised to leap into his eyes. "What took you so long?" she said, caressing the baby's fine black hair, a gurgling noise rising from his throat. They seemed to belong to each other, a peaceful ease in the way she handled him. "When I saw you fly by the first time," she said, "I thought for sure you were running from that little wife of yours. But I was wrong, wasn't I?"

He grabbed the baby off her lap. He was not angry, not even at Sterling when he erupted into tears the instant he realized whose hands held him, whose scent he breathed in. How light the boy was! After all that, he was such an insubstantial thing, his bones marrowless, his skin almost translucent, the veins visible like kelp barely below the surface of the sea. Holding the boy, tracking the journey of each of his pinguid tears, staring into his toothless, purple mouth, his tongue curled with anger, Lung more than ever believed her baby could have been his. One was allotted only a finite amount of passion in a lifetime, a few ounces, as a person was born with adult-sized eyes that the rest of its face would grow into. With Lucy he had used his share, his account empty by the time his wife appeared, and as he looked at Lucy now it was still at zero.

LUNG MOVED THE FAMILY to Lynbrook a month later and opened a new laundry. He was hiding his family from Lucy.

Days after the incident his wife insisted the baby was not the same baby that had been stolen from her. In the short time they were apart something had happened, though she was unable to pinpoint a single characteristic that was different. She just knew. He said she was crazy, even while he nurtured suspicions of his own. But he was not sure if the changes were in the boy or came from within himself. For a time he thought it was in the boy's smell: past the talc and sweet baby flesh he detected her perfume. And beyond, if he inhaled until his lungs imploded, he could sniff, high in the nose, the spiky odor that fluffed his head that day, inside the car wedged in the bushes, the metal smell of her infant's last breaths. It was centered in his face. Had he nuzzled at her breast and drunk her in? Was that what his wife sensed was wrong too?

He picked up their son more often now, held him to his face, tucked him against his neck, walked him through the store. Early on, his wife welcomed this: it was about time he took an interest in his son. She noticed—and he had noticed this too about himself, before she said a word—that he never went to comfort the boy, never handled the boy with purpose, only at his pleasure, lifting him from the bassinette while he slept or lay serenely, dry and full-bellied. Something in this behavior seemed to trouble his wife. Once he had the baby in his arms, within seconds she would wrestle the boy from him.

At the same time his wife talked less and less often. Eventually, what she had to say she said through their eldest, Lucy, who, hardly embracing the role, listened lazily and relayed the rare messages sloppily. And his wife abandoned the clothes he had dressed her in, acting as if she had a mind of her own. One night she stuffed every garment he liked into a laundry bag and, while the children slept, burned the clothes, a spectacular cotton-and-silk pyre in the lot in back of the store. On consecutive Saturday nights she took money from the cash register, and in Chinatown the next day bought fabrics she liked and hired a seamstress. He did not interfere. What was she thinking? He was all she had, even if she could not admit this now. One day she would wake up old, and the new dresses that fit her body now wouldn't suit her spirit anymore. Her babies wouldn't talk to her, they wouldn't even speak her language. And if she didn't watch out, her baby boy would grow up and might hit her.

THEN SHE GAVE Sterling away. Without consulting Lung, she loaned the boy to the Chins. He was a cook, and she was the seamstress who sewed her dresses; they lived in Chinatown. Lung's wife originally had met Chin-Moo on Ellis Island, and had remarked that her new friend was such an old sow, she could not understand why she would bother coming so far at her age. While the Lungs had four children, the Chins had none. Either Chin-Moo was barren or Chin-Bok was not a man. So, in a single act of goodwill, Lung's wife eased her burden and the loneliness of her friends' childless lives. Lung did not object too strenuously. Her stated reasons for the giveaway: She no longer could manage the three youngest children and cook and clean and work in the laundry, especially during the business hours when Oi Ling, the only hands that helped, was off at school. When it was time to say good-bye and his wife held the boy up to his face, like a flower for him to sniff, Lucy was there again, in the vague particles rising from the creature's flesh. He realized then his wife's true intention was to hold the baby and him apart, exiling each from the other—father from son, her no-good husband from his American wife. He reached for the baby, wriggling his hands playfully in the boy's bland, red face, but she jerked him away and deposited him in Chin-Moo's waiting arms.

Lung abruptly walked away from them. He could not stand the sight of that woman's lustful eyes, her hunger to possess, or his wife's frank self-satisfaction. He returned to his work. Once he was standing at his ironing board he felt better. He pushed his iron furiously across the front of a shirt. He grabbed the water pistol out of the air and dampened the fabric. When he was through he gave the water pistol an extra tug, then let it fly from his hand, and it bobbed up and down, the long steel spring contracting and expanding, the nozzle dipping dangerously close to his head, like the attack of an irate bird. He watched as the contraption settled, the red rubber hose quivering, the dangling pistol slowly wagging, its deranged, jumping rage all but spent. Then it bobbed its last, and came to rest at the end of its restraint, hanging heavily like a bloom on a vine. He remembered the strong young body that had jury-rigged similar systems for other laundrymen (which he did gratis, refusing the indelicate exchange of coin for favors to friends). He was something then, hammering together ironing boards and counters and shelves, erecting walls between public and private spaces, partitioning rooms, wiring and plumbing the store. A maker of things! He was no longer a young body, with hands that built things and hungry eyes and legs ready to go; now he had grown roots beside the ironing board, his right hand an iron, limited in its usefulness. How else could he explain his failure to pluck the baby from that woman's arms while he was still safe inside the store?

He heard the *clack* of the deadbolt. The Chins were leaving with the baby, and they were saying their final good-byes. As he watched, he thought, I have come to this, I have come all this way to come to this. Then he realized this was not a struggle between him and his wife, or between him and the Chins. The matter rested on the baby's little shoulders. If the baby would only cry during the abduction, even a few weak tears, then Lung would know that the boy sensed something was wrong, that between them existed ties bred into their blood. As Chin-Moo carried him over the threshold, the baby looked over her shoulder, past his mother, at Lung. The only thing on the boy's shapeless face was a rabbit's dumb, wide-eyed stare: no grief, no recognition, no pang for the loss to come.

For the entirety of his American life, he saw now, he had been unhappy. An immigrant has no business even contemplating such a luxury as happiness. It was an American affectation, slipperier than Chinese luck or money lust. He had come this great distance to witness extravagant things, not monkeys, not peacocks, not buffalo, but American genius, motorcars and highways, movies and appliances, airplanes for leisure travel, and wars in Europe and Asia. Yet he had been only an observer, admiring America from afar, driving a car but not on a road, a woman having him without his having her. He was outside now, watching his son being taken away. Even in his own family he was outside, watching.

H IS WIFE WAS STANDING at her ironing board weeping, ruining some guy's shirt. The boy had been gone for an hour. She returned to work as soon as the Chins left. He said some things to her then, to which she offered no response. Now she was crying, even though she had no right to put the demands that a woman's tears put on a man, not when she had orchestrated her own misery.

When he finished with the shirt he was folding, he locked the front door, returned the key to the nail under the counter, unplugged his iron, turned off all the lights. He said nothing and left her in the dark store, illuminated only by the glow of the streetlamps. He smoked a cigarette inside the family quarters, and as he listened to the radio he watched her past the partially drawn curtain, her legs unmoving, her sobs uncontained by the volume of the music. He closed his eyes, and as the smoke pried at his lids he said, "Why is she crying?" He is yours, and you gave him away; he is yours like the others are yours, starting with the oldest, who despises me because she knew from the beginning she was not mine but yours. What died inside him when he crashed his car into the bushes died again when she gave the boy away. He quit. He washed his hands of them. They were all hers. When were they not?

A hand touched his shoulder. He opened his eyes, and she was standing at his side, sobbing quietly. She told him she missed the boy, and that had triggered the tears. She reached for him then, as if feeling her way in the dark. He stood up from his chair and closed in on her, but once he felt the damp heat of her weeping body he stepped free. Now she wanted him to protect her against her own cold heart. He moved into her, and nudged her backward against a wall. He stiffened his thumbs and pressed them against her breasts, until they sank so deep he could feel the hard nodes of milk. She winced, her head thumping lightly against the bare, unpainted wood separating them from the sleeping girls. She closed her eyes, and shunning him she seemed to abandon her body, to hollow out. What pain she felt, she would not show him; she would not let her hurt wake her daughters. He saw then that she had to have sorrows beyond those he made for her. Other sorrows existed inside her body like stillborns in her womb. He could not name them, just as his were unknown to her. But their sorrows showed in the sag of their shoulders, the starchy stiffness in their necks. He did not want to hear about the depth or variety of her sorrows. With such knowledge he might have to think of her as someone with a private life, separate from his, with feelings he did not understand and passions he would never know.

She tipped her chin and opened her eyes, and he was shaken by the sight of his son's eyes in her head, the same ambivalent look he had perfected as he was borne away. Those eyes alone were enough to sting his hands from her body. From that day forward those eyes kept him at a safe distance. She would not have him, and he did not try.

T HE CHINS OCCASIONALLY VISITED with the baby on Mondays, Mr. Chin's day off from the restaurant, but a busy work night at the laundry. Some Sundays the Lungs took the train into New York to see the Chins. These visits were usually brief affairs: tea, steamed sponge cake, and the girls' lavishing their attentions on their little brother. Lung stayed on the fringes. At home he drifted back to work; in Chinatown, he drank coffee with his buddies on Mott Street.

After a year, the boy was back for good. He was walking and beginning to talk. The girls adored him like a pet. In turn, he was dazzled by his newfound sisters. But he soon discovered Lung. He was drawn to the curling smoke and the bright orange embers at the end of his cigarette. One day soon after his return, the boy toddled to his father, who was seated on a milk crate, taking a break, smoking, his legs crossed demurely. The boy tried to sit on his dangling foot, and Lung just let him fall off. He had kept his distance from the child; the boy was hers now, they all were. But the boy was stupidly insistent. He climbed up his father's leg like a squirrel up a tree. He clambered onto his thighs, and grasped his shirt collar for support. He stood face to face with his father. The boy reached his little hands toward Lung's eyes. Perhaps he was attracted to the light reflecting off the lenses, or he glimpsed himself there. Sterling knocked the frames off his father's nose and left them hanging precariously from one ear. The boy was laughing at his handiwork, his mouth wide open, showing his tiny teeth like grains of rice embedded in the gums. For the moment Lung forgot the boy was hers. He buried his nose into the boy's soft belly and inhaled deeply, involuntarily seeking Lucy's scent. To his surprise he did not find her there, and to his greater surprise he did not care. He bounced the boy on his knee, thinking that he liked this, a sturdy, playful son. Sterling laughed and laughed, then cracked into hiccups, Lung holding him by his soft puffy arms.

This was their secret, this playing, at least until the day his wife walked in on them. She laughed, clapped her hands together. How pleased she was to see the affection bud between them. Lung glared at her, trying to bend the grin off her face. He set the boy on the floor.

When he wanted to climb back on, his father did not allow him. Lung simply stood up and walked away. Later, as the weeks passed, whenever Sterling came, closing in with his unsteady, headlong stagger, hoping to play, his irresistible cuteness notwithstanding, Lung flexed his foot and flicked him off with a single brutal tap of his shoe. Which the boy registered as play, until the foot grew meaner, smacking him so soundly he toddled backward and fell. Lung never wavered, even though he saw his son's tenderness was crushed. To the boy's credit, it was not long before he was trained to keep his distance.

THE MAN LUNG WAS before his wife and daughter joined him in America wouldn't die. He was supposed to die the instant they arrived. But for his whole married life that man would not let go of him; he clung to his shoulders, dragged him down. If Lung ever looked fondly at his family, that man was there, poised to divert his gaze. At the hospital, that man had sat on Lung's chest like a massive stone, and together they sank so far, so deep, Lung had to drive here this day.

Part Four

Cooking is like matrimony:
two things served together must
match.

— YUAN MEI

Chapter 18

WE DRIVE TO CALIFORNIA in separate cars. Bliss and the two boys in the Volvo wagon, me following in the Valiant. Each day we leave the motel parking lot and head for the interstate in tandem, Bliss leading, the cars ten or so yards apart. But a few miles after we merge with 80, she takes off, vanishes at the horizon, and we don't see each other until we hook up at whatever motel we have reservations for that evening. "What is your big hurry?" I ask, when we meet in whichever anonymous room or parking lot.

"If it matters so much to you, then you have to try harder to keep up with me. But don't expect me to slow down," she'll say. Or, "Is it really that important? We're headed for the same place, only at different speeds." Or, "Of course I'm in a hurry! California, Silvy! The future is waiting for us there."

We are moving because Morton Sass has sold me to San Francisco public TV, sold me like a used car, and there isn't anything I can do about it. He broke the news to me this way: "Congratulations, you finally turned a profit!" When I went to tell Fuchs the news I was leaving for good, he said, "I don't know if you want to hear this, but it looks to me you're less a son-in-law than another of the big man's acquisitions. He holds on to you for a while, maybe fixes you up a little, and then peddles your ass for considerable financial gain. That's what I do with my meat."

"So now I'm a piece of meat."

"No, listen to Fuchs. You're being *sold* like a piece of meat. There's a difference."

I ordered a couple of chickens for the last supper I'd cook as resident chef at the Sass house.

"Sterling," Fuchs said, as I was about to leave the store, "I don't get it. Why California? People don't eat in California. They're all vegetarians."

I didn't want to move. I was comfortable where I was. And how could I in good conscience put all that distance between my parents and the kids, especially taking Moses away from Genius?

But Bliss was gung-ho about going. I suspect she conspired with her father to make this happen, but I can't prove it. When I've asked why she's so enthusiastic, she has consistently said one of two things: KQED is a good career move for me, and this is a fresh start for us.

AT BLISS'S INSISTENCE we live in Santa Cruz, a small city an hour and a half south of San Francisco. She and Moses spent an afternoon here when they came out to visit Lester, and she fell in love with the place. A friend ("What friend? Who do you know out there?") found a house for us to rent, Morton Sass writing checks for the security deposit and the first and last month's rent. It is a pint-sized Victorian, painted in different tones of blue, on a street lined with sycamores. For a range of reasons, literal and metaphorical, I've dubbed the place the House of Blues.

I start my new show for KQED, *The Peeking Duck* ("Evvy week I peek into you lifes!"—a voice I borrowed from another TV Chinese chef, Hop Sing, the houseboy on *Bonanza*); Bliss works, when she is moved to, as a dental hygienist downtown. Moses is four, Ira two.

The first year passes, geographically fresh, but otherwise as stale as can be. Our New Canaan life, only transplanted three thousand miles. It's like a marital McDonald's, the same no matter where you go.

I WAKE UP, flat on my stomach, and sweep my hand across the mattress, feeling for her. But the sheet is cold. A few degrees more in temperature she might still be in the house, getting the boys together for their preschool. But clearly she's been gone for a while.

I check the clock on her side of the bed. It's a plastic rooster wearing sunglasses, the clock face in its belly; as an alarm, the rooster crows: "Hey baby, shake that thing!" It's a gift to the boys from a friend of hers, a geologist, but for some reason she won't relinquish her hold on it.

Where has she gone at this hour? It's too early to wake the kids for school. I tap my forehead, thinking, thinking, and blame myself for forgetting, as if by my remembering, she would return bodily to me. As hard as I try to respect this latest absence as a unique, isolated occurrence, an honest-to-goodness surprise, I cannot beat down the familiarity of this feeling, of searching for an explanation, struggling to ignore the fact she's slipped away again.

I scramble out of bed and check on the boys. I worry she might take them, especially Ira. But they are in their bunk beds, asleep. Out of harm's way, and harmless themselves. I love to watch the two sleep. They are naturals, falling so deeply and so solidly asleep that this seems their very essence. Many nights I watch as sleep hits each boy like a bead of oil striking water, then plummeting to the depths of his being, before rising to the surface of his skin.

I look in on Ira in the bottom bunk first. I don't dare touch him, though as always I'm tempted. An hour earlier I could've combed my fingers through his sweaty curly hair and at most he might've yawned or swallowed, but now he's too close to the brink of consciousness. I step onto the first rung of the ladder and peek at Moses on the top bunk. I am relieved to see him without his glasses. They age him, and each time he glances my way I see Genius's face, and feel Genius's rebuke. That is why his sleep is so precious; he is biteless, and I start feeling he's mine again. I am brimming goodwill and pity; as I step backward off the ladder, my eyes catch on the scrap of paper he has taped to his headboard, a Xerox of a photo of six Chinese whom I have dubbed "the ancestors." I can't see it from this end of the bed, but I have the thing memorized. They are two generations of male Chinese, the elders seated on thronelike chairs, leather riveted to wood, a row of four teenage boys standing behind their shoulders. The men are bald (one is eyebrowless and wears glasses), the boys have thick hair greased and combed back from their angular faces (one also has bad eyesight). None of them smiles. They wear old-fashioned suits—the lapels rounded, the fabric coarse and bulky—and expressions of bewilderment, their eyes wide and searching. In his sleep Moses' head is twisted back, face turned in the ancestors' direction. Night after night he falls asleep this way, his neck bones locked in position like the final turn of a screw, staring at the ancestors he has chosen for himself until dreams come. Where Moses picked these guys up from, I don't know.

Bliss claims she doesn't either. "He's always finding things in the gutter," she once said. "One man's trash is that boy's treasure."

"You think it's cute, don't you? Why you want your son falling asleep each night with his head full of some stranger's garbage, I'll never know."

"Hey, don't put it on me. If you don't like it, take it away from him. Personally, it doesn't bother me one bit. He is Chinese, after all. He misses being around Chinese people. What do you expect—you took him away from your parents, and there are no Chinese around here."

"What do I look like? I *am* Chinese, you know."

"Then act the part."

"Act?"

"Yeah, cook the kid something Chinese. He misses your mother's cooking. Speak Chinese to him once in a while. Take him to Chinatown. You can do that much."

One morning while staring at the picture, I boiled over—I reached across his hot sleepiness and tore the ancestors from the headboard. They were like a bunch of squatters in my house, mocking me, occupying my kid's final moments of wakefulness each night. But as I held the ancestors in my hands I saw what Moses saw: Genius's face blooming on the face of one of the elders, the gentleman in wire-rimmed glasses, and Moses' in the bespectacled boy over his right shoulder. Genius and Moses, like father and son, skipping my generation, as if I didn't exist. Wood-pulp-and-ink DNA. Then Moses woke up, and caught me with the paper ancestors in my hand. Without a word, I laid the Xerox on his mattress and left the room. Behind me, I heard his chubby palms anxiously smoothing the picture back onto the wall, his flesh against the paper making a watery sound, like swishing amniotic fluid, that curdled my heart.

SOMEONE KNOCKS at the front door.

When I go to see who it is, the sight of the spaceman there almost kills me. It's too much, especially at this hour of the morning, with Bliss's absence hanging in the air—his goldfish-bowl head, mirrored like a mafioso's limo, protection against solar glare and lunar wind. He talks at me, but all I hear are muffled sounds: "Vuhvuhvuhvuhvuh . . ." Behind him are two other spacemen. I watch the pair over their leader's shoulder, their silver suits gleaming in the morning light. Each is working the same strange instrument—an aluminum pole ending in a Frisbee-sized metal disk—that appears to be a natural extension of the bulky, otherworldly gloves he has on. In ultraslow motion the spacemen move across the lawn, wagging their instruments in front of them, over the tips of grass, as blind men wag their canes. I keep expecting the spacemen to bounce as Neil Armstrong and Buzz Aldrin did, like hunks of interstellar debris across the lunar surface.

Moses and Ira come to the door to see what's going on. My first impulse is to block their view, protect them from uncertainty, mystery, to keep them within the bounds of earthly society. I shoo them from the door. But they come back. I pick Ira up, nudge Moses aside with my hip.

They can't take their eyes off the spaceman. I can't take my eyes off the three of us reflected on the spaceman's glass face. What a queer sight it is: Ira riding my hip, a miniature of his Jewish grandfather, bearing no resemblance to his brother, Genius's twin. Genes tell you nothing. The spaceman points at the Valiant parked in the driveway; he points at Moses, at Ira, at me, at the car again. "Vuhvuhvuhvuhvuh . . ." he says.

"I can't understand you." I shake my head, leaning closer to the spaceman's helmet, my reflected face on its surface growing larger, coming into sharper focus. "What do you want? Why are you here?" I say, as if talking to myself in a mirror.

The spaceman unscrews his head. The boys gasp; they're in awe. The man's new head is long and skinny like the tongue of glass inside a lightbulb. "You shouldn't be in there," he says, holding the helmet aloft, poised to be popped back on at any moment. He shows me a job-order form; a box is checked that says no one'll be in the house when he and his crew come to do their work. "Get out!" he says, plunking the helmet over his skull. Then he removes his head again. "Oxygen break," he says. "Hey, cute kid."

My liver curls. I don't know which "kid" he means. I feel he's testing me. He knows that I have a preference, that I find more beauty in one son than in the other, that I am an imperfect father. In the end, I ignore the spaceman's remark. I ask, "What are you doing here?"

"What are *we* doing here? What are *you* doing here?" he says. "A Mrs. Lunge sent for us." He shows me the job order again.

"Who?"

"Lunge. Bliss Lunge."

She was doing it again. At parties, among a roomful of strangers, I have heard her do that, Frenchify my name, bleach its single syllable of any possible Chinese associations, and in that act blur the bond between us.

"You must have some problems here," the spaceman says. "Nobody calls Home Wreckers unless there's a serious problem on the domestic front."

"Oh, there are problems, all right." I try to remember if she had said something about these guys coming.

Not long after we moved in, we suspected something was wrong with the house. Neither Bliss nor I could pinpoint the problem, but we sensed one existed. We described it as a general "bad vibe," a sense that the place was haunted, that something bad was about to happen. A major pipe about to burst, Jack Nicholson running loose with a hatchet, a tidal wave washing the works into the sea. The people our landlord sent over to inspect the house dismissed our claims. Our landlord suggested we were imagining things. Over long-distance, Selma Sass hinted we look into marriage counseling, in essence siding with the landlord that the problem was with us, not the house. Undaunted, over the last few months Bliss and I have paid an army of specialists to inspect the property, inside and out. They crawl under the foundation, up into the attic; they replace pipes, check the wires in the walls, and finger the usual suspects: lead, arsenic, carbon monoxide, microwaves, toxic wastes. Everything negative. They test the soil, water, air, paint, and electricity. They spray for phantom rats and bugs, and want to tent the house for termites. A quack digs a hole in the front lawn searching for a renegade uranium deposit. The county radon man, the city asbestos man come and go, gloved, masked, and goggled, leaving slips of official paper with seals and signatures that rule out any danger. A hundred dollars is lost on the tree surgeon; her theory is that roots, burrowing and seeking moisture under the house in this season of drought, are easing it a millimeter at a time off its concrete anchors. So she prunes the trees and, risking the wrath of the city's water commissioner, floods the offending pair of eucalyptus.

For the price of a Sterling-cooked meal, Bliss hired a geologist from the university in town. She had seen him give a lecture on campus about earthquakes, a preoccupation of hers since our move to California. She came home smitten with the brilliant Mr. Pierce, who saw far into the future and deep into the earth. She relayed what she had heard, her voice charged with an alarming enthusiasm: The Big One will happen sometime in the next thirty years! Against my objections—what was a geologist going to tell me about what ailed my house?—Bliss invited him, using me for bait. "What harm can he do?" she said. "Besides, he's a university professor. He comes cheap."

The geologist raced down the hill, armed with specialty maps and satellite shots of the San Andreas Fault. He walked the property line, poked under the house. He told us that the house sat on bedrock, that plate tectonics wasn't to blame for what was troubling our home and our lives. "I can't find fault here," he said.

The spaceman motions for Moses to come closer, which he does, and instructs the kid to unzip a zipper on the hip of his spacesuit. The unzipped zipper opens to another zipper, which opens to a third, which opens to a pocket that holds a dozen or so lollipops of different flavors. "Take one for yourself," he says, "and one for—" His eyes jump from Moses to Ira, from Ira to me, from me to Moses. He's not sure if we're all a single family. "And take a sucker for the little one."

"Say thank you."

"That's okay. My personal touch. I love kids. Usually don't see too many kids on the job. By the time I'm called they're not feeling so good. Most Home Wreckers problems don't come with people inside. That's why we wear these suits. We can walk through a nuclear reactor in this thing, wade waist-deep in a chemical swamp, survive days in an oxygen-free environment, dance through wildfire, play golf on Mars."

"Wow!" Moses says.

"Wow!" says Ira, imitating his big brother.

"Wow is right! We inspect every square inch of your domicile, ten feet below ground, twenty feet into the airspace overhead. We start with radioactivity. Very nasty stuff, just a few milligrams will make you feel lousy, sick in the blood. But we have very sensitive instruments, top-of-the-line Geiger counters, and my men are the best. They'll find something. That's why you and the kids ought to get out. We always find something terribly wrong—that's the Home Wreckers guarantee."

"Let's go!" Moses says, agitated by the spaceman's talk of radioactivity, toxic fumes, chemical spills, ancient spells infecting the house. "Let's go before we get killed. Come on, Ira!" He makes a grab for Ira, pinching his leg, and Ira squirms in my arms, suddenly cranky, ready to follow his brother, who darts from the house to the safety of the car.

W HERE'S MOMMY?" the boys ask, first Moses, then Ira copying him. "We have to get Mommy!"

Moses thinks Bliss is still in the house. As I back the Valiant into the street, I'm tempted to let him hold that thought, to let it overwhelm him like odorless, tasteless carbon monoxide, until he blacks out. He's fretting about her well-being, when it's she who's jeopardized our well-being, casting the three of us from our home, forcing us to roam the streets like refugees. Moses and Ira are riding side by side in the backseat, both unbuckled, Ira not even in his kiddie safety seat, because it's in the Volvo, the car we drive the boys in, the one she took off in. The Valiant, in her opinion, isn't safe, especially for a child Ira's age. "Don't worry," I finally say, "your mother's not in the house. She's been out since before you woke up."

"Where'd she go?"

"Moses, why're you even asking? You know the answer to that one."

"I don't know where she is."

"That's what I meant. Nobody knows."

After a prolonged silence Moses says, "Well, let's go find her."

We should send the spacemen after her; maybe they have a gizmo that can search out vanished wives and mothers.

"Yeah," Ira says, "let's find Mommy!"

"Sure! Why not?" I tell Ira. "Let's find Mommy!"

FIRST, I BUY BREAKFAST at Spudnuts. We are not a minute away from the Spudnuts parking lot, and Ira's already covered with powdered sugar and purple jelly; Moses nibbles his doughnut—honey-dipped, of course, nice and boring, a taste he learned from Genius—which he wears like a ring around his finger.

I steer the car downtown, and onto the main drag, a narrow street lined with antique lampposts and potted trees. We are looking for their mother. At this hour most of the pedestrians are parents with kids or homeless people. Except for the cafés and coffeehouses, most businesses are closed. But employees are preparing for the workday, hosing down the pavement, hauling racks of discounted clothing into the sun, arranging cut flowers in buckets of water. We are cruising, my eyes on the lookout for Bliss.

In the backseat the kids torment each other. I can't tell who the instigator is. I watch in the rearview: Ira tries to grab Moses' uneaten breakfast; Moses holds the doughnut out of his brother's reach; Ira doesn't quit, leans into Moses, leading with his jelly-fingers, until Moses plants his free palm on Ira's forehead and shoves him back into his seat; there's a momentary truce, and then Moses teases, wagging his doughnut under his brother's nose. It starts over. "Moses, give Ira the doughnut if you're not going to eat it," I say, turning my head from the road to let the boys know I mean business.

"It's mine," says Moses. "I'm saving it for later."

"I don't think that's true."

Sensing things are breaking in his favor, Ira seizes the moment and lunges for the doughnut. "I need it!" he whines. The urgency in his voice spins my head around. This is parental instinct in operation, for which a glance at the rearview won't do. "Moses," I say, "let him have it."

He does, whacking Ira on the top of his head until he falls back in his seat. I expect him to start bawling, but he doesn't. I stop the Valiant in the middle of the street. "Moses, what's wrong with you?" I tell him to leave Ira alone, to hand over the doughnut, and to buckle his brother's seat belt. I supervise the operation, but Moses struggles just locating the metal ends; I can't tell whether he really can't find the buckles or is fooling around. A car approaches from behind. "Shit!" I turn and face front, but keeping my eyes on Moses for as long as they'll stick. I ease off the brakes. The car rolls a few feet before I abruptly slam on the brakes again. Tires squeal, the boys tumble forward, someone's limbs bump the back of my seat.

A man stands in front of the Valiant. He stares menacingly, as if I had hit him. He looks mean, his face consumed by beard. You've done nothing wrong, I tell myself. "Everything's okay! Everything's okay! No one's hurt here!" I yell at the kids, who are rearranging their bodies into their seats. "I want Mommy!" Moses says, his glasses crooked on his face. This sets Ira off. He wants Mommy too.

Things get worse. The car behind us honks. I wave for it to pass. It's an eternity before the driver gets the message. When the car finally squirms past, Moses shrieks, "Look, Jack!"

"Mommy!" Ira says.

The guy I almost hit, but didn't, kicks my front bumper, then mercifully leaves us alone.

"There goes Jack!" Moses says.

"Mommy!" says Ira.

Their voices shrivel my heart to a prune. "Who's Jack?"

"Mommy's friend!"

I know whom Moses is talking about. That Jack. Jack Pierce, Bliss's dirt-doctor geologist friend.

"You saw Jack Pierce?"

"No, his car!"

"How do you know it's his car?"

"Because he always drives the car to my house."

I HEAD TO THE MEDICAL PLAZA where Bliss sometimes cleans teeth. It's a Spanish-style hacienda, with stucco walls, orange terra-cotta tile roof, and a verandah hung with pots of fuchsia. The medical plaza is located in the general direction Moses claims he saw Jack Pierce navigate his car to. Once we come within sight of her building, Ira starts shouting, "Mommy, Mommy!"

"She's not here," Moses says dismissively.

I scan the cars parked along the curb, I circle the adjacent blocks, I creep through all four levels of the municipal lot she sometimes parks in. Moses is right; she's not here.

I DRIVE THE KIDS to the park. I don't know where next to look for her, and my parental instincts tell me I'm losing the boys. Do something before they explode with boredom. A preemptive strike.

Swing, slide, and sand. I watch the boys and marvel at the high seriousness of their play, and their self-sufficiency just now, as if all they need for their survival is the pleasure of their creativity. Ira rolls his body in the sandbox and discovers the grains will stick to the patches of jelly on his shirt, arms, and face, like sesame seeds to breadsticks. He doesn't even know I'm here. He's so lost in his fun, there's no future, no past, just this crunch of shoulder, hip, leg into sand. His easy joy stings my heart. For him, life is nothing more, nothing less than swimming in the sand; he's like a blue crab newly shed of shell, highly vulnerable until his tender self ossifies again, oblivious to danger. I tremble at his nakedness, the bone-blue purity of his desire laid open. Anything can happen to him: it would be so simple, a hand breaking the surface of the water, ripping him from the sea. I feel helpless.

I envy Ira, insane with play, his mother drained from his body. If only I might bleed her from mine. Where is Bliss? Why has she done this to me? And why is Jack Pierce, his face and his car, so everyday for the boys? My knees knock, my breath shallow and sore. Why is there so much uncertainty, and why is there so much misery in the uncertainty, and why is the earth shaking and falling away beneath me when there is this beautiful, brilliant, lovely child, in the middle of all this chaos?

At the height of its forward arc, Moses flings himself off the swing he's been riding. He lands on his butt, then falls backward, and knocks his head on the ground. He lies there, supine, and I feel my heart flaming into my head, but I don't move, because I'm expecting Bliss to go to him. Then he gets up on his own, dusts off the seat of his pants, and runs over to us. And before I can ask how he is, Moses stares at his brother, screws up his face, and says, "He's so dorky!" I almost hit him—what Genius automatically would've done to me. But instead I reach down to protect Ira, and scoop his sweet, sweaty, sandy body into my arms, and rush him, torn from his pleasure, twisting and crying in protest, to the safety of the car.

Ira is so upset he won't let me help him climb into the Valiant. I'm still mad at Moses, and he seems to know it and gets in without fuss. I park Ira next to him, and secure the seat belts around their waists. Once in motion, Ira unleashes tears for the sudden loss of playtime; next to him Moses is seething and sullen, arms crossed over his chest, his eyes drilling holes in the back of my head. A few blocks later, when Ira quits crying, Moses shouts, "He's trying to take off his seat belt!"

"Let me go!" he screams, struggling with the buckle.

"Ira, I can't do that right now. We're in the car, and when we're in the car we all wear seat belts or ride in the car seat. Now isn't it special to be sitting next to your brother like a grown-up, instead of being stuck in the car seat?"

He's silent, thinking things over carefully, and finally he says, "Yes." I hear in his voice a body full of resignation.

"That's the answer! It's special, isn't it, Ira? It's so special, let's make this our special secret! You, me, and Moses. Okay, Ira?"

Ira's not saying a thing. I find Moses in the rearview. "Does he understand what I just said?"

The kid leans over and stares straight into his brother's face, nose to nose. "I think so," he says with a shrug.

Bliss will kill me if she ever finds out. She'll accuse me of not loving the boys. "Ira, are you with me? We're going to keep our secret from Mommy, okay?"

"Where's Mommy?" Ira's voice soars with hope. "Where's Mommy?"

"We're looking for her, stupid!" Moses says, kicking the back of my seat.

OUR SEARCH TAKES US to a block of Water Street that fronts a row of stores Moses and Ira have a fondness for, a fondness that has everything to do with the fact their mother likes to bring them to this part of town to fill the hours of her day. I wouldn't be surprised to find her here. "Okay, you guys," I say, trying to talk us all into a better mood, "it's fun time!" I park the car. Their eyes are plastered on the happy destinations: a bookstore, a toy store, an Italian deli, a gourmet cookie shop, a pet shop, a taco stand. "We'll read books, check out the animals, then everyone gets a treat!"

Immediate dividends: Ira claps his hands.

Moses scowls at his brother. He has been trying to act cool, but I detect in his posture an eagerness that belies his behavior. "Can I take my seat belt off now?" he asks.

"Sure."

He struggles with the buckle. "Push the metal in the middle," I say, which is what he is doing.

"It won't work," Moses says, panic creeping into his voice. He's afraid he'll be left alone, tethered inside the car, while his brother and father play.

"Stop," I say, "before you break it! I'll help you."

I turn and unbuckle both of them. When I turn back around I see in the left edge of the windshield the geologist's car. I start the engine— "Hold on!" I say—and shift into drive.

"Hey," Moses whines, "the puppies!"

"Birdies!" Ira says, longingly, reaching his arm back, as if he could grab the pet shop as we pull away from the curb. "I need birdies!"

Moses kicks the back of my seat. "Stop!" he screams. "Ira's seat belt isn't on!" He's right, but I don't listen, it's just his grandfather Genius's bossy genes acting up. I keep after Jack Pierce's shit-brown car.

"This is a temporary change in our plans. You know what that means? Daddy has to drive around the block first, then Ira can see the birdies. Which birdies do you think we'll see today?"

Up ahead at the corner, fronting the laundromat, parked behind a sky-blue Chevette in the opposite traffic lane, is the shit-brown car. Two people are wedged between the cars. The traffic moves slowly, backed up by the signal at the intersection. Ira weeps. Moses demands he shut up.

"Don't talk that way to your brother."

"He's a baby. You always let him cry."

The next few minutes of my life, I know, are important, and won't come easily.

Jack the geologist leans against the shit-brown Barracuda's hood. He's laughing, his shoulders bouncing like an earthquake is rolling through him. It's not until I drive past that I glimpse his companion. To my relief, it's not Bliss. Though they seem to be the same height and weight, the spread of their hips about equal, this woman is wearing a miniskirt over black tights, a floral print blouse on a shiny synthetic fabric that hugs the curves of her body. Much too youthful for Bliss's tastes. There's something weirdly erotic about her, the way she has her knees bent, her hands resting on her thighs, her head dangling massively from her neck, like a ripe sunflower on its stalk, her wavy hair cascading forward, a perfect match to the Barracuda's shit-brown.

I drive a few more blocks, keeping sight of the geologist and his friend in the side mirror.

Ira is sobbing. Between sobs he calls for his mother. I tell Moses to sing. "Come on, Moses," I say, losing patience, while my eyes roam from the road to the rearview to the side mirror. "Ira, what should your brother sing?"

He's keen on the idea and he's thinking it over. How simple and uncomplicated life is: a song, a tumble in the sand. This is all I really want. Our eyes meet in the rearview mirror. Ira asks for "You Are My Sunshine."

"How about it, Moses? Ira wants to hear 'You Are My Sunshine.' "

Moses crosses his arms and glares out at the window.

"Don't be that way. Lead us, Moses," I say.

He won't do it. But Ira picks up the ball, and he starts singing, sweet and pathetic, his puny voice barely making a dent in the car's bleak interior, its rough atmosphere. He rocks back and forth in his seat, eyes blank and unfocused, as if his singing were a form of self-hypnosis and he were slipping into a trance. He doesn't care that his brother and father won't sing. He's absorbed in the pleasure of his clever body—lungs, breath, mouth, ears, memory. He reminds me of when they were little, their mindless sucking of fists and feet, lusting after touch and bright light and tuneful voice and sweet drink.

When he comes to the end of the song, Ira looks infinitely pleased with himself, six feet deep under his own spell. "Do it again," Moses says. He's goofing on his little brother, I know that, but Ira doesn't. He gathers his breath and lets loose, louder this time, his push for volume throwing him further off-key.

WE ARE WAITING for the green at the intersection of Ocean and Water. Ira's singing for his life. Moses scowls, staring at his uncool brother, mouth open with astonishment. He can't believe how Ira delights in being a kid.

By the time the light is green, *Please don't take my sunshine away,* there are tears in my eyes. I can't take it anymore. Ira's pristine joy and my own fuck-up. The tears seem to have always been there, too many years to count.

"What's the matter with you?" asks Moses.

"Nothing." I turn right. Ahead I see the Barracuda. Suddenly Ira breaks off his song. He leaps to his feet: in advance of downtown's gold coast, he is keenly attuned to the conflation of sensual signals hanging in the air: dust mites from spines of books; salami on sourdough; dander from cockatoos, rabbits, and ferrets; taco shells sizzling in lard. He shares the genius of animals—cattle anticipating storms by sniffing ions escaping the soil, birds agitated by electromagnetic disturbances before tornadoes. Standing on the car floor he surveys the street, seeking visual confirmation of what his body senses.

"Sit down!" Moses says, strangling on his irritation.

Which Ira does, kneeling on the backseat, and gazes out the window, registering each store we pass with a nod.

AHEAD OF US, to the left, the shit-brown Barracuda, the khaki-and-plaid geologist planted on its hood. We are driving at the rate of a tour bus cruising a monument. We pass the toy store, bookstore, deli, the whole scene—kids, parents, sidewalk cafés, balloons on strollers. Moses is sunk deep in his seat. A look of puzzlement has congealed on Ira's face; his hands press against the window and he bounces anxiously on his knees. "I want to go home," Moses says, and again kicks the back of my seat.

Red light. We come to a stop just shy of the Barracuda. Ira starts in with his song again, "You are my sunshine, my only sunshine," very softly, as he used to serenade himself in his crib. The black-tighted, miniskirted woman, as before, is bent at the waist, her mass of shit-brown hair cascading, scraggly as an artichoke plant. I have her figured out: She's drying her hair in the sun. From the way she's dressed, her figure, my guess is she's a grad student. Stupid Bliss, thinking she can compete with a younger woman.

The light changes, and I ease off the brakes. The car starts rolling. Ira's still singing into the window, in that same eerie, out-of-body way of his, as we pull even with the Barracuda.

"There's Jack!" Moses says. "Jack!" he calls, as if he hopes the other will rescue him.

"Where?" asks Ira. "Let me see." He scrambles over Moses.

"Get off me!"

I ignore them. But I can't take my eyes off the geologist either. Jack Pierce is raking his mineral-encrusted fingers through her thicket of hair. His touch seems to jolt her; she whips her hair in crazy circles, like a go-go girl on *Hullabaloo,* every hair in her scalp a wire, each wire connected to a nerve.

"Mommy?" Ira says. "Mommy!" The word comes out like a revelation. He throws himself against the window.

"Where?" says Moses, springing from his seat. They're both plastered to the window, banging their palms against the glass.

"What're you talking about?" I say. "Settle down. I just need a few more minutes, and then we'll do something special." I scan the pedestrians on the sidewalk. If she's there she's an easy one to spot—that mop of silver hair of hers.

"Mommy!" Ira calls.

"Jack!" says Moses.

The boys shift from the side window to the rear, as we leave the Barracuda behind.

"Mommy and Jack! Mommy and Jack!"

Ira's yells are suddenly loud and forceful, his voice a knife to my neck. Something wakes in me. I see the boys are right, though I can't say how they recognized her in clothes I've never seen her in before, and with her nimbus of silver hair dyed shit brown. I try to fix her in the rearview mirror, but the boys' heads are in the way. I adjust the side mirror; she's in there cavorting with the rock lover, as if she had no sons, as if she had no ties to the world, as if she were a stranger in town and no one knew her. Could it be that Moses and Ira have seen her this way before? That would explain why they recognized her so easily.

I'm watching her in the side mirror. I can't get enough of her. I realize then that she has known Jack Pierce since she and Moses visited Lester. I'm such an idiot! She was too chummy with him from the very start of our life out here. Earthquakes, my ass! He must be the "friend" who helped find the house for us. What does she see in him?

The boys are pounding at the rear window, and shouting, "Mommy!" and "Jack!" I'm watching Mommy and Jack receding, and as they recede they loom ever bigger in my life. My insides have been scooped out and replaced with the two of them. The car's rolling, I'm watching the mirror, I'm thinking, How dare you? I'm hearing Genius thump his chest, saying, "Yuk never would've done this to you." Then Moses kicks the back of my seat, kicks me in the kidney. I turn around and face him, "Don't do that!"

"I want to go home."

"What home? There is no home!"

"Mommy!" Ira whines.

"Yeah, right! 'Mommy!' She's nobody's mommy!" I slam my hand on the dashboard, over and over. "Let's go home!" Moses kicks with both feet to punctuate each word. "Quit that!" I yell. Ira's kneeling on the seat, his face buried in the backrest, his little shoulders rising and falling. He's trying to hide from me the fact he's crying. I think he's afraid he might make me madder at him, meaner toward his mother. "Hey, Ira, it's okay. I won't raise my voice again. I promise." I stare into the rearview. I feel so sorry for him: having me for a father. Tears burn in my eyes. Why is this happening? "Ira, turn around, look at me. There's nothing to cry about, okay?"

He rotates on his knees. When I see his broken face, I know we have gone past the point of love and disappointment, into sorrow. Forget Bliss; I'm the one who's done it, and dragged Ira in neck-deep.

I don't know why, but I hit the accelerator—I hope to outrace the moment, the sorrow, the life, speed Ira out of there.

Cars honk. I look at the road, and the red light, and everyone is stopped or stopping, except me. It happens in a heartbeat: The distance between me and the car ahead rapidly closes, I brake, the Valiant fishtails, Moses kicks, I shout, *"Shit!"* Ira's mouth is wide open, as if he were singing with all his heart, but nothing comes out.

T HE VALIANT RAMS into the car ahead of us, an old, beat-up Cadillac hearse. My head bounces off the windshield. The boys scream. Their bodies thud against the front seats, muted echoes of the automobiles colliding.

"You guys all right back there?" I say, knowing nothing is. "Everything's fine, okay? We're all okay, okay? Everything's going to be all right."

Ira, dear little Ira, is nowhere in sight. I turn, and find him face-down on the floor behind me, one foot—its shoe improbably knocked off—hooking the steel door handle. He whimpers, a muffled cry into the carpet, in sharp contrast to Moses, who is wailing about his hand hurting. He must've jammed his wrist when he was flung forward, before his seat belt grabbed. He tilts awkwardly to his right, half sitting, half reclining, his legs crossed serenely at the knees like an adult's. I reach for his injured hand; it burns in mine, life's heat already abandoning me. I pat Ira's back; his shoulder blades bulge like newly sprouted wings. "You're okay, right? Don't move, I'll come around and get you, okay?"

I pull the Valiant over to the curb, and the hearse follows my moves. Cars in both directions of traffic are slowing to rubberneck; people gather in distinct clumps on the sidewalk. Bliss is going to kill me. I release myself from the seat belt. The driver pops out of the hearse. She's a hippie girl, probably an undergrad at the university. "Did you hit me, or did I hit you?" she says. "Was I going too slow? My boyfriend says I go too slow and that I'm gonna cause an accident one day." Her car is cratered with dents, only a patchwork of original paint remains.

I don't answer. I eye her suspiciously and hurry to Ira. "I'm Summer," she says, over my shoulder. "My car's such a boat, I hardly felt a thing. I'm cool. But how's the baby?"

An alarming blood mustache, like two, thin strokes of a red Magic Marker, branches across his upper lip. Ira clumsily wipes his nose with the back of his hand and coughs. Anytime he's under the weather I've felt helpless, overmatched by circumstance. At least he isn't crying. Just blinking and staring. Dazed. Hasn't cried since I extracted him from the car. A good sign: Things can't be too messed up if the child isn't crying. Besides, Moses is squeezing out enough tears for both of them. "Aww, little baby boy!" Summer says, patting Ira's head. He looks groggy waking from a nap. He reaches out to the girl, I lower him into the stranger's arms. "If you don't mind," I say. "I need to check on his brother."

In the distance sirens sound; someone must have called 911. Moses jumps into my arms. On the curb Summer holds Ira on her hip, an expert and motherly pose. She's trying to wipe the blood mustache off. Ira lets her have her way, but the blood won't come off; it seems to permanently stain his face. Passersby gather on the sidewalk. But what's there to look at, really? There's no broken glass, no spilled oil, no crushed steel, no carnage. There's a hearse and, parked behind the hearse, an old but reliable sedan; there's a child with a bloody nose, and a girl who might easily be mistaken for his mother by the casual observer. Still, people stop and gawk, they go up to Ira, especially women, pet his head, chuck him under the chin. Poor Ira, his arms looped around the stranger's neck, looks spooked.

I put Moses down on the hood of the Valiant and massage his wrist. "Ouchouchouch!" he whines, sucking air through his teeth.

"You said your wrist hurts."

"You're making it worser!"

An ambulance arrives and double-parks beside the hearse. The paramedic wants to take someone to the hospital. I point Ira out to him. "You okay, kid?" he asks Ira. Moses slides off the hood of the car, pushes between me and the paramedic and says, "He's okay." I restrain Moses, my hands on his shoulders.

A commotion breaks out in the crowd. "Moses! Ira!"

Bliss. She breaks into the inner circle. Ira looks at her and blinks and stares, his hand swiping at his nose. She reaches for him. "I'm his mother," she says.

But Summer won't relinquish Ira to her. Bliss stares me down. The geologist comes after her, and stands just behind her shoulder like a bodyguard. Bliss mouths something but I can't catch the shape of it. "What?" I ask, across what's nothing more than a square of sidewalk, but emotionally continents apart. "Moses," she says, "come here!" I don't frame Moses' going or staying as a test of loyalty, but when the kid squirms free of my grip, I see, once again, what a little traitor he is. He hugs her black-tighted leg, and she bends and pecks the top of his head. It's the first step in her rehabilitation.

I'm standing alone, staring at my sons, the hippie Summer, Jack Pierce, my wife: I'm looking at an ad for auto insurance: the geologist and Bliss, the typical upper-middle-class couple; Summer the au pair girl; Ira their child; Moses their adopted refugee from an Asian war. The crashed car. A perfect picture. You're in good hands with Allstate. Now it makes sense to me. Of course she wants Jack Pierce. It's only natural. How can I blame her? I don't fit there.

BLISS MOUTHS SOMETHING again, her eyes darkened by anger. What is she so pissed about? Who is she kidding, trying to act so discreet, after the public spectacle she's made of herself?

"Nice hair," I say. "Nice outfit. You look ridiculous."

"*I* look ridiculous? What about all this?" She waves her arms to indicate the scene. "And who's this little tart?"

"Hey," Summer says, "I'm cool. Don't drag me into this. All I did was cause the accident. Nothing more!"

The paramedic comes over and says, "If there's no problem, I'm going to have to leave."

I look at Ira. He simply appears stunned and disoriented—no surprise after all that's happened, the accident, seeing his mother that way.

"We're okay," I say, sending the paramedic on his truck.

Once the ambulance leaves, and the crowd thins, I take Ira from Summer's arms. He seems so light, almost weightless. On the edge of flight. I wipe the blood under his nose. His skin feels rubbery, the dried blood is stubborn and ponderous. I can't make it go away. I forget myself for a moment, and look imploringly at Bliss for assistance, advice. But when she closes in on me, I take a quick, short turn, shielding Ira from her. She grabs my arm. I glare over my shoulder. She mouths something again.

"What?" I snap. "Why don't you just say it? What do you think you can possibly hide now?"

I challenge her, again and again.

Finally Moses says, "She said, 'How could you?' "

"How could I what?"

"How could you?" she says.

"How could you?"

Moses says, "I'm hungry!" A welcome relief, a merciful touch of normalcy.

But it comes too late.

Chapter 19

I LIFT IRA from his bed and transfer him to ours for
the night's sleep ahead. How heavy he seems now,
especially his head. My arms still remember his weightlessness downtown, his substance drying to powder. But now he is liquid again. He's
been sleeping for hours; after the accident, we came home, and Ira was
Ira on the verge of getting sick; that is, he was himself but a few seconds slower in the legs, not as chatty or hungry, less ornery with his
brother, who seemed, now that I think of it, gentler, even deferential,
toward Ira. After half a bowl of noodles and cheese sauce, he walked
himself to his room and climbed into bed.

I set him in the middle of our mattress. I put him on his back, his
hands at his sides, legs straight, close together. If he were vertical,
he'd be standing at attention. My little man! He is in such a deep sleep
his eyes look sunken in their sockets. His breaths rush in and out, as
if his lungs had shrunk. I sit next to him on the bed, push his hair
off his brow, neaten loose strands behind his ears. The ridges of his
ears are cool to the touch. That's odd, I think, but I wonder why it's

reasonable to expect the opposite. "Hey, Ira man!" Why am I talking to the kid when he's asleep? Why whisper? It was so close this afternoon, so scary. And it could easily have been worse. I indulge my fears. And feel I've been stabbed—first shock, then numbness, then searing pain. I struggle to inhale, my breath catches in my windpipe. No one else in the world is Ira—obviously, it's a stupid thought, it's stupid even as it hatches, but I lose myself in its deep folds. Tears sizzle in my eyes, then are dammed by Bliss and Jack Pierce; I see her on the street, her dyed hair, her college-girl getup, letting that man touch her in public.

I CHECK ON MOSES. His scalp is hot, hair damp. "Where did you take Ira?" he asks.

"He's in my bedroom."

"Where's Mommy?"

I want to say: "Aren't you tired of that question?" I suppress my anger, my desire to say: *She stepped out for milk, but she's probably running around with our favorite geologist and home-wrecker.*

Instead I tell him, "She's at the store. She'll be back soon."

"Where are you going?"

"It's hard to say. This is entirely new ground. I've never been here before."

"Huh?"

"You want to sleep in the big bed too?"

He jumps up and hurries from his room before I can change my mind. I don't blame him.

"I THINK YOU SHOULD go back to your room," I say.

"Okay." Moses' antennae are out.

"I'll be right there."

"Okay."

Ira hasn't moved. He's in the exact same position I left him in. Arms at his sides, legs only slightly apart. His breaths, as before, rapid and coarse.

"Ira!" I say. "Don't do this, you hear me?"

I RA SEEMS TO FLOAT like a little cloud, free of the rancor everyone confuses with sorrow. He is pure, and will always be. Loving evenly, never choosing sides; he has shown what love is, but no one's learned the lesson. Ira passes the iron gates of the cemetery. I can't take my eyes off the bright white coffin, as perfect as a white chocolate confection. But I can't penetrate the paint, the wood, the love-your-loved-one-to-death steel sheet that shields his body, no matter how hard I stare. When I think of Ira now, I picture him in that hippie girl's arms, his wrist swiping under his nose, a look of dreamy amazement in his eyes; I see him tottering off to bed.

Like Ira, I am riding alone. Mine is the limo directly behind the hearse, closest to Ira, the one the funeral home reserved for me and Bliss. I refused to ride with her, and she clearly shared the same sentiment toward me. Now she and Moses are with her family in the limo behind mine. My family's in the one behind theirs. These last forty-five minutes alone have been a blessing. I don't have to look at or listen to any of them. A rest from their stares and accusations. One after the other at the memorial service they took their shots, hanging the blame on me. Morton Sass, assuming the mantle of family patriarch, stood beside Ira's casket, his big hand caressing its brass handles, his eyes hidden behind aviator sunglasses, like a Secret Service agent, and concluded his eulogy by saying, "I should never have let things get this far." Then Jack Pierce spoke. I had stupidly assumed the geologist wouldn't dare show up at the funeral. But there he was, huddling with the Sasses. After the rabbi spoke and a woman sang ("Sunrise, Sunset"), he had the nerve to address the mourners, stand before us like family, like someone who might've mattered to Ira; he delivered a long, rambling speech that encompassed the beginning of time, shifting continental plates, dinosaurs, and finished with this: "Once Peking Man assumed a vertical posture, he had the new-found advantage — an enhanced field of vision. It is the difference between what is eye level for a toddler like Ira and what is eye level for his father. The adult should be able to detect danger approaching long before danger catches scent or sight of him, while his son won't see the same danger until it is too late and already upon him. But such an advantage is moot, unless the adult, our Peking Man, is vigilant, is diligently, excuse the pun, peeking, that is, keeping his eyes open to potential trouble." To top things off, my own father rose from among the assembled, and I was still so stunned by his predecessors that I thought he was planning to defend me against the attacks. He bowed to everyone, acting chinky, and in the worst English I'd ever heard from him said, "Big sadness." He bowed repeatedly, hand patting his chest. "I sorry." As in, I'm sorry my son caused the death of my grandson and so much sadness for us all. He stood there, showing off the top of his head, not moving, until Moses went to him, took his hand, and led him away.

The limo rolls past the cemetery's lush green lowlands, the grass dense and manicured so each blade is the same perfect height. The place reminds me of the lawned suburbias I used to covet when I was young. Rest under shade trees. Play catch. Picnic. Here death doesn't look all that bad. The graves themselves are like miniature estates, with well-maintained flower beds and decorative shrubs. Ira and his pretty little white "house" (as Zsa Zsa, at the memorial service, called his coffin) belong among this pampered nature, tucked away in this piece of earth like a jewel in a velvet pouch. I expect the limo's brakes to grab at any second; I exhale, and my heart clutches; I feel the end coming. This is it.

I shiver, and wedge my hands between my thighs to control the feeling. Tears cloud me. I turn around quickly in my seat and peek out the rear window; I want to see if Bliss and the others notice the salt in my eyes, the grief thick in my throat.

The limo motors past the genteel flats. We follow the hearse and take the right fork, and immediately the landscape changes, and we're in a different neighborhood, the graves more congested, the headstones smaller, the grass taller, less green. Soon the road snakes up the side of a hill, and the higher we climb, the more depressing the graves; the ground is barren, rocky yellow dirt littered with scraps of paper, and unloved, untamed clumps of crabgrass sprouting like fright wigs from deep inside the inert earth.

The hearse parks. My driver sends the limo rocking into park. He shoulders the door and steps out. "What's going on? Why're we stopping here?" I say.

He opens my door. He offers me his hand as if I were old, a woman. But I take it, and let him help me out.

The headstones stacked on the hillside are crawling with Chinese characters, with peonies and bamboo cut into the granite slabs. This is the Chinatown of cemeteries. There's a mausoleum topped with a pagoda-style roof. Old Chinese grannies in blue silk vests are sweeping some of the graves, and black-haired boys in tight black slacks run among the headstones playing tag.

The funeral home workers open the tailgate of the hearse. Everyone is pouring from the other limos. This is Ira's new home? I look down the hill, surveying the lush, lovely lowlands and the good plots we have just left, cool and fertile, an invitation to croquet, and gin and tonics. Bliss made the funeral arrangements with my parents; she and I were hardly speaking, and she thought she was doing the right thing, getting me involved by getting my parents involved, and they bought into this ghetto of a graveyard. All the residents here are Chinese:

Chan	Lo
Wang	Chin
Li	Hsu
Fan	Ling
Yee	Fu
Ng	Liu
Cheung	Yip
Leong	Chang

Wong	Louie
Lee	Yep
Fong	Fung
Hong	Wing
Young	Low
Ching	Eng
Chu	Chow
Lu	Nee
Fang	Lum
Huang	Chiu
Yung	Lung

ZSA ZSA AND GENIUS come up behind me. I'm okay with Zsa Zsa, but I'm still mad at Genius for apologizing to everyone. I'm not the only one who's done wrong.

"What are we doing here?" I ask Zsa Zsa.

"Are you dreaming? Dead boy! Your own son!" she scolds.

"We're here because your son's Chinese," Genius says, tugging at my sleeve. "Isn't that right?" Then he changes his tone, and adds, "Where he is, is the best. It's good he's not too high. At the top there's no protection in the rear." He reaches around and taps his back. "Excellent location. He couldn't ask for better. Facing south. Sheltered from the winds. The rain will rush down the hill and he'll always stay dry. . . ."

"What're you talking about?"

"Don't ask. Trust me, this is the best! You *juk-sing*'s don't understand!"

WE STAND in two semicircles around the grave, the Sasses on one side, the Lungs on the other, Rabbi Ron separating Bliss and me. Ira's coffin is floating over the opening, perched on ribbons slung across a steel frame. We're waiting for Genius. He is taking a tour of Ira's new neighborhood, strolling from grave to grave, hands clasped behind his back, a solitary figure without a care in the world. I watch him walking alone, among the headstones inscribed with Chinese characters, looking for family and friends. All those Chinese dead. For thousands of years my forebears have survived dynastic shifts, barbarian conquests, mass conscriptions, universal starvation, pestilence, and superstition to ensure that I would have this day on earth, on this spot, at this moment, to watch my youngest son be buried. Will the ancestors recognize Ira as one of theirs without Genius at his side or there to welcome him? And will those same ancestors claim me, after my breakneck dash from them and into the arms of any willing American girl who would have me—my desperate attempt to overcome the unremarkableness of being a Lung, and create a family more to my liking? I embraced school because school wasn't home, European cuisine because Escoffier wasn't home, Bliss because she wasn't home. My sons were the blades of scissors that were supposed to snip me permanently, and genetically, free from home, from past and present, from here and over there. (With Ira, whom everyone deemed pure Sass, I thought I had succeeded in erasing every trace of myself, committed genealogical suicide.) But centuries from now, a stranger roaming the grounds like Genius will happen upon Ira's grave among the thousands staggered along this slope, and when he encounters Ira's names carved in Chinese and English on his headstone, he will conclude one thing: There lies a member of the One Hundred Families, a black-haired, American-born scion of the Lungs of Toisan, Guangdong, China. So sad, dying so young! His poor parents! His white-haired grandparents!

"Your mother's exhausted," Bliss says. "Let's get going."

When I don't respond, Rabbi Ron intercedes like a Kissinger. "There's no point in putting off the inevitable."

"Go get Genius." She points at him. Does she think I don't know my own father?

WHEN I COME UPON Genius, he immediately starts talking to me, as if we were in mid-conversation: "Oh, this is a most auspicious site! Up so high, he'll have a fine view. And below is the very worst. Rains run downhill and flood the flatland and drown the people's good luck and fortune. The barbarians don't understand these things. If they did, they'd be up here and the little one would be down below. Do you understand what I mean?"

I nod. I believe I got it. Ira's in the best place he can be. Standing on this portion of the hill I feel its slope in my body, and I feel what I've imagined my father must've felt all these many years—lopsided. Maybe I'm the one who's lopsided, I'm the one who's off balance. Genius stares ahead at the distance. There's a shimmer in his eyes, and in this drop of liquid light I see for the first time Ira's face in his, and seeing Ira in my father, Ira comes to me vividly, not the stunned boy in Summer's arms, life already draining from his body, but Ira in his bed singing, his eyes unfocused and dreamy, his pajama bottoms pushed down, his hands playing with his little dick, his sugary voice vibrating in my chest, before rising through his brother's bunk, through the ceiling, into the trees, the sky, the roof of heaven. And there he is, alive in Genius.

As GENIUS AND I make our way to the others at Ira's grave, a yellow taxi pulls up behind the limos.

"She's here!" Genius says.

"Who?"

"She's brought the food."

"What food? Who can eat now?"

He peels away from my side, and at the same time Zsa Zsa leaves the graveside, screaming something. Both converge on the taxicab. They seem far from their bodies, transported in space and time, the days of inevitabilities gone.

The taxi driver unloads colorful plastic shopping bags from the trunk. As soon as his fare exits the cab, Genius and Zsa Zsa swarm her. The passenger is a Chinese girl, probably a waitress or someone's relative at the restaurant Genius ordered the food from. They kiss and hug her; they keep touching her as if the cab had just delivered her from the dead. I am awed by their capacity for affection. This side of their grandsons, I have seen them like this only with my imported bride, Yip Yuk Hing.

I hurry down the hill toward the taxicab. As I close in I'm sure I see Yuk, and even that slightest hint of her being there tickles me, and instantly, thankfully, I am transported from this day. For one glorious instant I return to prehistory, the time before marriage, sons, and death. Soon enough, I see it's not Yuk. This one's hair is too hip, cut short, buzzed on the sides, spiky as a pineapple on top; she looks taller than Yuk; and I can't imagine Yuk in the almost too mini minidress, the black-for-mourning tights.

"Mr. Sterling!"

I fly into Yuk's arms, and weep. The comfort of the long-lost, and regret for the what-could-have-been. "I'm sorry," I say, meaning I wish I had listened to my parents.

"I'm sorry," she says.

The spell breaks: she is crying, her body shaking. More tears want to come, but I'm all out. For those five days when Ira was in the hospital, under the ocean of sleep, I'd caress his cheeks, sing into his face, and when my tears fell on his skin, I wanted to believe I could wash him back to me.

HER DRESS IS her stewardess uniform, midnight blue with a pair of gold wings over her heart. Everything about her seems different, and it's not just her hair, her clothes, her professional, flying-high-above-the-Pacific face. I don't need to stare too long before I can identify the main change: Those years ago when we first met, Yuk still had a traveler's gaze, eyes fixed on a point in the distance, a traveler shipboard, straining for a glimpse of land; there was nothing inside backing up those eyes, the candle or bulb or electric spark that illuminates a person missing. But her eyes now are bright as new pennies, lucid, inviting contact, darting like hummingbirds from person to person.

From the bags Zsa Zsa and Genius unpack food—thick slabs of boiled pork belly, strips of glistening *cha-siu,* a hunk of roast pig with crispy skin the same hue as the dirt. Four pounds of meat. Oranges, sweet tricornered muffins, sponge cakes. And a giant whole chicken, at least five pounds, all appendages attached, unsavory black feathers poking from its bald yellow head. They call Yuk to help. She crouches, her back to me, the soles of her feet springing free of her shoes, the balls of her fleshy heels doming white like eggs through her black stockings.

Bliss glares at me. I feel the burn of her eyes. "When did that happen?" she demands, "that" being Yuk. She pinches my arm, and I have to shrug free of her. "She was at Moses' banquet. Don't think I don't recognize her. Is she a girlfriend from before or after we met?" she asks. "You have to tell me." Is she joking? I'm amazed she doesn't recognize my "cousin." Right then, I fall in love with the symmetries of our respective jealousies and hurts, the turbulent yin-for-yang, the eye-for-an-eye, the world descending into a chaotic balance: my Yuk and her professor.

"Why does it matter?" I say. "You tell me: Will it bring Ira back?"

AT THE FOOT of the grave they've arranged a picnic buffet. Tinfoil trays full of food. I hear Selma Sass whisper, "Food is very important to Chinese culture." She's explaining us to the rabbi and the geologist. What viciously stupid talk: isn't food important to every creature that ever walked, crawled, or swam this earth? She continues, "They don't do anything without food. They're like us that way."

Isn't this weird, though? Who has a stomach for eating now? This is a burial, not a picnic. Only scavengers have appetites so close to the dead. There are specific occasions for food, but this isn't one of them. I shudder at the thought of Zsa Zsa and Genius down on hands and knees urging Morton Sass to the brink of the grave to dine. We are dangerously close to civilization's end when we dispense with tables and chairs, when the decorum of dinner gives way to displays of teeth, and the hips of all manner of men and women grinding together as they jostle for position while they feed off the ground.

Yuk smooths the dirt in front of the trays of food, lays down three pairs of red chopsticks, six inches apart, and beside each a thick-bottomed shot glass. Next candles, bright red candles on sticks. While she's forcing the last one into the ground, Moses snatches a muffin from the impressive mound of sweets. "That's not for you to eat!" Genius snaps, and makes Moses put the muffin back. What then? Bury the goodies along with the dead? As in the pyramids of ancient Egypt, the imperial tombs of China. What would Ira want with this stuff? Better to throw in his tricycle, jelly doughnuts, his collection of plastic ponies. Why not mimic the ancient Incas? In their priests' tombs servants were inhumed, teenage boys and girls whose feet were cut off to ensure their loyalty. Perhaps I should accompany Ira into the afterlife and serve him in ways I've failed to do in this life.

"STERLING." Bliss comes up to me. "What's going on here? That's pork!"

"So?"

"There's a rabbi here!"

"What are you trying to say, the ground's kosher? Ira's Chinese too, you know."

The flames tremble in the breeze. Yuk lights three sticks of incense, and hands them to me. "What? What is all this?"

"Not important," she says, "for you to understand. Just do for your little boy." She bows to the grave. "Three time," she says. Once that's done I'm supposed to stab the sticks into the ground.

I hate the smell of incense, which Zsa Zsa and Genius used to burn at home on certain holidays; it's dirty to my nose, not fragrant or sweet. And I hate all the eyes circling the grave watching my every move: some angry at the sacrilege; others comforted by the familiar, the return of the world to its proper spin; and then there's Moses, who shifts his gaze from Yuk (he's been staring up at her like a tourist admiring the local architecture) to me, and who seems impressed by just how Chinesey I can act. I close my eyes and bow from the waist, a stiff, slight tilt forward. The greasy smoke burns high in my nose, lifting off the top of my head. I feel free of the others, the hillside falling away beneath my feet. Yuk squeezes my elbow. "Mr. Sterling, you bow too much already," she says. I kneel and, surrounded by the smells of the roasted meat, the incense, the citrus oils, try to dig the delicate, spider-thin sticks into the hard yellow dirt. I notice I am doing this with the same laser-dense concentration Ira brought to his playing and singing, and I want to do this for him, with all my heart, and do it right, without splintering even a fraction of the wood, even though I don't understand why that should matter or what any of this means.

Genius summons Bliss. It's her turn. Yuk smiles, waves, holds the incense out to her. "I'm sorry. It's against my religion," she says.

My parents burn incense for Ira; then my sisters, then Moses. We offer wine, and after that we burn fake money and gorgeous gold-leaf paper, a bouquet of flames in my hands, its heat bringing my tears to the boil.

Rabbi Ron says a prayer in Hebrew. At his insistence, the food has been cleared from the grave. I don't understand a word, but his voice, the melody, vibrates in my knees. Moses hugs Genius's legs and buries his face in my father's crotch. I know it's long been too late, but I want some of that. I am the bridge between them, the reason they look upon each other and immediately love.

THE HORRIBLE MOMENT COMES. Yuk's arrival, the ritual, my parents' relief the right thing's been done, and the Sasses' refusal to take part were welcome distractions, but once the workmen release the pulleys and Ira is lowered into the ground, all the world is in that shiny white box. Every tree, every stone, every breath, every scrap of love. He drops from plain sight like the daily sun tucked behind the horizon. Only, this time it is permanent and won't rise again in the morning. As soon as

he's gone, the world dims—light itself breaks. I register an actual physical difference, all that's visible has faded, taken down a notch in brightness. And just as the body reacts to changes in light, I feel a change
happening inside me. What I feel is a blind spot forming, like a cancer
crowding out healthy tissue, and into it Moses falls, Bliss is lost. No matter how strong my gaze is, I don't see either of them.

Chapter 20

O N THE DAY Genius and Zsa Zsa are scheduled to leave for home, Genius crumbles at the departure gate. His legs dissolve from under him, the floor suddenly cloud. The plane takes off without him.

Exhaustion. Stress. Heartbreak. Whichever is the cause of the collapse, he needs rest. I bring him back to the house and put him to bed. Bliss insists he go see a doctor. Between the geologist's friends at the university hospital and people she knows at the medical plaza where she cleans teeth, she is certain she can obtain the best care for my father. It's Bliss to the rescue again, trying to look good in front of my parents. Save face. I might be slimy toward your son, but I can still be nice to you. "This isn't your business," I tell her, "anymore."

"He's sick, Sterling. Isn't that obvious?"

"He's just tired. He's been put through enough," I say. "No one's dragging him to a doctor."

THE NEXT DAY I have to shoot my show at KQED in San Francisco. I am happy to have the distraction. As I stare into the camera and reel off my intro, "I am Sterling Lung, the Peeking Duck, peeking into your kitchen, as I do, each week at this time . . ." I happily relinquish my skin, and become someone else, someone whose son is at home minding his own business, singing in some corner, out of harm's way. What joy it's been to contemplate nothing but food, even if it is Chinese.

"Today I make velly famous dish," I say in my Peeking Duck voice. "Shlimp and robster sauce! This one velly good and velly chlicky dish. Aw time peoples say, 'Wah! Where is robster?' . . ." I laugh. I pepper every third or fourth sentence with laughter. To the right of the camera the show's producer, Nadine, gives me the thumbs-up. She is always after me to crack myself up periodically and wag my head and show a lot of teeth. That's to remind my audience the show's an entertainment, the viewers shouldn't take me too seriously. I peel a couple of shrimp. "Wah, so easy!" Next I demonstrate the proper way to clean them. With the tip of the knife I pick the black vein from the gray-pink glistening body. I hold it out to the camera for a close-up. "Unberievable! That's too good. You want me to do that one more time?" I slice into a second shrimp. Its flesh squirts and cracks, the sea rushes into my brain and knocks my head backward. When I dip the blade's tip in and eviscerate the black vein, my hand trembles. Lifting the dancing worm, I feel like a surgeon holding a heart, which later, transplanted, will give life to another. But here the heart is mine, I am opening my own chest, holding up my own heart, and frantically searching for a substitute. My Ira! I slap my hands against the chopping block and say, "Wah!" It's automatic by now. But this time I hear myself as I never have. I hear myself as Moses must, as Genius, as Yuk, I hope, never will. I hear a loud clank, the sound of a shank bone dropped into a stockpot, what hollowness is. If Ira had grown up and gotten a faceful of my act, I would have died. Tears bead at the corners, hot and stinging, and I stretch wide my lids and create wells into which they drain. Nadine holds both palms up, What the hell are you doing? I'm thinking about Ira, his not liking me, his not finding an ounce of me to respect; I'm thinking about the direction not-liking flows, Genius not liking me, and me not liking him back, the simple equation that has summarized my understanding and lowered my expectations of us. While the mere hint of Ira's disapproval sends me reeling, it chills me to think Genius has absorbed all these years of my meanness and indifference, accepting it as duty, the life of a parent. My tears rise like high tide, then burn down my face, and leach in the corner of my mouth. When I taste the saltiness I know they're Genius's.

Nadine fakes a belly laugh. She's prompting me: Snap out of it!

I nod. The camera lights star in my eyes. I dab the tears with the back of my knife hand. But I can't crank out any laughter.

I survey my ingredients arrayed on the countertop—shrimp, scallions, pork, eggs, garlic, and salt. Salt in tears. Salt the only edible rock. Staple of life. At the CIA we learned all about salt. The Jewish people used it in sacrifices and ceremonies. Homer described nations as poor whose citizens didn't mix salt with their food. The Roman Empire paid its soldiers a wage called *salarium,* or "salt money" (the root of our own *salary*). In the Middle Ages, the salt routes were the basis for the flow of trade. Across the centuries, state monopolies in the production and sale of salt brought wealth and power to nations and impoverished those so taxed. Gandhi in 1930 as an act of civil disobedience scooped up a handful of salt crystallized from the evaporated waters of the Arabian Sea, symbolically breaking his British master's monopoly and striking a blow against the Empire.

I look straight into the camera and tell my viewers this. At first my voice quivers; then it strengthens with each new bit of history remembered. I'm on a roll. The facts come quickly and naturally, like breaths I exhale. And like breathing, the recitation is involuntary and necessary. Then I hear myself saying, "Salt was invented by the Chinese. . . ." That's what some scholars claim. I never put much stock in it myself. They say the Chinese invented salt in the way some say the Chinese invented agriculture, around 6500 B.C., or human civilization began with Sumerian society three thousand years later. The Chinese were the first to cultivate salt. "We flooded fields with seawater, and after its evaporation, we harvested the remaining crystals from the soil. . . ."

I hear myself say "we," as if I were there with the ancestors, among the world's first Lungs, smoothing the pans of seawater, pulverizing large sediments into edible grains. Or better yet, Ira and Genius and Moses and me, the four of us together working the salt, barefoot in the brine, and when it inevitably happens that someone picks on Ira because he looks different, calls him a barbarian, we will close ranks and protect him, and I will make the claim, "He's one of us."

Nadine's listening intently. She has on her pinched-brow, puckered-lip look. She's watching like a viewer somewhere, waiting on my next word; she wants to hear the rest of the salt story and then a tidy segue back into today's recipe. But I've run out of things to say. I'm empty, as though I've just exhaled my final breath.

She wags her hand, Come on, come on, encouraging me to speak, trying to coax me back to life. What comes to mind is the phone conversation I had with Genius when I broke the horrible news. He was dead on the other end. After the initial utterances of disbelief he said nothing, and I heard his anger in the prolonged silence, and all I could do was be angry back. Then he spoke up: Did I touch Ira? Of course I touched him. After he passed away? Yes (I had cupped his cheeks for as long as I could). He said to get off the phone and ordered me to wash my hands immediately with salt. To cleanse and purify myself, ward off bad luck, the "bad wind" of coming in such close contact with the dead. He hung up on me, so I would go do as I was told. And of course I didn't. I thought he was out of his mind. Dumb Chinese superstition!

I pick up the little white dish of salt. I'm thinking, Who knows? Maybe Genius is sick, the way Bliss insists he is. Maybe I'm the cause, something I did or refused to do. Maybe I did get too close. And the bad wind is in me, hissing in my bones. I feel it now, a tingling sensation, like teeth grazing my skin. I pour the salt in my hand, then rub my palms together. The salt falls through my hands. I know what I'm doing is not nearly enough.

WHILE I WAS at the studio, Bliss took Genius to see her doctor, even though I had told her not to. Thanks to her connections she was able to circumvent red tape and speed him up the medical hierarchy, from specialist at the county hospital to Stanford all-stars, from stethoscope to MRI, all accomplished in the hours I was gone. When Bliss is on a mission, her body grinding in rescue mode, she is unstoppable, will not relent until she gets results. After logging countless miles and waiting-room hours, after filling out dozens of forms, she was rewarded for her efforts when the Stanford doctors insisted he spend a few nights in the hospital.

NOW HE'S DEEP in hospital hell. Twenty-four hours in, he's tangled in a web of wire and tubing, a forest of machines and monitors, a bag of salt water dripping into his body, a bag at his bedside catching what seeps out. Years ago the doctors at Sloan-Kettering said there was a good chance the disease that had claimed his kidney might still be alive in his body. They just couldn't make a definitive diagnosis. Then came his miraculous recovery around the time of the wedding, and ever since he has confounded his handlers, "a medical wonder." Until now.

He is sleeping. The nurse has told me he sleeps whenever the doctors aren't working on him. Still he looks exhausted, depleted, his face brown and lean, the silver stubble on his chin pinpricks to my eyes. I want to put his glasses on his face, make him look more everyday, and his arms, poking free of the stupid gown and bare up to his armpits, scare me with their utter uselessness. I lean in close. His face is locked in a grimace, the look of a man in pain or a child being scolded.

BEFORE ZSA ZSA FLIES back to Long Island, I arrange for Lucy to help run the laundry until Genius gets better. I am surprised Zsa Zsa even contemplates leaving. But she says the store's been closed too long. That's the way she and Genius are, so Chinese. On the way to the air- port she has a brainstorm. She wants to detour to San Francisco Chinatown and buy medicine for Genius. What she has in mind are those herbs—twigs and berries, leaves and grass—that she brews into a thick, black tea. "We don't have time," I say. After I drop her off she expects me to pick up the herbs—she names a forestful, but how am I supposed to know what's what?—then drive over to the hospital and brew Genius up a batch. "I can't do that! It's a hospital."

"What hospital doesn't have a kitchen?"

"They're not going to let me bring your medicine into the hospi- tal. That's like you bringing food to a restaurant."

"I never did that."

"Good. Don't ask me to either."

"Take me to Chinatown. I'll cook the tea myself."

"You have a plane to catch."

"*Ai-yah!* You have a father."

"Oh, come on. You know what I'm saying. I'm a cook, but not in a hospital."

"You cook in a TV, you can cook anywhere."

"But food, not medicine."

"Medicine is food if you're sick."

"These American doctors won't let your medicine into his room."

"Stinky American doctors. What do they know? They've already ruined him. Look how bad he's gotten in just a few days in the hospital."

O NCE ZSA ZSA LEAVES, I decide to move out of the house. From the time of the accident my brain has been frozen. With her departure a segment of the nightmare ends. I take a cheap apart- ment in Half Moon Bay, halfway between Santa Cruz and San Francisco, about twenty minutes from the hospital. Bliss didn't want me to move out, but she didn't seem to want me there either. She thinks that this is a temporary thing, that I have to do something to make a dramatic statement, blow off steam. Maybe she's right. I just know I can't stay there.

By agreement with Bliss, I plan to visit Moses twice a week, but I anticipate uncomfortable hours with him, bookended by bitter pick-up and drop-off encounters with his mother.

My new place isn't much of a home yet. At Bliss's request I left most of my belongings at the house, for Moses' sake, to keep things intact for him until the grown-ups decide what course ultimately to take. So I brought a box of clothes, a few cookbooks, and nothing else. My only piece of furniture is a mattress on the floor. It's a bleak space, in a building constructed hastily, with cheap materials—a transient structure designed for a steady stream of transient residents. You're in trouble if you stay more than a year. But its dinginess, its naked walls, its mustard-brown carpeting that lunges at you each time you step indoors suit me to a T. It is interior design's answer to how I feel inside: dirty, empty, and ugly; and the succinct answer to the question, Why am I here?

I'VE BEEN GONE for about a week when I notice Bliss in the Volvo, parked across the street in front of my building. I wait for her to buzz me, and fret over what to do when she does, whether to let her in or not. But she doesn't get out of the car. Mostly she stares in the direction of my apartment, like an undercover cop, a secret agent, or a hostage-taker guarding her prize.

I'm stuck inside, the front door the only way out. But that's okay; I can wait her out. I don't need to see her, especially here. This is my place, untainted by what's come before. Unadulterated, as it were. All I brought to these walls from then is Ira, and why shouldn't I protect the purity of that?

I call Genius's hospital room. The line rings and, as usual, no one answers. The phone's unplugged or he's away from his bed, getting worked over by the doctors. I call Zsa Zsa but she's too busy to talk. That's fine with me; I only wanted to check in, let her know I am thinking of her. As I'm about to hang up she asks, as she has every time I've talked to her this week, if I've bought the herbs for Genius yet. Before I can bark my usual "No!" she's already running through a recipe for a medicinal bowl of tea, a pinch of this, a handful of that. "Why am I telling you? The apothecary will give you what you have to have," she says.

"He doesn't need me to brew him your tea. He already has doctors."

"I'm not asking you to be a doctor," she says. "I'm asking you to be a good son."

"Look, even if I did brew him a bowl of tea, he wouldn't drink it anyway. You know how he is, he won't eat anything I cook." I remind her of this fact as a joke, a diversionary tactic.

She sighs, then finally says, "I can't tell you how much it frustrates me to have to rely on you."

After we get off the phone I look for something to eat. The refrigerator is empty, and it's then I remember I was on my way out when I spotted Bliss and the Volvo on the street. I sneak along the wall over to the window. Nothing's changed; she's still below. I can wait her out.

I stand in the middle of my apartment. I don't know what to do with myself (I'm sure she has a few ideas). I'm not here much; even on days I'm not working, preparing for work, or visiting Moses, I get out as soon as I brush my teeth.

I lie on my bed and stare at the cheap cream-colored paper lantern flush on the ceiling. I turn onto my side, balancing on the edge of the mattress. I play a game I've played before: I rock my body forward, in the direction of the floor, and try to see how far I can tilt and still maintain my balance. If I fail, I fall on the mustard-brown carpet, its matted grime and the spent lives that preceded me in the fibers.

I teeter, on the brink of toppling over, my body stiff and trembling from the effort, my head swirling with dust and evaporants of spit and sweat. When I see a crescent of some loser's thumbnail rising from the carpet, I feel like a patient in an ambulance watching helplessly as the world in the window rushes by, and I huddle with myself, as Ira must have, as Genius must. And because they can't, I pick up my bones.

ONCE I STEP from the building, Bliss rises from the Volvo, leading with a crown of silver hair, her shit-brown dye job restored to the old state of shock for the occasion, a return to the days before shifting continental plates and sudden death. We look at each other across the street and freeze: Who's going to cross first?

She holds up her hands signaling me to stop, making a great show of how she is willingly yielding to me. As she approaches, her eyes blaze like yolks; she shakes her hair so that even if I missed her nest of wires before, I have to see it now. She comes on like a teenager parading her unbreakable life. Her chest heaves, she's breathless. As she approaches I feel Ira in my arms again and I squeeze him for as long as I'm able, but he twists and kicks at the sight of her, his little body a fleshy spring I can no longer suppress. He breaks free and runs to her, innocent to the very fact of her, her cunning heart, her changing hair, her fickle loyalties. He speeds into the harsh world's gaping mouth, poised to swallow him whole. She gathers him hungrily into her arms, and he never looks back at me.

She comes up to me, bumping her chest to mine, and she smiles a smile from a long-ago past. "Moses needs you," she says. "Come back home."

"Bliss, I've hardly been away yet. I spend more time with Moses now than when I was living there with him. At least now he doesn't hide from me."

"It's different living with us and visiting us."

"I visit him, Bliss."

She grins, her irritation checked. "He misses you. He misses your Chinese food."

"Take him to a restaurant. They have better cooks there."

"At least they're real Chinese." She laughs uncomfortably; she knows her joke hasn't found the right audience this time. "Come on, Sterling, you've cooked Chinese for us. Remember how Moses couldn't believe you could cook like that? Remember how he stared at you like he was in the presence of some wonder, a carousel pony or a daring cat? Remember what he said? 'Chinese food is my favorite!' Now do you see how much he loves you? Misses you?"

"Don't use Moses, okay? My not living in the house has nothing to do with Moses. It's what's between us."

"And what's that? What's between us?"

"Nothing. That's what."

"Why're you like this? Ira's dead, for God's sake!"

I know how it pains her to admit this; it pains me to hear it again.

"I want you to come home. Forget what I said Moses wants."

"Okay. But you have to tell me something first."

"What?" she says sweetly, a single bright expectant syllable.

"Are you still having sex with that guy?"

"How dare you!"

"Yes or no?"

"You're incredible. I don't have to answer you."

"Yes or no? Or is that too hard? How about, Is he so amazing in bed that it's worth trashing your family for?"

"Honey, I'm not the one who can't operate a motor vehicle safely."

"It's like you ate poison," I say. "But instead of killing you it sits in your blood and makes you cruel."

"I just followed your example."

"Fine. Why don't you stop sleeping with the professor."

"Sure, when you stop crashing into other cars."

I RECEIVE A TELEPHONE CALL from my father's day nurse, Florence. When I hear her voice I think the worst. But she's only dialing for Genius. He gets on the line and says Yuk's in San Francisco and I have to pick her up, later that afternoon, in Chinatown, at the corner of Jackson and Grant, and bring her to the hospital.

I FIND YUK sitting on a bus bench. At her feet is a black carry-on with wheels, and beside her is a pile of white paper packages, each the thickness of a paperback book, but irregular in shape, stacked one on top of another, secured with twine. She stands and waves. My heart speeds from me. She looks particularly lovely today, in a sleeveless turtleneck top and a skirt embossed with two enormous tigers hiding in a bamboo grove.

"These things are for you," she says, referring to the tower of white parcels she puts between us.

"Really?" I'm elated. "You didn't have to do that."

"But Mr. Sterling, it is most important."

I'm flattered, even though I'm certain the gift is nothing more than Chinese custom, never go visiting empty-handed; I remember Genius and Zsa Zsa schlepping a bag of oranges each time we dropped in on their friends. I'm touched—she truly is the gem of a person my parents have been selling these many years. And now, more than ever, I'm sold.

I fondle the packages, playing at guessing at their contents. "Feels like twigs," I say before I can stop myself. Instantly I realize how insulting that must've sounded. I try to backtrack. "It's not twigs. Who'd give twigs as a present?"

"Twig is not present," she says.

"That's what I said. So what's inside?" Then I playfully add, "What did you bring me?"

"Twig," she says matter-of-factly. "But twig is not present, twig is for your father. I buy, you cook. Your mother tell me you already understand all about this."

"My mother put you up to this?"

"Of course! She loves your father. She wants for you to cure him."

There is more than twigs in the packages. Roots and herbs, berries and leaves. Very high-quality ingredients, she assures me. The plan is to fortify his body, restore his strength, and then deliver Genius back to New York so Zsa Zsa can turn the full force of her kitchen loose on what ails him.

WE INCH THROUGH the Chinatown streets, looking for a way out. I'm surprised by how well Yuk seems to know the place, even though she doesn't live in the city. She points out the shops and restaurants she has frequented. "You purchase black chicken there," she says. I'm supposed to boil the twigs and herbs with a black chicken, which, she informs me, is available only at "respectable" markets.

Once we find the freeway we roll the windows down, inviting a stiff wind to pound our faces, thunder in our ears. Yuk puts on a pair of sunglasses that look like an identity-hiding strip of electrical tape across her eyes. We're heading south to the hospital, driving along the coast, past beaches and rocky cliffs, past eucalyptus groves, strawberry fields, kiwi and ollalaberry farms, rolling hills with brown cows and stands of trees like giant broccoli. The wind, the sun, the salt in the air, Yuk beside me grinning into the bright silver light. I feel carefree, the burdens of the past years blown off my shoulders. I smile, the wind on my teeth, spit evaporating to a cold glaze; and my insides bubble as on the day Ira was born.

On our left we pass the cement plant, decorated year-round with Christmas lights. Workers on the grounds are covered in ghostly ash-white powder. On a bluff on the ocean side of the road, migrants in straw hats and baseball caps man vast fields of artichokes. The laborers are in rubber boots and blue jeans, red or orange bandannas around their necks. At the edge of the field, close to the road, a group of men with silver canisters strapped on their backs and rags over the bottom half of their faces spray the artichoke plants. Yuk has her eyes fixed on the road ahead. I don't think she's even noticed the migrants. They're just a part of the general landscape, like trees, gulls, grass, and chaparral. I close in on a white school bus towing a pair of blue Portosans, and as I switch lanes and pass, I notice its passengers are migrants as well, their gazes fixed on the world outside, with no expectations, only weariness and dread. For Genius, his American life began here, and from here he worked and walked across the country. Now he's back at the beginning, having flown three thousand miles to watch me bury his grandson. Is there a man who prepares himself for that? I'm sorry, after all he's done, that I put him through so much.

"HORSE!" I say, pointing left, at the brown, sunburnt hills. It's a habit. We call out livestock sightings on the road, especially the rare horse. I do it for the boys. Ira's horse love was just peaking. "Horse!" I would say. "Where?" he would respond, pushing his body so hard against the straps of the kiddie seat I could feel the Volvo lurch. "On the hill. You see him?" And invariably Ira would answer he had—it was a matter of pride for him—even if a bend in the road or a rise in the land had obstructed his view. "Are you sure you saw the horse?"

"Uh-huh."

"Did it have a long tail?"

"Uh-huh."

"And a mane?"

"Uh-huh."

"I guess we saw the same horse."

"Did you see that horse?" I say to Yuk. She doesn't hear me. I tap her arm and she leans closer, and I repeat myself. She shakes her head. I tell her about my game with Ira.

Miles later I spot another horse, black and shiny in the sun. "Horse!" It escapes from me. I'm not even thinking; it's second nature.

She hears me this time. "Why you do that way?" she says. "This is Yuk, not Ira."

"Sorry." This has never happened with another passenger. There's something about Yuk that triggers this reaction. I break it down this way: I can visualize each step diagrammed in my head: I see [an arrow represents my line of sight] a horse; the image [a picture of a horse done in broken lines] is carried to the place in my brain that houses tenderness and affection [a spot on my brain with pink cutouts in the shape of my boys]; the message [a row of pulsing dots] is then routed toward the centers of speech [a podium and microphone superimposed on the same brain]; and involuntarily I say, "Horse!" With anyone but the boys or Yuk, the horse sighting just passes.

I LOOK OVER AT YUK. Her hair seems magnetic and holds the shape of the wind. Her cheeks have a twenty-four-carat glow. She is high-polish. Road dust doesn't stick to her skin. Against the backdrop of the rushing world, her posture perfect, her serene stillness, Yuk seems noble, almost floating along the earth's surface. Above it all. Remember, she spends most of her days thirty-five thousand feet in the air. In her Hong Kong life she was far removed from the dirt-under-the-nails masses. Her people own factories, they're white-collar, she had servants, a chauffeur, attended the best schools, studied English. Had our families known each other in Hong Kong—that is, imagine a Genius who never set foot in America, and a Sterling who was China-born—she would not be Genius's favorite "daughter," an honorary member of the clan; if we were lucky we might know her family as our bosses, Genius in a factory making plaster Davids, me slaughtering a duck for her family's table. She won't look at the migrants in the fields, can't abide their sweat, the grease on their brows, their preference for bright colors. I am closer to this than she is, closer to Genius: thirty years ago he was a man like these.

WE COME to a stretch of highway dotted with farmstands. Yuk bumps my arm; she wants to stop. At the next chance I pull over.

We are the only customers. The farmstand is actually an old-style wagon, on which corn, tomatoes, eggplant, zucchini, melons, and arti-chokes are displayed in rows of rough-hewn crates.

I'm glad for the break from the unrelenting blasts of sun and wind. The air is heavy, cool, damp, briny. In the field behind the farmstand a fog rolls in off the ocean. Migrants move slowly down the rows, their colorful cloth fog-muted. Some of them are harvesting artichokes, oth-ers are spraying the spiky plants, holding the spray hoses delicately in their fingers, as if the tubes were lengths of other men's bowels.

A worker in a yellow cowboy shirt with red piping and fringes emerges from a Portosan near the edge of the field. As he approaches us at the wagon he shows off his bad teeth. He is small and thin, field dust molded into the shape of a man. He keeps smiling at us, and soon enough I can tell that's about all we'll get out of him. He can't speak to us—it's written on every inch of his face. To him, we are visitors from overseas, Japan or China, as English-poor as he. Yuk can crush him with her thumb. "What you want to buy?" she asks, her fingers flitting across the produce.

"What's he going to do with any of this stuff?"

Undaunted, she picks through the basket of large artichokes. They are the size of my fist, two for a dollar. There are some in another bas-ket for seventy-five cents each, as big as an infant's skull.

"Which is good one?" she asks.

Those that look heavy, unblemished. "He doesn't know what those are," I tell her. Artichokes are as foreign to his experience as rocketships.

"No matter," she says. "It is never too late to try new thing."

"What's he going to do with an artichoke?"

"You bring to your father," she says, "and let your father decide what to do." She drops the artichokes she has selected into the bag the worker is holding open for her. As she hands him the money he is momentar-ily fixed at the center of my world; my heart shakes, flutters, and flies. Time fills the hole my fleeing heart leaves in my chest: The migrant is Genius, it's not just his complexion or wiry frame, but his stupid smile, eyes cast down, head bowed and bobbing, the obsequious professionalism that I hated, and inherited. How did he come to that? I have seen photos of the young Genius, mugging for the camera, loose-limbed, hat tipped low across his brow, hands on hips, legs crossed in a figure four, in his leather shoes, a Chinese Fred Astaire. Cocky, self-possessed. But years of work transformed him into groceries and rent, and soon the family showed in his posture, and the son put a stitch in his side.

IN THE HOSPITAL's plate-glass sliding doors I see an attractive couple coming toward us, he slightly taller than she, their chests high and proud, his arm brushing against hers, their faces somber but alert. Genius would love this picture. Yuk and me together, as he and Zsa Zsa had planned. Seeing us looking like a couple might put a charge in him, knock loose whatever it is that's taken hold of his body. I imagine the two of us entering his room together, shoulder to shoulder, his face exploding into a smile, the one he keeps in reserve for Moses, which springs from a tender spot he holds, secretly and greedily, for me.

Yuk leans into me. In the glass she looks like she's snuggling, her head on the man's shoulder, and they're tight, oozing love. But in reality that's not it at all. She tells me she's scared, she hasn't seen Genius since before he was put in the hospital. And she wants me to reassure her he's fine, she'll be fine. I put my arm around her, pull her in tight. "He'll be so happy to see you," I say, "he's going to jump out of bed and come home with us." I like the sound of "with us," as if we were a couple, and when she doesn't dispute it I take that as a sign she likes the sound of it too, and I snuggle my cheek against her spiky hair, and she doesn't dispute that either. Then the pneumatic doors slide open, and with the jolt of a dream coming to an abrupt end, the couple disappears.

GENIUS IS ASLEEP, with loud, vigorous exhalations that shake the glasses crooked on his face. TV light flickers across the lenses. His teeth aren't in his mouth. I've always been spooked seeing him this way, his facial architecture collapsed, aging him beyond his years. Today it's worse, his face seems layered on his skull like a heavy coat of paint. His hands clutch the top of the sheet, drawn neatly across his chest, an IV needle buried in one, the other an easy target for the nurse who takes his blood. Despite the violence of his breaths, his body is disturbingly still. Ira comes to mind—the frantic steady breaths that were his last, sleep-filled forty-eight hours. I tell myself, That's not happening; Genius is fine; the doctors said he was a goner more than five years ago; he's as stubborn as they come.

"I'll wake him for you," I say.

"No, don't." Yuk squeezes my shoulder. "Your father looks too tired." She pushes aside the small TV set, silent and suspended inches above his face, then reaches past me, her arm grazing my belly, and touches the blue-green bruise that IV nurses have tattooed to the back of his hand. She lets her finger run delicately along his skin, applying the same slight pressure one would when selecting a fillet at market. Watching her, I feel queasy, it's as if she were poking at a wound, testing his threshold for pain. I hope she hurts him, just enough to pop his eyes open a few seconds, so he can take us in. But he doesn't stir. She reaches up and plucks the glasses off his face—how's he going to see us without them?—and sets them on the nightstand. She retreats to the foot of the bed and says, in a voice I imagine she uses to calm passengers during the worst turbulence: "Your father needs long good sleep. Next time you come, you bring tea for him to eat."

WE'RE KEEPING VIGIL by his bed, in case he wakes. Yuk is watching TV. *General Hospital.* She needs to be at the airport within the next two hours. I've offered to wake him, but she's begged me not to. She promises to fly up from Los Angeles when she returns from China. I want to believe she is right, there'll be a next time, and we'll hook up, and Genius will be around to witness that all is not lost, that he has not completely failed, that his son, in the end, has learned to behave in a manner that will not shame him, that he's not such a barbarian after all. Then Genius can brag, as he always wanted to, My son, my son, my son . . . Genius shifts his body, and when he comes to rest again, his untethered hand lies awkwardly on his stomach. His palm shines up at me, blindingly empty. Zsa Zsa has said of her husband, "His whole life, he can hold a hammer, but not a dime." That's why he needs to see us together; then he'll have something to hold on to.

"Is that you, Mr. Sterling?" Yuk says, pointing at the tiny TV set that appears soldered to her face. She motions for me to come watch.

She's changed channels and has found me doing my Peeking Duck act. It must be one of the promos the station runs for the show. My heart rushes to my brain, pumping wildly: I am all beat. I have never thought of someone like Yuk as in my audience. "Wah!" she says, squeezing my arm tight as a tourniquet. "Look at you on television, like 'Mr. Sterling and Hutch'!"

On the screen I am chopping onions. Celery. Cabbage. I can't even recognize the dish I'm preparing. Yuk turns up the volume. She watches, grips my arm ever tighter. Is it possible she likes what she sees? But when I unleash my trademark "Wow!" after I toss the ingredients into the smoky wok and break into my toothy smile, Yuk pushes the TV away, as if rejecting the advances of a lover.

She clucks her tongue. "Who is that person, Mr. Sterling? Why you do like that?"

"I'm acting. Like Starsky and Hutch aren't real people but characters played by actors."

"I know those mens are acting. But how television watchers know you are acting?"

I shrug. I feel stupid. I glance at Genius, and even with him in his less than intimidating state I can hear his admonition: You grow up with wolves, you are theirs your whole life. You howl like them, rip the meat like them. They raise you from infancy, and then the day comes when you wake in dew-wet grass, your feet aching from a hard night's hunt, and you realize you're not a wolf after all. The wolves, of course, have known this all along. That explains why no one in the pack ever follows your lead. So you go to town. But the people see the wilderness in you. They joke and laugh, and the hairs at the back of your neck stand on end. You are confused; you think you had unlearned your wolf days, but the wild's furry edges still must show. As you shake your head, vehemently denying you ever ran with wolves, your lips involuntarily peel back, baring your teeth, and you snarl and growl.

What did he expect? I was born here, among the wolves. If he wanted a clone of himself, if he wanted Yuk for a child, he should've stayed in China. All my life he's killed me over this. He and his Chinese-from-China brothers and sisters. I am unfilial because I don't know Chinese ways. I am stupid because I forgot my Chinese. I am useless, despite all my labors since the age of six in his crummy businesses, because I am so far removed from Yuk's perfection, her tongue, her appetite, her palate pure, unadulterated by her American days, her skin that will never hold the *fahn gee lo*'s scent. I act like an ass on TV because I don't know how else to act. How am I supposed to be Chinese? By being myself? I'm not the kind of Chinese that viewers want to see, I'm Sterling, graduate of the CIA. So I try to give the people what they want: a goofy bucktoothed immigrant bastard who is humbled and grateful he's been let into their homes.

"I'm acting like Genius," I say. Truly, I've modeled Peeking Duck, at least in part, after Genius, only jazzed up for TV. Doesn't Genius see that he too has lived among the same wolves, and having failed to adopt to their ways, he also has, in his own right, been devoured by them?

"Act like father?" Yuk begins. "Why say such mean thing? He loves you."

WE SIT IN SILENCE. Yuk tapping Genius's thick fingernails like a set of typewriter keys. She stares at what she's doing. Her eyes are rocks. She looks scared.

Finally she says, "We must move bed." She pats the mattress and waves me closer, her fingers tickling the air. "It is answer to all your problem."

At first I can't believe what I'm seeing and hearing. But as I watch her hand urge me toward the bed, there is no way of mistaking her meaning. Her English no longer staggers. With the exception of interior decorators, people talking about "moving the bed" are talking slang for sex. Is she crazy? What kind of crowd is she flying with? I ask her to repeat herself, half hoping her immigrant shyness will seize her and swallow her words. But without hesitation she says, "We must move bed," her voice strong and unequivocal. She wants to make the mattress dance, the springs scream.

"What about my father?" I nod in his direction. What about the time? What about the nurses?

"We can move bed with your father inside."

Wild Yuk! "There's hardly any room."

"No problem. We don't have to move bed too much." She nudges the mattress's edge with the tops of her thighs, thrusting her pelvis delicately forward. She's getting started without me. With a flirtatious tilt of her head she motions for me to come to her. "Help me, Mr. Sterling." I step cautiously toward her. My animal brain slumbers. All I want is for Genius to pry open his lids and wake to an eyeful of us, his chosen daughter-in-law and his disappointment of a son. Finally, not so bad anymore. But sex? She has to be kidding! "What are you doing, Mr. Sterling?" she says. "Let us not delay. Bed must move immediately. Push, push!"

I position myself behind her, and as she requested, from the waist down I push, my legs brushing against the backs of hers. *"Vay, vay . . ."* she says like a warning, anger rustling in her throat. "We have no foolaround time. I must soon go to airport. Your father is right, you all time fool around. Never serious."

"You're the one who wants to fool around."

"Not true. I only try to help your father. Look at him, look at location of bed, look at window behind his head," she says, like a physician pointing out the suspicious gray spot on her patient's X ray. "Oh, you American-born Chinese don't understand. Just come, help Yuk move bed," she adds, thrusting her pelvis against the mattress again.

I tell her, "I can't do that. Not *now*." I throw my eyes at Genius, in case she's missed my meaning.

She glances his way, then turns and faces me. "No, now is good! We have to move bed and make father better."

We're on the same wavelength, different as we are. We both want him to see us together, only I think a glimpse of us is therapy enough, while she's committed to "moving the bed." What a sweetheart: her lack of inhibition teems with hope. She nudges the bed again, this time with such force Genius moans. His head flops heavily from side to side, and once he settles back into a sound sleep, she says, "If you don't want to move bed now, Mr. Sterling, you can move bed with nurse. I will tell you how."

"I'm not one of those people who'll move beds with just anyone."

"Why not? You can move bed with any available person." She shrugs. "It is not significant who moves bed with you, as long as you move bed. You can move bed all by yourself."

"I don't want to move the bed with the nurse, I don't want to move the bed alone, I want to do it with you." As I say these things I step toward her, feeling I have no choice but to comply with her demand or risk losing her altogether. My animal brain still hasn't stirred. She looks at me, her pupils wide with surprise. I close my eyes, and when I'm close enough to feel the heat of her face, she spears me in the chest, a straight-arm to the heart, as if trying to gauge what's going on inside.

"So crazy," she says, as she sidesteps me. I stumble forward and bump the bed.

"*Ah-Mah!*" Genius yelps, sitting up, calling for his mother.

Yuk jumps, I jump. Genius scans the room but his eyes appear raw and disconnected. Yuk is silent and still. She seems shocked by Genius's sudden life. I'm waiting for her to shift into stewardess mode, act cheerful, be chatty, tend to his every need. Where is Yuk, the legendary daughter-in-law who never was, who nonetheless outstripped all the Lung children in love and filial piety? She hangs back and watches Genius lift his arm in slow motion, his hand trembling, the fingertips magnets repelling. He swipes at the wild white halo of hair that radiates from the back of his head. He wants it combed. He wants to look sharp for Yuk. In the nightstand drawer I find his comb, lost among plastic spoons and forks, packets of sugar and salt, and unused napkins. As soon as he recognizes I have the comb in my hand, he tilts forward, bending loose-hinged at the waist, and I catch him, his forehead pressing heavily on my palm. I work the teeth slowly through his pillow-flattened hair. He no longer smells of cigarettes and fresh-pressed cotton. He might be any old man.

When I hear Yuk choke back tears, my eyes start to ache, my throat stings, as at the sour burst of salted plums in my mouth. Why is she crying? Yuk's here, I tell Genius. I tell him I'll let him have his glasses as soon as I'm finished with his hair. I tell him I've got something to show him. My chance for final redemption, in this man's blank eyes: His worthless Taoist-dumb son, weak in Buddha love, has come with the gift of peace of mind.

Just as I finish prettying him up, Yuk comes to my side; I am relieved she has snapped out of her funk and is going to take over. "Don't stand so close," she says, tugging at my arm. "Don't touch! Let nurse touch." I realize I'm hearing old-country talk, Genius's talk of "bad wind," my holding Ira too long, too close to death. She pulls my sleeve again. "Don't breathe your father's air. You don't want him to get inside you." I don't completely understand what she says next, but she's back to moving the bed.

"You mean you wanted to move the bed from this wall to that wall because of 'bad wind'?"

"Of course. What else could I mean?"

She talks about the dangerous position of the bed in the room, the window behind his head, the door opening onto another blind spot, the good wind making a beeline from door to window, window to door without properly circulating through the space; or worse, the bad wind enters, catching Genius from behind and roosting in his body. That's why the bed needs moving, why Genius needs the medicinal herb teas, why I need to check the location of the beds in Moses' house, why I need to eat a bowl of tea myself, why I need to keep my distance now from Genius.

But he has to see us. I raise his bed to an upright position, then gently relinquish him to the forces of gravity and his relentless fatigue. I position Genius against the pillows, holding him by his shoulders. The man is all bones. He looks as parched as a New England autumn, brown and crisp—the sixty-five percent of him that's water has been drained, leaving only the dry ingredients in the recipe for a man: carbon, nitrogen, hydrogen, oxygen; air, fire, earth, wood. The crystalline residue of urine, perspiration. He lodges high in my nose, my mind blanks, my heart seems to stop. This must be the agitation of animals before the slaughter, when they smell death on the killing floor, and the glycogen in their tissues converts to sugar for strength and energy against the looming attacker. My throat aches, as if with the worst thirst. I retrieve his glasses from the drawer and hook them behind his ears.

"Pop, do you see who's here with me?" When he opens his eyes, the globes underneath don't shine, don't spark, don't emit anything, don't let anything in. From her safe distance Yuk calls to him, her voice loud enough to go through stone. And it works, because he seems persuaded, roused as with a whiff of smelling salts. "Have you eaten yet?" she asks, as Chinese do. Anyone can see he hasn't taken a bite in days, in perhaps more than a week. "Can you hear me? Would you like something to eat?" She reaches into her plaid tote for the bag of artichokes, which I'd forgotten about. She hands me one. What does she expect me to do with this thing? But she nods, as if to say, "Go ahead. Do it!" I hold the artichoke for Genius to see. It's possible he's never seen one before, and even if he has, in the supermarket, or in a field, I'm sure he does not know its purpose, how it is eaten. He'll be surprised to learn artichokes are members of the sunflower family. If left to bloom, an artichoke will mature into a beautiful purple thistle-like flower. "This is the bud," I tell Genius, using the same let-me-try-to-shout-through-oblivion voice Yuk employed. "What we eat are the petals." I try to peel a petal off, but it's impossible, the thorn at its tip tears my skin. But I'm determined: "An artichoke won't sustain a person. It is decorative eating, a bourgeois repast, what lace is to clothes." Meanwhile, I struggle with the artichoke. "You don't eat the whole thing. Most of the petal is too tough, too fibrous, the cell walls too strong. What you're after is the tender fleshiness at the base of each petal." I wrestle the artichoke for one of its petals, I want to show Genius what I mean, show him I know what I'm talking about, prove that what he hears and sees is real. The artichoke, Yuk and me together. Pulsing with urgency I double my efforts, pull with all my strength. It slips from my hands. The thorn pricks my thumb meat just under the nail. "Sonuvabitch!"

"Fuck you! Fuck you!" Genius barks, springing forward off his pillows, as if he were riding in a car and the brakes suddenly slammed, his powder-blue gown billowing from the momentum. Whom is he cursing? His eyes open, yet I detect none of the undulations of comprehension on their glassy surface, no signs of his synapses sparking. I urge Yuk to come closer, so Genius might burn a picture of us into his brains. But she won't budge from her place at the foot of the bed.

We meet each other halfway. She puts her hand on my shoulder, then I turn into her, and we hug. I feel sorrow shoot through her like waves of sexual feeling, the tiger on her skirt leaping against my groin. She is hot, liquid, and runny; eyes, nose, and mouth. My hand roams freely across her back. I nestle my face into the humid nexus of cheek, neck, and hair. At this she sobs and pulls me tighter to her. My fingers scale her spine, like a thief up the rungs of a ladder. When my lips harvest the salt off her cheek I realize the tears are falling because she believes my father's dying.

I know she's wrong. She's wrong, she's wrong, she's wrong. I look over at him. He's staring at us. His yellow glare, his slack-skin bitterness as strong as ever. Yuk's wrong. Then, before my eyes, something seems to come over his being. A greasy luster coats his skin, as obvious as the film of protein that floats on boiled milk. To Yuk's horror I lay my hands on Genius, easing him back against his pillows. I settle him in, smoothing the sheet around his stick legs. Doing so, I notice bleeding on the cloth, a liquid turning the white cotton gray. Genius has pissed all over himself, and the piss has already gone cold—life's heat vanished. Maybe Yuk's tears are justified: Genius has passed the point of indignity and insult. Decay finally has outpaced regeneration. The ongoing violence in our cells. I have made a career out of this violence. Cooking is nothing more than disguising death and decay with heat and seasoning; we serve the food prettily to distract us from our own mortality.

I move to comfort Yuk. I now realize what she must have seen. But she backs away—I know she's worried I've let myself be contaminated by bad wind again. How do I explain to her that Genius is okay; he has been in better shape, of course, but he's not what she thinks he is, and therefore her concerns about bad wind are unfounded. Right? Reflexively, I turn to Genius, seeking his counsel and comfort. This is its own revelation: In his peculiar way he must have counseled and comforted me in the past. Why else would I seek these in him now?

"You can't go yet!" I want to say, but of all times, now the words form in my mind in Chinese, and I am too self-conscious of my poor pronunciation, my bad accent to release them with Yuk standing so close. The moment passes, and nothing is said. Our paths have crossed in this manner countless times. I grab the artichoke from between his legs. It beats in my hand like a heart. I hold it in front of his face. More show-and-tell. Distract him from the biology that must run its course. I see the artichoke's reflection on his lenses, like two eyes wide open. I run through as much as I know, confident he's listening and taking us in. Then Yuk says, "I go for nurse. You stay in here. Don't touch your father, okay?" I watch her leave. She is so agitated.

When I turn there's nothing on his lenses. I catch him inhaling a shallow but labored breath. He holds it in and won't let go. I wait for its release, pretending he's just lost his train of thought mid-sentence. "Pop. Pop!" I shout, trying to reach him through a stiff wind. His lips move slightly. He wants to tell me something. His face clenches, he seems on the verge of an eruption. He's going to curse me, as he did before, "Fuck you!" as if I'd just ruined him. I can taste his anger, like salt sniffed from the air. I feel it finding its target inside me. I understand this is being his son. I wait for him, the exhale, the words, the curses. I wait, and nothing comes. His mouth is as tight as a seed, his lips the color of cork, his eyeglass lenses themselves seem closed. His skin, now as pale as lard, leaks light. I wait, but nothing's coming. He's just being himself, which, under the circumstances, is its own comfort. I can throw it back at him, have our usual standoff, but I decide, Enough. I step closer to the bed, and reach for him. But stop my hand—Yuk's admonition, Genius's own: "Bad wind."

Behind me Yuk and a nurse enter the room. Before the nurse touches his neck, his wrist, before she puts the stethoscope under his gown, before she catches my eyes in hers and shakes her head, I know he has spent his final moment on earth with me. Was he aware he wasn't alone? That I was at his side? Or did he feel abandoned, unloved, even though he knew I was there?

Chapter 21

EVERYONE MOBILIZES for the funeral. Yuk pulls strings with the airlines and has my father flown east for burial at a cut rate. My sisters Lily and Patty arrive in New York ahead of us. They insist on buying him a new suit because they hate the one he's worn his entire American life; this suit will be a dark navy businessman's special, with European tailoring, modest lapels, and pinstripes as fine as the lines of a dollar sign. Dressed for success. A new man. No trouble is too big for my sisters; they hit mall after mall, finding nothing that satisfies their needs. They train into Manhattan, shop Macy's, Bloomingdale's, Barneys, at each stop describing their enterprise, his dimensions, the shade of his skin, their wish to send him off looking to the world like he's made of money. With a single, multisegmented act, they hope to expiate the lifetimes of indifference they've shown the man. Let them make nice now, I think. Who am I to accuse them of too-little-too-late?

I accompany my mother into Chinatown to finalize the funeral arrangements. During the train ride into Penn Station she doesn't cry or sob. A first in her thirty-six-hour-old widowhood. Too many other kinds of people around.

We enter the funeral home. Little men in black suits scurry like rats at the sudden intrusion of light. The place is small and dingy, the air heavy with incense. I can feel greasy smoke residue sticking to the walls. One of the men leads us downstairs. He's a chair of a man, lean and dark like a fieldhand, cigarette dangling at the edge of his mouth. As we descend, I stare at the bald spot at the top of his head, at the sparse hairs like guitar strings stretched across the pink-yellow void. I worry he's taking us to see my father. That'll probably set Zsa Zsa off. I'm relieved when he leads us into a room with a desk and folding chairs. Once we sit down, the undertaker offers his condolences. Zsa Zsa bows her head and nods. When she shows her face again I expect to see tears, but to my surprise she's all business, she's not interested in a stranger's kind words. Then he says something directly to me in Chinese. When he sees I don't understand, his face brightens, and he switches to English. "Why you mahdha mad for me? I goot man."

"She's upset."

"Sure. Sure. She not think straight, rye? She velly sad, rye? You do for mommy. We work together, you and me, rye? You pick good house for you *baba*." He shows me a loose-leaf binder full of Polaroids of caskets. He flips to the expensive models: cherry wood, mahogany, semi-precious metals. "You smart guy, rye? You buy dissa one for you *baba*. A-number-one best. Look like gold but much more cheap." It's the bronze model. I offer Zsa Zsa a look but she doesn't want to. She stares at the filthy floor between us, at the cigarette burns like cockroaches on the carpeting. I ask her how much we should spend. She shakes her head.

"See, you mahdha want you to pick. She know you be good son, you pick best house for you *baba*."

I flip the pages of the binder, feeling tremendous pressure to prove to the guy I am a good son. I am a good son. I settle on a handsome walnut-looking number, which to my surprise is actually made of steel, at a quarter of the bronze price.

"Wah! You go college, rye? You not stupit. Dissa one for poor man. Dissa one cheap one. Not velly strong house."

"It's steel!"

He turns up his lip at me. "Everybody think you cheap, think you hate you *baba*. You try this one. You *baba* more safe in dissa one." He points to another casket in his binder.

"Copper?"

"Look like bronze, rye? Look like gold, rye? Copper is best."

"For cooking."

"Why you make joke for? I try help you mahdha, rye? You buy steel house, no probrem for me. You boss. You son."

I check the price of the copper casket. About a thousand dollars less than the bronze.

"This one, everybody think you good son. Everybody think you buy you *baba* bronze house."

I take the binder and flip between the copper and the steel models. I lean toward the modestly priced casket. I mean, isn't everybody going to decompose? Still, I do wonder if my father might prefer a fancier "house," to go out in style. Hasn't his earthly life been a cheap steel box? Why settle on copper? Go with the bronze, and install radial tires to the casket, a V-8 engine, steering wheel, then fill 'er up with a tank of high-octane gasoline, and personally chauffeur him into eternity. I ask Zsa Zsa which she prefers. She tells me the undertaker is trying to rip her off, "trying to catch a pig." She calls the man a maggot, a bastard, a dead snake, as if she were cursing out one of her customers, and the undertaker can't understand a word she says. Finally she glances at the photos and shakes her head. She wants me to decide. She wants to see what fate awaits her, a deluxe copper house or a steel tenement.

I opt for the good son.

"You smart. You see everybody say you be good son now."

A FTER I CLEANSED my hands with salt (Yuk found plenty of the ribbed packets stashed in the nightstand drawer), and made the call to my mother, and signed the hospital papers, and accepted a plastic bag of Genius's belongings (teeth, eyeglasses, shoes, the artichokes), I drove directly to see Moses.

I didn't know he was my final destination at first. I just got on the coast road and drove, my windows down, the wind bursting in my ears, blasting away at my mother's weeping in my head. Each time a jet climbed the skies over the ocean I imagined Genius on board flying back to China, smoking free cigarettes, drinking free liquor, a favorite of the stewardesses; but I couldn't hold him there, I couldn't bring him all the way home. How could I land on ground whose look and smell I didn't know? With that, the spell was broken. Immediately, I abandoned Genius flying indefinitely in the heavens, my thoughts turning to this most recent failure, this rich hole in my life. I imagined myself on the plane, escaping the familiar and sad, but I couldn't sustain this flight either, too much turbulence—my mother's wailing like an alarm, my father's dead, Ira's dead. I pulled the car off the road, to an unofficial parking area tourists and surfers use, and inched to the edge of the cliff overlooking the ocean. I killed the engine. The sudden stillness jarred me, as when my baby boys asleep in the car would awaken once the rocking stopped. A single, discrete shiver rattled my body. I expected tears, but nothing came. I was, I thought, still dry from Ira.

The sun was setting. A flock of cormorants flew past. I remembered Genius telling me about the black birds when we drove this road home from Ira's funeral. Like everyone else in the car, he was left mute by what he had just witnessed. Then, at Dead Man's Slide, he slapped my arm for attention and pointed at cormorants soaring over the surface of the ocean, searching for fish. When he was a boy in China, he told me, he kept cormorants to catch fish for him. He put brass rings around their necks, which would prevent them from swallowing any fish they caught. They would dive into the sea, surface with their catch, and he would harvest the fish from their bills. I didn't say anything back. He must've thought I hadn't heard him. I was annoyed he was bothering me, especially during this dangerous stretch of road; I had to concentrate on my driving, and he was distracting me with his ridiculous story. I was quiet and stared at the road, and he didn't say another word. That was the last time he really talked, as if he wanted to be heard, had something important to say. He was telling the story to me, and I shut him up. Wasn't that what I had done my whole life? Devising new and more potent ways of shutting him up, pissing him off so he wouldn't want to look at me, let alone speak to me from the heart. He had just buried his grandson, he was thinking of his own boyhood, of a time and an age Ira would never know, and he probably knew he was sick, and he wanted to tell me something that would transport me, take my mind off Ira, soften the sorrow for just one moment—in other words, he was trying to be a father to me. I cried, big noisy tears, because he had to endure me, my meanness, because too late I missed him. From the dirt and dust of these feelings I realized Genius had gone to follow Ira, to make sure he was taken care of, to protect and guide him, to show him the tricks of the trade, the ring around the neck, how to exploit another's appetite in order to satisfy one's own. I filled the emptiness with longing: I had to see Moses. It just came to me. He saw Genius better than any of us, and loved.

I drove to the house and walked right in; I didn't bother knocking. "What is it?" Bliss said. "What do you want?"

"Where's Moses?"

"I've told you before, Sterling, I want some warning before you show up here. I need time to prepare myself." Her voice was brittle and world-weary. She asked about the blue plastic bag I gripped in my hand.

I didn't tell her Genius was dead.

"Why're you here?" This was Moses, popping from his room. "It's not your day."

I was wounded by that. Moses, the closest thing to Genius on earth. I hadn't planned what I'd do once I arrived.

Then he also asked about the blue bag.

I seized the opening, and knelt beside him.

"He has to go to bed soon," his mother said.

I reached into the bag and its pieces of Genius. "This is an artichoke," I began.

"I know that," he said.

"It's a member of the sunflower family. What this is is the bud of a flower. The part people eat is the petal."

"I know, I know."

"Of course you do. You're a smart boy, aren't you? Just listen to me anyway." I wanted to finish saying what I hadn't finished saying to Genius. I held the artichoke up to his small face. "Smell. It smells like the ground, like the outside." We inhaled together. I sighed. "Ahhh!" and Moses sighed, "Ahh!"

"Moses, bedtime!" Bliss took a step into the bedroom, then stopped. "Sterling, it's bedtime. He's tired. Can't that wait until next time?"

I ignored her. "You don't eat the whole petal. There are these prickles at the end, and things too hard to chew in the middle. This is tricky food, dangerous food."

She ordered Moses to bed. My eyes snagged hers: Not now! I told her, "I'm not done yet. I have something important to say to Moses."

"What's so important?"

I shook my head. "Technically speaking, these petals are called scales," I said, bending one back. "There are musical scales, weighing scales, fish scales, and people scales, which is an illness that happens sometimes to those who are unhappy. These are the only scales we eat." Moses was between my legs, leaning against me, letting my arms encircle him, his hands toying with but not demanding the artichoke. He was listening intently. "You pull off a scale, she loves me, pull off a scale, she loves me not. You take away all the tough stuff, the prickles and pokey parts, and every time, inside, you find a heart."

A T THE HEAD of the black room, the coffin lies on a cloth-draped platform. The place is unbearably cold, to suit the dead not the living. From this distance Genius looks as good as one could expect. I had dreaded seeing him again, but it's not so bad. Except for the color they've smeared on his cheeks and mouth, he is my father. The suit my sisters bought fits nicely across his chest.

We are seated in our mourning chairs in the front of the room, near the casket, more or less at Genius's feet. I have a clear view of him—with his gray hair darkened and his glasses off his face, he looks youthful, as he must have lying on the rocky shore, soaking in the rays, while his black birds did his work for him. Zsa Zsa is on my right, Moses is on my left. My sisters fill out the row. I wonder if anyone else sees this. "He looks so young," I say to Zsa Zsa. She nods. "He is young," she says.

My friend the undertaker and an assistant, a young woman with square glasses, emerge from a curtained entryway on the wall opposite us. She positions small square pillows in a row in front of the casket. He unwraps packages of incense and lays the sticks on top of an altar, a small ebony table with a decorative urn filled with sand. The undertaker signals for me to kneel on the first pillow, my special place as number-one (and only) son. "Which one you wife?" he asks. I tell her she's not here. "You boy?" I nod. He fetches Moses. Next to him, Lucy, Patty, then Lily. The assistant hands three sticks of burning incense to each of us. She tells us to bow in Chinese. "Bow three times," I whisper to Moses. "I know," he says, "like with Ira." He performs three deep, reverential bows. Witnessing these acts of love, Zsa Zsa wails.

We are invited to approach the casket, say good-bye one last time, face to face, private, in the American way, before the mourners arrive. Up close Genius looks puffy and strange, the embalming fluid ready to overflow the limits of his flesh, his skin rubbery and wrinkle-free. His complexion has gone from tobacco to ham.

Soon the mourners arrive, friends of my parents', mostly men my father's age, lifelong bachelors, the old guys we used to have coffee with during our Sunday excursions to Chinatown. They light incense, hurry down the row of us, shaking my hand, stopping to say a few things to my mother, before they pay their last respects to Genius. To a man, when they come to Moses, they point at him and say to me, "You boy, rye?"

Many mourners come to the refrigerated room to visit Genius. I never knew he knew so many people, had so many friends.

THE AFTERNOON passes slowly. Except to go to the bathroom, we're expected to stay glued to our chairs. Moses, though, keeps getting up and going to Genius. He stands there, arms at his sides, head tilted to his left. Zsa Zsa sends me after the boy. He obediently returns to his seat, and then a few minutes later, when the flow of mourners ebbs, he drifts back to his spot. "Do you understand what's going on?" I ask. He nods. I'm not convinced. "Are you waiting for Ah-Yeah to wake up?" He's staring at Genius, trying to detect some movement. He shakes his head. "Ah-Yeah is with Ira," he says, without lifting his gaze from his grandfather. It feels like he's mad at me. I remember this feeling from the day I buried Ira. When they all hated me, and Ira, the one I loved best, was gone, and Moses, I'm sure suspecting this, was in his own way also gone.

And throughout the wake Zsa Zsa worries me. She has cried so much and with such ferocity. *"Ai-yah! Ai-yah!"* she wails, so soulfully my body aches. I try to comfort her, but all she wants from me, it seems, are tissues. She calms herself, then her tears and sorrow flare again.

I'M GLAD for the steady stream of visitors. I'm not sure when the undertaker brings us the squares of rice paper stamped with smaller squares of canary-yellow ink and decorated with a sheet of gold leaf. He teaches us how to fold these into origami tubes, which he says are gold bars for Genius to spend. Moses picks up the instructions easily. We work diligently, quietly, each in our separate compartments—our lives seem to depend on it.

Yuk enters. She's come all the way from China. I've not seen her since that day in the hospital. She sweeps in alone, a fantastic creature among this congregation. She's everything in this room, the incense, the bows, the Hell Bank notes, and she's none of it. After she lights sticks of incense and bows—everyone watches, the grannies and old men reminding one another that she was the one Lung wanted for a daughter-in-law—Yuk shakes my sisters' hands, then hugs Moses. He won't let go of her, the weight of his skull pinning her against his arms.

The chrysanthemums on the many wreaths throw their perfume. The gladioli pulse like hearts. I am certainly persuaded by Yuk's argument, the eloquent statement she makes with her appearance today, for his sake, and mine. But when my chance finally comes, and I rise out of my chair to meet her, our arms fold around each other naturally, her body crumbles against mine, her sobs rival those of a professional mourner, of Zsa Zsa herself. I fight back my own tears, a precious fluid I cannot live without. I don't know why I am so stingy. Why I feel I must hide my grief. Or whom I'm shielding it from. I see Moses, his edges blurred by my tears. Is this what I look like to him without his glasses on? Seeing life through a thin wall of tears. Is that their special link, Moses and Genius, a constant world of sorrow that glasses mask only temporarily?

Yuk leans heavily against me. I take her weight, and she melts into me. The wails increase, so much so that I snap to alertness, lifting my chin off her shoulder, my gaze off Moses, and listen, my eyes falling on the grannies and old guys in the folding chairs, in their silk vests, disco suits, pointing and whispering. I turn in the direction of their collective stare-down: My mother's in her chair, one hand over her eyes, her arm extended, her hand clutching Yuk's. I'm sandwiched between them, separating the two. I let Yuk go. As the heat of her body evaporates through my mourning clothes, and Yuk embraces my mother, who grabs the sleeves of Yuk's black jacket until her knuckles bleach, I see that in the high rev of emotions this afternoon it's too easy to confuse one's heart's flutter with the truth. Of course, my sorrow is true; my sadness for Zsa Zsa is true; my regrets are true. But the tenderness I feel, the bright yearning she wakes in me, is grounded in history, something that shined in the past, and as such it is merely nostalgic.

Now Zsa Zsa visits her husband. She lets Yuk lead her. They stand side by side, Yuk so much taller my mother seems the child. When Yuk drapes her arm on Zsa Zsa's shoulder like a guy on a date, I expect her to shatter at the sudden human touch. But from my vantage point Zsa Zsa reveals nothing. She's statue-still. How to explain that peace? Then Moses gets out of his seat. I grab for him, hiss, "Moses!" but he gets away and slices between Yuk and his grandmother. The three of them stand like travelers waiting for a train to take them home.

A NEW MOURNER, an old guy in a shiny gray suit jacket and black slacks, enters and takes their recently vacated places. He lights incense, bids his friend farewell, then goes to Zsa Zsa, skipping the row of children. He seizes her hand from her lap and shakes it in that weak-wristed Chinese manner, a bloodless rendition of Western flesh-pressing. He mutters a few things to her, which prompt a new bout of weeping. I put my hand on my mother's hot back. Once the man takes a seat with the other mourners, Zsa Zsa's grief evaporates. "I don't even know who that old corpse is," she says. Then, in the same breath: "Aren't you hungry? Your boy must be hungry. Why don't you go get something to eat?"

Out of respect for my father I know I'm supposed to be selfless, abstemious in the way of personal comforts. But that's thinking only of myself. I haven't given Moses' needs a thought. I glance over my shoulder at Moses, sitting in the congregation with Yuk. On looks alone, they might be mistaken for mother and child; seriously, some of Zsa Zsa and Genius's friends have asked if she's my wife, if she's his mother. One of her friends, Chin-Moo, who knows better, has asked the same question. Moses is fidgeting; even though Yuk's there, he's struggling to keep still in the chilled and incensed room. I'm so busy tallying up my regrets and trying finally to be a good son, seizing this last opportunity to dedicate myself to Genius's needs, that I've forgotten I am the father now.

Zsa Zsa tells me the "dead corpse" had promised there would be some food here.

"Where?"

"You're a cook. Where do you think the food is?"

When I go to fetch Moses he doesn't want to leave Yuk. Then he wants her to come with us. But she declines. I invite her also. When she declines again, saying, "You two go," Moses brusquely slides off his chair and marches past the others in the congregation, past the incense altar. He stops in front of Genius. My mother calls him, motions for him to come to her, and when he doesn't budge she raises her hand to her lips and makes like she's shoveling rice into her mouth. She points with her chin, and he turns obediently. His eyes find the curtained entryway to the left of the casket. He looks at her again, and she nods. As he moves toward the crab-custard-green curtain, his eyes are screwed on the casket, feeling the disquiet of leaving something valuable untended in a public place.

I get up and follow. Moses leads me into a kitchen. A kitchen in a funeral home! I don't know why I'm so surprised; after all, I did grow up in the back of a laundry. We had to eat.

I tell Moses to sit, pointing to the milk crates that ring a small oil-cloth-draped table shoved against the wall opposite the stove. The oil-cloth, cracked and greasy, is white, with a pattern of red roses. The L-shaped Wedgewood range is a classic, a four-burner with eye-level oven. But the oven door is missing, the space functioning as a mini-pantry, inside it Quaker instant Oatmeal, Domino sugar, Borden condensed milk, Chinese tea, Lipton tea, bottles of mushroom soy sauce, boxes of Diamond Tip matches, Chock Full o' Nuts coffee (at least eight tins, stacked), Premium saltines. The kind of stuff we had in our kitchen when I was growing up. A giant panda-shaped thermos perches on top of the stove, beside it a Budweiser beer tray, and on the tray a stainless-steel napkin holder, a soy sauce dispenser, salt and pepper shakers, a shot glass filled with toothpicks—the typical setup in any Chinatown greasy spoon.

The rest of the kitchen: To the left of the Wedgewood a water heater. To its left, on the adjacent wall, a tiny bathroom, a double-spigot sink, nails on which facecloths hang. In a corner stands a plunger in its brick-colored bell, and wherever I look there are towers of takeout containers, red and white cardboard as well as plastic.

On the table are a big pink thermos and a box from On Luck Coffee Shop. The promised treats. The red strings that once held the box shut have been cut, the lid gaping inches. Invitation enough. It's the way things were done at my parents' place; Zsa Zsa rarely bothered to transfer, for instance, English muffins (an old favorite of mine, split, steamed, and then served with so much granulated sugar they crunched) from the steam pan to a serving dish—a ritual display of sharing. Why do more work than necessary; isn't there enough to do already? Who cares how food is served, just as long as there is food to serve? After my sisters and I visited the nice homes of our American friends, we were shamed and mesmerized by their table manners, by their glasses for cold drinks, cups and saucers for hot, dishes of different sizes for different purposes, the dizzying array of utensils, big and small, the beautiful gilt-edged platters on which food was served. I quickly learned to cut, then transfer the fork to right hand, then eat. By increments we imported these customs of the table into the laundry, even though they seemed strange, foreign, and had made us, at one time, feel dumb, cloddish, inadequate, like dogs trained to walk on their hind legs. But mimicry, even coarse mimicry—what did we own in the way of dishes, flatware, serving sets, anyway?—was belonging. So an after-school snack, say, my mother's ultrasweet tricornered muffins, minicakes which, when steamed, would crown and cleave (if you were skilled) into three equal parts, were no longer held in our hands and eaten but plunked into individual rice bowls and dissected with spoons.

I flip open the box from On Luck Coffee Shop, show Moses what's inside. It's the usual mix, he has seen it all before: shrimp dumplings, *cha-siu bao,* sweet lotus-seed *bao,* egg custard tarts, *har-gow,* beef balls. "What do you want?" Moses shrugs.

I unpack the box, the varieties of dumpling, *bao,* the aluminum-cupped tarts. I offer each item to Moses and in succession he turns them down. Before I realize, I feel anger building inside me, as if he were rejecting food that I'd personally prepared. I have to resist the seductive power of a swift, tactical blow delivered to back of the boy's head. A Geniusesque maneuver, appropriate for the occasion, that will knock some sense into him, kindle appetite, duty. "Hey, you have to eat something," I say. "You love these." And he does. This is Moses food. Genius would make special trips to Chinatown to buy these things if he knew Moses was coming to visit. I put an egg custard tart under his nose. "Ah-Yeah used to buy these for you. You remember what you call them in Chinese?" Moses shakes his head. But I know he knows, he just doesn't want to play along, in a funk, as he is, about his grandfather. I answer the question for him: *"Ahn tot."* Moses nods, letting me know that I got it right. He's staring down at his lap. In his hands is a small metal car, a longtime favorite—he must've sneaked it out of the house this morning, and the picture it makes in his small caressing hands drains me of my anger. This is what is precious to him. And I'm such a bad parent I never considered bringing a toy for Moses. I suppose with me for a father he's learned to be resourceful. "You have to eat something," I urge, as I uncap the pink thermos on the table to see what's inside. Boiled water. I go to the Wedgewood and grab some napkins from the dispenser. I spread a napkin on the table, then lay one of each type of goodie on the napkin in front of Moses. As I do so I give its Chinese, then its English name: *cha-siu bao,* roast pork bun; *voo tee,* taro root cake; and so on.

Moses says, "I'm not hungry."

"Sure you are," I say. "I am." I peel a sticky gray shrimp dumpling free of its partners in the paper boat and pop it into my mouth. "Wow, really good," I say, Peeking Duck style. It slips out, I didn't mean to do it. As far as I'm concerned, Peeking Duck's dead. Moses narrows his eyes and looks vaguely at me. "Just eat something," I say. "Once you do, you'll see how hungry you are."

"My appetite is lost," says Moses.

"Then we have to find it." I look under the table, in the pastry box, in the boy's ear, searching for the lost appetite.

"Quit it," Moses says. "Why do you think you have to do that?"

"You said your appetite was lost. Well, I'm looking for it." I keep fooling around. I am keenly aware my father never did this for me.

"I found it!" I hold my fist up to Moses' face. "It's a big one."

"What, what? Let me see!" says Moses, grabbing the fist, trying to pull it apart. I resist; I am playing, extending my own lame joke, and I am withering inside, already feeling the glare of his disappointment. I see Moses getting frantic, his glasses are tilted, the flesh in his face is tightening, his baby-fat cuteness disappears, in its place a tissue-paper layer of skin over a demonic mask of bone. I can't stand seeing him wound so tight and distraught. I unlock my fingers. "Look how big your appetite is," I say. Of course, nothing's there and Moses calls me on it. He slaps at my open palm. "Okay, I can't fool around anymore. I need to get back out to your grandfather." I grab a *cha-siu bao* and split it down the middle. "Halfsies," I say. I put Moses' half in his hands. "On the count of three: Wwww-one, two-ooo, three—"

I pop my half into my mouth, but Moses doesn't follow suit. I stare him to pieces as I chew. Then I see what's the problem. It's there on his face. "That's enough," I say. "Your grandfather can't come in here. He can't come in here so you can feel like eating again." I avert my eyes from the boy because he's ready to cry. In a corner of the kitchen I see the towers of red paper takeout containers, and get an idea. "How about some long noodles? Or some wontons, or you can have them both together, wonton noodle soup. You like that. I'll go get you some." But Moses shakes his head, glasses left crooked by the force of his refusal. I position the black frames back onto the boy's face. As I make the final adjustment, tipping the glasses on the bridge of his nose, I see myself reflected in the lenses, the same way I saw myself in my father's. My whole life I believed I could never go further, penetrate any deeper into his life than the reflective surface.

"What's the matter?" I ask. "What can I get you?"

Moses bows his head and cries. Over the top of the frames he has no eyes, just his long lashes, damp black smears like tiny minnows washed onshore, graceful and helpless. I feel I'm torturing him. We sit in our places. His tears drip off the insides of his glasses and onto his white shirt. I wait out the flood, until enough time passes and he pulls himself together, his eyes turning arid, the red run from them.

High in one corner of the room there's an altar, a drawing of the kitchen god, spindly sticks of spent incense, two oranges on a plate. Hanging on an adjacent wall are a wooden back-scratcher, a flyswatter, three calendars—a Hong Kong starlet; a lake in Switzerland; a Chinese immortal, the old man with the cauliflower forehead, huge smile, and entourage of laughing children. For a moment I'm in the back of the laundry again, a kid at the dinner table, tears flaring in my throat; I'm staring at the calendars, pretending the man who just caused the newest bruise inside me isn't there, but I don't hate Genius, or fear him, or know how to unlove him—I only wish I could step free of him, off to France, hanging on the wall.

I close my eyes and shake loose the memory. When I come back, Moses is staring at me. "I miss Ah-Yeah," he says. "I miss Ira."

He slides off the milk-crate chair and steps in my direction, and wraps his arms around me, holding on tight, my body all that's solid in a liquid world. In that moment my body stiffens, like an animal full of fear and suspicion: Is he hugging me, or am I a convenient substitute for his brother, his grandfather?

But aren't those the same?

I hold him close. He buries his head in my chest. Then he wipes his nose with the back of his hand, takes a deep, quivering breath, and exhales, his little body trembling so hard I fear he might break apart. I hold him tighter, as if he were Ira and Genius rolled into one, because he is, and by my holding on they won't get away.

WHEN WE LET GO, we're both thinking food. Moses looks in the On Luck box and surveys the possibilities. We have returned to our bodies, to the day-to-day. I see what will satisfy our longtime hunger. "If you can wait a second," I say, "I know the perfect thing. It's what my father used to make for me for a snack when I came home from school." While I was hugging Moses I spotted the cans of condensed milk again—Elsie the Cow's face centered on the petals of a daisy—in the oven turned pantry. I remembered Genius making me the concoction of saltine crackers, sweet condensed milk, and boiled water, especially on cold days. I don't remember the last time I had it; I certainly have never made it. But this is comfort food, warming and soothing. The mere thought of a bowl of Genius's cracker stew evokes good, safe, happy times.

I ask Moses to help. He goes to the Wedgewood and fetches the box of saltines and one of the "cans with the cow on it." Meanwhile, I find little pink bowls, stacked on the toilet's water tank, and spoons in a coffee can. When I return to the kitchen table Moses is kneeling on a milk crate, palms flat against the oilcloth, ready for action. "This was so good on cold days," I say.

"Like today," he says.

"Even inside."

I ask him to break some crackers into the bowls. "How many?" he asks.

"Ten. No, make it twelve."

"Twelve all together? Or twelve in each bowl?"

I consider his question. It's the first project we've done together since he was tiny, back in the carriage house apartment in Richfield, those days of building towers with blocks. "Twelve and twelve," I say, pointing at the two bowls.

Moses works diligently. He's inherited from me a fastidiousness in the kitchen. He breaks the crackers one at a time, halving, then quartering each. I open the can of condensed milk. "You'll love this stuff," I say. "There's almost as much sugar as milk in here."

I hand Moses the can and tell him to pour. "Say when," he says.

The thick yellow milk oozes from the can. I remember Genius letting me put my finger in the path of the pour to steal a dollop of the sweetness.

Once Moses is through I pump the thermos, and streams of hot water shoot out over the broken crackers in the pink bowls. "We have to let the crackers get nice and soggy," I say. "But we can't wait too long, because you want the water hot. I liked it best when it just about burned my tongue."

"Not me," he says.

"You're right," I say. "I used to rush. I couldn't wait. You're right to be patient. Good things won't get away from good people."

I slide a bowl in front of Moses. He lowers his head for an appraising whiff. He frowns, disappointed, You're psyched up over this?

"It's Chinese," I say.

He stares harder at the bowl. I can see his exertions. His temples pulsing, his glasses fogging up. He looks over the top of his black frames at me. He doesn't believe.

Trust me. If you can only know what I know. Let the steam caress your face, smell the roasted sweetness, the milk's own sugar, and feel the glow of well-being radiating from within. I don't blame Moses his skepticism, because until this moment I wouldn't have believed either. But I'm not making these feelings up, they are as real as the food is pure: just flour, water, sugar, milk, and salt. I spoon some of the cracker stew from my bowl, blow, and offer it to Moses. He won't bite. "It really is Chinese, you know. Ah-Yeah used to make it for me. It's a special recipe he brought from China. And think about it, you and I just whipped this up together!"

I see Moses' brain processing what I've just said. Finally he claps his hands and says, "We just cooked Chinese food!"

"That's right. The real thing!"

Moses opens his mouth, and lets me feed him.

Acknowledgments

THIS BOOK was written and rewritten over a six-year period, and no one was more instrumental to its completion than my wife, Jackie. I am deeply indebted to her for the wise and loving readings of the countless drafts, and for enduring life with a house full of my characters, and with me.

Heartfelt thanks to friends, readers, and lifesavers Holly Bergon, Stephen Tukel Mills, Elaine Markson, and Marian Wood. My admiration and appreciation go out to Lynn Itagaki, my assistant, and Anna Jardine, the copy editor.

I wish to express my gratitude to the Committee on Research and the Asian American Studies Center at UCLA for the generous financial support both have provided. I am happy to acknowledge the encouragement and support that Don Nakanishi, director of the AASC, and Tom Wortham, my chair in English, as well as former chairs Eric Sundquist and Jonathan Post, have given me over the years.

Beyond words, I owe too much to Ken Offit and the other doctors, nurses, and staff at Memorial Hospital in New York, whose collective good work and wisdom, in very basic ways, made this all possible.

Last, more than anything else, this book is about family and love. I could not have written such a narrative, at least not in its present form, without my son, Jules, who taught me to respect family and how to love.

About the Author

D AVID WONG LOUIE is the author of the story collection *Pangs of Love,* which was a *New York Times* Notable Book of 1991 and a *Voice Literary Supplement* Favorite in the same year. One of the stories in that collection was included in *Best American Short Stories of 1989,* and the book itself won the *Los Angeles Times* First Fiction Award and the *Ploughshares* First Fiction Book Award. Louie teaches at UCLA and lives in Venice, California.